The Odyssey
of Geronimo

The Odyssey of Geronimo

TWENTY-THREE YEARS
A PRISONER OF WAR

W. Michael Farmer

THORNDIKE PRESS
A part of Gale, a Cengage Company

LIBRARY OF CONGRESS CIP DATA ON FILE.
CATALOGUING IN PUBLICATION FOR THIS BOOK
IS AVAILABLE FROM THE LIBRARY OF CONGRESS.

ISBN-13: 978-1-4328-6849-9 (hardcover alk. paper)

Published in 2021 by arrangement with W. Michael Farmer

Printed in Mexico
Print Number: 01   Print Year: 2021

For the *Odyssey of Geronimo,* the epic warrior's journey after ten years of war and surrender, a paraphrase invocation from the beginning of *The Odyssey* by Homer:

Sing, O *Di-yen,* man of great medicine, of that ingenious warrior who traveled far and wide after he surrendered to the lies of the famous *nantan,* Miles. Many cities did he visit, and many were the nations whose manners and customs did he see; moreover he suffered much trying to save his own life and those of his people to bring them safely back home; but do what he might, he could not save them all, and he perished in captivity longing for his home in a far land. Tell me, too, O *Di-yen,* about all these things, from whatever sources you may know them.

For Corky, my best friend and wife

TABLE OF CONTENTS

ACKNOWLEDGMENTS

There have been many friends and professionals who have supported me in this work and to whom I owe a special debt of gratitude for their help and many kindnesses. My longtime editor, Melissa Watkins Starr, provided independent eyes, valuable technical suggestions and corrections, and shined a light on passages that needed clarification.

Lynda Sánchez's insights into Apache culture and their voices are a major point of reference in understanding the times and personalities covered in this work.

Good friends, a rare and a true gift, Pat and Mike Alexander, opened their home to me during numerous visits to New Mexico, allowing me time and a place from which to do research that otherwise would not have been possible.

The histories listed in Additional Reading that I found particularly helpful were those by Angie Debo; Eve Ball, Nora Henn, and

11

Lynda Sánchez; Alicia Delgadillo and Miriam A. Perrett; Lynda Sánchez; Sherry Robinson; Woodward B. Skinner; Edwin Sweeney; H. Henrietta Stockel; Robert Utley; and John Turcheneske.

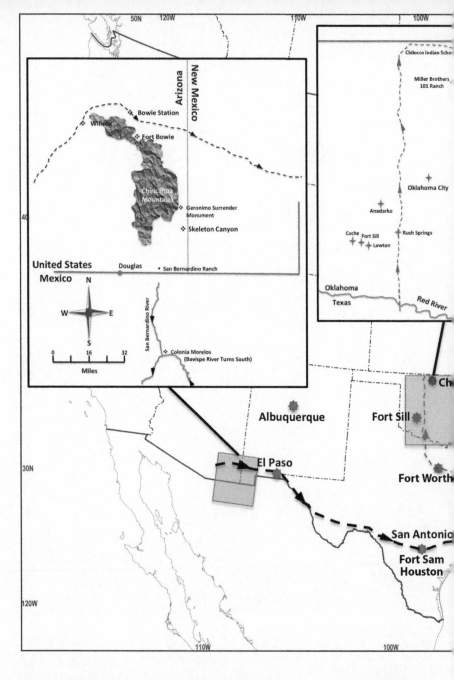

The odyssey of the Naiche-Geronimo band of Chiricahua
Apaches beginning at Fort Bowie, Arizona, in 1886 an

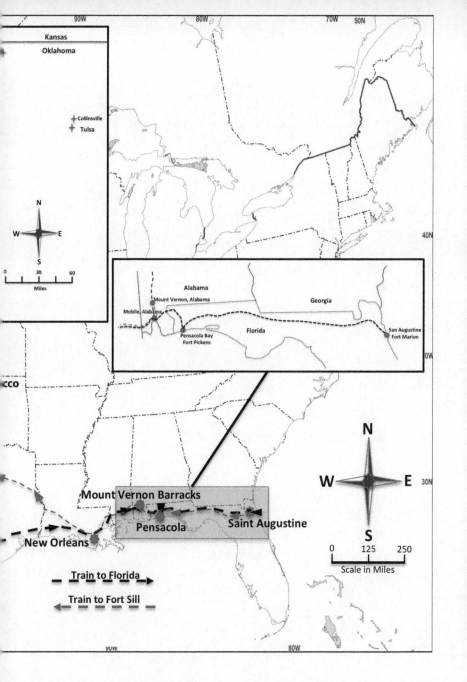

...nding at Fort Sill, Oklahoma, in 1914 when the last Chiri-
...ahuas were released as prisoners of war.

FICTIONAL AND HISTORICAL CHARACTERS

FICTIONAL

Grayson — Man with a pistol and gray beard who was always watching

HISTORICAL

Apaches

Geronimo's Family

She-gha — Wife to Geronimo

Zi-yeh — Wife to Geronimo

Fenton — Son of Geronimo, mother was Zi-yeh

Eva — Daughter of Geronimo, mother was Zi-yeh

Ih-tedda — Mescalero wife to Geronimo, taken in 1885, divorced in 1889

Lenna — Daughter of Geronimo, mother was Ih-tedda

Robert — Unknown son of Geronimo until 1904, mother was Ih-tedda

Chappo — Son of Geronimo, mother was

Chee-hash-kish

Dohn-say — Daughter of Geronimo, full sister of Chappo, mother was Chee-hash-kish

Thomas Dahkeya — Grandson of Geronimo, mother Dohn-say, father Mike Dahkeya

Sousche — Wife of Geronimo, married three months in 1905/1906 and then divorced

Sunsetso (aka Azul) — Last wife of Geronimo, married 1907

Daklugie — Nephew of Geronimo, married Ramona Chihuahua at Fort Sill

Jason Betzinez — Geronimo's cousin and an acolyte

Fun — "Brother of Geronimo" (second cousin), Segundo in Naiche-Geronimo band

Perico — "Brother of Geronimo" (second cousin), major warrior in Naiche-Geronimo band

Ahnandia — "Brother of Geronimo" (second cousin), first cousin to Betzinez, major warrior in Naiche-Geronimo band

Geronimo's Warriors

Jasper Kanseah — Youngest warrior in Naiche-Geronimo band

Yahnosha — Major warrior in Naiche-

18

Geronimo band and training warrior for Kanseah

Chiricahua Leaders

Naiche — Chief of Chokonen Apaches, youngest son of Cochise

Chatto — A chief of the Chihenne Apaches, famous warrior and scout

Chihuahua — subchief of Chokonen Apaches, protégé of Cochise

  Ramona Chihuahua — Oldest daughter of Chihuahua

  Emily Chihuahua — Daughter of Chihuahua (about the age of Eva)

  Eugene Chihuahua — Son of Chihuahua, younger brother of Ramona

Nana — Married to Geronimo's sister, Nahdos-te, leader of the Chihenne Apaches

Loco — Chief of the Chihennes

Kaytennae — Second in command to Nana and later leader of the Chihenne Apaches

Mangas — Chihenne chief, son of Mangas Coloradas, named Carl Mangas by the army

  Frank Mangas — Son of Mangas

Kayihtah — Scout who talked to Geronimo about surrender

Martine — Scout with Kayihtah who talked to Geronimo about surrender

Anglos

George Wratten — Interpreter for Chiricahuas

Lieutenant Charles Bare Gatewood — Chief of scouts who helped talk Geronimo into surrender

Captain Henry W. Lawton — Commander of a cavalry troop that supported Gatewood at the meeting with Geronimo

Lieutenant William Wallace Wotherspoon — Commander of Apaches at Mount Vernon Barracks

Lieutenant Charles C. Ballou — Successor to Wotherspoon as Commander of Apaches at Mount Vernon Barracks

Captain Marion P. Maus — With Lieutenant Scott determined interest of Chiricahuas for leaving Mount Vernon Barracks

Lieutenant/Captain Hugh Lenox Scott — First Commander of Apaches at Fort Sill

Lieutenant Allyn K. Capron — Successor to Ballou at Mount Vernon Barracks and second in command under Scott at Fort Sill, second commander of Fort Sill Apaches

Lieutenant Francis Henry Beach — Third commander of Apaches at Fort Sill

Lieutenant George A. Purington — Commander of Apaches at Fort Sill at time of Geronimo's death

Captain Farrand Sayre — Commander of Apaches at Fort Sill during 1904 Saint Louis Exposition

Lieutenant Colonel Loomis L. Langdon — Commander of Apaches at Fort Pickens, 1886

General George Crook — Led effort to get scouts released from captivity and a Chiricahua reservation

General Nelson Appleton Miles — Made surrender terms to Geronimo that were never kept

General D. S. Stanley — Commander of Department of Texas, headquarters at Fort Sam Houston, managed Naiche-Geronimo band at Fort Sam Houston, took a census of families, interviewed Naiche and Geronimo on their understanding of the terms of surrender

General Oliver Otis Howard — Pushed for humane living conditions and a reservation for the Chiricahuas

S. M. McCowan — Head of the Indian School at Chilocco and Geronimo supervisor at 1904 Saint Louis Exposition

Jimmy Stevens — Interpreter for Miles-Geronimo debate in 1898

Stephen Melvil Barrett — Transcribed Geronimo's memoirs

Elbridge Ayer Burbank — Portrait painter

of Geronimo and friend

Leonard L. Legters — Minister for Dutch Reformed Church at Chiricahua Mission

Frank Hall Wright — Choctaw minister for Dutch Reformed Church

Walter C. Roe — Helped Frank Wright establish a Dutch Reformed Church mission at Fort Sill

APACHE AND SPANISH
WORDS AND PHRASES

Be'idest'íné — binoculars
Casa — house (Spanish)
Di-yen — medicine woman or man
Enjuh — good
Googé — whip-poor-will
Hacendado — wealthy landowner (Spanish)
Haheh — puberty ceremony
Hoddentin — sacred pollen
Ish-kay-neh — boy
Ish-tia-neh — woman
Iyah — mesquite bean pods
Llano — dry prairie (Spanish)
Nakai-yes — Mexicans
Nakai-yi — Mexican
Nantan — big chief
Nantan Lupan *(Chief Gray Wolf)* — the Apache name for General George Crook
Nish'ii' — I see you
Nkáh — We will go
Pindah-lickoyee — White-eyed enemies

Pesh — iron

Río Grande — Great River (Spanish)

Teniente — lieutenant (Spanish)

Tobaho — tobacco

Tsach — cradleboard

Ussen — The Apache god of creation and life

APACHE RECKONING OF
TIME AND SEASONS

Harvest — used in the context of time, means a year

Hand width *(against the horizon sky)* — about an hour

Season of Little Eagles — early spring

Season of Many Leaves — late spring, early summer

Season of Large Leaves — midsummer

Season of Large Fruit — late summer, early fall

Season of Earth Is Reddish Brown — late fall

Season of Ghost Face — lifeless winter

PREFACE

The Odyssey is a Greek epic poem attributed to Homer that describes the long ten-year journey home of Odysseus at the end of the ten-year war the Greeks finally won using the famous deception of the Trojan horse, as told in Homer's *Iliad.* The story of Geronimo's wars and the way General Nelson Miles finally deceived him into surrendering with false promises is an epic story that mirrors *The Iliad* with its mighty warriors, innumerable battles, and those who fell on the field of battle.

Geronimo was a prisoner of war for twenty-three years. Those years are his Odyssey. They are filled with trials and years of wandering across the land claimed by the White Eyes as he worked to return to the land of his birth. Geronimo's odyssey is an epic that reveals his strength and character and that of the Chiricahua Apaches working to be free and independent of the White

Eyes. Geronimo's death was the key that unlocked the door for the Chiricahua Apaches to escape their captivity four years later and continue as a people. His memory and his spirit continue to this day.

Six weeks after his surrender, the beginning of his odyssey, Geronimo and his warriors narrowly escaped hanging by white settlers in Arizona. In the years that followed, he became a national "superstar" and an astute businessman. He was invited to three world's fair expositions in Omaha, Nebraska, Buffalo, New York, and Saint Louis, Missouri, and numerous parades and fairs in Oklahoma. He rode with five other famous warriors and chiefs in Theodore Roosevelt's 1905 Inaugural Parade, in which Geronimo's popularity was second only to the president's. During his time in captivity, Geronimo became an entrepreneur, a schoolmaster, a justice of the peace, and a village chief, and he earned pay as an army scout. At the 1898 Omaha Exposition, Geronimo publicly debated General Miles about the lies Miles told him to orchestrate his surrender.

During his captivity, beginning when he was about sixty-three years old, Geronimo fathered two children, lost three wives, and, near the end of his life, married two more women, the last being more than twenty years younger than he. He and his warriors were deliberately separated from their families for eight months, a promise to allow them to rejoin their families a major reason for their surrender. He saw his people dying from White Eye diseases at a rate nearly three times the national average. He became a Christian but decided the missionary rules for the Jesus road were too strict and returned to a belief in the Apache creator god, Ussen. When he died, he had over $10,000 (about $277,000 in today's coin) deposited in a Lawton, Oklahoma, bank earned from selling his autographed pictures, headdresses, canes, and bows and arrows. Some of his own people hated him, while others loved him, but they all respected him.

My rendering of Geronimo's years in captivity has been drawn primarily from the classic biography, *Geronimo,* by Angie Debo; the oral histories of the Chiricahua, as recorded in *Indeh* by Eve Ball, Norah Henn, and Lynda Sánchez; old newspaper and other accounts in *The Apache Rock Crumbles* by Woodward B. Skinner; *Apache Voices* taken from the oral history files of Eve Ball by Sherry Robinson; and *From Fort Marion to Fort Sill* by Alicia Delgadillo and

Miriam A. Perrett.

I've told the story of Geronimo's twenty-three years as a prisoner of war through his eyes to give the reader a sense of his humanity, what he personally endured in those years, and the impact government decisions, based on determined ignorance (uninformed assumed superiority of white culture, education, and religion), had on the lives of the Chiricahua prisoners of war. Everything Geronimo thinks or says in my novel that is not recorded by historians comes from my imagination and my understanding of his terrifically complex personality. He had great charisma for leading men in battle and a brilliant, tactical mind for raiding and war. He was often brave in battle to the point of foolishness, but he believed Ussen had told him no bullet would kill him. He was a tender, loving father, but also a hard-eyed killer who hated Mexicans so deeply that he had no reluctance throwing Mexican babies on cactus thorns or roasting them over a fire to kill them.

Geronimo was paranoid (at times justifiably so), often believing White Eyes and Apache scouts had or would betray him. After he became a prisoner of war, he continually worried that the army's execution of all the Chiricahua was imminent.

Geronimo was never a chief. He was a *diyen,* a medicine man, a man of supernatural power so great, many Apaches feared him. Naiche, son of Cochise, and who became the Chokonen Chiricahua chief when he was nineteen, had no experience leading the People, no supernatural powers to assist in war fighting, and knew little of battle tactics. Because of this, he asked Geronimo to become his counselor and assume the chief's duties as war leader. Geronimo accepted being Naiche's counselor and war leader rather than being a chief as is commonly supposed.

Geronimo was a man of many contradictions and personal conflicts. This is the story of his "Odyssey," a journey across the end of his life and the revelations, achievements, and bitter disappointments during his twenty-three years as a prisoner of war.

W. Michael Farmer
Smithfield, Virginia
September 2018

CHAPTER 1
KILL THE SCOUTS

I am Geronimo, *di-yen,* counselor, and war leader for Chiricahua Chief Naiche. When the soldiers of the Great White Chief drove my people and me from our home, we went to the mountains. When they followed us, we slew all we could. We said we would not be captured. No. We starved, but we killed. I said we would never yield, but one day from our camp on a flat-topped mountain in Sonora, Mexico, I heard one of my young men say, "Geronimo! Scouts come!"

I took the soldier glasses Kanseah offered me and looked down the mountain trail. Far below, the Bavispe River sparkled in the midday sun, and heat rolled off the boulders and sand among the yuccas, junipers, and grass across the steep slopes reaching up to us, making the land appear to weave and stagger like a drunk man. Still looking in size like they were not much more than small insects, I saw two men running, one waving a white cloth held high on a stick. Kanseah was right. They were scouts. No White Eye could run up this mountain, especially in this heat. I thought, *Fools, they betray us again. I should have killed them long ago. Now they'll go to the Happy Place wishing they had never seen this mountain.*

"Hmmph. You have good eyes, Kanseah. While I watch, run to the camp and tell the other warriors I want a council here now. Be quick!"

As the runners came closer, warriors began appearing around me. I knew their rifles would be loaded, and they would be ready for a fight. *Enjuh* (Good). I handed the glasses back to Kanseah. "Don't lose sight of them."

I sat down near Kanseah, and the rest of the warriors joined me in a council circle in the shade of a big pine by the edge of the trail down the mountain. I said, "Two scouts are coming with a white cloth tied to a yucca stalk." The warriors frowned and looked at each other.

My brother Perico said, "Good. Maybe they come to ask for peace. I'm tired of this never-ending fighting and running."

Still holding his glasses on the runners, Kanseah said, "Ho! The scouts are Kayihtah and Martine."

"It doesn't matter who they are. They betray us. If they come closer, shoot them."

I saw heads shake and jaw muscles tighten in the yellow light brushing the sides of my warriors' faces and falling in bright pools on the pine needles and dust where we sat.

Yahnozha, one of my best warriors and Kayihtah's cousin, clenched his teeth, shook his rifle, and, almost shouting, said, "They're our brothers. Let's find out why they come. They're brave men to risk coming here."

I felt rage boil up in me at all the betrayals we had suffered since Clum and his scouts had, nearly ten harvests ago, taken me, Ponce, and five others from the Ojo Caliente Reservation in chains and left us to sweat and die in the filth of the San Carlos guardhouse. I trusted none of them. I shook my fist at Yahnozha. "They don't risk this for us, but for money from the White Eyes. When they get close enough, shoot them!"

Yahnozha's eyes narrowed, and I saw rebellious fire burning in them. He looked around the circle, his teeth clenched, and his face squeezed into a frown of fury. His thumb pulled back his rifle's hammer, and his finger curled around its trigger. "We won't shoot. If there's any more fighting done, it will be with you, not them. The first man who lifts his rifle, I will kill."

The warriors lowered their heads looking from under wrinkled brows and peered at me. Fun, my best and bravest warrior, my *segundo* (my number two), stood with his rifle cocked, finger on the trigger, and glanced around the circle. *Good,* I thought, *Fun will stop this foolishness.*

But Fun said, "And I will help you."

I shook my head, thinking, *Fools. Those scouts deserve to die, but I know Yahnozha and Fun never bluff.* I saw the looks among the warriors. We couldn't be fighting among ourselves over traitors coming to us. I said the only thing that might save our little band. "Let them come."

Yahnozha took Kanseah's glasses and climbed up on a boulder to stand in the shadows where he couldn't be seen while looking down the trail. I smiled. Yahnozha might be a fool for saving his cousin, but he hadn't forgotten to be a wise warrior. Soon he lowered the glasses and yelled, "Why are you coming?"

I recognized the puffing voice of Kayihtah from not far down the trail. "We come . . . with a message from General Miles . . . and *Teniente* (Lieutenant) Gatewood . . . who

want to discuss peace with Geronimo."
Yahnozha stepped out of the shadows and
motioned them to come on.

We met Kayihtah and Martine at the top of
the trail. The scouts, blowing and sweating
like horses after a hard gallop, had become
soft living at Fort Apache Reservation. The
only weapons they carried were their knives.
We let them keep the knives and led them
to our camp where we sat down in council.
We made cigarettes with oak leaves and *tobaho* and smoked to the four directions,
but it took all my self-control not to betray
Ussen's law of asylum for visitors to the
camp and kill these traitors with my own
knife, even though they came with a white
cloth and a peace offer from the Blue Coats.
My guts were on fire for their blood. We
finished the smoke, and I said through
clinched teeth, "Speak. We listen."

Kayihtah folded his hands and leaned
forward to rest his elbows on his knees
before looking around the circle at every
warrior. He said, "The Blue Coats are coming after you from the east, west, north, and
south. Their chiefs have told them to kill
every one of you, even if takes fifty harvests
(fifty years)."

A breeze glided through the tops of the

pines where we sat, and I heard the soft murmurs of our women, who were working nearby, commenting on what Kayihtah had just said. Even children hid behind bushes around us, still and listening to what was said. I hoped my warriors didn't cringe in fear like the women. A big, black vulture riding on the breeze floated over the trees below us, and I wondered if it was sent by Ussen to take care of our bodies that were sure to die soon if we listened to these scouts.

Kayihtah continued, "Think on it. I know all this fighting must be a heavy weight on your minds. Everything is against you. If you're awake at night and a rock rolls down this mountain or a stick breaks, you run. Why, you even eat running. You have no friends anywhere in all the land. Even this mountain is a spear and a shield. You can live up here, but if the trail is destroyed, you'll be prisoners here forever. You who still have families will never see them again. You're not like me."

Thank Ussen for blessings, I thought.

Kayihtah smiled and nodded at us. "I get plenty to eat. I go wherever I want, and I talk to good people."

Ha! You talk to cowards and Blue Coats.

Kayihtah continued, "I lie down whenever

I want and get all my sleep. I have nobody to fear. I have my little patch of corn. I'm trying to do what the white people want me to do. There's no reason you people shouldn't do it. Don't you think my words are true?"

I made a false smile and said, "How do we know Gatewood will keep his promise to take us to our families?"

"He's given his word. He'll take you first to Fort Bowie, and there he'll put you on the iron wagon to go to your families in Florida. In three days, five at most, you'll be with them."

"You well know how many Apaches have been taken under safe conduct and then murdered." I slapped the earth in front of me. "This is my home. Here I stay. Kill me if you wish, for every living thing has to die sometime. How can a man meet death better than in fighting for his own? It's every warrior's dream to die this way."

"But your men don't have their families with them as you do. If you don't quit fighting, soon there will be none of you left. The Chiricahua will be exterminated."

"I prefer death to imprisonment."

"You won't be imprisoned. *Teniente* Gatewood has said so. He asks only that you meet him in council."

"Mangas Coloradas trusted the white flag. What happened to him?"

"Gatewood will keep his word. Think of the women and children with you — your own wives and children among them."

Kayihtah, you're a fool. The Whites Eyes wipe themselves with you after they make dirt. They always lie. You can't trust any of them. I looked around the council circle, and all the warriors were slowly nodding their heads at Kayihtah's words. Their faces told me they were willing to hear Gatewood's offer from Miles. *Lied to by traitors, and they still believe it. They're men with the understanding of children. I know they're tired of fighting and running, but in war you have to be strong. This meeting is like a game of Monte. I have to play the next card, or I will no longer deal.*

I said to Martine, "You go to Gatewood . . . you say . . . Geronimo wants to talk. You come back with Gatewood. Kayihtah stays with us until you return."

Naiche, the warriors' hereditary chief, tall and thin as a pine and stronger than oak, said, "Tell Gatewood if he comes, I give my word he won't be harmed." He lifted his jaw and flashed his eyes toward me, and I gave a small nod to show I understood.

Martine stood. "I tell Gatewood what you say. He comes. He speaks straight. This you will know after you hear him."

Naiche and I decided to meet Gatewood at a place on a bend in the Bavispe River where, if trouble came, we could defend ourselves hiding in the bosque and get back to our trail up the mountain without wasting bullets. Naiche sent Perico, my son Chappo, and Kanseah to Gatewood's camp in a canebrake on the east branch of the river. The warriors stayed hidden, watching the camp and waiting for the dawn.

The sun came painting a gold line on the eastern mountains against a gauzy, turquoise sky and throwing shafts of light through the treetops. Martine crawled from his blankets and went into the canebrake to make water. As he stood there, Perico told me he said to Martine's back, "Meeting place we want upriver. Only you, Gatewood, and an interpreter come. Leave all other scouts and Blue Coats with Captain Lawton. Ride south. We show the way."

Martine, sweating in the cool morning air, nodded he understood, and the warriors disappeared into the shadows. Martine told Gatewood the words from the warriors, and Gatewood did as they said. He was not afraid. He wanted our war to end. One of the warriors told me Gatewood had said to

Martine that he understood what was required and would come.

I thought, *This is good. Maybe now we'll get to live in peace.*

CHAPTER 2
TALKS WITH
TENIENTE GATEWOOD

The place we picked to counsel with Gatewood had clear views up and down the river and a good way to get back under cover to the trail up the mountain. It was shady and cool by the Bavispe, and there was plenty of grass there for our horses and Gatewood's mules. We stayed hidden where we could see the place and waited to be sure Gatewood brought only those we said he could bring and not a hidden troop of cavalry to attack and kill us. When we saw Martine come with Gatewood and Wratten, who would serve as the interpreter, and no one else, I had the warriors slowly drift down to the place and turn their ponies loose to graze with Gatewood's mules.

I followed Naiche to the meeting place. Sliding off his pony, Naiche went to Gatewood and shook hands with him after the White Eye custom. I was last to come in. I slid off my pony, rested my rifle against a

43

stone to keep the barrel clean, and pumped Gatewood's hand as Naiche had done. Through Wratten, I told him we wanted to hear what General Miles had to say after chasing us with so many soldiers for so many months and not catching or killing any of us. "Maybe," I joked, "General Miles has decided to surrender to us." Gatewood smiled on one side of his mouth but said nothing more.

We sat down to counsel in a good, shady place where the rocks were smooth. It was cool, and we heard the river gurgling and a canyon wren's occasional sharp *Jeet! Jeet!* High above us, ravens flew squawking down the river toward Colonia Morelos. Gatewood pulled tobaho and papers from his shirt and passed them around for cigarettes, but since this was serious business, we made our cigarettes out of our own oak leaves. After we smoked, the warriors leaned in to listen to Gatewood.

I looked at him and said with some impatience, "We come to hear General Miles's words. Give them to us!"

Gatewood held out his right hand palm-up and looked around the circle. "These are the words of General Miles. Hear them. Surrender, and you will be sent to join the rest of your friends in Florida. There you'll wait until the president, the Great White Chief, decides what he must do about you. Accept these terms or fight until you're all dead."

Do Miles and Gatewood think we're fools? Do they think we believe them? They'll be gone long before we are. The warriors looked at each other and frowned. I decided to play a little game with Gatewood. I held out my hands in front of me and made them tremble. I saw Fun smile. He knew I had done this before when we talked to *Nakai-yes* (Mexicans) and I wanted a little whiskey. It always got us a drink. "Gatewood, I'm a little shaky in this new sun. I need whiskey to calm and steady me. Don't you have some?"

"Sorry, Geronimo, I don't drink, and there's none with me or the other soldiers."

I knew he was lying, but I didn't show bad manners by saying so like a White Eye would.

I stopped my hands trembling and looked Gatewood straight in the face, practically insulting him, and said through clenched teeth, "I leave the warpath only if we can return to the reservation and live as before."

Gatewood shook his head. "General Miles's words won't change."

"Has he heard of all the things that happened to us that made us leave the reservation?"

"I don't know. I doubt he has, but I know General Crook did. He didn't believe you, and now he's gone."

"Then listen. I tell you."

Gatewood crossed his arms and nodded. "Speak. I listen."

"Let me tell you why we left the reservation. I lived quietly, and I was content at the White Mountains. I did no harm to Chatto, Mickey Free, or *Teniente* Davis. I would be happy to know now who started those stories of my intention to harm those men. I was living peaceably with my family, having plenty to eat, sleeping well, taking care of my people, and perfectly contented." I looked at Naiche and my son Chappo. They both nodded, so Gatewood could see they agreed with me.

"I hadn't killed a horse or a man, American or Indian. I don't understand the people in charge of us. They knew this to be so, yet they said I was a bad man, the worst man there." I stopped to gather my thoughts as anger about those times gathered in my mind.

"I didn't leave of my own accord." I paused, and Gatewood nodded for me to go on.

"Sometime before I left, an Indian, Nodiskey, had a talk with me. He said, 'They're going to arrest you,' but I didn't listen to him. I'd done no wrong. Huera, the wife of Mangas, told me they were going to seize me and put Mangas and me in the guardhouse. I'd seen the inside of that nasty guardhouse before, and I wasn't going back. I learned from Chatto and Mickey Free the Americans were going to arrest me and hang me. This was the same thing Tribolett told me six moons earlier the night after I'd agreed to surrender to Crook. They said the White Eyes would hang me after I crossed the border, so I left both times. I left once from Fort Apache and once from Crook's camp."

Anger grew in me as I told Gatewood these things, and I said, louder than I intended, as I pounded my thigh with my fist, "I want to know now who ordered me to be arrested. I was praying to the light and to the darkness, to God and to the sun, to let me live quietly there with my family." There were grunts and nods all the way around the council to affirm that I spoke the truth.

"I've asked for peace several times, but trouble came from the agents and interpreters. The agents cheated us, and the interpreters lied about what we said. I don't want that to happen again." I paused a moment to gather my scattered thoughts while Gatewood rubbed his chin and watched me. "The Earth Mother is listening to me, and I hope all may be so arranged so that from now on there will be no trouble and we will always have peace. Whenever we see you coming to where we are, we think it is God — you must always come with God." Again, there were grunts and nods of agreement around the council.

"Whenever I have broken out, it has always been on account of bad talk. Very often, there are stories put in the news-papers that I'm to be hanged. I don't want that anymore. When a man tries to do right, such stories ought not be put in news-papers."

Gatewood nodded he understood but said nothing. I looked around at the council faces and saw my warriors were listening to my every word. *Enjuh. They need to hear this and judge whether the reservation is how they want to live or whether they will be wild and free.*

"There are very few of my men left now. They've done some bad things, but I want the memory of those things all rubbed out, and let us never speak of them again.

48

Sometimes a man does something, and men are sent out to bring in his head. I don't want such things to happen to us. I don't want Apaches killing each other. We think of our relations, brothers, brothers-in-law, fathers-in-law, all of them over on the reservation, and from this time on, we want to live in peace, just as they are doing, and to behave as they are behaving. I want this peace to be legal and good."

Gatewood said, "You're right to think that way. That's what the Great White Chief always wants."

I frowned. "I don't believe that is so, Gatewood. When Crook went to the reservation, he put agents and interpreters over us who did bad things. I want the Great White Chief to treat us right. I want to have a good man over me. I want to live well. I know I have to die sometime, but even if the heavens were to fall on me, I want to do what is right. I think I'm a good man, but newspapers everywhere say I'm a bad man, but it's a bad thing to say about me. I never do wrong without cause. There's one God looking down on us all. We're all children of the one God. God is listening to me. The sun, the darkness, and the winds are all listening to what we say now. That is all I have to say."

Gatewood nodded he understood. He looked up to where the sun stood and said, "In a hand above the horizon (about an hour), the sun will be at shortest shadows. You and your warriors hold a council without Wratten, Martine, Kayihtah, and me and talk about what General Miles has told me to tell you. I have food for a meal a packer will bring to us at the time of shortest shadows. He comes unarmed. We'll eat and then counsel again. Is this good for you?"

I looked at Naiche, who nodded. "We will counsel for a while and talk on your words. Then we will eat your meal."

CHAPTER 3
THE CHOICE

In our council, we talked of surrender and going to our people in the place the White Eyes called Florida. As the warriors talked, I saw that those who had their families with us wanted to continue the fight, but those with families in Florida wanted to quit fighting and be near their families. They wanted to surrender, regardless of the cost.

I thought, *Fools, be men. Steal yourselves new women and make more children for yourselves. Fight. We can live in this place until we die.* I spoke my heart and encouraged them to be strong and fight on. By the time we were ready to eat, we had decided to surrender only if we were allowed to return to the reservation and the Blue Coats returned our families. I was glad we had decided this. If the Blue Coats accepted this, it was the best thing for us, but I knew it would never happen.

We ate a meal with Gatewood, Wratten,

Kayihtah, and Martine, but some warriors didn't like the food. It was dry and too salty, something men carried with them to eat in a time of raiding and war, but there were sweet cakes at the end of the meal, and all thought these were good. We finished eating, washed in the river, and again sat with Gatewood in council.

Gatewood looked at me and said, "Now that you've talked on my words, will you surrender to General Miles on his terms?"

I looked Gatewood in the eye, as the White Eyes do when they want you to believe they speak the truth, and said with a little snarl and growl, "Take us to the reservation or fight."

Gatewood looked surprised and glanced around the circle, but he saw no guns pointing at him. Naiche held up his hand and said, "Whether we continue war or not, you'll be allowed to leave in peace." There was a long silence broken by only the canyon wren's *Jeet! Jeet!* I wondered what it was trying to tell us. Gatewood took off his hat and ran his fingers through the water in his hair. He looked around the circle. "Geronimo demands to return to your reservation on Turkey Creek. But you have no reservation to which you can return. All your people have been sent to join Chihuahua in Florida."

The warriors' eyes flew wide open, and their jaws dropped. This news was more surprising than an ambush. The council moved back to the place where it sat in private before the meal.

There was no place for them to return. They had thought their families were at Turkey Creek. That was why they'd wanted to return to there. Now their families were many days' travel east, and our men had to go there if they wanted to see them again.

Naiche was anxious to learn about his mother, mother-in-law, father-in-law, wives, and children. He told Kanseah to go find a beef so they could make meat, cook, and talk all night with Gatewood to learn all he knew about our families. Kanseah came back empty-handed. He could not find a beef.

We returned to our council with Gatewood, and I said, "Tell us about this General Miles."

Gatewood nodded, "All right. What do you want to know?"

"How old is he?"

"He is forty-seven harvests."

I continued asking Gatewood questions about General Miles long into the time after shortest shadows before the night came.

"How big is he? What are the colors of his hair and eyes? Is his voice hard or easy? Does he talk much or little? Does he mean more or less what he says? Does he have many friends among his own people? Do the soldiers and officers like him? Does he have experience with Indians? Does he keep his promises?" Gatewood answered all the questions, and we all watched his face when he answered.

I never thought Gatewood lied when answering any of my questions. I liked Gatewood and what he said about General Miles. Miles sounded like he understood us much better than Crook had. I didn't like Crook, who had said I lied six moons earlier when I spoke with him to discuss surrender terms. I didn't lie. I was glad Crook was gone.

I had no more questions for Gatewood, and looking around the council fire, I saw the warriors were thinking hard about all they had heard that day. I said to Gatewood, "Miles must be a good man."

Gatewood made a little smile and asked, "Why?"

"The Great Father sent him from Washington, and he sent you all this distance to us."

The sun was falling behind the mountains in a golden haze. Frogs in the river began their noise, and the ravens came flying and squawking up the river to the trees in the canyons where they had their nests. One of the warriors began making a fire to keep away the cold night air as the youngest warriors went to the riverbank to gather wood.

Gatewood said, "My men and I will leave you to your talks and go downriver to Captain Lawton's camp to eat and sleep. I know you have much to discuss and think about. It's for you to decide what you'll do. I hope you decide the best trail for yourselves."

"Hmmph. This we will do. We will give you our answer when the next sun's light comes."

Gatewood motioned to Martine, Kayihtah, and Wratten to gather their saddles and catch their mules before it was too dark. Martine waved and said, "I catch your mule, *Teniente,* and Kayihtah will get Wratten's." Gatewood gave a Martine a little two-finger salute from the brim of his hat and waited, standing with me.

"Gatewood, I think you speak with a straight tongue. We want your advice. Consider yourself one of us and not a White Eye. Remember all that has been said today.

As an Apache, what would you advise us to do?"

Gatewood puffed air with his cheeks and crossed his arms as he stared at the fading light on the eastern mountains across the valley. He thought for a while until Martine and Kayihtah brought the mules for him and Wratten. Then Gatewood picked up his saddle and turned to me. "I would trust General Miles and take him at his word."

As Gatewood saddled his mule, the warriors gathered behind me, and I tried once more to get better terms of surrender. I already knew from the faces of the warriors that they wanted to see their families. The battle was lost.

"Gatewood, why can't you take a man and go to the nearest army post — I think maybe it's Fort Huachuca — and use the talking wire to ask General Miles to change his terms? I'll send some warriors with you to protect you from other Indians and *banditos,* so you won't be in any danger."

Gatewood finished tightening the cinch on his saddle. "I wish it was that simple, but General Miles has made up his mind and won't change his terms. I know I'll hear your answer in the morning. *Adios.*" He leaned over his mule and shook my hand.

I felt as if I stood tottering on the edge of

high cliffs looking into a darkness filled with shadows and shifting light. "*Adios,* Gatewood."

My son Chappo liked *Teniente* Gatewood very much and wanted to learn more about him and from him. He asked to go to Gatewood's camp and sleep there. I said, "Go." But soon he returned and said Gatewood was afraid some scout might try to kill him while he was sleeping. Gatewood had told him it would be better if he stayed in our camp. This only increased our respect for Gatewood and his judgment.

We talked in council long into the night as the river frogs and tree peepers sang their songs. We came to a time where there was no talk for a while as the warriors thought about what had been said as the fire sputtered and crackled lower. Then my brother Perico, like unexpected lightning in a summer night, said, "I'm going to surrender. My wife and children have been captured. I love them and want to be with them."

My heart fell. I knew there would be others making this choice. This meant the end of us. It didn't take long for Ahnandia, a powerful warrior whose wife Tah-das-te I sometimes used as a safe messenger to the White Eyes and Mexicans, and then Fun to say they, too, were going to surrender. I stared at the fire and then stood to look at them all. It was hard to speak. It felt like thorns were in my throat. I croaked, "I don't know what to do. I've been depending heavily on you three. You've been great fighters in battle. If you're going to surrender, there's no use my going on without you. I'll give up with you."

We spent the rest of the night deciding how we could get to the border without being attacked and surrender to Miles there.

Mists floated off the river, and the air was cold in the gray light of the new sun when we rode to Gatewood's camp and sent a scout picket to call for Bay-chen-daysen (Long Nose, who the White Mountain scouts called Gatewood). We saw Gatewood coming, his shirt bottom hanging over his pants, his suspenders not yet on his shoulders. The warriors all dismounted except me. They quietly unsaddled their ponies, put the saddles on the ground, and, as if approaching Ussen with a gift, laid their rifles and pistols on them and stepped back.

Gatewood came to stand beside my pony. I hadn't dismounted and still wore my big pistol in a fancy *Nakai-yi* holster. Gatewood gazed at the saddles with the arms lying on them and slowly nodded. He glanced at me and said in his rough, halting Apache, "What is your answer, Geronimo?"

"We will surrender to General Miles and ride the iron wagon to this place called Florida. We'll go to our families and make war no more."

"I think you've done the best thing for your people."

"We ask that you ride to this General Miles with us, and when you can, sleep in our camp. We also ask that we keep our arms until we cross the border and that Lawton's troops accompany us to protect us from the *Nakai-yes* and other American patrols. Do you agree to this?"

Gatewood said, "Yes, I agree for my part. I'll ride with you. I believe Lawton will also agree to accompany you, but that's his decision. Wait here and I'll ask what he chooses to do." He turned and walked back to Lawton's camp, disappearing into the mists off the river.

We didn't wait long before Gatewood returned. As he approached us, he nodded. "Lawton agrees to ride with us and to give you safe passage to meet with General Miles. He's sending a rider now to take word to General Miles that you've chosen the good way and surrendered. There will be no more killing."

"*Enjuh*. Let there be peace between us."

I swung off my pony, Gatewood and I shook hands, and then each warrior came forward to shake his hand. I saw relief in my young men's eyes that at last they would see their families soon. I prayed to Ussen that it would be so, but I had known the White Eyes for many harvests. I knew better. Ussen had told me I would die in a bed. Even now, I wished I had already died fighting, had died like Victorio, out of bullets and stabbing myself in the heart before the enemy could take me.

Chapter 4
The Train

The Plains of West Texas, September 9, 1886

The windows on our iron wagon were fastened shut. The air inside felt like that in the bread baking ovens of the Pueblo people, but our warriors had endured worse heat hiding in dust under ambush blankets. The stink of the dirt and water we made in the buckets and some on the floor at each end of the iron wagon crawled through the wagon to burn and tear at our noses, but we had smelled worse odors when we killed *Nakai-yes* and White Eyes with our knives and fire.

The worst thing about the buckets was not their stink, but the lack of privacy when we had to use them. At least the women were covered with their long skirts when they squatted, but we men could only turn our backs to the people while they looked away from us. It was a hard thing to lose

61

my privacy when I was full of harvests and a war leader of my people. I wondered if perhaps the heat and stink were the way the Blue Coats thought to torture us before they stopped the iron wagon to shoot us.

I thought, *Ho! Make the wagon hotter. Make the stink worse. We'll say nothing. We won't beg the White Eyes to end our misery. We're Chiricahua Apaches. We never give our enemies pleasure when we suffer.* Even our little children, red from the heat and covered with sweat, raised no cry as their mothers, whose shirts were dark from body water, offered them their water-covered breasts. I was proud of my people. They were strong.

This was the first time I had ridden an iron wagon. I looked through its dusty windows glowing in the afternoon sunlight to watch the creosote bushes, mesquite trees, and cholla cactus pass by faster than I had ever seen it from a running pony. I thought, *This is the way the land must look to birds swooping into the brush.*

The sun had fallen two more hands toward the horizon since the Blue Coats last stopped to get water and load more wood or black rocks to feed the demons in the belly of the iron wagon. Soon we would stop to get more.

■ ■ ■ ■

The iron wagon began to slow, and a Blue Coat chief with a yellow bandana held over his nose and mouth opened the door on one end of the iron wagon. He coughed and sounded like he was near to losing his stomach. George Wratten, our interpreter, his face twisted by the stench, stood behind him. He had agreed to ride with us as an interpreter of our language after helping Gatewood talk us into surrendering.

The Blue Coat motioned for Naiche to come to the door where he and Wratten spoke loud in each other's ears, trying to hear each other above the rumble and steady thump of the iron wagon's song. Naiche soon waved his hand parallel to the ground, came back to my place, and sat beside me while the Blue Coat shut the door. At least the air was a little better, with the worst smells going out the door with the Blue Coat and Wratten.

Naiche leaned next to my ear and said, "The Blue Coat says soon we stop at a small town. A crowd waits for us there. They come after long rides and want to see the Apaches they fear, who killed many White Eyes, burned their lodges, and took their horses

and cattle. The Blue Coat asks all the warriors leave the iron wagon and sit on the
iron road bank so White Eyes can look at
us. He says the women and children don't
have to come out. I told him they, too, want
to breathe air not filled with stink. In case
the crowd attacks us, I want the warriors
closest to the crowd so we can strike quick
blows, even if it's only with our bare hands,
before they kill us. We'll sit close to the bottom with you and me in the center. The rest
can sit up the bank behind the warriors."

I nodded as I rubbed my nose. "It's a
good plan. Perhaps while we sit outside,
some Blue Coats will empty our buckets
and wash the floor."

The iron wagon began passing White Eye
casas and soon stopped by a tower that
held much water. The doors on each end of
our wagon opened, and two young Blue
Coat boys, who must have been doing their
White Eye novitiates, came through a door
in our car. They sounded like they were
about to lose their stomachs as they carried
the buckets away. Two more came with
buckets of water and brooms to wash the
floor. Blue coats, standing on the platform
before the doors, wrinkled their faces in
disgust as the boys walked by. Then they

motioned us out of the wagon and down to the bank, where soldiers stood shoulder to shoulder with rifles ready in a big half circle outside of where we were to sit. In front of the Blue Coats were many White Eyes of all ages, men and women, boys and girls, who stretched their necks and leaned to look around those in front of them to get a better view of us.

A White Eye stood a head above all the others in the crowd nearest the soldiers, his shirtsleeves rolled up his arms showing his red "long johns" sleeves, as the White Eyes called them. I could smell him from where I sat, smelled like he hadn't bathed in moons, smelled worse than inside the iron wagon. We locked gazes. He pointed a finger on his big, meaty hand at me, turned to the crowd, and started speaking.

"That ol' bastard there with slit eyes and mouth, the one with new duds and fancy boots, yeah, that one, the evil-lookin' one, that there is Geronimo. He nearly scalped me one time when I was wounded and playin' dead over west o' th' big river in New Mexico, but the cavalry come an' run him off 'fore he could do it." He nodded at a soldier standing right in front of me, "Hey, you, Private! Cut me one them buttons off his shirt fer a soovynear. Then I'n say I's th' one that scalped him and now, aye God, he ain't ever gonna scalp me. Them bluebellies is likely gonna hang him. Haw! Haw!"

The crowd's total attention was on the soldier in front of me. He looked up and down the line of soldiers standing between the crowd and us, licked his lips, cocked his rifle, and shook his head. "Those ain't the orders I have for these prisoners. You folks look and move on, and leave these Apaches alone."

I knew the tall White Eye spoke about me, but I knew too few Anglo words to answer what he said without sounding like a fool. I had been around the White Eyes and soldiers long enough to understand what he said. I wished I still had my knife. I would make him regret those words. I could only sit there, smell his stink, and say nothing.

Black rocks rattled into the little iron wagon behind the iron wagon filled with demons, the ones the White Eyes called the coal car and the engine, which they continued giving a drink from the tall tower. Behind us, George Wratten and the Blue Coat chief stood on the platform outside the iron wagon door. I heard Wratten say something to the Blue Coat chief, who grunted in response. Then there came the sound of boots down the platform steps and then on the rocks under the iron road.

In a couple of breaths, Wratten stood beside me, speaking low in my ear. "Geronimo, that White Eye wanted a button off your shirt to remember you and how you almost, to use his word, 'scalped' him. I know that part isn't true. Apaches don't take scalps, at least not very often. Why don't you sell it to him? Your wife can sew another back on for you, and you've made some easy money."

Wratten had worked at the trading post on San Carlos and knew how to make a good trade. I liked the idea of making money. Maybe I could use it to pay a guard for looking the other way when I ran off. I nodded.

Wratten said, "How much do you want for the button?"

I looked down to think over a price, saw my new boots, and remembered the scouts used to brag they earned fifty cents a day for their work, the same as a soldier. "I want fifty cents for the button. That's what the scouts and soldiers earn in a day." I wanted to show them my buttons were worth as much as they were.

Wratten grinned and nodded, then turned to go back to the Blue Coat chief waiting on the iron wagon platform. I heard the

Blue Coat chief laugh, and Wratten told me later that he said, "He'll never get that much."

Wratten yelled down to the tall White Eye who stood staring at me with his arms crossed. "Hey, you! The one who wants a button off Geronimo's shirt. He'll sell it to you for fifty cents."

The tall White Eye frowned, started to shake his head, but then reached in his pocket and held up a silver coin for all to see. "Bring me that there button, and I'll give you fifty cents."

Murmurs lifted from the crowd, but the tall White Eye turned to them and shouted, "That there button will be worth a lot more than fifty cents when that old murderer is hung."

Wratten jumped off the platform, slid down beside me, and handed me a folding knife. The Blue Coat chief made a signal, and three soldiers pointed their cocked rifles at me. I opened the knife, cut the middle button off my shirt, and handed the knife and button to Wratten. He said in a low voice, "I'll be back."

The soldiers with the rifles pointed at me returned to their positions facing the crowd. Wratten, squeezing between soldiers, carried the button to the tall White Eye, took his money, and, with a big smile, brought it to me. He laughed as he laid it in my hand and said, "Geronimo, one day you're going to the Happy Place a very wealthy man."

I looked out over the crowd thinking, *Maybe so, George Wratten, but I'd rather be free and sitting in a wickiup on the Río Gila in the land of my fathers. These Blue Coats will shoot us all soon anyway.* As I looked at the faces in the crowd, I saw an old man standing apart from the others. His lower face was covered with long, gray hair like that of *Nantan Lupan* (General Crook). A scar on the left side of his face ran from his eye all the way down to his jawbone, making a deep, narrow canyon through the gray hair. I had seen him before, but I couldn't remember where. His rheumy, dead eyes never left me as he slowly chewed tobacco and spat the juice between his boots. He wore a long, black coat over a white shirt and vest. The coat was unbuttoned, and I could see a shoulder holster holding a revolver.

Then the demon carrying iron wagon made the same long moan it always made when it was full and ready to run down the iron road again. The Blue Coat in charge motioned for us to get on board.

69

CHAPTER 5
SAN ANTONIO

On the third day after we left Fort Bowie, we still rode in the stinking, hot iron wagon pulled on the unending iron road faster than the fastest pony, never tiring, but stopping every two or three hands against the sky to feed and water the roaring, moaning demons pulling us. It was not time to feed and water the demons again, but the iron wagon slowed as we passed many White Eye *casas* and scattered groups of White Eyes standing near the iron road to see us.

I looked at Naiche and frowned. He came and sat beside me. "Wratten says the Blue Coat chief was given words from the talking wire at the last stop. They said for him to stop the train in the place the White Eyes call San Antonio while the big chief, the one they call the president, makes up his mind about what he'll do with us."

I knew this would happen. "Hmmph. Soon we'll all be shot. I told you we must expect this. Miles said too many pretty words on the way to Fort Bowie about a reservation of our own where no White Eyes will bother us. I should have never believed him. I made a mistake. Now we're all dead."

Naiche shook his head as he stared past me out the window and watched the White Eyes and their houses pass. "Wratten doesn't think so. He says the White Eyes want to enjoy looking at the prisoners they fought so long and want to show us off in their fort so the other White Eye tribes know we surrendered to them. Maybe you can sell another button for a piece of gold. Who knows?"

I crossed my arms and shook my head. "Wratten's a fool. We'll all die, except Wratten. He's a White Eye."

The train stopped near the iron bar gate of a fort with high walls holding two rows of windows. A big crowd of White Eyes had gathered. From the door of our iron wagon, Blue Coats with rifles stood shoulder to shoulder in two lines, facing each other, to make an open path for us to walk through to the fort gate. Wratten told us the high walls were Fort Sam Houston in the town of San Antonio and that Big Chief Cleveland, the one the White Eyes called the president, had ordered us to stay here while he and General Miles talked about our surrender.

Naiche led us off the train. Many hands pointed fingers at me as we walked straight and proud into the center of the fort, the place the White Eyes called the quadrangle. The roar of many voices in the crowd behind the lines of Blue Coats sounded like the Gila River rushing over the rocks in a narrow place. I was glad when they shut the gate of the fort behind us and kept the crowd out. In walking places above where we stayed, many soldiers with rifles surrounded us and watched our every move.

Big white tents sat inside the quadrangle walls, each big enough for four grown people to sleep. Nearby, long tables heavy with soldier food had been set out for us along with buckets of water. Wratten told Naiche we were to take a small pan from a big stack, a thing the White Eyes called a spoon, and a metal cup for water and help ourselves.

Naiche, as chief, and his young wife Haho-zinne took the first tent closest to the stockade gate, and I sat in front of the next tent while my good wife, She-gha, brought me food. I was hungry, so I ate. Some did not. They believed, as I did, that the Blue

72

Coats would kill us soon. I wondered why they were feeding us. I didn't know and didn't care. I ate their beans and bread, but not the roasted pig meat they gave us. I would never eat pig meat, not even if I were starving.

Seven suns passed, and nothing happened. I thought the White Eyes were having a hard time deciding how they would kill us. It seemed the one called the president must be weak and could not make a decision without many voices telling him what to do. I thought often of my other wives, Zi-yeh, with our little son, Fenton; and Ih-tedda (Young Girl), who had carried our first child in her belly when I sent her to Fort Bowie after Crook and I spoke during the Season of Little Eagles. I especially missed Ih-tedda and wanted to see her and the baby I had never seen. She and Zi-yeh had been sent to the fort in the place the White Eyes call Florida moons ago. I hoped she was all right. I was in a hurry to know if our child was a daughter or a son.

I understood now I was a fool to have listened to Miles's pretty words. He had said we would be back together with our families in five days. He had said we'd have our own reservation. Where was it? Had Miles also lied about our reservation? It had been more than twenty days since I gave him my rifle, and still we had not seen our families. I knew it would be many more days before we saw them again if the Blue Coats didn't kill us first. All this we did not hold against Gatewood. I thought Miles had lied to him, too.

Another seven suns passed. Riding on the iron wagon had made us and our clothes dirty from the black soot made by burning black rocks in the demon wagon that blew its smoke into the air. We asked the Blue Coats to let us bathe, and places were fixed for men and women to wash separately. Another place was given for the women to wash clothes.

The only things for us to do were to talk, walk about the quadrangle, or play Monte with the White Eye cards Wratten found for us. Wratten said the president still had not decided what to do with us. One day, Wratten told me privately that he was also worried the Blue Coats might be planning to shoot us. He said he had a few rifles and ammunition in his tent where he stayed with us, and if shooting started, we should take them and defend ourselves. I thought then George Wratten was a better White Eye than I had first believed.

The Blue Coats let the White Eyes from the town come to stand and walk where the guards were so they could observe us, like some kind of fancy *Nakai-yi* birds in a cage. One day, I saw the same old man with a scar and beard who had watched us at the place where I sold a button off my shirt. I found Naiche to show him the old man watching us, but when we looked, he was not there. Naiche shook his head and, making face wrinkles like he thought I was an old fool, said, "Even at Fort Apache you thought there were White Eyes out to get you."

George Wratten came into the stockade with two soldiers who carried their big rifles in front of them across their chests and walked in perfect harmony their legs moving as one. *So,* I thought, *at last the killing begins.* Wratten motioned to Naiche and me to come.

Wratten said, "The president has asked the chief of this place, General Stanley, to speak with each of you apart and record what you say, so that he might understand what General Miles has told you. With General Stanley will be those who make tracks on paper of your words spoken, so everyone will know what you said, and there'll be others to listen who will be witnesses to your words. Since Naiche is chief, General Stanley will speak with him first." He motioned for Naiche to follow him, and they disappeared through a door. I leaned against the stockade wall to wait, still wondering when they would shoot us.

Two hand widths of the sun's path across the sky passed before Naiche returned with Wratten and the soldiers. He made a little sign with his face that nothing had happened. Wratten motioned for me to come with him and the soldiers. We went to a room where General Stanley sat behind a big, shiny table. A man on either side of him held a little spear writing stick in his hand ready to make black water tracks on paper of what was said between us. Those there to listen as witnesses sat in seats scattered around the little room. General Stanley motioned for Wratten and me to sit in chairs in front of him, where he could see our faces, watch our eyes, and know we spoke true.

General Stanley, his face covered with much hair, nearly all white, looked directly at Wratten and spoke in the White Eye tongue. Wratten turned to me and said, "General Stanley thanks you for coming. He asks if you agree that I can tell him what your words say in the White Eye language, and these will be made into tracks on paper."

I nodded. I already understood most of what was said. I would know if Wratten lied. Wratten spoke Apache better than any other White Eye I had known. He never deceived us like Mickey Free, who was always starting trouble at San Carlos because he lied about what we said or didn't make our words right in the White Eye tongue.

General Stanley said something to the paper track makers, who then made tracks on the paper and waited as he spoke to Wratten. Wratten said to me, "General Stanley asks that you tell us how you surrendered to General Miles and what he told you would be the result of your surrender."

I collected my thoughts and then spoke, waiting after each thought for Wratten to tell General Stanley and the track makers what I had said before he nodded for me to continue.

CHAPTER 6
MY STORY OF THE SURRENDER

I began my account, saying, "A moon ago early in the Season of Large Fruit (late summer, early fall), we were camped and resting on a flat-topped mountain at the big bend of the Río Bavispe, where it turns from running north to south at Colonia Morelos. Scouts came to us from *Teniente* Gatewood, who said he had a peace offer from General Miles and wanted to speak with us. We agreed to talk with Gatewood the next day at a place of our choosing.

"We met with Gatewood, and he said, 'These are the words of General Miles. Surrender, and you will be sent to join the rest of your friends in Florida. There you'll wait until the president decides what he must do about you. Accept these terms, or fight until you're all dead.'

"We tried to negotiate better terms, but Gatewood said Miles had made up his mind. We wanted to go back to the reservation, to Turkey Creek, but we learned in these talks that our families had already been sent to Florida. We wanted to see our families and, after much time in councils, decided to agree to what Gatewood said Miles wanted.

"After we decided to surrender, we decided how to do it. We would travel with our rifles to the American side of the border and surrender there to this General Miles if Captain Lawton would ride with us to protect us from Mexican and American troops, and if Gatewood stayed with us when we traveled, and, when convenient, slept in our camp.

"When we came to the army camp the next morning, we called for Gatewood. He came, and we told him we would surrender and the way we would do it. Captain Lawton and Lieutenant Gatewood agreed to what we wanted. We moved our camp, including the women and children, down next to Captain Lawton's camp. Captain Lawton sent a rider to General Miles to tell him we had decided to surrender and that we would hand over our arms to him at Skeleton Canyon. Miles agreed to all of this.

"We started north with Gatewood, Wratten, me, and the women and children in the lead, flankers on the sides, and Naiche and the other warriors in the rear to watch for and defend against attack. On the third day, a big party of Mexican soldiers on foot, two hundred or more, came toward us from the direction of Fronteras. Lawton stopped to speak with them while we ran on ahead while the sun moved for the width of a hand against the horizon, and then we stopped to see if there would be a fight between Captain Lawton and the Mexicans.

"There was no fight. A rider came to us from Captain Lawton. He said the Mexican *comandante* demanded that I come and tell him personally I had surrendered. I agreed to meet with him but far from his army. Each side agreed to meet and bring only seven men. The American soldier chiefs stood between us for the meeting. Gatewood told me who the Mexican *comandante* was, and then the *comandante* pulled his revolver holster around to the front of his pants. I wasted no time pulling my revolver halfway out of its holster, and I stared at him with angry eyes. I was ready to kill him. I would have enjoyed seeing him die. The Mexican put his hands behind him, and I dropped my hand to my side.

"The *comandante* wanted to know why I didn't surrender to him in Fronteras. I told him I didn't want to be murdered. Then he asked if I was going to surrender to the Americans. I said I was, because I could trust them and that they wouldn't murder my people or me. He said he would go with us to be sure we did surrender. I told him, 'No. I go north. You go south. I have nothing to do with you or your people.'

"The Americans spoke with the *comandante* and then asked me to let a Mexican soldier come with them to carry word back to the *comandante* that we had surrendered to General Miles, and I agreed to this.

"When we came to Skeleton Canyon, General Miles was slow to meet with us. We waited while Captain Lawton used a talking wire many times to tell General Miles to come and answer our questions. We were ready to surrender, but Miles wouldn't come. I sent my brother Perico with Wratten to Fort Bowie to tell General Miles that we wanted to surrender. Still, he was slow to come.

"He came late one day when the sun's shadows were long. I rode down from our camp unarmed and shook hands with him. We talked and laughed a little, and then he stated his surrender terms. He said we would be sent to Florida. He said, 'Lay down your arms and come with me to Fort Bowie, and in five days you'll see your families, who are now in Florida with Chihuahua, and no harm will be done to you.'

"Miles drew a line in the sand. He said, 'This line is the great water in the east.' He put a small rock the size of a sling stone next to the line and said, 'This represents the place where Chihuahua is with his band.' He put another stone some distance back from the first one and the line and said, 'This represents you, Geronimo.' He put a third stone down, bigger than the other two, and another distance from the rest. He said, 'This represents the Indians at Fort Apache.' Then, picking up the last two stones, he put them together with the one representing Chihuahua at a different place. He said, 'The president wants to get all of you together.'

"I smiled at Gatewood and said, 'Good, you told the truth.' I told the general of the plot by Chatto and Mickey Free, scouts who were telling lies and saying I would try to kill *Teniente* Davis, that made me leave the reservation, and he listened. He said he believed me. While we talked, Naiche waited in the hills to see what would happen. The next day, Gatewood and I brought Naiche in to talk. Miles gave Naiche the same terms he gave me, and Naiche also surrendered.

"General Miles had a big surrender ceremony. We stood between his soldiers and my warriors and placed a big stone on a blanket. This stone made our treaty. It was to last until the stone turned to dust. We raised our hands to heaven and took an oath not to do any wrong to each other or to scheme against each other.

"The next day, Naiche and I rode to Fort Bowie with General Miles in his wagon. Now we are here." I looked at General Stanley and said, "That is all I have to say."

General Stanley told the one who made tracks on paper to read back the tracks of what I said, and Wratten said the words to me in Apache. When they finished, Chief Stanley asked me if they had my words right. I said they were good. He thanked me and said I should return to my people.

Chapter 7
Broken Promises

The Blue Coats left us alone for ten suns after I talked to General Stanley with his makers of tracks on paper. I paced the place where they kept us, expecting every day the Blue Coats would shoot us. Every day I waited and told myself, *Stand strong and straight when you're defenseless and they aim their rifles at your heart.* Every day I thought about battles I had fought, the faces of my children, and the looks of fear in the eyes of the White Eyes and Mexicans before I killed them. I thought of the old man I had seen twice, once in a town near the iron road and once watching us in the quadrangle. I tried to remember where I had seen him before but failed.

Most White Eyes were very weak. I didn't understand how Ussen let them conquer us. Ussen told me I would die a natural death, and I had lived through many bullet wounds. I wondered if I would I die in bed like a woman. Wasn't a natural death for a warrior to die from wounds his enemy gave him or by his own hand, so enemies wouldn't take him? I thought of this often. I even dreamed of it. The answers to my questions I didn't know. I expected to learn them soon.

On the eleventh sun, after Naiche and I gave General Stanley our surrender stories, General Stanley came to the place of our tents with armed Blue Coat soldiers who carried a table and chairs. Wratten and the two men who made tracks on paper came, too. Wratten spoke to Naiche and me and said the president had told General Stanley to make an accounting of us with our names, number of harvests, wives, and children. He wanted us to make a line like the Blue Coat soldiers do when they march. Naiche and his family would give their answers first, then me and my wife She-gha, and then the warriors with their families. After each warrior and his family gave their answers, we were free to go about our business.

General Stanley asked the warriors if any bad men lived among us and if the others spoke straight. The warriors just stared at him. They wouldn't speak to the White Eyes about their brothers, even if those brothers were enemies.

When the shadows stretched long, Naiche and I spoke after General Stanley and the soldiers left us. We didn't understand why the president wanted to know these things about us. Who cared about the harvests a warrior had or whether he spoke straight when you were about to kill him?

Eight suns passed after we gave General Stanley our answers to his questions about our families and us. Then Wratten came with four soldiers and said General Stanley wanted to speak with us. We followed Wratten and the soldiers to the place where General Stanley did the business of a soldier chief.

When we walked into his place, he motioned us to sit in the chairs before him. Naiche sat, but I stood with arms crossed and waited to hear what he had to say. Through Wratten, he said to us, "President Cleveland has decided that you and your warriors will not be given to civil authorities in Arizona for trial. You'll go to Fort Pickens in Florida and be guarded by soldiers. Your women and children and Martine and Kayihtah will go to Fort Marion in Florida with the other Chiricahuas, the scouts, and Chihuahua's people."

Naiche sprang out his chair like a cougar, and I stepped toward General Stanley's desk. The soldiers standing behind us shouldered their rifles, ready to fire. General Stanley held up his hand and motioned them to stand back. Naiche threw his arms out to make his words sound stronger as Wratten spoke for him. "This is not what General Miles promised us when we surrendered. He said in five days we would be back with our families. It's been nearly forty. He said we would be reunited with all our family members, including those with Chihuahua, not torn away from all the Chiricahuas, including the families here with us. Does the president not know what General Miles promised us? Do White Eye chiefs always lie? This is not right." Naiche stared at the old man's face as Wratten spoke his words so he understood them. When Wratten finished, Naiche crossed his arms and nodded.

Through Wratten, I said to General Stanley, "Make tracks on a paper to the president. Tell him this is not what Miles told us when we surrendered. Tell him we ask him to keep the word of his soldier chief. We want to join our families, wherever they are, and not be torn from them."

General Stanley held up his hands and said, "I believe you. I'll send a written appeal, using your words and saying I agree with you. Perhaps the president will change his mind. It's all I can do. At least you're not being turned over to those in Arizona who would surely hang you. I'll wait for his answer before I move you."

Naiche said to Wratten, "Tell General Stanley we thank him. The White Eyes never do what they promise. Their words are like bitter water to a thirsty man."

I thought Naiche spoke well to the general. He spoke the truth. We turned and walked back to the place of tents.

That night after the meal, Naiche and I held a council with the warriors, and our women and children listened. Naiche told them what the president had decided. I heard low moans and wails like those for the dead from some of the women. It seemed that night the darkness grew blacker and the firelight weaker.

Naiche told the council he and I had told General Stanley what the president told him to do was not what General Miles had promised if we surrendered. He explained that General Stanley said he agreed with us, and would send our words on the talking wire to his soldier chiefs and ask the president to change his mind. I saw the men look at their women and children with the wish that it would be so, but I knew it wouldn't happen.

Two days after the meeting with General Stanley, Wratten came to us and said, "The president just sent word on the talking wire to General Stanley about Miles's lies. The president won't change his mind. The train to Florida leaves in the morning. Tell your wives and children goodbye tonight. It may be a long time before you see them again."

My heart wept. Women wailed, and children cried. I had never seen such a thing except when a great chief died. I held up my arms as a sign I wanted to speak, and they all grew quiet.

"Again, the White Eyes have not kept their promises. Again, we suffer because they speak their lies, but we must not cry, weak as babies wanting milk from their mothers. We must grow stronger. We will survive, no matter how long they keep us apart. Ussen won't scatter us to the winds. Ussen will bring us back together. He has given me Power to know the future, and I know it will be so. Be strong."

My nephew, Kanseah, standing off to one side, raised a fist and shouted, *"Enjuh!"*

Soon all shouted, *"Enjuh!"*

That night, the men told their children soon they would see them again, and after the children slept, the men laid down with their wives and promised to return to them. When I lay with She-gha, she told me she would be strong and carry word to Zi-yeh and Ih-tedda that I missed them and would come to them when I could. She-gha, a good woman, gave me many happy times. She made me happy I took her for a wife.

Before dawn the next morning, the soldiers opened the big gate with the iron bars and walked us out of the quadrangle surrounding us. No White Eyes in the town watched us leave. At the iron road, an iron wagon waited, its demons already snorting and groaning, and behind it, four iron wagons in which to ride. The first and last iron wagons carried soldier guards.

When we reached the middle two iron wagons, the soldiers took the women and children and Martine and Kayihtah from us and ordered them to climb on the second iron wagon. I remember the look of pride and sorrow in She-gha's eyes, the same as when I rode off to fight and kill Blue Coats and Mexicans. I said to her, "Soon I see you, and we're together again." She nodded and disappeared up the steps into the iron wagon.

In the iron wagon for the men, the windows were again fastened shut and there were buckets for when we made dirt and water. As I sat next to a window, I smiled and thought, *And the White Eyes think they're our betters.*

Chapter 8
Fort Pickens

The iron wagon never paused to watch the dawn come, never slowed as the land of grass gave way to brush and then tall pine trees, and the pine trees to great, ugly trees and bushes standing on water. Water lay everywhere, black and shining in the shadows of the trees. In all my years in the mountains and deserts, I had never seen so much water, so many green plants, so many trees with roots like fingers grabbing at the earth under the water.

On the second day after we left the stockade in San Antonio, at the time of shortest shadows, we saw great lizards resting in mud on places rising out of the water. They were big, long things, two or three times the height of a man. They had long mouths like the bills of birds, and some lay with their mouths spread wide in the heat of the sun, mouths filled with great teeth that could cut a man in half in one bite. I wondered if they belonged to the White Eyes. Who else would want them? Great white birds with long legs and long bills walked in the water, plucked up fish, and swallowed them whole. These I had seen before in the *bosque* of the great river, but not this many. Here there were enough to look like clouds on the water. There were snakes, too, big brown and gray ones that hung from trees. Such snakes I had never seen, and I hoped the Blue Coats sent us where none made their holes.

Deep in the night of the second day, the iron wagon's slowing shook me awake. I looked out the window at the stars. They had not turned enough for us to need more black rocks and water to feed the iron wagon demons. I looked at Naiche, who shook his head. The other men were awake, too. I looked out the windows to see what kind of forest we were in, but I saw nothing but sand and water on one side and big rough trees and tall cane on the other.

We moved slowly around sharp curves in the iron road and came closer to the sand and water. Points of light seemed to float far out on the water. Then the iron wagon stopped. I saw a White Eye come walking down the iron road with a lantern. He did something that made a loud hiss, and there was a banging *pesh* (iron) noise while the guard soldiers stood back to let him work between the iron wagons. Soon the White Eye held his thumb up, and the soldiers nodded. The demon wagon made a long moan, and I could see its lights begin moving up the iron road, but our iron wagon and that of the soldiers behind us didn't move.

The demon wagon had left us, taking our women and children with it. We watched its lights disappear in the trees and brush. I shook my head and stared at the floor. The White Eyes were good at torturing the spirit of a man.

Wratten came in the car with a soldier chief and told Naiche and me that Fort Pickens was the place with the points of light out on the water. We were to stay in the iron wagon until the sun came, and then a boat would come to carry us to it.

Naiche frowned. "A boat?"

Wratten nodded. "Like the White Eyes use to carry wagons and horses across the great river at Hot Springs when they want to stay dry, but this boat will be bigger and it looks different."

"Why not let us swim to Fort Pickens?"

"You might get away, and the water you cross is much wider than any river. We're sitting on the edge of the big water in the south."

"Will there be White Eyes who come to watch us ride this boat?"

"Yes, most likely."

Naiche laughed. "Then we'll get some sleep. The White Eyes will want to see us at our best."

The dawn showed us the big water. It was bigger and wider than any *llano* I had ever seen. It went as far as my eyes could see, fading into the gray distance. In the direction where Wratten had pointed last night, I saw the top of a great stone house and the tops of a few trees in the distance. Wratten was right. It was too far to swim. I knew we couldn't escape that place, and we wouldn't even try until we had our families back again. The air was thicker than it was in San Antonio. It felt like we breathed through wet bandanas, and we took a long time to get used to it.

When the sun came, so did Wratten and the soldiers. He gave us bread and coffee and said we could sit outside until the boat came. Naiche led us off the iron wagon into a light wind coming off the big water. It had a faint smell like wet mud in the canebrakes on the great river. I never liked that smell, but I learned to endure it.

Our iron wagon sat next to a wooden road leading out into the big water but soon stopped.

Different kinds of boats were tied like ponies to the wooden road over the water, and some carried nets Wratten said were used for fishing. I asked, "Will we ride one of those boats to Fort Pickens?"

"No, the one that carries you will also carry soldiers and supplies. It will be bigger, and steam will make it go like the iron wagon that pulled us here."

"There is an iron road for it on the water?"

Wratten shook his head. "No, it floats on the water, and its steam turns a big water-wheel to push it across the water wherever the driver wants it to go."

"Hmmph. Then it will be like nothing I've seen here or anywhere else."

We sat and watched big white and gray birds circling and swooping down close to the wooden road running out into the water. Sometimes they caught a fish or just landed on the water to float awhile, or they landed on top of one of the big, wooden posts holding the wooden road up high off the water. The birds made much noise as the sun rose, and their crowd grew. White Eyes, who gathered in groups to stare at us, threw little pieces of bread at the water for the birds to eat, and some grabbed a piece out of the air before it hit the water. Both crowds, birds and White Eyes, grew as the sun floated up off the edge of the big water.

Soon we saw a column of black smoke on the big water coming in our direction. A soldier chief came to tell Naiche and me the smoke was from the boat that would take us to Fort Pickens. We watched in silence, but there was much talk about it among the White Eyes who came to stare at us.

Soldiers formed two lines for us to walk between when the boat stopped at the end of the wooden road and was tied there by two men who jumped off. By this time, the crowd of White Eyes was big, and many fingers pointed at us. I heard the words *Apaches* and *Geronimo* coming from the crowd. The crowd pushed and shoved each other to get a look at us, and some grew angry that they were being pushed out of the way.

Naiche laughed at this, turned to me, and said, "Maybe we get lucky and the White Eyes kill each other because they can't see us. This is the easiest and best way to kill White Eyes."

I nodded and smiled. I looked over the crowd, and I saw the old man with the long, gray beard and black coat watching us and wondered why he followed us and why I couldn't remember where I had seen him before. I looked at the boat and the big water. When I looked for him again, he was gone.

When we were all on the boat, it was untied from the wooden road and pushed away. The great waterwheels on the sides began to turn, and it began making a wave as it turned in a big arc toward Fort Pickens. The noise was loud on the boat with the demons moving the waterwheels, and a great flock of birds that had caught food thrown to them by the White Eye crowd flew and squawked around us. Great gray fish Wratten called dolphins ran before us, jumping out of the water in big leaps, seeming to lead the boat forward. Beshe, the oldest among us, father of Naiche's wife Haho-zinne, watched them and gave big whoops of pleased surprise and pointed when he saw an extra high or long jump from our new friends leading the way.

We watched the strip of white sand and brush where the dirty brick and stone of Fort Pickens stood grow closer. It didn't seem as though anyone had been there for a long time. The men who operated the boat tied it at the end of a long, wooden road over the water leading to a road that snaked out through the brush to Fort Pickens. Wratten told us the boxes and barrels around us on the boat were our supplies, and we had to take them off the boat to be hauled to Fort Pickens. This we did. As the sun rose higher, the air seemed thicker and hotter. We had all made much body water in our shirts and on our faces when we finished unloading the boxes and barrels onto wagons that would carry them to Fort Pickens. We walked behind the wagons, the soldiers behind and in front of us as we went to the fort.

When we reached the fort, we were told to sit in the shade of a big, high wall. The commander came and spoke to us. He told us where we would sleep and cook inside the fort, and that we would work half a sun for five suns out of seven. Our work was to make Fort Pickens a good place for us to live by clearing the place of weeds, brush, and overgrown trees. I noticed one tree was even growing out of the bricks of the smoke pipe connected to a fireplace inside the fort. On the sixth day of the seven, we were to wash and patch our clothes and then, for the rest of the day and the next, we were free to rest or do whatever we wanted. The rooms we had to sleep and cook in were large. We had plenty of room for many bed sacks we filled with straw and slept on under blankets they gave us. We chose the youngest warriors and novitiates among us to cook our food and split wood for our fires. Our clothes were like those the soldiers wore when they did work at the forts.

CHAPTER 9
NEW PRISONERS COME

We settled into a schedule, and although much of what we did was women's work — chopping bushes, pulling weeds, and washing our clothes — its sameness helped make life smooth again. Perhaps, we thought, these Blue Coats won't kill us under these chiefs, but every time a chief changed, we knew he might order us killed. We often spoke of our families. We wanted our women and children back.

Six suns after we came to Fort Pickens, the *nantan* (chief commander) of Fort Pickens came to see us. Wratten said his name was Lieutenant Colonel Loomis Langdon, former commander of Fort Marion and now *nantan* at Fort Barrancas and Fort Pickens. He looked at everything we had done in those first six suns and said he liked what he saw. As he walked among us, I asked Wratten if I could speak to him. Wratten told Langdon I wanted to speak with him, and he said he would listen.

I said, "I thank the colonel who comes to watch over us. I think he doesn't know the rations we're given to eat aren't enough. We're hungry. The sergeant says, if the rations aren't enough to fill our bellies, we can fish and eat all we want. The sergeant doesn't understand Apaches. We won't eat food Ussen doesn't want us to have. Apaches won't eat fish. Fish aren't food for us. When will the colonel give us more to eat?"

Naiche looked at me while Wratten told Langdon what I said. Naiche said to me in a low, angry voice, "What are you doing? Be quiet, Geronimo. Complaining about little food won't help and might get us all in trouble. He might take all our food away."

When Wratten finished telling Langdon my words, Langdon frowned, stuck out his lower lip, and nodded before he replied.

Wratten said in a loud voice, trying to be heard above the birds that had started squawking overhead, "Colonel Langdon has already sent word to his chiefs that the rations they send for us aren't enough. They're less than the soldiers get, and he asks for more. He hopes more will come soon, and we won't get too hungry until then. Colonel Langdon says he wants to speak with Geronimo in private."

Naiche crossed his arms, shook his head, and turned away. Wratten and I followed Langdon to the shade beside one of the big fort walls. I thought he might shoot me for complaining about inadequate food rations. Instead, he grinned and stuck out his hand for mine. We shook hands.

Wratten translated Langdon's words as, "I just came from being commander at Fort Marion. You and your men have a better place to live here than the people over there. I like the way you and your men are behaving. Every day, I've received good reports of your work and how you care for yourselves. I wanted you to know your young wife, Ih-tedda, had a baby girl almost two moons ago and that both were in good health when I left. I recorded the child's name as Marion, but I think your people may have given her another name."

I grinned and shook his hand again. I was happy and relieved to know Ih-tedda lived and our child had come safely into this world. All I could say was, *"Enjuh. Enjuh."* I said to Wratten, "Tell Colonel Langdon he has made my heart glad with this news. He's a good man." I could speak a few of the White Eye words, but I wanted my thanks to Langdon spoken well.

■ ■ ■ ■

The next day we did what we wanted as long as we stayed in sight of soldiers watching us, so we explored the old fort and the land around it, the place the White Eyes called Santa Rosa Island. Across the big water from where the boat picked us up was Fort Barrancas. We could see there was much work for us to do. I thought that was a good thing. It would keep our minds off being separated from our families.

The day of washing and patching clothes came again, and we finished before the midday meal. After we ate, we sat on top of the fort wall, enjoying the sun's heat in the cool breeze, and watched the boats on the water. We saw a boat, different from the one we had arrived on, coming to the island's wooden road out over the water. I thought, *Maybe they bring us more food.*

Kanseah, who had good eyes, watched as soldiers led four figures off the boat and walked with them toward the fort. Naiche, sitting nearby, said, "So the Blue Coats bring more prisoners here. I wonder who they are." We climbed down from the top of the fort to meet and welcome our brothers, whoever they were, and waited in the shade of a wall.

When they walked out of the trees, I was surprised to see Mangas with the youngest of his two warriors, Goso, and his adolescent son, who we now call Frank, and my nephew, Daklugie, who was near Frank's age. I was happy to see them, but sorry they had been taken. The soldiers led them past us to see the Blue Coat officer in charge.

After speaking to the officer in charge, the new prisoners came to stand among us, and we greeted them as long-lost brothers. As the birds squawked and water splashed and rolled to the white sand and back out again, we found a place away from the fort in the shade of a few tall pine trees and sat in council. We found *tobaho,* rolled it in oak leaves, and smoked cigarettes to the four directions.

Naiche said, "Mangas, tell us how you surrendered to the Blue Coats, and we'll tell you our story."

Mangas looked at each one of us and then said, "For a long time, I've yearned to return to a place near the great river at Ojo Caliente, a place all the Chihenne enjoyed. After we traveled as far south as the great Canyon del Cobré in the land of the *Nakai-yes,* I decided it was time to return to Ojo

Caliente. Staying out of sight and living mostly on venison we took with bows and arrows so we wouldn't give ourselves away with our guns, I started moving north. We stayed away from *Nakai-yes* and White Eyes and avoided raiding. When we got out of the mountains, we traveled at night."

Mangas looked at Daklugie, who nodded and made part of a smile with one side of his face.

"No one knew we were in the country until Daklugie and Frank drove off a mule herd from the Corralitos Ranch. I didn't approve of taking the mules from that ranch, but I permitted it. We needed mounts, and we needed meat. Britton Davis, the *teniente* who Geronimo planned to kill at Fort Apache, left the American army and is now the *nantan* for that ranch. I think he knew Apaches had taken the herd and headed north, and he used the talking wire to tell General Miles this. I knew our chances of running into soldiers were much greater after we took the mules."

Daklugie lifted his chin, nodded his agreement with Mangas, and then shrugged his shoulders like a boy caught stealing something sweet from his mother's food supply.

Then Mangas said, "In the mountains east of Fort Apache, we discovered a Blue Coat camp. I knew then we could never get around the scouts and soldiers looking for us. I sent Daklugie to the camp to talk about terms for a possible surrender. Daklugie waited three days until he could talk to the scout cook alone to find out the situation, and it was then he learned that you had surrendered a moon earlier. I knew then our freedom was ended, and we surrendered to the officer in charge of the camp as soon as we could find him. His name was Cooper. Then General Miles put us on an iron wagon going east.

"Old Fit-a-Hat, my oldest warrior, was weak from all the running we did. He died, and we buried him at Fort Union on the way. I heard the soldiers talking about assaulting our women. Since we couldn't defend them, I preferred dying to watching such an outrage, helpless to do anything to stop it. I tried to escape the iron wagon and kill myself by jumping out the wagon window while it was rolling fast, but landing beside the iron road only stunned me. The Blue Coats backed the iron wagon up and found me lying near the iron road with a few scratches and bruises.

"We rode a long time, night and day, before the iron wagon stopped at a wooden road over the water. They took the men off, but the women and children went on to Fort Marion. I could hear them crying and screaming for us as they went away, and I wanted to run after them, but the soldiers had us, and we could not. That is all I have to say. Tell me now of your surrender."

We told them about the coming of Kayih-tah, and Martine, to our camp on the flat-topped mountain, why we decided to surrender, the hard trip on the iron wagon, the stop in San Antonio, and finally coming to this place.

Mangas shook his head and said only, "I'm glad we stayed out as long as we did."

Daklugie and I sat together in the cool of the evening and watched the sun drop into the big trees across the water to the west. The oranges, purples, and reds of the clouds reminded me of the sun disappearing in the mountains of the desert. We spoke of how General Miles had lied about a new reservation and bringing all the Chiricahuas together on it.

"Uncle, what do you think the White Eyes will do with us?"

"I don't yet know, my son. Ussen has not told me except to say that I'll die a natural death. I expect they'll kill us all sometime soon. But I think there's a way you might escape being shot."

"What way is this, Uncle?"

"There's a man who chooses Indian children to be taken away to a place called school where they can be taught the evil ways of the White Eyes. The *nantan* of this place, Captain Richard H. Pratt, was taking Apache children and some warriors to a school place called Carlisle, Pennsylvania. I know this is so because Wratten told me after he interpreted for Pratt. I plan to save Chappo this way, and now that you're here, you must go also."

"Uncle, I won't do this. I won't leave you or the people."

I knew Daklugie had decided many things for Mangas, but I wouldn't tolerate a boy not yet even a warrior telling me what he wouldn't do. I stared at him for a few breaths to let him feel my Power.

"Nephew, don't speak to me of what you will not do. I have the Power. I make the medicine here. You'll do as I tell you. One day you'll have Power. One day you'll lead the People. Unless you know the ways of the White Eyes, the People will never be able to compete with them. My medicine shows me this. You must go to Carlisle."

"Why not Chappo? He's your son. Why will I lead the People?"

"Chappo is my son, and I have much love for him. He has light behind his eyes and is a good fighter, but he doesn't have leadership qualities. Not many do. Your father possessed them to a high degree, and though I was never elected to the chieftainship, I had this thing also, and men knew it. Had Naiche been older, experienced in warfare, and a *di-yen* with his own Power, as I was, he would never have depended upon me to exercise many of his prerogatives. But he was wise enough to know that the life of his people depended upon someone who could do these things. And I, rather than see my race perish from Mother Earth, cared little who was chief so long as I could direct the fighting and preserve even a few of our people. You're always to remember that it matters little who gets either credit or blame, as long as it's for the good of the tribe. And you, you also go to Carlisle."

Daklugie argued with me more. He didn't realize it then, but he was just proving my point that he should be trained because he had leadership skills.

"Chappo is going to this place where we'll be taught to lie and cheat. Why can't he learn the things needed by a chief as well as I can?"

"Nothing taught to anybody puts within

him the things needed to lead a people. Haven't you seen enough of these White Eye *nantans*? What does Miles, though a general, know about chieftainship? What do any of them know? They're *nantans* because they served their time in this thing called school, not because of their ability to fight or their ability to get others to fight. Don't their warriors desert in flocks? Don't their men hate them? Don't they send their men into battle instead of leading them? And don't they use stupid tactics that cost many lives instead of using strategy in the selection and management of their fights?"

Daklugie sat back on his heels and stared at me. "My uncle is a wise *di-yen.* I'll go to Carlisle."

I told Wratten and Langdon we believed Chappo, Daklugie, and Frank Mangas should go to this place called Carlisle and learn the ways of White Eyes. Langdon seemed happy with the idea. He said one group of children and young men and women from Fort Marion had already gone. Another group was being formed, so in a week or two, he would send our young men to Fort Marion to be included in that next group.

I thanked him, but I was thinking, *This*

time I have outsmarted the White Eyes. At least the White Eyes won't have a chance to kill these young men, even if they learn nothing there.

CHAPTER 10
OUR FAMILIES RETURN

Five days after Daklugie and Frank Mangas came to us, the Blue Coats put them on the iron wagon to Fort Marion. Langdon told me they would be sent to the school at Carlisle within a moon. Langdon also thought Chappo would go, but he would be in a later group of older boys and warriors.

About the time Daklugie left, Langdon began giving the White Eyes tracks on paper that allowed them to come on boats across the water to see us. The White Eyes had to stand behind the soldiers watching us. Every day, new White Eyes came on a boat and stood around looking at us. Every day, when we worked outside, there were always twenty or more watching us, and on the day we washed our clothes and on our free day, many more. Some saw Wratten interpreting for the Blue Coat in charge of us as we worked around the fort. They talked to Wratten to ask our names. They always knew my name when he pointed me out, because it was in their newspapers.

One day, after talking to some White Eyes, Wratten asked if I wanted to sell another button like I had that time the iron wagon stopped for water. I said, "For five dollars, I'll do it."

He laughed. "I told them that's what I thought you might want."

I let him cut a button off the lower part of my shirt and take it back to the White Eyes, and I saw them give him several pieces of silver for it. He brought it to me at the evening meal and said, "I have an idea how you can make money without selling your buttons." I raised my brows in question. "I can teach you to make the tracks on paper that speak your name to the White Eyes. If they saw you make the tracks, they would buy the paper with the tracks from you. You could probably sell one for twice what you do a button."

"Hmmph. George Wratten has light behind his eyes. Show me how to make these paper tracks."

Wratten took a stick that makes tracks on paper and a piece of paper from his pocket and wrote on the paper, GERONIMO. Handing it to me he said, "Each symbol on the paper is called a letter and represents a sound in the White Eye tongue. The letters are put together in a particular way to form what's called a word or a name, and there are rules to say the letters together in a certain way so they sound like the word they represent. Any White Eye who understands letters will see those tracks and know they say your name, Geronimo. When you make the tracks, the White Eyes will say it's your autograph and will pay you money to put those tracks on paper or anything else."

Wratten made a smooth place in the sand where we sat and, taking a stick, made my name in the sand. Then, he handed the stick to me and smoothed out the sand. "Look at the paper with your name and learn how to make its letters in the sand with a stick. When you can do that, I'll get you a pencil and paper, and you can practice."

"I'll learn to do this. George Wratten is a friend. I'm grateful. I'll show you I can do this soon."

It only took a few suns for me to learn to make the tracks on paper for GERONIMO, and soon I was selling them to the White Eyes who came to stare at us. I asked Wratten to keep the money for me, but he said it was best if I kept it separately in a leather pouch he gave me. He said, "Maybe someday the White Eyes will let you keep it safe behind a big *pesh* door in something they call a bank."

I nodded, but I had no idea what he was talking about.

The moons passed through Ghost Face into the Season of Little Eagles and then into the Season of Many Leaves as we waited at Fort Pickens, did the same work, and watched the White Eyes who came to watch us. The seasons were not as cold as they were high in the mountains west of the great river, and there was no snow. The wet air and cold winds in the Seasons of the Ghost Face and Little Eagles made staying warm hard, but we didn't complain.

Every seventh sun, the free, no-work sun, I sang ceremonies for my men. I asked Ussen to restore our Power, give us our families back, and let us return to our own country, but Ussen didn't speak to any of the other men or to me. Still I dreamed often of returning to the high country to live my last days in the land of my birth. My dreams told me Ussen listened.

One sun in the Season of Many Leaves (mid-April), as we rested from our work, Wratten walked toward us from the commander's place. A big smile on his face, he motioned for Naiche and me to join him.

"Colonel Langdon has asked me to tell you the army is moving the Chiricahuas from Fort Marion to Mount Vernon Barracks a little west and north of here." He saw our squints of disgust and shook his head. "There's more. In seven suns, the iron wagon on the way to Mount Vernon Barracks will stop and leave your families with you." Wratten laughed aloud when he saw us look at each other with grins on our faces. Ussen had answered some of our prayers.

Wratten told us Langdon had decided each family would have its own room among the ones where officers used to live inside the fort on the far end of the walls from where we now lived. The unmarried men would stay together as we all did now. All the moons we had spent cleaning up the brush around the old fort included work on the officer apartments Langdon assigned us for our families, but they needed more work. We still had to scrape walls free of lichens, make sure the *pesh* (iron) stoves worked, gather wood to burn in them, fill sleeping sacks with fresh straw for us and our wives and children, and make places to lay the sleeping sacks. The days were long, and we even worked on our free day to finish preparing for our families' arrival. We didn't care. Our women and children were at last coming to us.

The sun when our families returned rose out of the big water red and mashed flat on the top and bottom. I remember it well. There were few clouds, little or no wind, and the sun's path across the bright, blue sky was slower than I could ever remember. Langdon didn't have us work that sun. Wratten told us it would be late in the afternoon before the iron wagons stopped to let our families off. Naiche, the other warriors, and I sat on top of the fort walls and stared as if we could will the appearance of our families at the far shore near where the iron wagons would stop.

While we waited, I sat against a wall running along the edge of the top walkway of the fort, felt the sun warming my face, smelled the sweet air from little vine and tree flowers, and let my mind wander through memories of my wives.

She-gha I had taken many harvests ago when I lived with Cochise, fighting the White Eyes after Bascom hanged the brother and two nephews of Cochise. She-gha was a Nednhi woman, strong, brave, easy on the eyes, and her blood relatives were close to Cochise's family. I chose her after her brother, Yahnozha, and I grew to be friends. He always showed great power and became one of my best warriors when we fought Crook and Miles.

War is hard on women. They have much to do in taking care of their husbands. They have to change camps, sometimes often and on the run, and take care of themselves and their children. After a time, it was clear She-gha needed help to support me, so I took another woman, Shtsha-she, but Blue Coats killed her when we first escaped from San Carlos. I killed many Blue Coats for Shtsha-she.

The second time we escaped from San Carlos, we stayed with Juh in his mountain stronghold on the east side of the Blue Mountains. She-gha was glad to return to her people. Despite her age and the hard times in war, she could still run with the best of them, but she needed help supporting me.

Zi-yeh was a young girl who lived in the camp of Juh. Her father was a White Eye, taken captive as a child. His name was Je-likine. He had become Apache in all things except blood. Her mother had connections to Nana and the Chihenne People. Zi-yeh was strong and fearless. I thought she was a fine woman. Many thought she was too small, not big enough or strong enough to make a good wife, but often I saw her do more work than most of the other women. She-gha said for me to take Zi-yeh for a second wife, and I did. I never regretted taking Zi-yeh.

After we broke out the third time from Fort Apache, soldiers and scouts under that traitor Chatto captured She-gha, Zi-yeh, and others, including the wife of Yahnozha, and returned them to Fort Apache. We needed and wanted our women back with us in our camp in the Blue Mountains. Five of us decided to return to Fort Apache and take our women back. We ran on foot from our camp in the Blue Mountains and slipped back across the border. At Fort Apache, we glided like ghosts in the night past the scouts watching our women. We were able to take back She-gha and Shtsha-she's daughter of three harvests, but I couldn't find Zi-yeh and our little son, Fenton. We did find a White Mountain woman named Bi-ya-neta alone and took her. Perico took her to replace the wife he couldn't get, and they lived well together.

We took the women we could and headed to the Blue Mountains, passing through the mountains of the Chihenne people in southern New Mexico, where we were lucky to find some Mescalero women with a few children. The Mescaleros were part of a group permitted off the reservation to harvest the good crop of piñon nuts in the southern mountains that year. We took the Mescalero women and children. Among them was a young girl who had no husband. She had not yet married. We called her Ih-tedda (young girl). She was strong and handsome and worked hard for us, so I kept her for myself when we returned.

Now I had She-gha and Ih-tedda. Between them, they were strong and fast enough to move camps and keep us fed when we had to move fast. I was gentle with Ih-tedda in the blankets, and eventually she came to think of me as a good husband of her choosing rather than her captor. She-gha, Ih-tedda, and I had happy times together in the moons before Crook sent Captain Crawford and Lieutenant Maus to ask for surrender talks.

We were tired of running. *Teniente* Maus spoke straight to us in council after Mexicans killed Crawford. I told Maus we would meet with Crook in two moons to discuss our surrender. As proof of my word, I sent nine of my people for Maus to keep until I met with Crook. They included Ih-tedda, who had my child growing in her belly; old

Nana, with stiff knees, barely able to walk; my sister, who was Nana's wife; a wife of Naiche; and several children, including one of my own little girls and one of Naiche's children.

I hadn't seen Ih-tedda in over a harvest since I sent her off with Maus. Zi-yeh with my son, Fenton, I had not seen in over two harvests. She-gha, I hadn't seen in six or seven moons, and she had seemed sick and slow when we left San Antonio. I hoped they were all well. If they were, I would soon have three wives back to keep satisfied and two children to begin training. That was the way it should be for a man to have a good life.

The sun was falling into the big water to the west and painting the sky in oranges and purples. But we looked to the east, where there appeared a little plume of smoke on the water. The plume grew and came toward us. We climbed down from the top of the fort and started a fire so our women and children might see us and have its warmth when the soldiers brought them down the trail through the sweet smell of the flowers in the trees and vines and the welcome songs of insects and peepers. We lighted the lanterns Langdon gave us and carried them to light the rooms we would have. Then we waited by the fire for our families to come to us.

There was only a fingernail moon, and it was a very dark evening. We waited, staring into the darkness, listening for them to come. It seemed like we waited a long time, and then, as if by some magical, silent ceremony, their faces showed at the edge of the firelight. Children ran to their fathers, who swooped them up and held them close. Our women came forward proud and full of grace. She-gha came hurrying out of the darkness followed by Zi-yeh, holding Fenton's hand, and then Ih-tedda came into the light with our daughter in her arms. I took Fenton in my arms and swung him out in a wide circle while he giggled, his eyes shining. My women came to stand around me, and I looked each of them in the eye before I spoke.

I said, "My women and children have come. Turn yourselves and let my happy eyes see you." They turned. She-gha looked thinner than I expected. Maybe she needed medicine. I would speak to her of this when we were alone. Perhaps I could make her some medicine and do a Sing to help her.

She-gha laughed and said, "Husband, your women and children have returned.

Our hearts are warmed to see you."

Zi-yeh, her eyes sparkling in the firelight, said, "Husband, it has been two harvests since the White Eyes took me and your son, Fenton. Ussen has returned us to you. He has answered our prayers."

Ih-tedda came forward with a bright smile, laid our baby in my arms, and said, "Husband, I bring you our first child, a daughter. I ask that we name her Lenna."

Lenna was a fine baby. She was asleep when Ih-tedda gave her to me and stirred just enough to chew her fist as I rocked her in my arms. I said, "I don't know where you found this name, but I'm happy with it. She is Lenna, daughter of the Chiricahua Apache Goyahkla, the *di-yen* the *Nakai-yes* call Geronimo."

She-gha saw me glancing over the other children for Shtsha-she's child. I didn't see her, and when I glanced at She-gha, she looked at the ground and shook her head.

I saw my warriors talking calmly with their wives and children, not publicly showing their great affection for them with bad manners as the White Eyes did, and I was proud of them all. I reached down, took Fenton by the hand, and said, "Come, my son. I show you where we live here on the big water."

CHAPTER 11
HOPES FOR THE FUTURE

Soon after our women and children returned, we settled into our normal ways of dividing the labor of living. The women took care of the children, cooked, washed clothes, and made our lodges comfortable. The men did the work the army asked, brought supplies of food to our lodges, and planned for how and when we could go back to our own country.

Of my three women, She-gha was first wife. She'd given me children in the long-ago times, but they had gone early to the Happy Place. I stayed with her the night our families returned. After a long, hard time apart, her warm body felt very good next to mine, but I felt her bones in places I knew I shouldn't. Her bones told me she hadn't been eating enough. The sound of her breathing, a low, gurgling, rasping sound, and her body's working like that of a long-distance runner to get enough air worried me most. The next morning, we talked. Rising before her sisters, she built a fire in the *pesh* stove and made coffee.

Standing together, we gazed out the opening at the big water. I slurped the hot coffee and said, "Your body felt good next to mine last night. I've missed you, but you feel too thin. I feel bones in your back and hips that I didn't before the Blue Coats separated us at San Antonio. Your hip bones show where they shouldn't. Your breathing sounds like you've run a long way. You work to breathe."

"My husband thinks now I'm ugly? Does not like to hear me breathe? You divorce me?"

I held up a palm and shook my head. "No, no. You're a fine woman. You're first wife. I'm very worried about you. Are you sick? Has someone witched you? Do I need to make medicine? Maybe do a Sing for you? How can I help you?"

She sat down, shook her head, and spoke, her voice sounding like a frog croaking. She had a need to clear her throat often. "I haven't felt good since Crook brought us back from the Blue Mountains over four harvests ago."

"But you went out with me. You kept up. You ran hard. You did more work than two or three other women combined. You never complained. I never heard you breathing like this before."

"A woman does what she must to help her man. Now I grow weak. I can't eat much at one time and keep it down, and sometimes I have to work hard just to breathe. If you can make medicine for me in this place, I'll be glad."

"Hmmph. I'll make medicine. First, tell me where you feel sick."

"When I feel my worst, the pain is great in my lower back and when I try to make water. Other times, I cough to clear my throat and can't stop. This started at Fort Marion in the bad, wet air there. Do you think I have worms, this thing the White Eyes call TB?"

"I'll think on this and decide how I can best use my Power to help you."

She smiled and motioned for Zi-yeh to sit where she had been sitting as Fenton came running to me with his mother behind him.

I picked him up, set him on my knee, and played a little with him as Zi-yeh sat down and said, "Ih-tedda comes soon. She nurses Lenna. You come to me tonight, husband?"

"Yes, woman, I come to you. We haven't been in the same place as husband and wife for a long time. I've missed you."

■ ■ ■ ■

Lenna, a pretty baby, nearly ten moons old and naturally quiet, gave me much pleasure. Ih-tedda had done well in training her, and I often walked, singing low with her in my arms, outside where the sun gave us its warmth and light. Many White Eyes came to Fort Pickens to watch us, as if we were chained, dangerous dogs. Their faces showed surprise that I carried my baby.

It was good to lie down and sleep with Ih-tedda, although it was still too soon after the birth of Lenna for us to know each other again. Ih-tedda was young when I took her, but she had learned much from me and my other two wives. She was a good woman, a good wife, and a good mother. I thought Ih-tedda would give me many more children.

As the moons passed through hot days, filling the Seasons of Many Leaves and Large Leaves with thick, wet air, I made medicine for She-gha and prayed to Ussen that we could return to our own country.

Naiche, Mangas, and I spoke with Wratten, who, to my surprise, had stayed with us, even after our families returned. He had no reason to stay. Perhaps he truly was a friend to us. We asked him to speak with Langdon and tell him, now that we had our families back, we wanted very much to live in our own lodges and to work our own land. We asked when this might happen. Wratten made tracks on a paper of what we said, read it back to us to ensure the tracks spoke as we had said, and, when we agreed its words were right, he folded it and said he would give it to Langdon and listen to his reply.

Later, Wratten said Langdon's face turned red when he read the tracks we sent. Langdon said for Wratten to make the tracks of what he said in reply. The tracks said we'd had our chance once to live as we wanted and had lost it. We were at Fort Pickens as a reward for not using our chance to live in peace and for making war on the Americans. A strong and powerful government had not killed us and had saved us from the Americans in our own country who had many claims against our lives. We should give thanks that we could disappear for a time; otherwise, those who had claims against our lives might take us. His words stung my ears. The words made me believe even more strongly that, unless the Blue Coats freed us soon, they would kill us all.

We asked Wratten to send General Stanley in San Antonio tracks on paper that spoke of our worries and desires. He understood the promises General Miles made to us after Naiche and I told him our stories. We asked General Stanley how long he thought the big chiefs would keep us in prison before they gave us the reservation Miles had promised.

Stanley sent tracks back to Wratten. The tracks said he didn't know how long the big chiefs planned to keep us, but he hoped we had the good sense not to lose patience and try breaking away. If we did, he said we would all soon go to the Happy Place. One thing Apaches learned from before they were off their *tsachs* was patience. We knew how to wait, whether in hunting or for the president to decide our fate.

My women spoke of seeing Daklugie and Frank Mangas sent with those nearly grown and younger children to the Carlisle school. It made me happy to hear this. At least a few might survive if the army chiefs decided to kill us. But Chappo had not left us. I wanted him to go to this place called school. His wife didn't get off the iron wagon with the others.

I thought at first she had divorced

Chappo, but my wives told me their baby had died in her arms at Fort Marion, and she could not face Chappo with this news. I again asked Wratten to make tracks on paper to Langdon and asked when Chappo might go to the Carlisle school. This time Langdon answered with a good tongue. He said Chappo would go soon, and he wanted other young warriors like Goso and other even younger ones also to go to school. Wratten made me glad when he read us these tracks on the paper from Langdon.

Within half a moon after our families came, my women told me that Hunlona's sister, Katie, who had fifteen harvests, was ready for her *Haheh* (womanhood ceremony). We asked Langdon to give us four days to hold one. After we explained the ceremony to him, he told us to wait a moon, and the night we had the Dance of the Mountain Spirits, he would let the whites from across the water come to watch it.

I didn't want our dancing watched by curious White Eyes who didn't understand why we danced. We didn't like waiting to hold the *Haheh* or letting the White Eyes watch it, but we decided in council that maybe the president would let us go sooner if we agreed. I decided, and the women agreed, that we could do the important parts of the *Haheh* inside the fort walls where no White Eyes could see Katie become White Painted Woman before they came to watch the final big dance for her.

We worked several days collecting enough wood for a great roaring fire in the center of the parade ground. It gave so much light, the White Eyes could even see into some of our lodges in the fort walls. We laid out my great buffalo robe with the dry skin-side up. Naiche, seven others, and I had switches we would use to beat on the hide like it was a drum. Another man had a drum we made by stretching a hide over a big pot half-filled with water. The drummer for the pot sat with us beside the hide. We waited for the women to start the dance.

When all was quiet, a low moan came. The moan grew louder and sharper, like a scream of joy. The White Eyes around us looked at each other with big eyes and appeared fearful of what this might mean. Women inside the fort were making the cry of joy from White Painted Woman when her son, Child of the Water, returned from slaying Owl-Man Giant, Buffalo Monster, the Eagle Monster Family, and Antelope Monster. Their cry of joy was the signal for the men to begin singing and beating on the robe and drum. Two masked dancers appeared and worshipped the fire, and a clown followed them to make us laugh and to bring healing.

The White Eyes watched us for a while, and then went to their boats to go back across the water. We danced all night while Katie became White Painted Woman and blessed us with her Power. As the sun rose out of the big water, Katie, now a woman ready for marriage, came back to us from her spirit meeting with Ussen in the sky. It was a good ceremony, and it raised the spirits of our people.

Ahnandia, my half-brother married to Tah-das-te, one of my fearless messenger women to the White Eyes, told Hunlona he was interested in taking Katie for a wife; and Hunlona, knowing Ahnandia was a brave, strong man who had helped kill many White Eyes, did not reject him. But Hunlona asked Ahnandia to wait a harvest or two before taking her, in order for Katie to grow stronger after being in the place of sickness at Fort Marion. Ahnandia agreed to wait.

Langdon didn't want Katie married off to a man who already had a wife. Before a harvest had passed, Langdon sent her to the Carlisle school. I didn't object to this.

The boys who survived in school needed wives. A harvest after Katie went to school, Hunlona told me she had died from the TB worms. White Eye diseases were killing off our best children. Our hearts wept that there was nothing we could do to save them.

CHAPTER 12
SHE-GHA GOES TO
THE HAPPY PLACE

The suns of the Seasons of Many Leaves and Large Leaves passed slowly as we lived in our confinement. We stayed out of the heat when the sun was hottest, working near sunrise and sunset. Near the time of no shadows, we stayed in the cool of our lodgings under the tall and wide fort walls. Every day, with the soldiers watching us, we trained to keep our strength, but our training was not like we did in our own country, and I could tell our warriors' strength and endurance had dwindled a lot since we surrendered. I could only hope Daklugie and the other boys sent to the school had enough strength and discipline to continue their running and other training at the school.

My women worked well together, but She-gha was not strong enough to do the work of Zi-yeh and Ih-tedda, chopping wood for our fire, washing clothes, and keeping our lodge within the fort walls clean and straight. She-gha spent most of her time cooking, looking after Lenna and Fenton, and resting in the cool darkness of the fort walls. Zi-yeh and Ih-tedda didn't complain about this and did everything they could to help her. We all saw She-gha growing weaker and prayed to Ussen that he would return her strength.

I decided she had the worms the White Eyes called tuberculosis, talked to Wratten, and asked him to make tracks on paper to a *di-yen* we knew at Fort Apache to ask for some *Perezia wrightii* (narrow medicine) so I might cure She-gha. I offered Wratten all the money I had and said to send it with the tracks on paper to pay the *di-yen* for the medicine. Wratten told me to keep the money and said he knew who to contact at Fort Apache for this medicine. He said he'd have it to me within a moon.

In half a moon, Wratten motioned me to meet with him one morning as we planned the day's work. Without a word, he smiled and handed me a leather *tobaho* pouch and nodded for me to open it. Inside were the roots of *Perezia wrightii.* Wratten said, "White Eyes may be no good at keeping their word, but they can travel far and fast."

I nodded and said, "Wratten is a man of his word."

Early the next morning, I ground up the *Perezia wrightii* roots and had She-gha take off her shirt and lie down on her belly beside the fire. I poured water in a bowl, added the ground-up roots, and heated the water with four stones, one for each direction. The water with the medicine foamed up. I sang the prayer to be used with the medicine, made a cross of pollen on the medicine, and then held the pollen to the four directions before I put it on her back and head. I took a cup of the medicine, held it to the directions four times, and then gave it to She-gha to drink. After she finished drinking the medicine, I told her to go lie in the sun and get hot, that soon she would have a bad stomach and vomit up the TB. This she did, but I saw no TB worm. I watched her close for five days, but she didn't seem any better. I tried the ceremony again with the root I had left, but still the medicine did not help her.

Every day I tried finding a new medicine for She-gha. During the Season of Large Leaves a powerful storm came across our fort. Lightning in a storm near sunset hit two trees. I thought, *This is a good thing. Even though She-gha no longer has moon times, perhaps flint medicine will help her.* I found a small, burned limb that had been knocked from one of the trees the lightning had hit and chipped the wood off to boil in water. She-gha agreed to try this medicine, and I made her comfortable near the fire. I poured some of the flint medicine in a cup for her and marked it with yellow pollen, sang a special ceremony, and then told her to drink it. When the ceremony finished, She-gha said she felt better, and the gurgling noise in her breathing was gone. I was glad, but the hard breathing came back a few suns later.

The many medicines and ceremonies I tried for She-gha did no good. She grew weaker, and her cough grew worse. One sun I saw blood on her lips, and she was so weak, she could barely stand to go where the women went for their personal business. Even the White Eye *di-yen* from Fort Barrancas, who came to do his medicine two times in a moon, told me there was nothing he could do. I prayed often to Ussen for Power to help She-gha, but Power didn't come. I felt like a man slowly sliding off the edge of a high cliff, grasping at every bush and rock, unable to keep from falling into the shadows far below.

One evening in the middle of the Season of Large Fruit, She-gha was too weak to stand, and with every cough, blood showed on the cloth she held over her mouth. I told her sister wives to speak to her before she left for the Happy Place. I sat with Lenna and Fenton outside in the warm night air, listening to the water roll against the rocks while Zi-yeh and Ih-tedda sat with She-gha. She-gha had been a good woman, and I had been glad to have her as one of my own. I never had to beat her. She slept close to me when I had need of her, made good food, kept our camp clean, ran when I had to run, and bore me children of whom I was proud.

I sat with She-gha through the rest of the night and heard her breathe her last as the gray light of dawn came. The last words she whispered to me were, "I'll see you again in the Happy Place, Husband. I know you'll take care of my sister wives and our children. They are good ones."

Soon Wratten came to serve as supervisor and interpreter for that day's work. I asked to speak with him alone. We walked to the wall shadows on the east side the fort and stopped to talk in the thin grass near the great walls still wet with night water.

I said, "She-gha has gone to the Happy Place. Where and when can I bury her? We must go to another sleeping place so we don't live where she did, in case her ghost tries to comes back."

Wratten shook his head and puffed his cheeks to blow a little air. "I knew this would probably happen. She looked sick when she came here. I've spoken to Colonel Langdon about what to do with bodies if we have people here go to the Happy Place. He'll want you to bury her in the place of soldiers across the water at Fort Barrancas. I've seen it. It's a nice place, and soldiers look after it. I'll send word to Langdon about this before we begin working, and I'll ask the local commander about where you can move. I don't think you'll have to work today."

"Hmmph. Wratten is a friend. I'll wait outside with Zi-yeh, Ih-tedda, and the children for the commander to tell us where to move."

Wratten touched two fingers to his hat in a White Eye salute and walked away to the commander's workplace in a different part of the fort wall. Wratten returned from the commander's office before the soldiers came to watch us on the work detail.

"The commander sends his regrets on She-gha going to the Happy Place. He says several empty lodge rooms are ready, and you're free to pick one that suits you. A boat comes with a box in which to bury She-gha. You and anyone you choose can accompany you when she is carried across the water to the soldier's burial place."

"This I will do. When do the soldiers come with She-gha's box?"

"Soon after the time of shortest shadows."

"We'll be ready. Now my family and I find a new lodging place. I would like Naiche, Perico, Ahnandia, Fun, and Yahnozha to go with me across the water to bury She-gha."

Wratten frowned when he heard the names, but then he nodded and walked away to tell them they were to stay with me. I went to my family. We found a new lodge place far enough away so She-gha's ghost wouldn't bother us. I sat and smoked an oak leaf cigarette to the four directions with the men I had chosen to go with me, while Zi-yeh and Ih-tedda moved the things from our lodge place to the new place. I told the warriors I had chosen them to go with me to bury She-gha so we might all know what it was like to go across the water to Fort Barrancas and to know Fort Barrancas in case we ever tried to escape.

Naiche looked at me with his brow wrinkled in an angry frown. He shook his head. "Geronimo, we'll never leave this place. The water is too wide. There are too many soldiers. We won't leave our families again. We're no better than dust in the wind."

"Perhaps this is so. But if we are dust, we'll blind their eyes until they can no longer see us. We must be ready if the time comes."

Naiche shook his head. "I won't go. We must learn to survive living among the White Eyes."

"Hmmph. You speak true. Still, we ought to be ready."

The soldiers came with a box made of pinewood in which we put She-gha wrapped in her best blanket. There was enough room in it for her body and her things we did not burn. We put the box on a wagon, carried it to the wooden road over the water where a boat waited, and made a fast trip to the place the soldiers buried their dead. An army *di-yen* asked if I wanted him to sing a ceremony for her. I said no, that I would do this since I was a *di-yen*.

We took the box to a prepared burial place. I sang for her. I told Ussen he should be ready, for a good woman was coming to the Happy Place. I put golden pollen on her pinewood box. I looked in all directions while soldiers lowered her box into the earth and saw many soldiers and fences that we might have to face if we tried to run. I saw little or no chance we might get away if we tried to escape this way.

We waited as the low light of the setting sun shone on the soldiers who worked to cover her box with black earth that smelled fresh and clean. When they finished, I put gold pollen on the fresh dirt covering her. Then the commander led us to the boat and took us back to Fort Pickens. As we crossed the water, I saw my best warriors study the place of burial and then turn their backs on it to watch the lights at Fort Pickens steadily approaching. I knew then we would never try to escape Fort Pickens. I was sad, but I accepted what Ussen had chosen for us. Still, I would pray every day for our deliverance.

That night, while the children slept, Zi-yeh and Ih-tedda gave me comfort on our loss of She-gha. I always chose good women.

CHAPTER 13
REUNION AT
MOUNT VERNON BARRACKS

Suns crept through the Seasons of Earth Is Reddish Brown, Ghost Face, and Little Eagles, but nothing changed. We continued to work five days to keep the fort and island clean and straight, and then, while the women washed on the sixth day, we gambled, ran races, and talked — never any action — just talk. Boats continued to bring the White Eyes who wanted to watch us as though we were cattle in a pen.

One sun when the White Eyes came, I saw the same man I had seen before at other places with the long, black coat, gray face whiskers with a scar through them, and a pistol under his coat. This time, he had no pistol. Perhaps the Blue Coats wouldn't let the White Eyes come if they wanted to shoot us. He studied the faces of all the people except mine. My Power warned me to stay clear, hiding in the open, so the White Eye couldn't see me.

144

One sun, a moon or two later, early in the Season of Many Leaves, we strained and grunted with pry poles and harnessed teams of sweating horses to move big stones streaked with green moss from the edge of the big water around the fort. A boat passed near where we worked. It had a great, white, canvas sheet, which would have made a good tipi cover, filled with wind that pushed it across the sparkling, bright, blue water. The same man I had seen earlier was steering the boat, while two other men worked to keep the sheet of canvas pointed in the right direction. This time, the man wore a pistol and stretched his neck, looking our way, trying to see our faces. Again, I stayed out of his sight. Now I was sure the man who carried the pistol under his coat looked for me. Maybe he wanted revenge. I had killed many White Eyes and Mexicans. Now I knew I must kill at least one more, but I wondered how I could defend myself when the White Eye came to take me. The Blue Coats only let me carry a small folding knife in my vest pocket.

A few suns after the White Eye with the pistol studied us from a boat, Wratten told us that in half a moon, the army would move us to Mount Vernon Barracks to live with the other Chiricahuas. I remembered hearing Wratten tell us Mount Vernon Barracks was the place where the others went when our families returned to us a harvest earlier. After nearly two harvests, the promise Miles made that we would all be together in five suns after we surrendered had come to pass.

I thought, *Now the White Eye with the pistol under his coat has a better chance to attack me since Wratten says there's no water around the Mount Vernon Barracks, only a river on the eastern side. There I must keep a sharp watch for ambushes.*

The boat came for us early one morning while wispy, gray clouds were still on the water, and the sun, shining through the clouds, looked like a great eagle's egg, golden on the edge of the big water. The women had already carried our things to the wooden road over the water where the boat stopped. It didn't take long to load our things and ride the boat across the water to Fort Barrancas, where we took wagons pulled by horses to the iron wagon waiting for us. The only good memory I had of an iron wagon was getting off and no longer smelling the stench from the buckets and hearing the constant noise from the demons pulling it. The windows were open on the iron wagon we mounted for Mount Vernon, but there were also many soldiers to guard us. Wratten told us we would get to see our brothers and sisters at Mount Vernon Barracks before the end of the day.

The iron wagon made many moans as it rolled west past White Eye lodges and then turned north. It passed a place of many iron wagons stopped on iron roads and soon rushed through forests of short pine trees. The iron road was long and straight, and the iron wagon seemed to go faster and faster as it made small turns to the east and then swung back west. It ran for a while along a great, wide mud flat with a brown river in the middle. After a hand width against the horizon, the iron wagon turned west and a little south.

The pine forests thinned, and we saw White Eye farms. Seeing them made me wish I were free on my own land raising my sons and daughters. I would teach them all the lessons I had learned in my life, and I would tell them they should learn the tricks of the White Eyes. One day it would be so. This I knew. Within half a hand width against the sun, the iron wagon turned farther south but still pointed a little west. Again, we rode through short pine forests, but soon we passed through another White Eye town. Then we crossed big, iron bridges across great, wide areas of grass and brush and great, tall trees standing on water like those I remembered from when we had first come to Fort Pickens. There, I saw one or two of the great lizards with their big mouths filled with their spear-point teeth while on mud islands as they warmed themselves in the sun.

The iron wagon followed the west side of the big swamp that gradually became a big river and into a place where were many iron wagons and great *casas* sat. Much banging and clanging happened when they changed the iron wagon that would pull us. It didn't take long, and soon we rode north through pine and oak forests with long bunches of moss, looking like gray-green hair hanging from the branches. Just to the east of us lay the swamp we had crossed earlier. We were on the iron road about a hand width against the horizon when the iron wagon slowed and stopped. Wratten came and told us we were at Mount Vernon Station, and the soldiers were ready to walk with us to the place where we would meet the commander.

I looked out the window at the place where other riders would wait to board an iron wagon or to see those who had come.

There were no Chiricahuas to meet and welcome us. I thought, *The nantan must be strict if he won't let our friends and brothers come to greet us.*

The women gathered what they had brought, and, with soldiers around us, we walked for a little while up a hill along the middle of the wagon road leading to the gates of the post. The chief Blue Coat who had come with us spoke with Wratten and then disappeared through the big, heavy gates. Wratten said for us to sit and rest. Soon the *nantan* would come and tell us where to go and what to do.

The post gates where we waited were on a hilltop barely high enough to raise us above the dark, green forest surrounding us. At the bottom of the hill, I saw a clearing filled with log cabins I guessed must belong to our people. I stood and walked a few steps to get a better view. I saw no one anywhere around the cabins. I wondered if the people were out somewhere working in the forests where we couldn't see them. A flash of fear and rage ran through me as I thought, *What if the Blue Coats have already executed them and we're next? We never know what the Blue Coats and their masters are thinking.*

I waited and watched the clearing as the

shadows changed, and a little wind rippled through the long grass, making tree branches and leaves bend and gently wave. A woman slowly came out of a cabin across the clearing, and with her head bowed, she crossed the clearing and came up the path to the place where we waited. Before she had walked ten steps from the cabin, my heart swelled in pride and joy. I recognized my grown daughter, Dohn-say. I wanted to run to her and throw my arms around her, at last to see her and my grandchildren and know they were still alive, but such a show of affection in public was not proper for a man, especially a *di-yen*. I kept my public manners and looked away, pretending she was not there.

Dohn-say raised her gaze when she reached the top of the hill and saw me look off in the distance across the forest top. She ran to me and threw her arms around my neck and wept, whispering, "Father, Father, at last I see you."

Water sat at the edges of my eyes as I stood there with Dohn-say. It was hard to speak. My throat felt filled with thorns. I croaked, "Yes, daughter, I'm here. Ussen gathers us together."

As she stood there holding on to me, I saw others coming from the cabins and running for the path up the hill. There were deep breaths of surprise and happiness from those standing behind us, and then movement, as they rushed forward to see those taken from them for many moons passing. I sighed. We were strangers in a strange land, but we were now all together, except for our children in the place the White Eyes called school.

CHAPTER 14
NEWS

The first moon at Mount Vernon Barracks, we slept with family or friends while the men enlarged the clearing, cut logs from the surrounding forest and swamps, and built more cabins. Sometimes we even had to work in hard rains and sticky, black mud to build the cabins. Each cabin had the same arrangement: two rooms, each about three paces on a side separated by an open place covered by the same roof over the rooms, and dirt floors. The army gave each family a *pesh* stove for heat in the cold times. The women cooked over open fires in the middle of the room. We had nothing to sit or sleep on, except blankets or rough beds we made from sawed wood the White Eyes gave us. My women and I slept on the earth. We didn't care. We had lived that way before we surrendered.

A two-room cabin with an open, covered walkway was a good thing for my family.

The walkway helped push air through and around the rooms. Zi-yeh and Fenton lived in one room; and across the open space, Ih-tedda and Lenna lived in the other. The women took turns cooking in their rooms for all of us.

We would have been comfortable except rain came almost every day, usually before the time of shortest shadows. The air felt damp and hot all the time, but it was worse in the afternoons. It made us feel as though we lived in a sweat lodge. If we didn't stay inside and close to a fire, our clothes remained damp and sticky, and black mud always covered our moccasins or shoes.

No-see-ums, tiny flying insects with bad bites, and the insects the White Eyes called mosquitoes, swarmed in great, thick clouds. Their constant bites made us all miserable, and even killed a few of our babies. Some said their bites caused the shaking sickness and even made the skin on some turn yellow. I knew of no ceremony to make the shaking sickness go away. Even the White Eye *di-yen,* who had a bitter, nasty-tasting medicine, couldn't keep the shaking sickness from beginning, but his medicine made the shakes go away faster than they did without it.

Even the workhorses and cattle ran in the

pastures and corrals swishing their tails to get away from the insects. We learned smoky fires helped keep mosquitoes away, and the army gave some of us thin cloth screens to put over or around us when we slept to protect us from their bites and let us sleep. The green and blue stuff the White Eyes called mold appeared everywhere — food, clothes, tools, even moccasins and shoes. The women had to work every day, scraping it away, to keep it from covering everything.

When I asked Wratten why the army had brought us here, he shrugged his shoulders, shook his head, and said, "The army believes Mount Vernon Barracks is better for the Apaches than Fort Marion." The other Chiricahuas who came the harvest before us said that, except for the fact there was much more room here than at Fort Marion, this place was worse because it rained nearly every day, there were many more mosquitoes, and there were so many trees, it was hard to see the sky. They said if you wanted to see the sky here, you had to climb a tree and look out its top. It was not that bad, but when the sun was out, our village only got little pools of its light. Compared to Mount Vernon, we'd had relatively little rain at Fort Pickens and very few mosquitoes.

The only one who died there had been She-gha, and she'd been sick when she arrived, but at Mount Vernon many had already died.

We had little to do after we built our cabins. The soil, full of sand, made it hard to grow much of anything. Small, productive garden space meant only a few of us could be farmers. None of the Chiricahua men wanted to be farmers. Farming was woman's work, and the place for gardens was so small, only a few women could work in gardens. The rest of the women had little to do after cabin and childcare chores. The women, like the men, often gathered to spend the long days gambling in games like Monte. They had cards we had taken from *Nakai-yes* or that had been given to us by Wratten when he could get cards from the Blue Coats.

Wratten suggested we make things to sell to those who came to watch us. But unlike the forts in Florida, few came or even knew we were at Mount Vernon Barracks. Our commander agreed to let Wratten take us to the place where we got off the iron wagon at Mount Vernon village and offer what we made for sale to the White Eyes going north or traveling south to the place called Mobile. We sold a few things each time we went, even the symbols of my autograph, but we didn't make as much money as we had in Florida.

The moons of the seasons passed, and the time of Ghost Face came. I had never seen a Ghost Face like this one in my own country. The rains only came every three or four days. The air was much lighter, making it easier to breathe. It never got cold enough to make ice on standing water during the nights, and the days were cool, requiring only a shirt with good, long sleeves for comfort.

One day Wratten spoke with the commander of the barracks and then asked to meet with the chiefs of our people, Chihuahua, Naiche, Loco, and Nana. Because I was a *di-yen* with Power and an advisor to Naiche, Wratten also asked me to come. On a clear warm day, we met under a big oak tree at the edge of the village clearing.

Chihuahua rolled a cigarette in an oak leaf, and we passed it around, smoking to the four directions. After Chihuahua finished the last of the smoke, he nodded to Wratten and said, "Speak. We listen."

Wratten spoke of news from the commander. "A band of women called the Massachusetts Indian Association live in the

156

White Eye town of Boston far to the north. They learned our children have no teachers for things they need to know to live in a good way with the White Eyes. Remember they sent two women to see how you and the children live in order to report to their band how they can best help you. The commander asks that I tell you this band of women has found the money to bring two women here to teach the children and hopes you'll send your children to learn at the school they give you, but the children don't have to go to their school."

I crossed my arms and said, "My People weren't here when those women came. Will someone tell of their visit that I might understand what they want to do?"

Chihuahua said, "I was at all the meetings, and heard the women when they talked to families in the village. We had a meeting like this one. Wratten told us the commander had learned these women were coming here. After Wratten said this, I looked around to see a council of frowning faces. Nana gave voice to what we all thought. He said to Wratten, 'Is this another White Eye trick to steal our children from us? Speak straight. We must know.'

"Wratten said, 'I believe they want to bring school to the children and have no intention of trying to take the children away from you.'

"The only way we could know the hearts of these women was to look in their eyes and listen to their words. My Power said to let the teachers come.

"The two women came in half a moon. They visited families and spoke with them, and they met with us in council. They promised us a school here. They promised they would not take our children away to the school. I believed them."

I nodded. "I trust Chihuahua's judgment and believe all he has told us. For my part, I say let them come."

Naiche nodded, and so did Loco, who said, "For a change, Geronimo speaks wise words. I, too, say let them come and speak with us. Tell the commander we will hear them."

Wratten waved an arm parallel to the ground. "*Enjuh.* The commander said, if you agree, the teachers will come. There is also other news. The Blue Coats have had many requests from the Mescalero reservation to free the Mescaleros here. The army has decided that any Mescalero who wants to return to the reservation can leave in two moons. If you or your People have Mescalero women or children living with you,

158

tell them soon so they can decide if they want to leave us."

At least, I thought, *some of us can escape this place of White Eye lies where we were never meant to live.* I looked around the circle again and saw all the chiefs nodding. Then, as if a lightning arrow fell from the sky, I remembered Ih-tedda was Mescalero.

Although no ice appeared on the morning water during the Ghost Face at Mount Vernon, the nights were still cold. The night after Wratten spoke of Mescalero prisoners returning to their reservation, I stayed with Ih-tedda. We sat together, warmed by her fire, after she had nursed Lenna and put the sleeping child in her *tsach* for the night.

I said, "You know this sun the chiefs and I met with Wratten, who brought us news from the commander. He says White Eye women want to send teachers here to teach our children White Eye ways."

Ih-tedda raised her brows. "They want to teach children White Eye ways here? They won't take them away to this place they call school?"

"So believes Wratten."

"Then that is a good thing. Would my husband let them come?"

"I said they should come, and the others

did not disagree. They come in a moon."

"*Enjuh.* My great warrior husband has a strong voice in the councils of those who lead. Husband, Lenna sleeps. Will you lie with me this night? I'm ready to give you another child."

"Something else Wratten told us."

She frowned. "What has Wratten told you that is more important than what I just offered you?"

"Wratten says the commander told him that in less than two moons the Mescaleros can return to the reservation if they want to go. You're my wife, but you're also Mescalero and can leave this place. Do you want to leave me and return free to the reservation?"

"My husband shames me to think I want to leave him. My heart overflows with love for a great warrior and *di-yen*. Already he gives me a beautiful child. I want another. I won't leave with the Mescaleros."

I studied her eyes and watched her face in the dancing, yellow light from her fire. She spoke straight. I was glad. I wanted her to keep our family together, but only if she wanted to stay. I saw desire for me in her eyes, and she stirred me.

I said, "*Enjuh.* Let us lie down in the blankets and keep our bodies and spirits

160

together and warm that another child might find us."

CHAPTER 15
IH-TEDDA'S DIVORCE

A moon before the White Eye women came to teach the children, a young boy, sent back to us from the Carlisle school, left for the Happy Place. I went with the family into the woods where they buried him. Women who knew him moaned and cried, and the men were somber and filled with sorry hearts over one so young riding the ghost pony. I sprinkled yellow pollen on the grave and prayed to Ussen to receive the good young man.

Walking back to our cabins in the falling darkness, I thought of all the people who had gone to the Happy Place since we had arrived at Mount Vernon Barracks. How many? Ten, maybe twelve? Too many had gone.

After my family ate our night meal around Zi-yeh's fire, Ih-tedda and Lenna went to their sleeping place across the walkway. That night, Zi-yeh kneeled on my blankets, and, as Fenton slept nearby, said, "Husband, I know you give Ih-tedda a chance for another child. Of this, I'm glad. In these hard times, we need to make as many children for our family as we can. I want another child, too. Help me also make one for you. Lay with me tonight."

"Wife, I'll give you a child soon, but now the day's ceremony is heavy on me like a great stone. Let me rest. One night soon, I'll come to you."

"Husband, we never know what tomorrow brings. Don't deny me tonight. Let me come to you."

I sighed, knowing I might as well argue against the sun hiding behind the western horizon. I threw back the edge of my blankets. "Come."

Zi-yeh gave me great comfort and peace with her body that night, and afterward, as I lay stretched out beside her, I fell into a deep sleep filled with dreams of the long-ago days.

Dreams floated across my mind like white clouds on a blue sky, and there was Alope, slender and beautiful. We had loved each other since the feelings of those who are no longer children began to stir in us. I killed *Nakai-yes* to get the ponies I gave her father for her bride gift, and they had been worth it. She gave me three fine children who played and learned our lifeways as we enjoyed our lives in the fine buffalo hide tipi I had traded ponies for from Lipan Apaches on the plains beyond the great river.

As I grew to be a strong warrior, Mangas Coloradas became my chief. One harvest in the Season of Large Leaves, our band followed him to peaceably trade with the *Nakai-yes* in the village of Kas-ki-yeh. We camped close to the village, and every day we left our families, horses, and weapons under the protection of a few watchful eyes to go into town to trade. We had no reason to distrust the *Nakai-yes,* but in case we had to scatter, we chose a place separate from the camp where we could gather after getting away from our enemies.

One day as I returned to our camp, an old woman called to me in a whispering, mournful voice from her hiding place by the trail. She said, "*Nakai-yi* troops from another town came to our camp when I went to the bushes on personal business. I saw them kill those who watched the camp and take the ponies and our supplies. We had no chance to defend ourselves."

My stomach churned as water fell from

her eyes.

I wanted to run to the camp, hoping to find Alope, our children, and my mother safe, but I knew we must wait at the gathering place until it was dark enough to enter the camp without being seen and ambushed. It took a long time for the sun to hide behind the mountains. As the sun's fire disappeared, a small ember of hope burned in my heart that Alope and the children had escaped.

At last, the darkness came, and we sent sentinels to watch as the warriors went into the camp to find their families. There I found my mother, her head crushed from the butt of a rifle, and Alope, lying in blood, her dress torn from her hips. She had been violated, and her throat was slashed. Our children, stabbed many times, lay nearby. Seeing my murdered family desecrated and covered in blood was the worst agony I had ever known. I slipped away and stood in the night by the river, numb to life, numb to living, staring into a great pit of darkness as the river gurgled by.

Something pulled me from my dreams. I sat up, only the orange coals in Zi-yeh's fire giving the room light. The memory that had appeared in my night vision still burned on my eyes. My breath came as though I had been running, and I felt as though Bear had been tearing at my guts with his great claws. I knew Ussen had sent me a message, and I needed to listen.

Zi-yeh sat up in her blankets and rested a hand on my shoulder saying, "Are you well, husband?"

I nodded. "I am well, woman. Ussen speaks to me."

I sat by myself under a big oak tree and smoked. I tried to understand the dreams of Alope and my family's slaughter. A memory came to me from six or seven harvests past when my People had come out of the Blue Mountains to take Loco and his Chihennes back with us to our camps, far from the misery of San Carlos. We thought we were finally safe in the land of the *Nakai-yes* where the American Blue Coats could not follow, but as Loco's People walked toward the Blue Mountains in Chihuahua, a *Nakai-yi* army under García attacked them at the edge of the big, dry arroyo the *Nakai-yes* call Aliso Creek. Many were killed and wounded, but we fought them off.

Fun became a legend among our People that day as he led the fight with Loco and Chihuahua against García's army, which made charge after charge against us. I stayed with the women and children in a dug-out place under the arroyo bank to protect them and to make medicine and calling on Ussen to save us. But many died that day, and many were wounded. Fun called on me to come out and fight and drive away the *Nakai-yes*. I fought and helped them. But after the fighting stopped, as the sun fell behind the Blue Mountains, we knew the *Nakai-yes* would soon start fires around us so they could kill us as we tried to leave the arroyo and escape. There was a short time while it was dark before the fires would start.

I heard Ussen say the most important thing was for the warriors to save themselves to fight the *Nakai-yes* and Blue Coats in the suns to come. I said to the warriors, "If we're to escape, we must leave the women and children and save ourselves." No others would do this, but I did. And the warriors who stayed with the women and children got them away from the *Nakai-yi* fire with not many lost. I still think I made the better decision. We lost a few warriors we needed in that escape through the *Nakai-yi* fire. We could always have stolen more children and taken other women when we needed them.

Now I realized the knife was in the other hand. We had to have our women and children if our People were to survive. Here disease might take them as it had the boy we'd buried recently. Here the Blue Coats might decide they should wipe us all out. Anyone who could get away from here must go. They must go to save the People, or the Chiricahuas might disappear forever.

My family ate our evening meal by Ih-tedda's fire. Zi-yeh looked at me with eyes filled with desire as she and Fenton went to their sleeping place. I looked away, and she knew I wouldn't come to her that night. I waited until Ih-tedda put Lenna on her *tsach* and came back to sit beside me at the fire. I rolled a cigarette in an oak leaf, lit it with a splinter from the cooking fire, smoked to the four directions, and then passed it to Ih-tedda. She smoked to the four directions, and, since she didn't smoke often, I knew she felt the smoke bite the insides of her mouth and nose, but she was pleased I honored her this way. She handed the cigarette back and waited with her hands folded across her belly, patient and ready to hear serious business.

I finished the cigarette and tossed the remains into the low, flickering yellow flames just above the rocks around the firepit. Outside, the winter wind swished through the tops of the tall pines, sounding like the big water rolling and crashing on to the edge of our island in Pensacola Bay.

Staring into the fire, I gathered my thoughts even as my heart said I must not speak to her of this. "Ih-tedda, I've decided you and Lenna must go." I waved a hand toward the door. "Leave me. Return to your mother and father in Mescalero."

Ih-tedda looked at me as though I held a stick of wood and was about to beat her, although I had never done such a thing with any of my wives. I tried to show only determination on my face, the same un-bending will that had carried me across many wars and the killing of many enemies. Ih-tedda stared at the dirt floor, her breath sounding as if she had run a race. I knew she spoke slowly to keep her voice from wavering.

"Why do you say this? I had no man before you. You stole me from my people. I hated you then, but I learned to love you. I've been a good wife for you. Our place is always clean. You never have to wait to eat. I've just come to you in our blankets that we might have another child. Our daughter is a delight, whole and perfect, and filled with laughter. Have mercy on us. I beg you not to send us away."

I remembered the dream of Alope and the memory of Aliso Creek and said, "You must go. The Blue Coats may change their minds any time and kill us all. You know, in less than half a moon, they'll free the Mescaleros they took to Florida, but not the Chiricahuas and Chihennes. You are Mescalero. I should be a Mescalero because I married you, but the White Eyes will never let me go. There's no reason for you to lose your life. Yes, I took you without courting you. Now you have a chance to be free. Take it! Save our People with your children and your knowledge of our lifeways. You're a fine wife. Our daughter, Lenna, is a good child, but if she stays in this bad air, this place of White Eye sickness, she'll soon make the journey to the Happy Place, and you won't be far behind her, even if the Blue Coats don't shoot us all."

"Please, husband, I want to stay with you."

"Woman, you must go. Take Lenna and go. That is all I have to say."

She buried her face in her hands. When she looked at me, there was water in her eyes, and she threw her arms around my neck and croaked in a whisper, "I'll do as my husband says I must."

I rubbed her back and said, "Ih-tedda is a

good woman. Save yourself and our child from this place of death."

Chapter 16
Schoolmaster

The White Eye teachers came to us, expecting to begin teaching our children White Eye ways in two days. First, the teachers walked through the village to cabins where families had children. At each cabin, the teachers said they would teach school in a building with one big room the Blue Coats had given them. The teachers asked the parents to send their children to school. Nearly all the parents agreed their children should go.

The next day, I met with the children by the tree where the leaders often had meetings. I told them to sit without noise and to listen to me. I stood on a stump and spoke slowly, looking at each one.

"White Eye lady teachers have come to teach you White Eye ways. For our People to live and do well in the White Eye world, you must learn from them. Some of your friends, brothers, and sisters have already been taken from us to a school far away. Some have returned sick with the disease the White Eyes call TB and have died here. Some will stay many harvests at this faraway White Eye school before they return to us. Your mothers and fathers want you to learn White Eye ways, but they also want you with them so you also learn Chiricahua lifeways. A group of White Eye women in a White Eye town far away agree you need to stay here with your parents and not be pulled from them, so they send these teachers to you. They will be kind and patient, helping you learn White Eye ways, like knowing how to make and read White Eye tracks on paper, how to speak the White Eye language, and to know White Eye lifeways. These things are as important for you to know as when I taught boys to be warriors by making them run long distances holding water in their mouths, or bathing in streams when it was so cold ice lay on top of the water. I'll help the White Eye teachers keep order and make sure you do as they ask. I'll be in the room with my stick where they teach. Be sure I'll use it on you if you speak out of turn, don't listen to the teachers, or don't act right. Do you understand my meaning and my words? Speak if you do not. I will tell you again."

I looked at them, each one, but not one spoke up.

"*Enjuh.* When the next sun comes, we'll meet together here when the sun is one of your father's hands above the horizon. I'll lead you to the building where your school is. When the lessons are finished for that sun, I'll lead you back to this place so you can return home. It will be so every day. I have said all I have to say."

The next morning I led the children up the hill and through the fort gate to their school as I promised them. The teachers, who spoke Apache, but not nearly as well as Wratten, told the students their names and asked each student to say his name and his family name and told them where they were to sit. The children acted well, and even though it was only the first day, we all learned much of the White Eye ways. At the end of the day, I led the children back down the hill to the village.

After the students left, I sat awhile by the council tree and smoked. I thought of Ih-tedda and Lenna. They had been gone half a moon. I prayed to Ussen for them to have good lives. When a woman went back to her parents, as Ih-tedda did, she was considered divorced and free to remarry. I didn't think her father would marry her off quickly, but he might.

Through the rest of Ghost Face, the Season of Little Eagles, and into the Season of Many Leaves, I led the children up the hill to their school, stood watch to discipline them, and led them back down the hill for five days out of every seven. I learned what the children learned and began to understand how the White Eyes had gained their great power, for they had learned many things, and their tracks on paper did not let them forget any of them.

One day as I stood in the back of the room, the door opened and I saw the fort commander follow another commander into the room. I could tell the other commander, who wore two stars on each shoulder, was a *nantan.* He had long, gray hair on his face, and when he turned toward me, I saw his coat sleeve on his right was empty. I remembered him as General Howard. He was the Blue Coat who had made peace with Cochise and given him the reservation he wanted that included his stronghold. General Howard was a good, fair man. When he saw me, he smiled and nodded. I ran to him and put my arms around him, telling him how good the school was and how the teachers were helping us learn. Soldiers started for me, but he held up his hand and said in a loud voice, "Wratten."

Wratten came quickly and worked his way between us. He said, "Slow down, Geronimo. General Howard remembers you and welcomes you. He wants to understand what you're saying."

By this time, the teachers and students were quiet and watching us. I said to Wratten, "Tell General Howard we have fine lady teachers. All the children go to their school. I want them to be like white children."

General Howard laughed. "Good. I can see you've changed for the better, Geronimo. I thank God for that. Tell me, have any children become sick here? Is there anything a White Eye *di-yen* can help with?"

"No, no sick ones here. The sick ones come from Carlisle."

General Howard shook his head. "I was afraid you might say that. Things would be much better if so many didn't get sick when they went to Carlisle. Do your people have enough to eat?"

"We have enough to eat. But we have only a small garden to plant, no big crops. There's no work for the men. We need work to support our families. Can you help us get the reservation General Miles promised us?"

General Howard lifted his chin and looked me in the eyes. "We're working on this problem now. Many in the government fight us, but we won't fail. Understand that it may take more time than we want it to or than it should."

I nodded I understood. General Howard went to speak with the teachers and even said a little Apache to some of the children, who solemnly nodded and answered his questions. Before he left us, he said to me, "Be patient, Geronimo. We're doing all we can as fast as we can to find you a home."

CHAPTER 17
GENERAL CROOK COMES

Throughout the rest of the seasons during that harvest, other Blue Coat chiefs came, looked at us, and left. Then in the Ghost Face, my old enemy appeared and spoke with many but not with me.

The last time I saw General Crook was at our meeting to discuss surrender terms in the Season of Little Eagles nearly four harvests earlier (March 1886). I had told him of my many desires and prayers to Ussen for peace. One was to see Kaytennae, the great warrior Captain Crawford had sent to prison. I wished Kaytennae would return to live with his family. Crook let Kaytennae out of prison and brought him to our meeting. I was glad to see Kaytennae. I had been afraid I might never see him again. Then I believed everything Crook told me was true. I told Crook all this with a good heart, but Crook looked me in the eyes, as White Eyes do, even though it is bad manners, and said I lied. I did not lie. I hoped someday it would be just Crook and me face to face with knives when he said I lied.

Crook and I argued back and forth about many things. I insisted we must return to the reservation if we surrendered. Crook said no, we had to spend two harvests in the East in this place he called Florida before the *nantan* named president would let us return. Naiche, Chihuahua, Nana, other great warriors, and I sat in council until the next sun deciding if we would accept Crook's terms.

Chihuahua decided first to accept what Crook offered. After he broke, others decided they would too, and I also agreed to accept them. But that night a White Eye, Tribolett, who lived on the *Nakai-yi* side of the border and often traded with us, brought us a barrel of whiskey for a few trade things we had taken from the *Nakai-yes.* We all needed a drink of good White Eye whiskey after surrendering to Crook and agreeing to leave our own country for two harvests.

Before the whiskey made me drunk, Tribolett spoke with me privately in the darkness outside the firelight. He said, "Old friend, you need to keep your eyes open. I'm a-hearing they's White Eye plans to turn you over to a sheriff as soon as you cross the border. That there means you an' your boys ain't goin' to no Florida. They gonna have they selves a little trial and jerk you all to Jesus."

"What means this 'Jerk you all to Jesus?' "

"Why it means, aye God, they gonna hang you, and it ain't gonna be quick neither. They all gonna stand around smokin' and watchin' your face turn purple whilst you kick and jerk tryin' to run in the air while you're swingin' by the neck."

"Hmmph. Tribolett, you speak true words?"

He nodded. "I shore as hell do. Know 'em for a fact. You better get your boys and git outta here plenty quick."

"Tribolett good *amigo*. I want more whiskey, and then Naiche and I speak on this."

Tribolett had always been a fair trader. I believed him and gave much thought to what he said as the whiskey made me feel better.

The next sun, I told Naiche what Tribolett said. Our heads ached from the big drunk we had the night before, but we were clear-minded enough to know we had to do something or die. Our heads hurt too much to ride a long time toward the border, and we made camp soon after the time of shortest shadows. I told my best warriors that

Naiche and I planned to leave in the night, and the warriors said they would come with us. And so we left.

Teniente Gatewood and two scouts, Kay-ihtah and Martine, came and talked peace with us the next time. They represented a new *nantan* named Miles. Crook had gone to the plains to oversee the reservations of those tribes. *Good,* I thought. *Crook called me a liar and spoke ugly to me. Miles speaks pretty and believes what I say.* I believed Miles was a good man. He promised us our own reservation. He said that after we lived two harvests in Florida, the president would leave us alone. And he said our families would come to us in five days. But since it was after three harvests in Florida and over a harvest in Alabama before we were re-united with our families, I knew Miles was a liar and much worse than Crook ever was.

Now in the middle of Ghost Face, nearly four harvests after we had surrendered, General Crook, with the great bush of hair on his face and two stars on his shoulders, appeared among us. He drove up to the commander's house and went inside. A boy saw him, ran to the village, and told Chi-huahua and Kaytennae, the first chiefs he saw, that Crook had come. Then he ran on breathlessly, spreading the word. Kaytennae, younger than Chihuahua, raced ahead but just barely won the sprint to the fence gate in front of the commander's house. There they stood, puffing like winded racehorses, making steam in the cold air.

General Crook came out of the commander's house. He was putting on his hat and coat when he saw them, and, with a big grin, raised his fist in salute. "Ho! Chihuahua and Kaytennae, I see you."

Laughing, they raised their fists. "Ho, Crook. At last you come. We've waited a long time to see you."

Crook strode toward them and out the gate, grabbed their hands, and pumped them. Crook walked between Kaytennae and Chihuahua, and they spoke with smiles on their faces, as friends do who haven't seen each other for a long time. When they reached the gate to the trail leading down the hill to the village, a crowd, most of them scouts, had come to meet General Crook.

Chatto, a big smile on his face, came up and shook hands with him. Other scouts and headmen came forward, all glad to see the soldier chief who had always spoken straight to them and had returned to make the reservations livable after he drove away the White Eye storekeepers who cheated us.

After many handshakes, Crook pointed to

a building inside the gates and asked for a council with the headmen. Kaytennae said he would find them and bring them there. He found me at the school and told me Crook had come and wanted to meet with the headmen in a nearby building. I told him I would be there soon and moved to tell the teachers I had to leave for a while.

When I came through the door, the others had already come and sat in a council circle with Crook. Kaytennae came in the door right behind me, and we were the last to take our seats in the circle. As soon as we sat down, Chihuahua rolled *tobaho* in an oak leaf, and we smoked to the four directions.

I leaned forward to tell Crook we were glad he came to us and ask how we could help him and to tell him how he could help us. But before I could say anything, Crook said to Wratten, "I don't want to hear anything from Geronimo. He's such a liar. I can't believe anything he says." After Wratten told me this, I sat back and crossed my arms to listen, still wondering what it was Crook wanted from us, except to call me a liar. I saw Chihuahua and others frown and shake their heads when Crook said this. There was no need for Crook to be rude and use bad manners with me.

Through Wratten, he leaned forward and said to Naiche, "You left with Geronimo and others. How did you come to leave that night?"

Naiche crossed his arms and said with a frown, "I was afraid I was going to be taken off somewhere I didn't like, to some place I didn't know. I thought everyone taken away would die. Since then, I have found out different. Nobody said anything to me that night. I worked it out in my own mind."

Then the general frowned. "Didn't you talk about it among yourselves?"

Naiche shrugged his shoulders. "We talked to each other about it. We were drunk."

"Why did you get drunk?"

"Because there was a lot of whiskey there, and we wanted a drink and took it. The others didn't want to go out. I don't know why the others didn't know of it. I thought they all did."

"So you broke away with Geronimo and others. I know Geronimo hates Mexicans and will kill every one of them he can. You left a trail of blood all across northern Mexico after you broke away, but you did the same thing across the border with the Americans. Before you surrendered, you killed everyone you came across on either side of the border. Why did you do this?"

Naiche pushed at the dirt with a stick and shook his head. "It was war. We were afraid. If we left anyone alive, they could give the Blue Coats information about us. We had to kill them if we were to live."

Crook looked around our circle of faces, slowly nodded, and said to Naiche, "How did you surrender? Were you afraid of the troops?"

"We wanted to see our people."

"Did the troops force you to surrender?"

"We were not forced to do it. We talked under a flag of truce."

George Wratten then began talking to Crook in the White Eye tongue. I heard my name and the names Gatewood, Kayihtah, and Martine. I understood he was telling Crook how the surrender had happened. When he finished, Crook asked him a question, which he translated for us all. "Could the surrender have been made without the scouts?"

Wratten shook his head. "I don't think so."

Crook shook his head and said under his breath, "Damn." Then he said, and Wratten interpreted, "Tell me what has happened to you since the surrender."

Those who had stayed on the reservation told him how they worked to keep their promise to keep the peace. They told him of all their losses in the work they had done — their animals taken and sold for nothing, their crops and equipment stolen, their labor to grow their farms and make a little money all wiped out. But still they hoped for a better future. They believed Crook would help them.

Chatto took the big silver medal given to him in Washington off his coat. When Miles had him lead a delegation to Washington to ask Miles's *nantan* that the scouts and reservation Indians not be shipped to Florida, the big chief had given him the medal and a paper they thought said they could stay on the reservation. But the tracks on the paper said only they had been there. The big chief let them return as far as Fort Leavenworth before their iron wagon took them to Fort Marion to live with the other prisoners.

Chatto said to Crook, "Why did they give me that to wear in the guardhouse? I thought something good would come to me when they gave me that, but I've been in confinement ever since it was given to me." Chatto talked about how he had given up everything to make the Washington trip. He had fields planted in wheat and barley; he had a wagon where he made good money hauling hay and other supplies; he had thirty sheep that were increasing all the time. He made money shearing them and selling their wool, and he had horses and mules that were worth a good deal of money. He didn't leave any of his property of his own accord.

Ha, I thought, *Ussen gives justice to traitors like Chatto. He betrayed us, but his reward was betrayal.*

Others told similar stories of the lives they'd had to give up on the reservation. The army had gathered up their livestock, sold it, and given them their money in five-dollar-per-month increments, but none got the money for what their property and animals were worth. Noche said he was paid for his horses but not for ninety cords of wood he had cut and piled up to sell. Kaytennae told Crook he had lost his crop and his wagon. Chatto showed Crook figures showing that payment for his livestock was much less than what they were worth.

Kaytennae reminded Crook of how he had gone to the meeting when I had surrendered in the Season of Little Eagles. He said, "I talked your talk to them and your mind to them. I never did anything wrong and never went on the warpath since I saw you. I tried to think as you told me to and was very thankful to you, and I was very glad to see you again this morning. All the Indians were, even the little children.

"Now my work does nothing for me or my family. It's useless work for me. I help build roads, dig up roots, build houses, and do work all around here. Leaves fall off the trees, and I help sweep them up. I was working this morning when you came here. I don't know why I work here all the time for nothing. I have children and relatives, lots of them, and I would like to work for them before I get too old to work. I'd like to have a farm long enough to see the crops get ripe."

Chihuahua also said he'd like to have a farm and wanted to support his family. He spoke of the wide, clear ranges of our homeland and the smothering forests of pines around us. I said nothing, just nodded at what the others said. I knew Crook saw me.

Crook said, "I've heard you. What was done to the scouts is unjust. It must be changed. Farms and land must be returned to you who were living and working in peace on the reservation. The president must give you land on your own reservation, as Miles promised. It's only right. I think the best place for you is in Indian Territory. Too many of your children have died at the Carlisle school. They should be taught and given their lessons close to your houses, wherever that may be. These things I will tell the president. Maybe he'll listen. If he doesn't, I'll tell anyone who will listen. I thank you all for coming and telling me with a straight tongue how your lives are."

CHAPTER 18
ASH FLAT

Our meeting with Crook had lasted for a sun. I was glad when he left in the dimming light of the coming darkness. I didn't like him, and his coming brought back many memories of times when we were free and the war was good against the Blue Coats, settlers, and Mexicans. I walked back to my cabin in the cold darkness, thinking of the good meal I knew Zi-yeh would have waiting for me. When I picked up Fenton, who waited by the door, and swung him, laughing, in a great circle around the cabin, I still thought of the good war, and I wished I had never surrendered. Zi-yeh had roasted meat and potatoes with onions and made fry bread for us, and great smells filled the cabin as she smiled and gave me a pan like the soldiers used to eat from. She and Fenton expected to wait to eat until I finished, but I wanted them to go ahead and eat, so they did.

When I finished eating, Zi-yeh said, "My husband doesn't have a happy face from his meal. It is not good?"

I shook my head. "Your meal, as always, is good this night, but sitting and listening to Crook all this sun brings visions of wars and raids from long-ago times."

She poured a cup of her good, strong coffee and handed it to me hot and steaming. "I'll put Fenton in his blankets and clean up from the meal. Then I'll come to you. Perhaps Ussen will make another child as you hold me tonight."

I smiled and nodded as I blew steam from the cup. I stared at the flickering yellow fire as a vision of Ash Flat ten harvests ago appeared before my eyes.

Ash Flat was on the trail we rode to free Loco and his people from San Carlos. We planned to take them with us to our camps in the Sierra Madre, where we believed the Blue Coats would never come. We thought we would be safe there. Near Ash Flat, we smelled and soon heard many sheep. I smiled when I smelled sheep were nearby. Sheep always meant *Nakai-yi* herders, and it was always a good time killing *Nakai-yes*. Naiche, Chihuahua, and Chatto rode with me in the front of our warriors, and they, too, smiled when they smelled sheep. They laughed and said our warriors would be hungry. It was time to stop and eat.

Outriding scouts came to us and said the sheep had nine *Nakai-yes* and three White Mountain Apaches herding them. Some of the *Nakai-yes* and Apaches had their families there. Twelve men with their families posed little danger for us. We were a big war party of more than seventy warriors. We quietly rode through the brush and appeared like ghosts at their camp where the women worked. I looked the camp over. It was a safe place to take time for a meal and take proper care of *Nakai-yes* — men, women, and children.

The man in charge came toward us unarmed. A *Nakai-yi,* he looked familiar, and I quickly realized it was Bes-das, once a boy I had taken in a raid in the land of the *Nakai-yes.* He had light behind his eyes. He learned quickly to speak Apache and worked hard around the camp, and I treated him well. I gave him a spotted pony, a saddle trimmed in silver, and shirts to keep the sun from burning his skin, but he was not happy with us. I think he was too old when we took him. It would have been better if I had killed him then and been done with him. I knew I couldn't trust him to stay with us, so I traded him to a White Eye rancher for a pistol, a box of cartridges, and two ponies. The rancher said the boy's *Nakai-yi* name was Victoriano Mestas, which he never told me, even though I speak good Spanish. I had not seen him since I traded him away. He had grown into a strong man, and his woman had made fancy designs with colored thread on his shirt. It was a very nice shirt. I liked it.

Bes-das walked up to us as we sat quietly on our ponies looking over his camp and deciding what we wanted, but he didn't seem to have much. He waved his arm parallel to the ground and said, "I see you, Geronimo. Welcome to my camp. Do you remember me?"

I swung down from my pony and walked over to him. Every *Nakai-yi* stood still watching us while the sheep milled about nearby making noise, and the children gathered around the skirts of their mothers, who held fingers over their mouths to keep them from screaming in fear of us.

"I know you, Bes-das. I took you from *Nakai-yes* to raise myself when you were small but growing. You grew into a big *Nakai-yi* after I traded you to the White Eye rancher, and I see you have a woman and three children playing around her. You are the chief of the *Nakai-yes* here? They do what you tell them?"

Bes-das cocked his head to one side and nodded. "*Sí,* I am the *jefe* here."

Warriors pushed the sheepherders over to the wagon where they made them sit down and then tied their hands together with one rope they found on a wagon, but they left the women free to work.

"I see another little camp of wickiups just over there." I pointed at them with my nose. "They look like Apaches, and they have their women with them. Who are they?"

"That's Bylas and three other men. They're White Mountains helping with wether lambs."

I swung up on my pony to visit the White Mountain camp. "Hmmph. I have lived in the White Mountains. I think I know this man Bylas. My warriors have ridden far. They're hungry." I smiled down at Bes-das. "We can have a few of your sheep?"

Bes-das smiled back, but I saw fear in his eyes as he turned toward the sheep and spread his arms wide. "*Sí, sí,* Geronimo. Take all you need."

I turned to the warriors and told them to take sheep they needed for a meal and then turned back toward Bes-das. I saw a fine sorrel pony grazing near to his wagon. To

Bes-das I said, "That's a nice pony that grazes near your wagon."

The smile left his face. He said, "The pony belongs to *Señor* Jimmie Stevens, whose father owns the sheep. I just ride him once in a while. It's not mine."

"*Enjuh.* I like horsemeat better than sheep." I killed the pony with an easy shot to its head from where I sat on my horse not fifty yards away. The rifle's report made the tied *Nakai-yes* jerk in surprise and look around in fear to see who was shooting. I laughed at them. It was always good to *Nakai-yes* flinch in fear. "Tell your women to prepare the meal. Is that Bylas's wickiup over there by those trees?"

Bes-das's fear was leaking out of his eyes and on to his face. He nodded.

I said, "I know White Mountains. I know Bylas probably has some whiskey. I'm thirsty. Maybe he'll give me a drink. Let's go over to see Bylas."

Bes-das told the women to fix whatever the warriors wanted and followed me on foot as I rode to Bylas's wickiup and dismounted. I sat by his fire and waited for him to come out of his wickiup. Soon he came. He smelled of good whiskey and could not walk straight. I said, "I know you. You lived in the White Mountains when I did. You always have some whiskey around. Give me a bottle."

Bylas shook his head as he dropped down in front of me. The whiskey stains on his shirt were still damp, its smell fresh and powerful. "I don't have any more. I drank it all when I saw you and your war party ride out of the brush."

"Hmmph. Not another bottle you have? None you can give me?"

"Whiskey all gone."

"That's too bad. I was hoping for a drink of good whiskey. You come eat with us. The women cook sheep and horse now. Maybe you remember where another bottle is after you eat."

Bylas and his White Mountains walked behind me as I rode back to Bes-das's wagons where cooking fires burned and the women cooked beans and tortillas along with the meat.

I sat with Bylas and his men, one a grown son of one of the men. I said to Bylas, "You still don't remember having any more whiskey?" He looked at his moccasins and shook his head. I spoke of old times with Bes-das, who relaxed a little. I asked Bylas to tell me if things were any better on the reservation while the warriors filled their bellies. After he spoke, I said, narrowing my eyes like I didn't believe his earlier answer, "Still you don't remember having any more whiskey?"

The grown son of one of Bylas's men had not grown enough to control his tongue. He said, "This man Bylas is not a boy for you to talk to this way and keep on asking for whiskey. He won't give you any whiskey."

I didn't need a boy to tell me how to act. He didn't look like an Apache to me. He looked like a *Nakai-yi.*

"This boy is a full-blood *Nakai-yi.*" I cocked my rifle. I was ready to kill him, but one of the White Mountains said, "No. He is not a *Nakai-y*i. He's a full-blood White Mountain, and his mother is of the 'black water' clan, so he's of that clan also."

I looked at Bylas and then the cocked rifle lying in my lap. "What is he?"

Bylas swallowed hard and then said in a croaking whisper, "He is White Mountain."

My anger grew. I didn't want to kill a White Mountain. They had many scouts who worked for Crook. Perhaps they needed to know we meant business. I said to Bes-das, "That's a fine shirt you wear that your woman decorates for you. I think I would like to have it. Why don't you take it off and give it to me so I can keep it clean?"

Bes-das's face froze. He stood, and his

fingers trembled as he unbuttoned the shirt and pulled it off his shoulders. I saw him glance at his woman, his head making a tiny shake most of the others did not see. She spoke to her children, and they climbed under the wagon, squatted there, and watched their father give me his shirt.

I laid it over my knees and took my time to fold it carefully, knowing Bes-das trembled inside. He knew what was coming. Most of the warriors had eaten and were leaning back on their elbows enjoying their meal, but a group near us sat on their heels with their rifles cocked, wondering what we would do next. I looked at Bes-das, grinned, and then said to the waiting warriors, "Tie the *Nakai-yes* together and kill them."

The warriors were on Bes-das before he could take a step toward me. They dragged him and the women, who screamed and begged to be spared, to the men who were already tied together. Bes-das's woman screamed at the children under the wagon and told them to run. They ran quick, like rabbits leaving a hole taken by a rattlesnake.

Warriors looked at me, and I nodded and said, "Yes, even the little ones. They must die like all my children did."

They caught two of the three and threw the smallest one on the thorns of a big cactus. It wailed for a long time. It was a strong child, like my children must have been. The other child they tied over the coals of a fire to roast. It, too, screamed a long time.

The warriors smashed the heads of the screaming women with rocks and bashed some of the men with their war clubs. They had knife-throwing contests at the bodies of some of the men, and two or three of the throws went straight and true. Those men didn't last long. My men found a loaded rifle in Bes-das's wagon and brought it to me. I tried it out on Bes-das, shooting him in his man parts. He screamed and groaned only a little while because he bled so much, and then I put a bullet in his heart.

The warriors found the third child, a boy, hiding under the skirts of Bylas's wife. They dragged him away from her while she pleaded for his life. When they looked at me, I nodded and said, "Yes, all must die. Die good in pain."

Jelikine squatted nearby leaning against his spear, watching what was happening and shaking his head, saying, "No good. No good."

Naiche said, "No! There's been enough killing here. Let the boy live."

"He dies! All *Nakai-yes* die like my children died. Kill the woman, too. She protected him." I felt the point of Jelikine's spear push against my chest. "Kill that boy and you die, Geronimo."

I heard the hammer click back on Naiche's rifle and saw the barrel pointed at me, not two bow lengths from my belly. "Kill that child and woman, and you'll die with them, Geronimo." Naiche was a good warrior, just soft sometimes.

I nodded and lifted my hands. "Naiche is chief. I obey Naiche. Let them go."

We took all the supplies we could from the camp, and Bylas and his people went with us on to Dewey Flat and the Old Wagon Road. Eating so well before we raided the reservation to take Loco and his people came as an unexpected gift.

For a long time, I didn't understand why I thought of Ash Flat that night, except I was remembering old war times after Crook left us, and Zi-yeh was anxious to make another child for us. It took nearly fifteen years to understand why I had that memory. Perhaps someday I will tell you.

Two moons later, Wratten told us General Crook made tracks on a paper to the president that said what he had told us. Three moons after he left us, Crook was no more.

I remembered then how, when we met in the Season of Little Eagles, Crook had said he had no intention of putting me in prison. I knew he had lied, and I was convinced he gave orders to put me in prison or to kill me, if I resisted. Ussen took his life as a punishment for all the evil things he had done. Of this, I was certain.

CHAPTER 19
EVA

One night, three Moons after Crook met us in council, Zi-yeh put Fenton in his blankets and came to mine. It was a warm night, and many frogs sang in the river, along with things the soldiers called peepers, which sang from the trees. I didn't like all that noise. Their songs made it hard to sleep and hard to hear enemies when they came. Sleeping was better in our own country, and it was easier to hear raiders coming in time to defend the camp.

Zi-yeh whispered to me, "Husband, I have news for you." I frowned. Zi-yeh and the other women often found out things sooner than Wratten could tell the leaders.

"Hmmph. What do the White Eyes say now?"

"The White Eyes say nothing. I say Ussen makes a child grow in my belly."

I laughed. "Hi-yeh. This news pleasures me much. When will the child come?"

"I think in seven moons. It's hard to count the seasons in this place of many tall trees and little change in seasons, but I think near the beginning of the Season of Earth Is Reddish Brown. Are you truly happy to have another child, husband, even if it is born while we are prisoners?"

"I'm happy to hear your news, woman. Ussen is good to us. Do you think it's a girl child or a boy child?"

"It's too soon to guess. I want a girl child who can bring a strong man to help us. But I don't care if it's a girl or boy as long as it's born strong."

"Zi-yeh is a wise woman. Ussen will protect her while she carries this child."

"I am my husband's woman."

"Enjuh."

Wratten said Crook's report prodded the army into sending *Teniente* William Wallace Wotherspoon to look after us, since the commander of the fort had many other things for which he was responsible and not much time for Apaches. *Teniente* Wotherspoon first fixed a place where White Eye *di-yens* could use their medicine to drive away sickness. Wotherspoon also gave us money so we could buy seeds and plant big gardens, and we had enough fruit, beans, and potatoes to feed us all through the Seasons of Large Leaves and Large Fruit, with some left over to sell the White Eyes in the village of Mount Vernon. As the fruit grew large and ripened, so did Zi-yeh swell with our child. I was glad she was my woman.

Through the harvest suns after Crook came to visit us, we did what Wotherspoon said we should do without complaining, even if the work was useless to us. He even let some of the men leave the village with their families to work on White Eye farms and earn money. Wotherspoon paid me and the other leaders to do things only a chief should do. I looked after the children when the lady teachers came and used my stick of correction on them if they needed it, but mostly all the students did as their teachers told them.

As a *di-yen* gifted with great Power, I also performed many ceremonies for the People. That year, I led *Hahehs* (womanhood ceremonies) for several girls. I conducted several healing ceremonies and advised boys who wanted a Power vision for what Ussen expected of them. These were hard times for our boys. Unlike girls, who became marriageable women after their *Haheh,* boys did not, in captivity, have a recognition ceremony showing them how to be men ready for marriage. Before the reservations, boys were novitiates for warrior raiding parties. The boys had to serve successfully in four raids to be recognized as a man and warrior. The other leaders and I struggled with the question of how and when boys were to be recognized as men. We finally decided there was no straight way to do this. We would have to let their fathers decide when a boy stood as a man and could marry.

After evening meals, clans often sat around fires as the old ones told stories. These stories were told many times so our children would know Chiricahua lifeways and remember their ancestors. Even though we were prisoners of the Blue Coats, we knew that to survive as a people, we must never forget who we were, forget our pride, or forget our history. We all knew that one sun we would be free People.

One sun after the time of no shadows in the Season of Earth Is Reddish Brown, I sat in council with the tribal leaders. A young woman came running and said to me privately that Zi-yeh's baby was coming and that my grown daughter, Dohn-say, and other women were helping her. With a happy heart, I told the others, "Ussen

blesses us. A new child comes to my lodge."
And they all said, as with one voice, *"Enjuh!"*

A baby girl came to us. She was small, as
girls usually are, but she was quiet and took
my finger in a powerful grip for one so
young. I named her Eva, a White Eye name.
I liked the sound it made when spoken. We
asked Dos-teh-seh, mother of Naiche, wife
of Cochise, and daughter of the great Mangas Coloradas, to make Eva's *tsach* (cradleboard), and she said she would do anything
she could to help the family of Geronimo,
Naiche's most important advisor, and she
was honored to do it.

We gave her four blue stones, golden pollen, a new cooking pot, and a basket for
making the *tsach.* Naiche gathered materi-
als for it. He found wood like black locust,
heart of pine, and long strips of hickory to
steam and bend into the rainbow (the
protecting top above the baby's head).
Where he got it, I never learned. Dos-teh-
seh used a piece of buckskin on it she had
long saved, hung small bags of pollen inside
the rainbow, and padded it with soft grass.
It was a fine *tsach.*

On the fourth day after Eva's birth, as
pools of sunlight were being formed from
great shafts of light thrown through the tall
trees, Dos-teh-seh performed the *tsach*

ceremony. First, she sang a prayer to Ussen.

"Good like long life it moves back and
  forth.
By means of White Water in a circle
  underneath, it is made.
By means of White Water spread on it, it
  is made.
By means of White Water curved over it,
  it is made.
Lightning dances alongside it, they say.
By means of Lightning, it is fastened
  across.

Its strings are made of rainbows, they
  say.
Black Water Blanket is underneath to rest
  on.
White Water spread is underneath to rest
  on.
Good, like long life the cradle is made.
Sun, his chief rumbles inside, they say."

Listening to Dos-teh-seh sing, I thought,
*Eva is warmed by the sun, rocked by the
winds, and sheltered by the trees, as other
Indian babes. She can go anywhere with a
good feeling.*
Then Dos-teh-seh pointed the *tsach* toward the east first, then south, west, and

207

north before taking Eva, naked in the cool morning air, from Zi-yeh, rubbing warm water on her, and three times pointing her toward the *tsach.* Eva was quiet, but awake, watching it all with her big, round eyes. She never even whimpered as the women sang their songs and prayers and warm water was poured over her body from the strong, callused hands of Dos-teh-seh. The fourth time Eva was pointed toward her *tsach,* Dos-teh-seh laid her within the cradleboard, and prayers continued with sacred pollen placed on both Eva and Zi-yeh's head and lips.

Although the feast we had to celebrate the *tsach* ceremony cost me much money from all I had saved selling my signature and bows and arrows to White Eyes, I was glad to share my happy time at the arrival of Eva, and so were the other families who celebrated with us.

Rains were heavy again that Season of Earth Is Reddish Brown. The cabins where we lived kept the rain off our heads, but the green stuff the White Eyes called mold was once again everywhere, and people were often sick. Every sun, with the coming of dawn's low, gray light seeping through the trees around us, I got up to listen and look at Eva, worried I would hear the gurgling sounds in her breathing that signaled she was sick. I picked her up and listened to her breathing while she still slept, but, even with my ear held close to her little chest, I heard only her gentle breath before I handed her to Zi-yeh, who sat in a rocking chair ready to feed her. Eva grew strong. I don't remember her being bad sick. I thanked Ussen for helping me drive the demons away that might have made her sick.

We had been much better off in Florida at Fort Pickens than at Mount Vernon. I told

Crook and others we should all be at Fort Pickens, but they wouldn't listen. *Teniente* Wotherspoon walked among our cabins with Wratten, looked at our lodges, and saw the mold and dirt everywhere that made it so hard to keep things clean. Then he gathered the leaders and spoke to us in a good way.

He said, with Wratten interpreting, "I've seen your lodges, and with my chief's agreeing, I want to build you a new village with good comfortable houses on the big sand ridge covered with trees a long rifle shot on the other side of the fort. I'm sure you've seen it and know the ridge. It's a much better place for your lodges. Water won't gather there when it rains, and maybe the mold and sickness will be better. What do you think?"

I stood up and said, "New lodges are good. Less mold and sickness are good. Where is the reservation Miles promised us? Why can't we have that?"

I saw the other leaders nod and grunt they agreed with what I said.

Teniente Wotherspoon shook his head. "I don't know where your reservation is. The *nantans* in Washington argue over it. You know what General Crook said in his report to them. He said they thought land the Cherokees would sell you was the best place in the East, and some place around Fort Sill the Comanches and Kiowa would agree to let you have was the best place west of the big Mississippi River. He thought that was the best place of all, but until the *nantans* agree, you have to stay here."

"I don't know the North Carolina land or the Fort Sill land the Kiowa and Comanches have. I don't want it. I want land in my own country. Give it to us as Miles promised."

"That I cannot do. Even General Crook said it would be bad for you to go back to Arizona because the Whites would probably attack you for old wrongs, and there would be war. That we cannot have. I ask again, shall I ask for new houses to be built for you in a village on the far ridge?"

I studied the young, serious eyes of Wotherspoon for a breath or two and saw he spoke straight. I nodded and sat down. The others asked where the lumber would come from and who would build the houses, but they all agreed a new village on the ridge was a good thing. *Teniente* Wotherspoon smiled and said one of the few Apache words he knew, *"Enjuh."*

Before the end of Ghost Face, Wotherspoon's army chiefs agreed new lodges be built for us on the ridge we had agreed to. Sawed lumber came within a moon by iron wagon to the place the White Eyes called Mount Vernon Station. I drove one of the wagons Wotherspoon sent to the station with three or four men on each one to help load the new lumber. I liked the good, strong smell of the sawed lumber, most of it hard pine, brown sand colored, and easier to handle than tree logs. The mules strained to pull the wagons to the top of the ridge on the sandy road where the wheel tracks got deeper and deeper each time we used them. The men unloaded the lumber where the village was to be, stacking it high as a man's head in big interlaced squares. If it wasn't raining, we could haul and stack two loads in a sun. It was hard work, but we were glad to be doing something that helped our families.

We made many trips hauling lumber from the station to the village site. After we hauled all the lumber, Wotherspoon hired two White Eyes called carpenters. When we first arrived at Mount Vernon, we built our cabins with some Blue Coat help, but none of us knew how to build these things called houses. The carpenters knew how to build houses, and they began teaching our men how to build them, too. The men watched the carpenters pile stacks of flat stones beside the level string lines tied to stakes that showed the size and shape of the house. The carpenters called the stacks of big stones the foundation. Then they laid wide, thick pieces of lumber between the corner piles of stones and nailed them together with crosspieces so the pieces beside the string rested on their edges around the stone piles to form what they called the floor frame. I watched them level the frame using thin stones and wood pieces between the stone pillars and the frame's wooden edges. When the frame was level, they stacked piles of stone up to level strings between opposite frame timbers. The carpenters nailed thick timbers on the piles of stone inside the frame to connect the frame pieces crosswise. Then the carpenters covered the frame top by nailing thin, wide boards across it to make what they called the "floor." This floor was very strong and flat. The carpenters even showed us it would support a horse. A smooth ball of string laid on the floor wouldn't roll anywhere because the floor did not tilt in any direction.

The carpenters showed the men how to make frames for the walls before raising them up and nailing them to the floor frame. And when the walls were up, they taught us how to make a roof frame and cover it with planks. I watched them work and teach our men how to be carpenters, measuring, checking the measure, marking, leveling, sawing, and nailing.

Very skillful men, very precise in their work, these carpenters, I began to understand the power of White Eye knowledge in everything they did, from the lodges they built that lasted many seasons to their weapons of war that killed many. My People had much to learn. Our men were glad to learn from them so they could do something for their families. I was glad to see this. I wanted them to learn all the power of the White Eyes.

Early in the Season of Little Eagles *Teniente* Wotherspoon met together with all the men. It was cool, the wind shook the tops of the trees, and we sat wrapped in blankets looking like boulders gathered on a creek bank watching him.

With Wratten again interpreting, *Teniente* Wotherspoon said, "You've all been warriors. You know how to fight. The big army chief in Washington has decided to use your skill in warfare and form an army company that includes only Apaches. It will be a company of infantry — soldiers who march and fight on foot — called Company I. You'll train together like regular Blue Coat soldiers. You'll train by learning to march together and by simulating fighting and learn the ways of Blue Coat trackers. You'll get the same pay as all Blue Coats. You'll get Blue Coat uniforms and other supplies, including rifles. You'll live together in big buildings called barracks. You'll build your barracks and more village houses like you are building now. The army will teach you to build bridges and to do other things it needs. To do this, you must enlist, make your mark on a paper with tracks that say for three years you promise to do only what army chiefs tell you. I think this is a good thing for you and encourage you to do it. Are there any questions?"

I stood and, throwing the blanket off my shoulders in the cold wind, said, "What if we get the reservation Miles promised us before our promise to the army is done? Will we be able to leave?"

Teniente Wotherspoon shook his head. "As long as you are bound by your promise, you must stay and do as the army chiefs say."

"When will we get the reservation Miles promised us?"

Wotherspoon frowned. "I don't know, Geronimo. As I've told you before, the *nan-tans* in Washington are trying to find you a place." He looked around at all the men,

"Are there any other questions?"

I threw up my hands in disgust. "Talk, talk, talk. That is all the big chiefs do. No wonder Blue Coat soldiers never caught us."

Fun said, "When must we make a mark on this paper to be a Blue Coat soldier?"

Wotherspoon smiled and nodded. "I think within two moons it will be here. I'll tell you when it comes and give a day for it to be signed."

Naiche stood said, "The Blue Coat chiefs will truly give us rifles and bullets?"

"Yes, you'll each have a rifle, and you'll have bullets. Until the chiefs tell you to do something, the rifles and ammunition will stay in one place. Any more questions?"

No one moved or said anything.

"Very well. That's all I have to say. I hope the chance to join the army appeals to you."

We all sat as still as stones as we watched *Teniente* Wotherspoon walk away.

Before they signed the paper, Naiche, Fun, Tsisnah, Ahnandia, Yahnozha, Toclanny, Haozous — all my best, most fearless warriors — sat with me in council, smoked to the four directions, and asked what I thought they should do.

Naiche, as their chief, said to me, "Geronimo, you're a good war leader. You've led us in many battles against many more Blue Coats than we ever had warriors, and we often won those battles. When the wars ended, we lived to be their prisoners, but we didn't die. Now the Blue Coats say we, too, can wear a Blue Coat. We, too, can feel the steel of rifles in our hands once again. They will give us money to give to our families. They'll teach us Blue Coat training and fighting ways. But if we agree to do these things, we must do as their chiefs tell us. We can no longer do as we want when we want. You have many harvests. You've seen many things, know many things, and have great Power from Ussen. The White Eyes say you're too old for their army. We all laugh at this and know you're stronger and can last longer in battle than their best soldiers. Now we ask what you think of this offer from the Blue Coats to join them."

I looked at each one around this circle of great warriors and fighters for the People. I said, "Warriors, you must decide your own path, but I will tell you what I think. When the soldiers of the Great White Chief drove us from our homes, we went to the mountains. When they followed us, we killed all we could. We said we would never be captured. We starved, and we killed. I said we would never yield. I was a fool. Now we're prisoners far from our own country. The Great White Chief has vast power. Only Ussen can give such power. I say we, from the youngest to the oldest, must learn everything we can from the White Eyes, but we must always remember that Ussen made us Chiricahua Apaches, not White Eyes. If we forget this, the Chiricahua will vanish in the harvests to come. What I hear Wotherspoon say through Wratten is that you must do as the Blue Coat soldier chief says for three harvests. Let it be so. While you are Blue Coats, learn everything you can from the White Eyes, do everything they tell you, and be glad Ussen has chosen this way to show you their Blue Coat lifeways. One day, you will be free. Your People will be free. You'll have Power from Ussen again, given to you through the Blue Coats. That is all I have to say." I looked around the circle at each one. Each nodded he understood.

In the Season of Many Leaves, my warriors became Blue Coats. Forty-six Chiricahuas at Mount Vernon, all in their prime, strong and able, joined the army. Thirty-one men from various bands living at San Carlos and some who had gone to school at Carlisle also became soldiers. Twenty-eight men had no desire to fight for the White Eyes and refused the Blue Coats.

The Blue Coats cut the hair of those who joined and gave them names the White Eyes could pronounce. Our men learned to dress and march as one man. Every day for the width of a hand on the horizon, the men learned to speak in the White Eye tongue and to read tracks and make numbers on paper that told them Blue Coat lifeways and what they must do to finish jobs they were given. In their training, the White Eyes showed them how to build bridges. They learned White Eye ways to scout and track, but they all knew our ways were better, and so did the White Eyes. There were trials where they pretended to fight to see who could outsmart and capture the other side. My People liked that work and training best. Soon Fun, now named Larry, and Tsisnah, now named Burdett, along with Toclanny and Naiche, were in charge as subchiefs. Fun was a corporal, and Tsisnah was a sergeant.

Teniente Wotherspoon quickly put all the Chiricahua Blue Coats to work building the barracks where he said they would live. The skills they had learned from the carpenters made the work go fast. Since they lived so close to their families, the soldiers visited them during the times the White Eyes called weekends and holidays. But the men had to return to their barracks by a certain time.

The Blue Coats used them to continue building houses after the barracks were finished. The men also made bed frames, tables, and chairs for each house. Wotherspoon provided an iron cookstove the women soon learned to use efficiently. They cooked meals on the stoves as well as they did over the open fires. Zi-yeh found ways to decorate our house inside with the many-colored blankets she made from scraps of cloth, a bow and arrows I had made, beadwork she had done, and other things she thought looked good in her house.

CHAPTER 21
LIFE AT
MOUNT VERNON BARRACKS

Naiche, Nana, Loco, Chihuahua, and I had
smoked together and talked many times
with other leaders of the Chiricahuas held
captive by the Blue Coats at Mount Vernon.
We spoke often of our worries about what
the White Eyes were doing to destroy our
lifeways. Our children, sent back to us sick
and dying from worms that attacked them
at the school at Carlisle, had told us how
they could not speak to each other in our
tongue or tell our stories, even in the White
Eye tongue. We asked ourselves why the
White Eyes did this and decided they
wanted to make our children forget who
they were and where they came from. They
wanted to destroy the Chiricahua as a people.

I thought it was important that our children go to the White Eye school to understand their secrets in making tracks on
paper and then reading them, how their

chiefs thought, how they decided what was best for their people, how they made medicine, and what they knew of Ussen. We talked long into the night about how to make sure our children didn't forget they were Chiricahuas, regardless of what the White Eyes did to them at school.

We also spoke of how our lifeways must change now that we were prisoners and what we would do if we became free and had to live on a reservation as we had before, unable to raid or make war.

We didn't begin answering our questions until old, arthritic Nana, Victorio's *segundo,* said to us, "The brown robe *padres* had a saying when I was a boy, and the longer I live, the more I understand it is true and one of our lifeways. It goes something like, 'Teach a child the road he should go, and when he is old, he won't leave it.' "

I thought, *That's exactly right, Nana.*

In councils, we decided we would gather the children around fires to tell them the stories they needed to know as Chiricahua Apaches. They would hear all those stories that taught us how to behave, who we were, and the importance of Power from Ussen. They would hear the history of our fathers and chiefs, the stories of White Painted Woman, Child of the Water, Killer of Enemies, the Slaying of the Monsters, and the Coyote stories. They would hear these stories many times, so they would always remember them and always remember who they were and where they came from. It was important they understand this, or the Chiricahua would surely vanish.

During our gatherings by the big fire, I told the children our stories of White Painted Woman, Child of the Water, Killer of Enemies, and the man-eating monsters, all giants, that Child of the Water destroyed. The children sat listening and watching with bright, shining eyes as I walked around the flickering yellow and orange flames sending sparks spiraling high into the blackness above us. I had to speak loud enough for them to hear above the frogs and the tree peepers. They always turned their heads so they could hear me, so I knew they heard and listened to me.

I told them, "In the beginning, White Painted Woman was with Ussen. She had no mother or father. Ussen's Power created her. Ussen sent her down to the world to live. Her home was a cave. In those days, they say monsters roamed the earth, and there weren't many people then. The monsters ate the people whenever they could catch them. The people who escaped the monsters had a hard time just living. There were four monsters hunting and eating people. There was Owl-Man Giant, Buffalo Monster, Eagle Monster, and Antelope Monster.

"White Painted Woman, in those days, had a boy named Killer of Enemies. He was either her brother or her son. Some stories say one, and some the other. Owl-Man Giant tormented the boy but never tried to kill him. I don't know why. He was just mean to him. He would watch Killer of Enemies go hunting and then take the meat away from him or mess up what he was trying to do. Killer of Enemies never resisted; he just cried and let it go. He wasn't much good, I guess."

I told how White Painted Woman became pregnant from water and lightning and had a baby. A spirit told her she must call the baby Child of the Water, and this she did. I told the stories of how she had to hide the baby under her fire so Owl-Man Giant couldn't find and eat him, and how one day Child of the Water battled Owl-Man Giant. With help from Water, he used a little bow and grama grass arrows to kill the Owl-Man Giant monster, and he eventually killed all the other monsters with help from the animals.

The children listened to these stories. They knew the stories were telling them things they needed to learn and remember. Telling the stories and watching their faces in the firelight gave me strength and hope to believe we would defeat our monsters, the White Eye giants, who were trying to eat us.

Singers for masked dancers also came to the fires and sang for the children, so they learned the masked dance. We didn't let them dress up, because doing so might bring evil influences. The children knew what to do in dance ceremonies by the time we needed them. And they knew who to talk to if they were uncertain about what to do. We also taught them the circle dance, so useful in the early days of courting when young women could choose with whom they wanted to dance. But we were careful not to let boys and girls dance together until they were ready.

As a *di-yen,* I continued to conduct womanhood ceremonies for girls who had become women. In the long-ago days, the girls and their mothers made dresses and costumes for the ceremony out of the finest leathers with much fringe and beadwork. At Mount Vernon, we didn't have the rifles or good bows to hunt the deer we needed for the buckskin and doeskin dresses, so the mothers shared with their daughters the dresses they wore for their ceremonies, reworking them to give the girls something truly new and made with the best buckskin or doeskin. However, finding trees to make the big brush tipi for the ceremony at Mount Vernon was easier than it was at Fort Apache.

As boys reached their time to begin receiving Power from Ussen and his spirits, we taught them to deny themselves for four days and how to use the sweat lodge to get them closer to their vision time, although only Ussen could decide when and where Power came and to whom it was given. When they were younger, we had hoop and pole makers give them small sets so they could learn how to play this game in which women could not participate. I believe Ussen used everything we did to keep our people together, no matter what we learned from the White Eyes.

At Mount Vernon Barracks, there were no tourists to buy the things we made. White Eyes in the town stores bought a few things we brought to sell, but most buyers were soldiers or farmers who had little or no money to spend on what we made.

One sun an iron wagon brought a new load of sawed lumber for our new houses. I rode with Fun to get a load of the lumber. White Eyes who rode the iron wagon had descended from it to watch us work. They didn't live at Mount Vernon, but they wanted to see the Chiricahua who were prisoners there. I sat on the wagon with my arms crossed and watched those who rode the iron wagons point at us and talk among themselves, then shrug their shoulders, throw up their hands, or scratch their heads in curiosity. I thought, *There are our tourists.*

I asked *Teniente* Wotherspoon if we could go to the Mount Vernon Station to sell what we made to the White Eyes riding on the iron wagons. He asked those who drove the iron wagons if we could do as I asked, and soon they agreed. He told us we could go, but that we must tell the gate guards we were going there when we left, and we must return through the same gate. He put me in charge of those who sold at the station and gave me a thing he called a watch. He showed me how to read when an hour passed on the watch and how to twist a little knob on top so it made the little pointing arrows turn around the center. I liked the watch and practiced using it often.

We did as *Teniente* Wotherspoon told us and sold many things we made to the iron wagon riders. So many White Eyes bought my toy bows and arrows that other Chiricahuas who had made them gave them to me to sell, and I did. I didn't tell the White Eyes I never made some of the bows. They knew I sold them, and thus believed I'd made them. The White Eyes even paid fifty cents more for my bow and arrows if I wrote or carved my name on the bow. For those bows I sold that I didn't make, the makers gave me some of the money from the sale. I refused the money at first, but they said they couldn't have sold them unless I handed them to the tourists. So I took what they offered and began to understand how storekeepers like Wratten made money.

In less than half a moon, I had sold everything Zi-yeh and I had made to the iron wagon riders. We took Eva and Fenton and went to a trading post in Mount Vernon that sold the things Zi-yeh and I needed in order to make things for sale. While we waited for the White Eye to gather what we needed, Eva, who was barely old enough to be walking, began playing with Fenton around a little red wagon with a long, silver-colored handle. Eva climbed in the wagon, and Fenton strained to pull her. While it rolled and bumped over the trading post's rough wooden floor, she laughed and clapped her hands and begged Fenton to keep pulling when he stopped. When the White Eye had gathered what we wanted and was ready to take my money, I handed him a roll of paper money to count out what we needed to pay, pointed at the wagon, and said, "I buy." The White Eye smiled, held up two fingers, and said, "Two dollars." I nodded. He counted out the money he wanted and gave the rest back to me. The roll of paper money was still thick. *Enjuh.*

I pulled Eva and Fenton in the wagon back to our cabin. Fenton didn't like the bumpy ride and got out, but Eva stayed put. She wanted to ride anyplace we could take the wagon. Zi-yeh carried what we bought, which was much lighter than Eva, and she was in good spirits. I smiled. I knew that night she would want to try to make another child. I never denied those requests. Ussen would not want me to do that.

In the Season of Large Fruit, three or four moons after *Teniente* Wotherspoon came to Mount Vernon, he sent a soldier to ask me to come for a talk at the place where he made tracks on paper. I went. I had no choice, but I asked Ussen not to let Wotherspoon order me shot.

I stood at Wotherspoon's door in the big building near the children's school and waited until he saw me and motioned me to a chair. He handed me a jar of *tobaho* and said, "Let's smoke. Wratten comes soon."

I reached in the jar and gathered enough *tobaho* for a cigarette rolled from papers *Teniente* Wotherspoon gave me. I was ready to light the cigarette when Wratten came through the door and sat beside me. After we smoked, *Teniente* Wotherspoon said, "Geronimo, I need a respected leader from your people to act as a judge for cases that involve them. I want you to be the judge."

I frowned. "You mean like a White Eye judge who puts people in iron cages or orders them hung or shot?"

Teniente Wotherspoon laughed. "If the law is broken by a Chiricahua, you can order him put in the guardhouse for a time of your choosing. You won't be able to order anyone put to death. That order has to come from the Great Father far away in Washington. For disputes between your people, you can make the choice of who is right, who is wrong, and what to do. When the tribal police bring before you one of your people

230

wronged by another, you can listen to the charges, hear the arguments against them, and decide who is right. I'll pay you ten dollars and fifty cents a month for you to do this. How about it?"

I stared at *Teniente* Wotherspoon. I knew nothing about being a judge, but ten dollars and fifty cents a month would buy supplies for making things that could be sold for much money. I nodded and said, "*Enjuh.* You teach. I judge. When you pay?"

Teniente Wotherspoon, in a happy mood, laughed again. "Excellent. I'll pay at the end of each moon that you're a judge. Mr. Wratten will go with you to watch and explain how a local White Eye judge works, and you do the same as he does when you work as a judge."

This sounded like a good way to learn, and I agreed. As *Teniente* Wotherspoon directed, I watched a White Eye justice of the peace work. He judged most people he saw were bad and sent them to stay for many harvests at a place Wratten told me they lived in iron bar cages.

When I did my first judge work, I heard charges of public drunkenness. One man, called One Foot because he had only one good foot, walked leaning on a stick. Blue coats found him lying in the weeds by the trail, passed out with a half-empty bottle in his hand. Fool! He was old enough to know that showing the Blue Coats he could get whiskey would get us all in trouble.

I looked at him and remembered he was a Chihenne who had helped me at Ojo Caliente before Clum came there. I said, "You have only one good foot. It's a reason to drink whiskey, but you do know whiskey isn't allowed at this White Eye fort because we live here."

He bowed his head, a smile nearing the edge of his lips. "Yes, Judge Geronimo. This I know. But I find a man who makes good whiskey. He gives me a little to sample. That is all I did." He knew the penalty for being drunk was half a moon in the iron bar cage. He thought the whiskey had been worth it.

"You make the Blue Coats watch your brothers with careful eyes. One Foot, you spend six moons in the place of the iron bars. Maybe then you will think about your brothers before you drink where everyone can see you. That is all I have to say."

I brought the wood mallet I held down hard, so it made a loud knock like I had seen the White Eye judge do. I liked making the knock. The sound let all who heard it know that I had spoken. But many murmuring voices of surprise said I had given too strong a penalty for drinking a little whiskey. They all knew I drank whiskey. I liked to drink it, but the Blue Coats never caught me.

Teniente Wotherspoon and Wratten told me the penalty was too hard for drinking. It should be something less than a moon. Six moons would be right for theft. I told them I understood and would be more lenient in the future. Still I thought One Foot deserved six moons' punishment, because he drank where the Blue Coats could find him drunk. We had to be careful with our drinking. Now One Foot wouldn't soon forget this important lesson, and neither would the others who learned of his punishment.

The Blue Coats brought another man to stand before me. He was chained about his wrists and ankles. The Blue Coat chief said this man, too, had drunk whiskey and become so aroused to anger by another man, he tried to stab him. I sentenced this man to one hundred years in the place of the iron bars, but I later changed it to three years. *Teniente* Wotherspoon and Wratten said three years was a better measure of punishment. Soon I began to understand what the Blue Coats thought were fair punishments, and I gave those when I sat on the judgment chair.

■ ■ ■ ■

The seasons passed, and we settled into sun-to-sun living and waiting for General Miles to keep his promise of giving us our own reservation, not this little thumbnail place, as Mangas called it, with many trees to give shade but that still burned your foot when you stepped on the ground.

CHAPTER 22
TALK OF A NEW PLACE

Chappo returned to us from the Carlisle school in the Season of Small Leaves in the harvest time the White Eyes called 1894. One morning on the rest day in seven, I pulled Eva, laughing in the red wagon, on the smooth floor in our new house. I heard an announcement cough outside our house door, and, looking through the doorway, I saw a tall, lean young man I had not seen for six harvests. A mix of feelings washed over me. Happy to see how he had become a grown man, now nearly thirty harvests, I saw he wore a fine White Eye shirt, coat, pants, and tie, but seeing him left the taste of ashes in my mouth. He was pale enough to pass for a White Eye, his face thin, and his eyes and cheeks sunken. He coughed often into a white cloth that showed traces of blood. The TB worms had taken him. He was not far from going to the Happy Place. Although he looked at me, Chappo smiled and made a little wave at Zi-yeh, Fenton, and Eva, who were gathered behind me at the door. He said in a rough, rasping voice, "Father, I've returned to the People."

"You make my heart glad to see you, my son. Come. Zi-yeh will give us coffee, and you can meet your sister, Eva, whom you've never seen, and your brother, Fenton, who was Eva's age when you left. Tell us of your days and all you learned at the Carlisle school."

Chappo smiled and leaned over to shake hands with Eva and Fenton saying, "My sister" to Eva and "My brother" to Fenton.

Fenton said, "I go to the school here. Sometimes Father comes and makes sure we behave, but mostly Chihuahua is there for us."

"It's good you have a school at this place. I had to go far away, three days on the iron wagon, to the place for learning the secrets of the White Eyes."

Fenton's eyes grew big, and his mouth dropped. "You must have learned much."

Chappo nodded. "Yes, I learned much."

Eva chirped like a little bird, "Soon I go to the school with Fenton. Father, can you pull me now?"

Zi-yeh smiled and said, "Come. We'll go outside and leave your father and brother to speak alone." She led the children outside, and Chappo and I studied each other as we sat at the table with our cups of coffee.

When Chappo had ridden with me in the days of war, I'd taught him to speak quick and straight to the point. He said, "Father, Captain Pratt, chief of the Carlisle School, has sent me home to die. I expect I'll soon go to the Happy Place. I expect my wife will soon join me there. I wasn't with her when our baby rode the ghost pony. I've missed her for a long time and the baby I barely knew before it went to the Happy Place."

I nodded. "*Teniente* Capron, our new commander, told me you were sick and thought you had the worms the White Eye *di-yens* called tuberculosis. I think the same thing made She-gah sick. I tried every ceremony and plant medicine I knew to help her. Nothing worked. Even the White Eye *di-yens* don't know what to do to make you better. I can only pray to Ussen for you."

I told him to tell me all he had learned at the White Eye school, but he began coughing hard, and I could see fresh blood on the cloth he held over his mouth. He ran out of breath and strength before he could finish telling me anything. He promised to come again soon and finish our talk.

"I hear you, my son. Come when you can. I will listen. Rest often. I will pray."

Rivulets of body water rolled down his face as he stood and steadied himself, holding on to the table. I followed him out the door. He waved to Zi-yeh and the children and walked to his house, coughing hard again.

Teniente Capron called the Chiricahua leaders together and told us there was talk between the Blue Coats and the Great White Chief to move us to the place of our new reservation. He had received talking wire messages that a *teniente* named Scott, from Fort Sill, and a captain named Maus, from General Miles, were coming in six days. I remembered Maus. He spoke straight when Crook sent him to find us. I liked him. The officers were being sent to talk with us about whether we wanted to stay where we were or move to Fort Sill.

We looked at each other in disbelief. Who would want to continue living in this place when we could have our own place on the plains with good water, away from all the trees and swamps? I thought, *Maybe with our own horses, there'll be a chance to slip away to the mountains in Arizona or the Blue*

Mountains in Mexico where the Blue Coats might search a lifetime and never find me.

Teniente Capron saw our frowns and said, "I thought that was case, but you need to understand you'll probably be starting all over again, and you'll be neighbors with Kiowa and Comanche all around you. I suggest you pick a speaker and let him tell the officers coming here what you all think as a group. I'll leave you here alone to make up your own minds."

We counseled about what to say and who should say it for all the Chiricahua. I never said anything about my thought of escaping. I knew many opposed any idea of bringing White Eye anger down on us by trying to escape, but I would take my chances to be free in my own country again if I thought I could get away. General Crook had said we would be two years in Florida before we returned to our own country. General Miles had promised us our own reservation. Ten harvests had passed, and still we waited. If I had a chance to leave, I would take it. At the end of our council, it was agreed that I should speak for us all.

Teniente Capron led us with Wratten to a big room he used to hold councils with his officers. In the council room, two officers sat side-by-side at a big table. I knew Captain Maus. He looked more like a chief, older and more experienced, than he did in the Blue Mountains ten harvests earlier when he told us he had come at the orders of General Crook to take prisoners or kill every one of us. Beside him was an officer with yellow hair cut short and becoming very thin at his forehead. *Teniente* Scott looked a little younger than Maus, wore the things the White Eyes called glasses to help him see, and had sheets of white paper stacked in front of him with the little spear-like writing stick and a bottle of black water beside them for making tracks on the paper.

Scott and Maus came from around the table and each shook our hands. Maus said through Wratten as we shook hands, "Geronimo, it's been many moons since I last saw you. I hope you and your family are well."

I said, "Maus, you're a good officer. I'm glad to see you. My son Chappo goes to the Happy Place soon. My children and a wife have died since we come here. Not a good place. When will Miles give us our reservation?"

Maus frowned and shook his head. "I hate to hear about the passing of your family members. We came to talk to you about the reservation."

I nodded thanks to Maus and then shook hands with _Teniente_ Scott. He had a clear eye and an easy way of speaking. I liked him. He said, "I'm _Teniente_ Scott, and I am glad to meet the great and famous warrior Geronimo."

"Hmmph. _Teniente_ Scott, I see you. I hope you give us our reservation."

Teniente Scott smiled a little. "We want to give you your land. We're working on that today."

"Enjuh."

After all the hand-shaking, we sat in chairs facing the table. Captain Maus stood at his chair and told us his chiefs in Washington were considering where they could send us so we might be healthier and happier. He said he was on General Miles's staff and that General Miles, in speaking with the chiefs in Washington, thought that the land at Fort Sill was a good place for us. He, Captain Maus, and Lieutenant Scott, who dealt with the Comanche and Kiowa who owned the Fort Sill land the army used, had been sent to Mount Vernon Barracks to ask us if we would rather go to Fort Sill or stay at Mount Vernon. Captain Maus then asked _Teniente_ Scott to speak.

Teniente Scott stood at his chair and said

he was happy to meet all the great Chiricahua warriors and scouts. He said he had spoken with the Comanche and Kiowa about Apaches using the land at Fort Sill only a few suns ago. Quanah Parker, the great Comanche chief, said the Comanche and Kiowa had been enemies of and fought the Apaches since the grandfathers, but if the Chiricahuas would stay on Fort Sill land, then they should come and be welcome. They wanted the Chiricahuas to have a home, and they would give the land to them when the soldiers went away. *Teniente* Scott said he would keep tracks on a paper for General Miles to read and to send his chiefs in Washington. He asked us to speak to the question concerning our wishes to be removed to some other locality. Then he sat down, placed a white sheet of paper in front of him, and, taking the little spear, got ready to make tracks on the paper.

All Chiricahua eyes turned to me. I stood and said, with Wratten interpreting so there was no misunderstanding, "I'm very glad to hear you talk. I've been wanting for a long time to hear somebody talk that way. I want to go away somewhere where we can get a farm, cattle, and cool water.

"I've done my best to help the authorities — to keep peace and good order and to

242

keep my house clean. God hears both of us, and what he hears must be the truth. We poor people, who have nothing and have nothing to look forward to, are very thankful to you. What you say makes my head and whole body feel cool. We are all that way. We want to see things growing around our houses — corn and flowers. We all want it. We want you to talk for us to General Miles in the same way you have talked to us.

"Young men, old men, women, and children all want to get away from here. It's too hot and wet. Too many of us die here. I remember what I told General Miles. I told him that I wanted to be a good man as long as I live, and I have done it so far. I stood up on my feet and held my hands up to God to witness what I said was true. I feel good about what you say, and it will make all the other Indians feel good. Every one of us has children at school, and we will behave ourselves on account of these children. We want them to learn. I don't consider I'm an Indian anymore. I'm a white man, and we'd like to go around and see different places. I consider all white men my brothers and all white women my sisters. That is all I want to say."

Maus crossed his arms, leaned back in his

chair, and said, "I understand it to be your opinion that all of you want to go somewhere."

I said, "We all want to go, everybody."

Naiche nodded and said, "We live just like white people, have houses and stoves just like them, and we want to have farms just like other white people — we've been here a long time and have not seen any of us get a farm yet."

Chihuahua stood and said, "God made the earth for everybody, and I want a piece of it — I want to have things growing. I want the wind to blow on me just as it blows on everyone else. I want the sun and the moon to shine on me just as everybody else does." He thought of his children and said, "I went to Carlisle to see them, and it made my heart feel good to see them in the white man's road. I want to have all our children together where I can see them. I want my children with me wherever I go." He recalled when Maus brought him back as a hostile and said, pointing to his chest, "I want you to look at me and see that I am not like I was when you saw me before."

Nana slowly stood on his stiff legs and said, "Although I am too old to work, I want to see young men have a farm. Then I can go around and talk to them and get something to eat."

Chatto said after Nana sat down, "If anything I said would hurry up the farms, I wish it would. You can find some of the old people yet, the grandmothers and grandfathers, but most of them are dead. That is why I do not like it here. I want to hurry. I want you to tell General Miles to get them away from here in a hurry."

Kaytennae, always close by Chatto so he couldn't get away with anything backhanded, stood and said, "I had lots of friends, cousins, brothers, and relatives when you saw me last, but since coming to this country, they have all died. I have children here, and all the time I'm afraid they will get sick and die."

Loco, with the sagging eye almost taken by a bear, pushed up from his chair and, after a pause as he stared at the floor, said, "For old ones and children, it is just like a road with a precipice on both sides. They fall off on both sides. Nobody killed them. Sickness did it."

Mangas, sitting beside Loco, stood slowly and said, "Since I got to Fort Pickens, I have been a good man and have never stepped off the good path. While walking around, I have always wanted to look pleasant at everybody. Here we are in this little bit of reservation, not bigger than a thumbnail. There are lots of trees here. Yes, they shade us, but when we put our feet on the ground, it burns them."

Chihuahua said, "If we want to see the sun, we have to climb a tall pine tree."

And to this truth, there were many grunts of agreement.

Teniente Scott smiled and said, "I promise you that at Fort Sill, you cannot only look up to see the sun when you stand on the ground, but in the distance you can see mountains. I'll send the tracks of your words to General Miles. Soon you'll know if the great chiefs in Washington will send you to Fort Sill."

As if with one voice, we all said, *"Enjuh!"*

Twelve suns after Captain Maus and *Teniente* Scott counseled with us, Chappo went to the Happy Place. *Teniente* Capron would not let us destroy his house. He gave us a strong-smelling pinewood box the Blue Coats used for soldiers to hold his body and assigned a sergeant to go with it for burial at the Blue Coat place of the dead in the town called Mobile.

Zi-yeh, his sister Dohn-say, and I went with the sergeant on the train south early the next morning with Chappo's body.

When we got to the place of the dead, a grave had already been dug, and a White Eye *di-yen* and gravediggers were waiting for us. The White Eye *di-yen* asked me if we wanted his ceremony. I no longer was sure what Chappo had believed about the White Eye God, and Zi-yeh and Dohn-say now walked the Jesus road. I said we wanted his ceremony, but I would also do mine when he finished. And it was so.

I had hoped Chappo could give much to his People after he returned from Carlisle, but he died far too soon. Those hopes, too, became dust on the wind.

We returned to Mount Vernon the same day we left. We walked back to the barracks up the dark road in the light of a fingernail moon, listening with the sergeant to the night birds, frogs, and tree peepers. I remembered the days I'd had with Chappo in our own country and prayed to Ussen to send us back to there. But Ussen had turned his face from me and didn't listen.

CHAPTER 23
FORT SILL PILGRIMAGE

The next full moon after Chappo went to the Happy Place, the women began gathering our belongings together after *Teniente* Capron told us we would leave soon on iron wagons. But big belongings like the boxes the White Eyes called trunks, with our personal things, the iron stoves we had in our houses, furniture we had made for our houses, even the lumber we had used to build our houses, were to be taken down so we could send it on separate iron wagons and rebuild at Fort Sill.

I told Zi-yeh we would not send our trunk separately with those of the others. I didn't trust the Blue Coats to leave my things alone, and my Power warned me against sending my trunk on that iron wagon. *Teniente* Capron wanted me to send it ahead, but I argued with him and would not agree. Annoyed, like a man with a barking dog, he finally told the sergeant in charge of collecting and sending our things on the separate iron wagon to let me take it on the iron wagon we rode.

My Power was right. The separate iron wagon carrying other trunks, stoves, furniture, and house lumber for our People caught fire and burned in the place the White Eyes call New Orleans. I was sorry to hear this and thought of the face of the man with the gray beard I sometimes saw in the crowds from the time we rode the iron wagon to Florida. But the White Eyes didn't believe the fire was set deliberately.

A half-moon was falling through the western stars when our People began walking toward the Mount Vernon Station to climb on the iron wagons that would carry us to Fort Sill. The iron wagon headed south at the darkest time just before dawn. Zi-yeh wrapped our children in blankets beside her, and the steady rhythm of the iron wagon thumping on the iron road soon had them sleeping. On this iron wagon, the windows could be opened a little to let in air from the cool night, and I heard frogs croaking down by the river, their music making even me drowsy.

Soft, gray light filled our windows as our iron wagons went around a long curve and began running west. As the sun came, filling the land with light, I watched big stretches of black water filled with big trees looking like boys wading in a lake, and I saw the long beard-like plants the Blue Coats called Spanish moss hanging from their branches. Outside the many houses around the place called New Orleans, a big crowd had gathered to watch us while the iron wagon stopped and took on more wood and water.

Some White Eyes saw me watching out the window. They began pointing at the window and yelling, "Geronimo, Geronimo!" Some, when they saw me, clapped their hands; others shook their fists. I thought, *How long would they do that if I were free? White Eyes have no honor. They would run, and I would kill as many as I could.* Fenton and Eva watched them with wide eyes, while Zi-yeh looked away.

Fenton said, "Why do the White Eyes do this, Father?"

I said, "Maybe because they have no Power, and they think catching a warrior who does makes them powerful, too. But the truth is, I don't know, my son. I think maybe the White Eyes don't know themselves why they do this. We're still prisoners far from our own country."

The iron wagon rolled on through the swamps, and I saw some of the great lizards with big teeth that live in the black water lying on the mud banks, letting the sun warm them. Zi-yeh uncovered a roll of dried meat, nuts, and berries, like she used to make for me when we were on the run, and we ate it and shared water from a canteen I had brought. We were glad we had something to eat then, despite *Teniente* Capron's saying the army would give us food on the way. I didn't trust the army, and neither did Zi-yeh.

We stopped for wood and water several times at little towns in the pine tree woods that began to grow thin as we traveled farther west. At each stop, there was a crowd of White Eyes who wanted to see Apache prisoners of war going to live at Fort Sill, and they always yelled, "Geronimo, Geronimo!" At one stop, a man wearing a hat like Chihuahua favored — I think the White Eyes called it a derby — had a picture box set up to capture a picture of us, but *Teniente* Capron said no, there was no time, and we rolled on.

By the time the sun was halfway past the

time of no shadows, we were out of the trees and rolling northwest. It was the first time in eight or nine harvests I had seen the prairie and great, blue sky running horizon to horizon without being shut out by trees, and it pleased me. Eva had never seen anything but the thick woods at Mount Vernon, and that was all Fenton could remember. They watched, unbelieving, through the windows while the grassy land rolled past.

At twilight, we began to see cattle on the grasslands, and the houses of the White Eyes standing closer together. We stopped in a big town with many corrals filled with cattle, and again there was a big crowd of White Eyes, twisting and turning their heads, trying to see us inside the iron wagons.

As at other stops, people saw where I sat, pointed, and clapped, yelling "Geronimo, Geronimo!" At this stop, I also heard yells of "Murderers, murderers!" A big, loud voice said, "They shoulda hung the old devil fifteen year ago." I looked at the crowd and saw, for the first time in several harvests, the gray beard with the scar running through it who wore a long, black coat over a pistol in a shoulder holster. This man had followed me all these years, dropping out of my sight for harvests and then reappearing.

I wished I could face him and learn why he followed me around the countryside. If it was a fight he wanted, I was ready to give it to him. It was another long time before I saw him again, and then it was for the last time.

A white board sign hung near our window. Fenton said it read, "Fort Worth." Soon, full of black rocks and water, the iron wagon moaned as it pulled out of the station into the darkness spread like a great, black blanket over the rolling plains.

I watched the stars and could tell we were traveling almost due north during most of the night. Before dawn, we slowed to a stop at a little town I heard someone say was Rush Springs. Soldiers came through the iron wagons and told us we would leave the iron wagons here, eat food, and then get on horse-drawn wagons waiting for us.

Getting out of the iron wagon into the cool night air, moving to take the cramps out of our legs, and smelling the great pots of food the White Eyes had on fires nearby lifted our spirits. We ate our fill of the food, and it was good. Some Comanches and Kiowa had come to welcome us, riding their ponies, and a few had wagons, but we didn't understand the waving hand language they used.

After loading our trunk, the soldier driving our wagon helped Zi-yeh and the children onto the back seat. There she wrapped her blankets around them and held them close as they leaned and stretched around her to see all the movement going on around them.

Many of our People would not ride the wagons, because their riding boxes looked like the boxes the White Eyes buried dead people in. These people let the wagons carry their things, but they decided they would walk with the marching soldiers instead of riding on the coffin boxes of the wagons.

Before climbing into the driver's seat, the soldier turned to me, patted his chest with one hand, stuck out his other hand for a shake, and said, "Me Sergeant Hoffman."

I nodded I understood, gave his hand two good pumps, patted my chest, and said, "Me Geronimo."

He swallowed and slowly nodded. He said, "Howdy, Chief. We ought to get to Fort Sill sometime after midday. If you need water, there's a canteen under the seat, and we'll take breaks for the horses and the people walking. We'll have bush visits for people on the wagons two or three times before we get there. You understand what I'm sayin'?"

I nodded. I understood every word, but I didn't yet want to speak the White Eye tongue. I knew I would make a mistake and sound foolish.

The road to Fort Sill wound across the prairie and around low ridges and little mountains. As the darkness gave way to dawn, we heard coyotes yip and call for the first time in many harvests. Some of the women wailed in joy when they heard them. It was like coming home. We crossed creeks and stopped for rest and water three or four times.

I tried to remember the land and where water was, in case I ever decided I needed to leave this place without a Blue Coat pass. There were mountains here, not big ones like in our own country, but high enough that no one said it was just flat land like we knew in Florida and Alabama. I thought, *This land is much better than where we were. We can see the sun and mountains, and the grass is good for cattle. Maybe we'll have a good reservation here.*

Our wagons passed between the posts holding the sign with tracks that Fenton said was Fort Sill. After a while, I could see in the distance many saddled horses and horse-drawn wagons and many people near the post buildings watching us approach. We came closer, and *Teniente* Scott came riding with several people on their horses behind him. He stopped at the lead wagon in which *Teniente* Capron rode. They made the touch-their-hat sign in respect to each other.

Capron looked down the line of wagons and pointed at me. Scott waved the Indians following him to come with him, and he rode to my wagon. He made the all-is-good sign, waving his hand parallel to the ground, and I nodded and did the same thing. Wratten had left his wagon and come to mine. Scott said through Wratten, "The Comanche and Kiowa have come to welcome the Chiricahua as some did when they left the train."

I nodded I understood.

Scott waved a Comanche chief forward. He looked at me, nodded, and then began making motions with his hands. I frowned and looked at Scott and then Wratten, shaking my head. I said, "I don't understand his meaning."

Wratten told this to Scott, who raised his brow and said, "Why, of course. Apaches are not plains Indians. They wouldn't know sign language." He thought for a moment, and then made signs to the Comanche who rode off to the group of Comanche and Kiowa waiting to welcome everyone. The Comanche rode back to Scott, followed by another Indian.

Scott said to Wratten, "The Comanche brings a Kiowa-Apache. Maybe they speak the same dialect as the Chiricahua."

After Wratten told me what Scott said, I nodded, and the Kiowa-Apache was waved forward. He nodded and said something. I understood a few of his words, but not enough to understand his message. This I told Wratten, who told Scott. Scott made a few motions with his hand, and the Kiowa-Apache shrugged and rode back to the waiting group.

Scott scratched his chin while he thought and then said, "Do you have any boys with you from Carlisle who speak English?"

Wratten grinned and nodded. While Wratten looked for a boy he knew could speak both English and our tongue, *Teniente* Scott motioned for the Comanche to come speak with him with his hands. After a few signs, the Comanche turned his pony and trotted to the crowd watching us.

In a while, Wratten found boys, now nearly men, who had gone to Carlisle and spoke the tongue of the White Eyes, and the Comanche returned with three of his own boys.

So it took two interpreters for Comanches and Apaches to speak with each other, but the Comanche and Kiowa chiefs and their people spoke to us, and we were glad to be welcomed in this way to the Fort Sill lands we would have one day.

CHAPTER 24
THE NEW LAND

The Blue Coats had put up tents in which families slept when we first came to Fort Sill, and they fed us an evening meal. We were all weary. We had come a long way from the woods around Mount Vernon, and although the trail was much easier, we were as tired as if we had been trying to escape Blue Coats or Mexicans in the mountains. The sound of coyotes in the distance, the snort of horses and mules in the corrals, and calls of night birds drew us into our new land.

The Blue Coats fed us again as the sun rose, glowing gold in the distant haze. *Tenientes* Scott and Capron met with the Chiricahua leaders. Scott told us there was not enough time to build houses before the winds of winter and snow came. He said he would give us canvas coverings and other supplies and let us build wickiups along a nearby creek he called Cache. Building shelter from the weather was the first thing we needed to do. He said he would give us a handful of days to do this, and then he would meet with the leaders again to discuss other business.

It helped that those warriors who had enlisted as Blue Coats were with us. They knew how to ask their chiefs for wagons and tools and other necessary things when we needed them. Many saplings and plenty of brush grew along Cache Creek. It was easy to make wickiup frames and cover them over with canvas. *Teniente* Scott made it easy for the women to get supplies we would need to live. While Zi-yeh finished our wickiup, I studied the land to the west in case I decided to leave the chains of the Blue Coats and tried to think what I had heard about the best way to get to my own land across this great prairie.

Soon the women had a supply of food, pots and pans for cooking, and had chopped some firewood. We were ready for the winds of winter. As the bright yellow glow from the sun faded into the western horizon, I sat near Zi-yeh's fire and smoked as I watched Fenton and Eva play in the brush and listened to the slow burble of water in the creek and the night birds.

The driver of the wagon who brought us

supplies stopped at our fire and said *Teniente* Scott would have a fire for all the parents of children in school that night. I wondered if the school here would be like the one at Mount Vernon, but the teachers at Mount Vernon had not come with us. We could not let the Blue Coats send our children to find the tuberculosis worms at Carlisle and come back to me to die as Chappo had done. Somehow, we had to stop that.

The fire cast its wavering light on us as we stood in a circle and waited for *Teniente* Scott to speak. Soon Scott stepped up the fire and using Wratten as his interpreter, said, "The teachers of your children at Mount Vernon were willing to come to Fort Sill, but neither my chiefs nor theirs were willing to pay them. They teach no more. It's important for you and for the Anglos that your children be able to speak the White Eye language and read and understand their tracks on paper. I'll send your children to the boarding school at Anadarko, Oklahoma, for their studies. This is the school the People of the plains use. It's a good school, a long day's ride from here, about thirty miles. I'll give you a pass to leave anytime you want to go see your children. They can return to help with the work in the Seasons of Large Leaves and Large Fruit."

The fire burned down, snapping and popping in the cool air, and we stood there quietly listening to him tell what the White Eyes would do with our children.

"In four days, the wagons will be ready to take them to Anadarko. I want the children ready to go, clean and neat, and prepared to begin their schoolwork."

No sound came from people standing around the fire listening to him. He waited, looking at every parent standing there. He nodded at Chihuahua, "Do you have anything to say?"

Chihuahua crossed his arms and said, "You know we don't want our children to go to this school place, but we have been prisoners long enough to know that an officer's orders are always obeyed. The children will be ready to leave, as you say, in four days."

Teniente Scott smiled and nodded. "*Enjuh.* Tomorrow I'll meet at the corrals with all the men at the time of shortest shadows. Please be sure your neighbors without children know this."

The next sun we all walked to the commander's lodge and waited near the corrals for *Teniente* Scott. Soon he came striding from the lodge where he worked and stood on a barrel where we could all see him. He looked us over and then said, "The big chiefs in Washington have sent me money to buy you cattle to begin a herd, which you can grow and make money selling. The money for this herd must be spent by the Ghost Face Season, or they will take it back. Every man will have work to do, whether it's with the herd, in the fields growing, or harvesting crops for yourselves and your livestock. When the Season of Little Eagles comes, we'll spend most of our working time on building houses in villages where you want to live. Today some of the men who want to work cattle will pick their ponies. Others must help herd the cattle without a horse for a time, and we'll all learn what we must do with the horses to herd cattle."

I thought, *Just give us horses, Teniente Scott, and we can leave when we want with the cattle. Ussen blesses us.*

"I know you're all good riders, but unless you've herded cattle like the White Eyes, you won't know what to do with them while riding your pony. There are Blue Coats here who have done this since they were children, and they will teach us. The cattle come in a few suns. We must be ready to ride and run with the herd and keep them together and off the land of the Comanches and Kiowas until we can build fences to keep them where we want them."

Ha. We won't be here when it's time to build that fence.

"There's something else you need to understand. You may be thinking that, with all this open range, this will be an easy place to leave whenever you want. The White Eyes are fearful of this."

They should be. We'll cut many throats on the way back to our own country.

"I've spoken with a Mescalero who lives with the Comanches and knows all the trails and water holes back to Mescalero. I have had a map drawn of these places. General Miles has a copy. I have a copy. I also have twenty days' rations and a pack outfit ready. This I will personally show you, in case you don't believe a Blue Coat's words. The Comanches who know these plains are my friends, not yours. They'll join me if we have to track you and bring you back. If you leave, we'll catch you. We'll bring you back, and you'll spend the rest of your time as a prisoner behind iron bars or in a stockade — not free, riding the range land and taking care of cattle, raising your crops, or being with your families."

Teniente Scott, you're a wise Blue Coat. I wouldn't want to fight you and your friends the Comanches in battle. I stay here.

Teniente Scott and his subchiefs, *Teniente* Ballou and *Teniente* Capron, told us we had to work every day except for half a sun on the day the White Eyes called Saturday and all the next sun, on the day they called Sunday. We were happy for this. It gave us productive work to do and time for our women to wash our clothes. The Blue Coat chiefs said they would give *Teniente* Scott mules and wagons for us to use to haul what we needed for our houses in the spring, and for making the earth ready for seeds we must plant. Before the mules and wagons came, we worked cutting logs we sawed for lumber to support the frames for our houses when we built them in the Season of Little Eagles. We also cut much smaller logs to use for fence posts when we stretched iron thorn strings around our villages and the edge of the reservation to keep cattle from trampling our gardens or wandering away from our land to be eaten by the Comanches and Kiowa.

Fifteen suns after we came to Fort Sill,

the other men and I returned to our camp after cutting logs all day along Cache Creek. It was early in the Season of Earth Is Reddish Brown and still warm. We all washed in the creek below our camp — cutting timber for logs and stacking the branches after they were trimmed soon makes a man covered with sweat and dirt and makes him smell bad, like a White Eye.

I was hungry when I went in Zi-yeh's wickiup, and Eva came running and laughing and grabbed me by the knees saying, "We found beans, father, we found beans." Zi-yeh was watching and laughed, as I frowned at what Eva was trying to tell me. I knew this was ration day, but I didn't think beans were anything to be excited about finding.

Zi-yeh said, "When we went for rations today, an old Kiowa woman was there. She was complaining to the clerk that her man was too old and slow to help her collect mesquite pods anymore, and what came out of her garden just wasn't enough. I got the clerk to help me speak with her about the mesquite pods. She told me there was a big grove of mesquite a long day's ride southwest from the fort. Even as she spoke, my mouth was watering for a bite of mesquite bean bread. We havn't had any for about seven harvests. The people around here say it has been a very dry season, so the pods will still be good. Please, husband, ask *Teniente* Scott to let us go to the mesquites to collect the pods."

Mesquite bread. Just the thought of it took me back to our own country. I nodded. "There is much light behind my woman's eyes. I'll speak with Naiche after I eat. Maybe we can convince *Teniente* Scott to let us go pick the mesquite."

After the evening meal, I went to Naiche's lodge and asked to speak with him. He welcomed me and told Hah-o-zinne to take the children and visit her parents for a while. She frowned but went without comment. He had trained her well.

He rolled a cigarette from *tobaho* and paper he had bought at the trading post Wratten was starting for us. We smoked to the four directions. Then he looked at me and nodded. We spoke of how life was in the camp. After we politely passed the preliminaries, he said, "What fills the heart of Geronimo?"

"Zi-yeh has learned a big grove of mesquite grows a long day's ride to the southwest. If we hurry and can get permission from *Teniente* Scott to harvest the pods, perhaps we can all have a little mesquite bread when the cold winds blow in the Ghost Face."

Naiche's jaw dropped, then closed with a big smile. "Hmmph. This is big news. I don't think I have eaten any mesquite bean bread since we surrender to General Miles. I can taste it already. I'll speak with *Teniente* Scott next sun. If he lets us go, we go quick."

The next sun, I saw Naiche leave his work detail cutting down trees and sawing logs to speak with *Teniente* Scott before the sun was halfway to the time of shortest shadows. It was a hot, bright day for the Season of Earth Is Reddish Brown, and from the looks the men on the detail gave each other, I could tell they were wondering why Naiche had left. Naiche returned at the time of shortest shadows riding on the fine pony given him by a Comanche as a welcoming gift. He dismounted and waved all the men over to him.

"Last sun, Geronimo learned that a day's ride southwest from here is a big place of mesquite trees. If we go quick, the bean pods might still be good, and we can gather enough for our women to make us bread. I have just spoken with *Teniente* Scott and asked for permission to go to the mesquites. He has agreed, but we cannot miss our work here. That means we cannot leave until the sun is at the place of no shadows on the day the White Eyes call Saturday, and we must be back ready to work at dawn on the third day, the day the White Eyes name Monday. I told him we would leave this Saturday. If you want to come, tell me. If you have a pony, bring it, but most who come will have to run like true Apaches. Those still in the infantry are welcome to come. It will be a test of our endurance and strength. What do you want to do?"

We all raised our arms and yelled, *"Nkáh!"* (We will go!)

He nodded. *"Enjuh.* Toclanny and Kaytennae will help me plan how we do this. Now let us return to our work."

Not everyone went on that trip. I had a pony the great Comanche chief Quanah Parker had given me, and I went as the medicine man. Some of the others, old men like Nana and Loco, or those who didn't want to run for two long days, didn't go. I thought, *Lazy Apaches didn't live long when I was a boy.*

Zi-yeh and other women who had to look after our small children didn't go, but several of the older boys and girls not yet gone off to the Anadarko school and wives who did not have young children to care for also went. And, as Naiche told them to do, they ran all the way to the mesquites and back, happy to test their endurance. Those who had horses carried sacks for the pods and the canvas we needed in case it rained. *Teniente* Scott gave Naiche a map that showed where the mesquites were, and Naiche, as a Blue Coat infantry soldier, knew how to use it.

We ran and rode until well into the night to reach the mesquites. There was water in a slow creek nearby, and we stopped and camped there. Next day, when the light was good, we gathered bean pods. We were lucky. Most of the pods were still hanging on the trees and had no black spots to show they were bad. We worked all day until dark and filled many sacks with the pods. It was very good to be close to the mesquite once more and to taste the pods. We all had scratches from the mesquite thorns, but we didn't care. Ussen was reminding us of our home after the Blue Coats let us go. We filled many sacks that day with mesquite bean pods, and as the sun was falling into the far *llano,* we loaded the sacks on the ponies and began our run back.

We had returned to our lodges and had

our ponies unloaded by the time the moon had done half its descent toward the stars on the southwestern horizon. I slept a little while with my happy wife and children, but I was up by the soft gray light of dawn, ready to cut more trees.

Later that day, *Teniente* Scott came to where we worked and said he admired how strong we were in what we did by gathering mesquite pods. By White Eye measures, we had ridden and run nearly ninety miles and gathered over 300 bushels of bean pods in less than thirty-six hours.

I thought, *Think what we could have done if we hadn't become soft living as prisoners of war.*

Every family got an equal share of the pods. Naiche, who as a Blue Coat soldier subchief had learned to do White Eye numbers, said that meant over forty pounds of mesquite flour per family. That mesquite bread would be good in the winter. As the White Eye farmers like to say, "It was a good day's work."

CHAPTER 25
DAKLUGIE RETURNS

During the Ghost Face, we enjoyed living in a camp of our wickiups. The cold was too hard on some of the old ones, and they went to the Happy Place. Some, even young ones, developed bad coughs and found it hard to breathe, but they grew strong again as the *llano* became green with the coming of the Season of Little Eagles.

In the middle of the Ghost Face, *Teniente* Scott became Captain Scott, a Blue Coat chief with more power than a *teniente.* We talked of many things after the sun set to end our work for the day. Captain Scott, with Wratten helping him, had decided there would be twelve villages based on the family groupings we had. The villages were located within easy walking distance from one to the next. Leaders of the family groups, headmen and scouts, were to serve as the chiefs for each village and would be paid as scouts by the army to ensure things were done in a good way. I was named the headman for my village and given a uniform to wear that was similar to the one I wore when I was a judge at Mount Vernon. The uniform I didn't care for, but they gave me money to wear it, so I wore it.

Mules and wagons Captain Scott had requested from the army finally came to us near the end of Ghost Face, and we began hauling the logs we had made into lumber and used for house frames at the village sites. With the coming of Little Eagles, wagons were sent for lumber and shingles at the iron wagon station at Rush Springs. We also used the mules to plow dirt in the fields near each village to make the land ready for seeds Captain Scott gave us.

Each family had an area the White Eyes said was ten acres where we planted eight acres of kafir corn, an acre of cotton, and an acre of some garden crop. Captain Scott said Kafir corn would not dry up and die in the Season of Large Leaves like other corn, when the hot winds and heat came.

I decided my family would plant pumpkins and maybe a few melons to sell to the soldiers at the fort. We worked hard in the pumpkin patch, pulling weeds and carrying water out of Cache Creek to the vines when the rains were slow to come. My family and

I worked our land and had one of the best fields of pumpkins and melons of any garden in our villages. We ate all the melons and pumpkins we could and sold the rest to the White Eyes and Blue Coats at the fort. I counted over four-thousand pumpkins and melons that first harvest in my garden patch. I was happy to see the plants grow and prosper, but the labor was woman's work.

I, as most of my brothers, would have preferred to be out warring and raiding, but I had promised to keep the peace, and our warring and raiding days were gone forever. We had to farm, doing the work of women, or die.

During the days I worked in the pumpkin and melon patch, I liked to sit in the shade of the breezeway of my new house. The shadows were cool, and air flowed through it when there was little breeze over the grass. I could sit back and see my pumpkins and melons and rest from my sunrise work before the sun reached the time of no shadows. At resting times I would listen to Eva play with the dolls I made her, Zi-yeh in the cooking side of the house as she prepared a meal, and Fenton playing in the house shadow behind us with the bow and arrows I had made him.

Now in the Season of Earth Is Reddish Brown, I sat in the breezeway out of the wind and studied the land where I had grown many pumpkins and melons in the Seasons of Big Leaves and Big Fruit. I had made a little money on my pumpkins and melons. Next year we would make more.

One afternoon as I enjoyed the breezeway and studied the land, I saw a rider on the Anadarko Road stop at the edge of the field where our crops grew. He stood in the stirrups to look over the fields already sprouting winter oats and then rode toward Cache Creek and my house on the other side. The way he rode seemed familiar, but he was dressed in good White Eye clothes, and he was too big for an Apache. He found the place to cross the creek and then rode for my house. As he approached the breezeway shadows, I knew I had seen him before. I told Eva to go inside with her mother, and she went, no questions asked. Even at that young age, she knew when she must obey.

The rider stopped his pony at the breezeway and leaned over its neck to see me sitting quietly in the dark shadow. The sounds of pots and pans inside had stopped, and I knew Zi-yeh watched him through the doorway. I saw his bright white teeth and flint black eyes as he grinned and waved his right arm parallel to the ground as he said, "*Nish'ii'* (I see you), Uncle."

I laughed out loud in pure pleasure, and I heard giggles from Eva and Zi-yeh. "*Nish'ii'* Nephew! Today I am glad I sit in this place. It has been many harvests, and you have become a man since I saw you last. Come, sit in the shade and tell me of all you have learned. Zi-yeh fixes our evening meal. We have mesquite bean flour. Maybe she will make us some bread. I missed it when I was in Florida and Alabama."

Daklugie dismounted, took off the saddle, and hobbled his pony in the shade of a tree nearby. I rolled a cigarette and we smoked. There was much to tell from the suns in our harvests apart.

The next day I rode with Daklugie to show him our new land. A scowl deepened on his face as he passed cattle grazing on the *llano* grass. The cattle carried a brand showing they belonged to the Chiricahuas, but he said they looked too thin to be of much value and pointed out one or two suffering from raw places on their backs, probably caused by ringworm, but there was no sign of treatment. Some were limping from bad hooves, and one seemed to have eye problems.

"If these cattle are like the rest of the herd, then the Apaches are being cheated again, like they were at San Carlos," he said. Having finished eight years studying cattle management and husbandry at the Carlisle Indian Industrial School, Daklugie said he knew cattle problems were usually fixable, but they should have been fixed as soon as they appeared and not allowed to fester.

We rode on toward the cluster of buildings called Fort Sill, and he scowled again when he saw Apache women at scrub boards doing laundry for soldiers. One was even shining leather for soldier boots and belts. The sign for the trading post stood out with clean, neat letters, but not many were in the store. It was near midday, and the cold wind made the store inviting. We tied our ponies to the hitching rail and went into the trading post, hoping to see George Wratten, the man with whom Daklugie had been friendly for many years, who ran the trading post.

Wratten looked up from a journal filled with long columns of figures and side notes when the doorbell tinkled and smiled. "Daklugie! When Ramona came in a few days ago, I knew you wouldn't be far behind. Welcome back to your people." He said,

"Good to see you, too, Geronimo."

We both shook Wratten's hand, and Daklugie said, "Ho, George. It's been a long time. I'm glad to see you're still with us. You haven't changed at all."

The curtain over the doorway to the supply room flew back. A tall, muscular boy in his mid-teens yelled, "Daklugie!" and ran up and grabbed Daklugie's shoulders. "Ramona told us you would be coming soon. I wouldn't know you, except she showed us a picture she had of the group at Carlisle. We're all happy you came back. Welcome!"

Daklugie, grinning, took the boy by his shoulders, lifted him off the floor, and put him down again. "Ho! Eugene. You've grown much, brother."

We talked a little while before Eugene said, "I'm working for George now. He's teaching me to read and do numbers so I can help clerk here in the trading post. There's a big order in the back I've got to unpack before I can go practice baseball. See you when you come to visit Ramona."

I sidled over near the stove as Daklugie nodded, waved him through the curtain, turned to Wratten, and said, "George, I need a job and a place to live. I've got to be earning money for a living before Ramona and I can marry. Any ideas?"

"Well, I know you can handle horses and mules, and you look big and strong. You can probably find work as a freighter here at the fort, but that seems like a waste of everything you must have learned at Carlisle. What did you learn there besides reading, writing, and doing sums?"

"Well, I studied how to raise and manage cattle. I spent the summers working for farmers near the school and learned how to take care of cattle. I think it's about the only thing Apaches can do that even comes close to hunting and raiding like in the old days. I saw some animals in sorry shape that were part of the Apache herd when Geronimo and I were out earlier."

Wratten scratched at his neck whiskers and thought. "Sounds like you ought to go see Captain Scott. He bought the herd for the Chiricahuas, but he didn't have time to pick out good stock because he had to spend the money quick or Congress would have taken it back. I'll bet he can use you."

"Where is Captain Scott?"

"I think today he's in his office in that big building across the quadrangle."

"Hmmph. Then I'll go ask him for a job. By the way, when I rode in, I saw Chiricahua women doing soldier work, washing their clothes and shining boots. Why are they doing that, especially out in the cold wind? I don't like it. It shows the Blue Coats don't respect our women."

I nodded in agreement. I was proud of the way Daklugie boldly spoke his mind.

Wratten shrugged. "Captain Scott wants everybody busy. If a woman ain't got children to look after, he wants 'em working, just like the men, to earn themselves a little money."

I said, "I'll introduce you to Captain Scott if you like," and Daklugie nodded. We said goodbye to Wratten and headed for Scott's office.

Captain Scott looked up as we walked into his office, and I introduced Daklugie as my nephew who had returned from the Carlisle school.

Scott nodded and said, "Good to meet you. What can I do for you?"

Daklugie frowned. "Well, for one thing, you can stop using our women and girls to do laundry for the soldiers out in that cold wind. That's a soldier's job, and they oughta be polishing their own boots, too."

I could tell Scott was taken aback by Daklugie's brusque reply, and I felt a surge of pride that Daklugie wasn't intimidated by the captain. Scott began to rise from his chair, saying, "Now look here —"

Daklugie, who was several inches taller and fifty or sixty pounds heavier than Scott, stepped up in seeming fury, put a hand on Scott's chest, and pushed him back in his chair hard enough to make it roll against the wall.

He stood glaring at him and pointed his finger. "No, you listen. I just rode through some of that so-called Apache herd you bought for my people. Those sorry cows ain't got no weight, some of 'em have blackleg, and there's some with hide sores that looks like ringworm to me. All that needs to be taken care of. You're a mighty sorry cattle manager. I know how to take care of 'em. Let me do it."

Scott was out of the chair and around the desk with his hand on his pistol faster than I thought he could move. Grabbing his hat as he went out the door, Scott ran to a horse at the hitching rail, swung into the saddle like an Indian, and rode off in a flurry of flying clods and dust in the thick, hot afternoon air.

Daklugie shook his head as if awakening from a dream, made a face, looked at me, and took a seat. "Uncle, I suppose I should wait here for the military police."

With a big smile, I said, "Probably so. We

talk later." And I left.

Being in no particular hurry to get back to my work, I returned to the trading post. Not long after, Captain Scott came in. He waited until Wratten finished with a customer.

Eugene came out of the supply room, waved at Wratten, nodded at Scott, and said, "Got to go play ball, Mr. Wratten." Wratten waved and the boy was gone.

When the customer left, Scott, tipping back his hat, walked over to the checkers table and sat down. Wratten joined him, slouching in a chair. I sat in a chair across the room behind a stack of flour bags, but I'm not sure Scott even knew I was there.

Wratten said, "Whew. Been a long day, and that wind has been whistling through the cracks in this old shack. Captain Scott, you look like you got something on your mind."

Scott eyed him and shook his head. "George, you know all these Indians. Who is this ruffian who came in my office today with Geronimo wanting to run the reservation? I thought I was going to have to shoot him to keep from being attacked."

Wratten laughed. "He's Asa Daklugie, Geronimo's nephew. He's been away at

Carlisle for the last eight years where, in addition to reading, writing, and arithmetic, he's been studying how to raise and manage cattle. He doesn't give a hoot about running the reservation. He just wants a job. He knows more about managing cattle than anybody here does, and he has the same charisma in leading and handling men as his uncle. His fiancée is Ramona Chihuahua, but he won't marry her until he's able to support her."

Scott sat, listening and staring at the shelves of cans and other supplies, as Wratten spoke and then rolled a cigarette. Wratten said, "Daklugie will have the support of every chief and influential man among the prisoners, except Chatto. As I said, he's young and well-educated. He could be extremely useful to you if he respects you. He may dislike you and you him, but to an Apache, respect is more important than liking. There's no real friendship without it."

Scott made a little tent with his fingers and sat thinking. He looked at Wratten and smiled. "George you should have been a lawyer. You made a very good case for your client. The Apaches have some mighty good cowboys, but overall their management hasn't been very efficient. I'll have to get Daklugie to join the scouts and pay him like

I do the others. I'll cut some orders the lead scout can give him that will make him the chief of the range. What do you think of that?"

Wratten nodded. "Captain Scott, I think you've made a very wise decision. I'll see Daklugie in a day or two and tell him to sign up with the scouts and what you have in store for him. I know he'll appreciate it."

Scott stood, and they shook hands. "Thanks, George. You're a real help and a blessing for the Apaches." He left without ever noticing I'd been in the room.

CHAPTER 26
THE ARTIST COMES

During the next two harvests, many of my family members and friends went to the Happy Place and the army's wooden markers with name tracks grew in the place where the Blue Coats said we must bury them. My granddaughter, Nina, daughter of my daughter Dohn-day and Mike Dahkeya, and little sister to Thomas and Joe, was the first to go. She road the ghost pony before the pumpkins were all out of that first garden. My old warrior friend, Nana, who staggered many harvests on crooked knees and a bad foot when he walked, left for the Happy Place the next harvest. He was glad to leave us. His legs could carry him no farther. My sister Nah-dos-te, wife of Nana, and my son Fenton followed Nana the next harvest. I didn't understand why Ussen took Fenton, so young, so fine, but he did, and I felt much sorrow.

But these times were not all sorrows. I

drew closer to my nephew Daklugie. He took his first wife when he made enough money to support her, marrying Ramona Chihuahua, daughter of Chief Chihuahua, headman at his village. Daklugie and Ramona had two ceremonies. Daklugie still followed the old ways and believed in Ussen and the Power he gave through the spirits. One of their wedding ceremonies followed this road with Ramona dressed in her beautiful buckskin dress, and they had a big feast. However, since Ramona had decided to follow the Jesus road, they also had a Jesus wedding ceremony, wearing White Eye clothes. After his ceremony, the White Eye *di-yen* gave them a paper with tracks that said Ramona was Daklugie's wife.

I thought, *This is foolishness. How can a paper with tracks make a woman a man's wife? It is her choosing and his promise, and it's not made by tracks on a paper.* But I'm an old man, and the world changes.

During the harvest Fenton and Nah-dos-te went to the Happy Place, Captain Scott left as our commander and went east to another place. I thought Captain Scott was fair with us, but we, Scott and I, were never friends. *Teniente* Capron became our commander in the last suns of the Season of Earth Is Reddish Brown that harvest. But the next harvest, the White Eyes were fighting the Spanish, and Capron left to fight in a place across the big water called the Philippines.

We understood the people there were like Mexicans. If that was so, I hoped Capron killed many of them before he went to the Happy Place. When *Teniente* Capron left early in the Season of Many Leaves, *Teniente* Beach became our commander He was a good Blue Coat, if there can be such a thing, and I liked him being the Blue Coat chief over us. By the harvest Captain Scott left, our people lived in good houses, worked hard, and had accepted the land we were given.

One sun in the Season of Large Leaves, the harvest my son and sister road the ghost pony, I left my house to gather my ponies that were grazing on the prairie out beyond my village. It was not hard to find them. I trained them well, and they knew by my call to come. I put a bridle on one and swung up on his back to ride back to my house.

When I returned, my grandson, Thomas Dahkeya, oldest son of my daughter Dohnsay, sat in the shade at the edge of the breezeway with a White Eye I didn't know. I slid off my pony, raised my hand to them in greeting, and said, "Ho!" I understood the language of the White Eyes, but didn't often speak it for fear of making a foolish mistake. I asked Thomas in our tongue, "Who is this White Eye, and why have you brought him here?"

Thomas said, "Grandfather, this White Eye says he paints pictures, and his chief sent him to paint you. He is called Burbank."

When Burbank heard Thomas say his name, he smiled, nodded, held out his hand for a shake, and said, "Chief Geronimo, my name is Elbridge Ayer Burbank."

I took his hand and gave it two good pumps. At least he showed me respect, even if I was not a chief as he said, but I didn't correct him. It took a long time to teach a White Eye the right things to say to a chief or a *di-yen*. The Blue Coat soldiers had started calling me Gerry. That was not my name, and it was disrespectful. I didn't like it. In the long-ago days, I would have killed them for it. One way or the other, I would have been satisfied, and they would have died screaming my correct warrior name fearful Mexicans gave me.

I said to Thomas, "You interpret for your grandfather exactly as I say so there is no misunderstanding between us. Say to Burbank: Where do you come from and why are you here?"

Burbank answered, "I'm from Chicago, and my uncle, my chief, sent me here to paint a picture of you."

"Where is this Chicago?"

"Chicago is about eight hundred miles northeast of here and sits on the edge of a big water called Lake Michigan."

"How many people live at this Chicago?"

"Maybe a thousand times fifteen-hundred people."

"Hmmph. Many, many I hear. How you feed all these people?"

"With cattle, hogs, sheep, and much grain."

"And there is a place for pictures that are painted?"

"Yes. There is a place for pictures. Many people come to see them. My uncle wants your picture there for people to see."

"Hmmph. This is a good thing, I think."

"I hope you'll let me paint your picture."

"Come."

I took Burbank in my house and went to the trunk Zi-yeh brought from Mount Vernon. I opened the trunk and found a picture like those I sold to people on the iron wagons that stopped in Mount Vernon. Now I would find out if Burbank had money and would maybe pay me to paint my picture. I handed him the picture. He took it, nodded, and said, "Good, it's good."

I said, "One dollar," like I did to the White Eyes on the iron wagons. Burbank reached in the fold of leather he had in his pocket and gave me a dollar. I smiled and nodded. A dollar would buy a good drink of whiskey.

Burbank said, "I would like to begin a painting of you tomorrow. You just need to sit still on something for a while. Will you do this?"

"Sitting while you paint will take time from my garden work. If Captain Scott says I can skip work while you paint, I will do it, if you pay me."

Burbank grinned. "Wonderful! I'll ask Captain Scott, and, if he agrees, I'll be back tomorrow to begin when the light is good. Is this good for you?"

I told Thomas to tell Burbank I said it was good and that I would be ready if Scott agreed. If Scott didn't agree, then Burbank should not return. After Thomas told him this, Burbank smiled, nodded, and went back to Fort Sill.

Burbank returned the next sun just as I came from my garden to sit in the breezeway. I was ready to sit awhile. He carried many brushes, and his paints were in little jars. He had square wood frames about the size of a window with white canvas stretched over them, and a tripod of sticks to hold the frame while he drew with a pencil and then painted to give the picture color.

Burbank said, "Captain Scott approves my painting your portrait and that of any other Chiricahua I choose. Are you ready for me to begin?"

Eva was playing by the house with dolls I had made her. Since she had heard both Apache and White Eye tongues all her life, she spoke the White Eye tongue as well as she spoke Apache. I waved her over to us and said to her, "I want you to interpret what is said between this White Eye and me. Always speak true and never change my words. Tell him I am ready to begin. Where does he want me to sit?"

Eva said to Burbank, "This man says he is ready. Where should he sit?"

Burbank smiled and nodded. "You speak very good English for a child. What's your name?"

"Eva Geronimo. My mother is in the house. Do you want to speak with her, too?"

"No, just your father and you. There are too many shadows here. Ask him if he can maybe sit on the bed I see through that door and look out his window."

Eva repeated perfectly all he said, and I was proud of her. I thought she had a gift from Ussen for speaking different tongues. We went through the bedroom door and moved the bed until I could sit in light he liked. He was already starting to sweat in the warm bedroom air. I laughed inside, thinking, *Burbank doesn't know what real heat is.* He looked around for a chair, but we had none. I asked if a box would do. He said it would, and while Burbank mounted a canvas-covered frame on his tripod, I found the crate to hold supplies in Zi-yeh's kitchen for him to sit on. Then he used a pencil and began to sketch me on the canvas. He worked for less than half a hand against the horizon (about thirty minutes) before I remembered we had not discussed the value of my sitting. I called to Eva, and she came running with another doll in her hand. I told her to ask Burbank how much he would pay me to sit.

Pointing at me while she tried to look at his sketch, she said, "This man wants to know how much you are going to pay him."

Burbank stood back and scratched his chin. "Ask him how much he wants."

I said to Eva, "Say to him, you get much money for that picture. Maybe you get five dollars. I want half."

When Eva told him what I'd said, he frowned and looked toward the bright, blue sky before he said, "Tell your father, if he will sit for two pictures, he can have the entire five dollars."

I nodded and said, *"Enjuh."*

Burbank put his pencil in his pocket, reached in his pants to bring out his fold of leather, and pulled five dollars from it for Eva to give me. I took the money and waved Eva back to her dolls. Burbank didn't use much paint that day. He did several pencil sketches first, and in the following days, he made two pictures with his oil paints.

I liked his pictures. They had good color, and the face was mine. I especially liked one he did with me wrapped in a red blanket. He also asked to paint Eva when he came back the next year. By that time, we had become friends, and I told him he could paint her without a sitting fee, but he insisted on giving her some money.

I watched him paint while he sat on Ziyeh's crate, and I knew she would soon want it back. I called Eva again and she came running. I told her, "Tell the man I know he would find painting easier if I had a chair for him to sit on. Maybe he wants to give me one."

Burbank frowned a little as I spoke to Eva, but he laughed when he heard what she had to say. He said to her, "Tell your father I'll bring him a chair soon."

I smiled and nodded.

Burbank was a generous man. Every day he worked at my house, he brought his midday meal. Sometimes he shared it with me, and it was good. He might bring meat between two pieces of bread, apples, boiled eggs, little dried biscuits he called crackers, sweets like brown or white cake, or cans of peaches with sweet syrup. I usually ate a midday meal Zi-yeh fixed for me when she came in from the garden. Once Zi-yeh fixed us a midday meal that included meat, mesquite bread, and coffee. We ate with our fingers, like any Apaches would, from a board she set between us. It was a good meal, and Burbank thanked Zi-yeh and me for it.

I knew Burbank needed me to stay still while he painted, but I had spent years being hunted by the Blue Coats and Mexicans, and the least unexpected noise by men or horses brought me to the door of my house to see if we were being attacked or watched by enemies. I knew they weren't there, but the Power Ussen had given me in the long-ago times warned me to check to be sure.

Some days I sat a long time being perfectly still and became very tired. Burbank would say when it was a good time to rest. During those times, he touched up his work while I lay on the bed. Sometimes I would sing, and that made us both relax. One of the songs he liked most went:

O, ha le
O, ha le
Through the air
I fly upon a cloud
Toward the sky, far, far, far
O, ha le
O, ha le
There to find the holy place
Ah, now the change comes o'er me!
O, ha le
O, ha le

CHAPTER 27
THE WHITE EYES PANIC

By the second harvest when Burbank came to paint us, he was one of my best White Eye friends. That harvest was a sad, strange time. My daughter Dohn-say went to the Happy Place, and the next harvest her son, Joe, and her husband, Mike Dahkeya, one of my good warriors, were gone. No *di-yen,* American or Indian, could explain why, but I knew. Ussen wanted them, and he took them.

Burbank's second harvest with us was also the one when the Americans fought the Spanish across the big water to the south for the land they called Cuba. I had heard a little about this place Cuba. It was where Mexicans sent Apache slaves to be worked to death in sugarcane fields. The Blue Coats told me it was like those places in the land they called Florida where we were prisoners.

It made no sense to me why the Americans

wanted the place. I don't know why they wanted it, but they took it. I remembered the Americans fought each other about slavery in the long-ago times, and the war decided there would be no slaves in the land. I thought maybe after they took Cuba from the Spanish, they would free the Apaches slaves there, but I never learned if this happened, and Ussen never told me.

That harvest in the Season of Many Leaves our villages were peaceful as we worked the cattle and the land, planted our seeds, and did our other jobs. The Blue Coats decided they only needed maybe twenty soldiers at Fort Sill to guard their supplies. The rest went to fight the Spanish in Cuba. *Teniente* Capron had already left to fight people in the Philippines. We had offered to go with him to help wipe them out, but he said it was better to wait until the Blue Coat chiefs decided they needed more help and then asked us. With all the soldiers leaving, except a few, and *Teniente* Capron gone, the village leaders held a council to talk over how the Blue Coats going to the war with the Spanish affected how we might continue to live in this new land that held our seeds, our cattle, and many long days of our labor.

The council met in an oak grove by Medicine Bluff Creek near Naiche's village. Many insects and frogs sang as we gathered around the fire, as in the long-ago times. Rather than using oak leaves to roll our cigarettes for a smoke to the four directions, we now used papers from Wratten's trading post. Maybe our lives were becoming easier. The night air was cool, and the warmth from the little yellow fire felt good to an old man's bones.

Standing in the flickering, yellow light, Naiche, as chief, said, "Soon, maybe two or three days, Wratten says most soldiers here will go to the Spanish place across the big water named Cuba. Maybe twenty Blue Coats and *Teniente* Beach will stay here to protect us and guard supplies. The Americans wait to see their need for soldiers before they call us to help them. Maybe they ask us to help them fight, maybe not."

He stopped to lay another log on the fire, which was fast burning down. More cigarettes were rolled as we listened and waited.

Naiche continued, "I worry that the White Eye settlers might see this as a chance to attack us, since they didn't want us here in the first place. I worry that the Comanches and Quanah Parker might want to take back the land they have given us, now that the

Blue Coats have gone. I worry that my family is safe here and at the schools in Anadarko and Chilocco. I ask what must we do to keep ourselves safe from the whites now that the Blue Coats are gone. What if the Blue Coats are gone a long time in this war? Maybe it lasts many harvests. We must be ready. Speak, members of the council. Share your wisdom, and we will hear you."

I'd been Naiche's counselor since he was barely a warrior. He had even turned some of his responsibilities as chief over to me. I always wanted everyone to understand that I was a *di-yen,* one with Power Naiche did not have, but I was never interested in replacing him as chief. When he finished speaking, all eyes turned to me.

I stood and looked around the circle at Naiche — who, in our torment of captivity, had become a strong and good leader — my brother Perico, Chief Chihuahua, Kaytennae, Noche, Kayihtah, Martine, Chiricahua Tom, and Toclanny, who spoke often of his medicine from Ussen and believed his Power was growing stronger than mine so that he should be Naiche's counselor. I looked at Loco, Chief of the Chihennes; Chief Mangas, whom the Blue Coats admired; and the traitor scout Chatto who many times was my segundo in the long-ago Sierra Madre days.

I said to them. "Brothers, the questions Naiche asks only Ussen can answer. I worry with Naiche that White Eye settlers may attack us. They're afraid of us. They don't know us. They don't know our hearts are good. My heart is good. I won't attack them, but if they come, maybe now is the time to return to our homeland. There will be few soldiers to stop us."

There were grunts of agreement around the circle, but Naiche held up his hand and said, "As Captain Scott told us, there is a map, and his friends are the Comanches, who will help him find us. *Teniente* French now has this map and Comanche friends. I won't risk my women and children and my parents or my wives' parents on anything like that."

I nodded. "Naiche speaks true words, but a time may come when we have to go or die here. Regardless of what is done, let us show Ussen we have pure hearts and hold a dance for the People to speak with him. Then we will all feel good, knowing Ussen sees our hearts and can give us Power to do the right thing." Again there were grunts of agreement around the circle and I heard voices saying, *"Enjuh."*

One by one, the others spoke while the

women and children, even those who had come back to us from Carlisle, sat and listened. I watched and saw confusion on the faces of the grown children who had been to the Carlisle school for many harvests, which showed they had forgotten — or had never learned — many of our customs from the long-ago times. This was not a good thing. White Eye power among our people had become stronger.

We held our dance for Ussen on a big, smooth place near Loco's village two suns later near a big fire. There were Mountain Spirit dancers covered in black with their headdresses carefully done. *Di-yens* beat stiff, dry hides with sticks rolled into hoops on the ends, and chiefs kept the rhythm as in the long-ago days when we were on the move. Though Naiche sang and I led a dance or two, the children back from the Carlisle school didn't dance. They didn't seem to understand what we did or why. Soon, we thought, they would learn. We danced until light came in the eastern sky and then went home. Because we knew we'd dance all night, we had chosen to hold the dance on the night before the White Eyes gave us a day to rest. Believing Ussen's Power would help us now that he had seen our hearts, we were all glad we had danced for Ussen.

The Blue Coats left Fort Sill at the rising sun on the day they name April 19, 1898, and rode to meet the iron wagons at Rush Springs that would take them on the big water boats to Cuba. Many of us did not even see them go because we were working our cattle and our crops.

The Fort Sill soldiers headed for Cuba had barely disappeared over the horizon before rumors at the post of an impending Apache uprising to murder everyone and then ride for Arizona and New Mexico started sprouting like toadstools after a thunderstorm. An "educated" Indian woman told Lieutenant Beach the Chiricahuas were "making medicine and holding war dances."

Wratten, in a quick check, heard that I had said if the White Eyes attacked us, we ought to leave for New Mexico and Arizona. He reported that there was a probability of an "attempt to escape to Arizona." Later, he told me there was also a story that once the troopers were gone, Comanches intended to attack the Chiricahuas. Soldier families were in near panic.

Wratten said Grace Paulding, an officer's wife, wrote, ". . . this looked to wily old

Geronimo as a heaven-sent opportunity to make one last stand for freedom," and show his "defiance of his captors by massacring" those who remained at the garrison. The White Eyes are sometimes brave people, but too often they lose the ability to think that Ussen gave them.

After the midday meal on the sun the soldiers left, I took the village wagon and a team of mules to get supplies for Zi-yeh, who had fallen sick and needed to rest. Eva, who had wanted to go with me, decided to stay with Zi-yeh in case she needed help. The sun was bright and the wind cool. It was a good day to be living and feel the warm sun and cool breeze on my face. The gentle rocking of the wagon as the mules walked along almost put me to sleep.

I passed a White Eye house near the post where a woman was sweeping her porch. When she saw me, she screamed for her children to go in the house. She was right behind them, slamming the door behind her. I felt so good, I started singing my riding song.

It was a strange thing when the wagon passed among the houses in Fort Sill to see no women around the post stores or children playing in the streets. I wondered if this was a White Eye feast day but decided it was not. I tied the wagon mules to the hitching post in front of Wratten's trading post and went inside the cool, low light. No one was there except Wratten standing behind his counter with a book of tracks opened in front of him. When he saw me, his eyes grew round, he looked to both sides of me to see if anyone else was with me, and then relaxed when he saw I was alone.

I said, "Wratten, where are all the White Eyes?"

He made a half smile and said, "They're all hiding from you, Geronimo. They think, with the soldiers gone, you'll attack and kill them all pretty quick now before you run for Arizona."

At first, I wanted to laugh, and then I grew angry. I stared at Wratten and said, "Every headman in the villages is peaceful and working hard, including me. Where did this belief come from?"

Wratten shook his head, "I ain't sure, but it looks like tales somebody made up added to what you said at your council meeting."

If my eyes could have thrown fire, I would have burned Wratten to a piece of fried meat. I roared, "But I'm a scout in the army. A headman. I have given my word to serve the army. I wear their uniform. Has someone stolen their senses? This isn't right."

He made a face and said, "I know. We'll get this situation straightened out soon. What can I get you, Geronimo?"

I unloaded supplies at the house and drove the mules and wagon to the barn where we kept them. After I rubbed down the mules and fed them, I walked back to the house. The sun falling toward the horizon was painting the clouds oranges and purples. Since I had left Wratten's trading post, I had tried to think why the White Eyes thought we would attack them. Some crazy Apache might have said as much to *Teniente* Beach. Maybe it was the Carlisle Apaches who had forgotten everything they had been taught before they went to school. Maybe it was a whiskey peddler trying to start a war for money, like they had in the long-ago days. Whoever it was, I wanted to find him and whip him with a stick.

As I went for the house, I saw six or seven riders coming toward the village. I stopped, waited, and soon saw it was Quanah Parker and his subchiefs. *Good,* I thought, *maybe he understands what's happening and can tell me.*

Quanah's face looked like a thundercloud as he left the others a little behind and rode up to me. I said, "Ho, Quanah! I'm glad you come. The White Eyes act strange today. Come sit with me, smoke, and drink a little coffee. Bring your chiefs with you, too."

He leaned forward on his pony and said, "Ho, Geronimo! We hurry here because the White Eyes believe you are about to attack them. Is this true?"

I knew my face must have become as dark as Quanah's. He leaned back from me, as I said, "No. It's not true. We have no desire to kill White Eyes now."

Quanah nodded and looked relieved. "Good. If you start killing White Eyes, they'll start killing all the Indians. Hear me, Geronimo. We go to each of the Chiricahua villages so there is no misunderstanding. If you'd like to start trouble, we'll take care of you."

I crossed my arms and looked up at him in the fading light. "We start no trouble. This is some fool's doing."

"Hmmph. Good. You should find that fool before he gets us all killed." Quanah jerked his pony around and led his chiefs towards Perico's village.

The next morning, soon after sunrise, *Teniente* Beach, with another officer and a troop of cavalrymen with rifles against their hips, came riding to my house. I went out to meet them, leaving my food to grow cold on the table.

Beach dismounted, and he and I spoke for a while. He explained that the White Eyes had heard we were going to attack and kill them and then ride for Arizona. It made me mad, and I told him, as I had told Wratten, I was in the army, and as far as I knew, no Chiricahua had any thought of attacking the White Eyes. We were more worried the White Eyes would attack us. As we spoke, I noticed *Teniente* Beach was looking over my shoulder and seeing the men in my village getting ready to work, rounding up and hitching up mules to wagons. Some were going to work their gardens; others, to our cattle. None appeared ready for the warpath.

Teniente Beach looked me in the eye and said, "Geronimo, I think there's been a mistake and a misunderstanding on my and other White Eyes' parts. I see now that you and your people have no intent except to work and live peaceably here. Go about your business, and I'll make certain the other White Eyes on the post no longer believe you'll attack them."

I nodded. *"Enjuh!"*

When the cavalry and *Teniente* Beach left,

I went back inside to my morning food. Before I went to my melon and pumpkin patch, Zi-yeh made me a new hot meal to replace the one I'd missed while talking to *Teniente* Beach.

CHAPTER 28
THE HORSE RACE

A few suns after the cavalry had come to stop us from killing all the White Eyes at Fort Sill and riding for the Blue Mountains in Mexico, they left to fight the Spanish in Cuba. The White Eyes no longer thought we would kill them, although sometimes I thought we ought to show what a liar General Miles had been to us. How I wished I could face him and call him a liar to his face.

A sun or two after the Blue Coats left, I learned my good daughter Dohn-say had gone to the Happy Place. The White Eyes had called her Lulu. She had been married to Mike Dahkeya and was the mother of Thomas, Joe, and Nina. Her mother, Chee-hash-kish, who had also given me my fine son Chappo, had been taken in slavery by Mexicans when we lived in the Blue Mountains fifteen harvests ago. On a later raid, I had taken six Mexican women, including one with a baby in her arms, to trade back for her.

When General Crook used scouts to find us in the mountains, he freed the Mexican captives I wanted to trade for Chee-hash-kish and made us return to San Carlos. I knew then I would never see Chee-hash-kish again. I didn't even know if Chee-hash-kish still lived after Chappo and Dohn-say were killed by the worms the White Eyes call tuberculosis.

My heart for many days was heavy with sorrow for Dohn-say leaving us. Then my friend Burbank, who had drawn and painted me and other Chiricahua the previous harvest, returned from the East and asked me to sit for him again, and I agreed. Sitting still in the hot shade for Burbank quieted my mind and let me offer prayers to Ussen for Dohn-say's early entry into the Happy Place. It made me feel smooth with the world again.

As he did during our first harvest together, Burbank shared his midday meals with me. Once Zi-yeh helped me prepare a meal for Burbank like the White Eyes make, with a cloth on the table and plates to eat from. He drew and painted his drawings of me until the big White Eye feast day they called

Fourth of July. There under the trees and cleared grassy places would be Monte gambling, horse races, baseball, and other games. I told Burbank I would not sit for him that day. I wanted to go to the Fourth of July feast day and asked him if he wanted to come with me. He said he would come, and I was glad.

The Fourth of July feast was a good one for Indians and White Eyes. Many people came. While Burbank wandered from game to game and talked to people, I found a Monte game and soon became the dealer. Most Comanches and White Eyes don't understand how to play well in a Monte game, and I won, maybe more often than I should. I had luck that day, and it made me feel so good that I gave a war whoop every time I won. The sun had begun painting the clouds when Burbank was ready to leave. My pockets were filled with Monte winnings, so I turned over the Monte game to another man and left with Burbank.

We were nearly to our horses when a young cowboy came up to us and said, "Ain't you old Geronimo?"

I understood what he said, and I felt safe to answer, with Burbank nearby. I nodded and said, "Geronimo."

He grinned and said, "You still have that

pony people say is a fast 'un?"

"Have pony."

"Well folks 'round here think my pony is the fastest in the Indian Nations. Wanna race to find out? Betcha ten dollars my pony's faster than yours."

Burbank stood nearby with his arms crossed, his head cocked to one side, smiling, and studying the cowboy.

"Where race?"

The cowboy pointed to a great tree growing near Medicine Bluff Creek and then to a flagpole near a horse corral."

"How 'bout from that there flagpole over by the corral to that tree down yonder and back?"

The race distance was about what the White Eyes called a mile. I was too heavy to race that far and win. I would need a rider much lighter than me. Zi-yeh usually rode in my races, but she wasn't feeling well and had stayed home. I knew Chiricahua boys who could ride and win. I just had to find one.

"You have ten dollars? Give to Burbank there." I had won much money at the Monte game. I found ten dollars in my pocket and gave it to Burbank. "He hold bet. Pay winner."

The cowboy nodded and handed his

money to Burbank. "That'll work. Goin' to get my pony. Meet ya by the flagpole in twenty minutes."

I asked Burbank to lead our ponies to the flagpole and went to look for a boy to ride for me. I hurried through the crowd but could not find one. I was worried I might have to ride, and knew I would lose. I was too heavy and too old to be racing.

Then I saw Eugene Chihuahua. He was a good pony rider, but he was at bat in baseball. I went to get him, thinking he could bat another time. Just as I got close to the batting place, he hit the ball a long way and took off running. I thought, *He has to help me,* and chased him to tell him I needed him to ride for me. While the other players chased the ball, he ran the bases back to place where he hit the ball, and I, afraid he might get away, chased and finally caught him at the ball hitting place. The Indians and White Eyes were laughing and yelling. Baseball is a strange game.

I caught up to Eugene and laid my hand on his shoulder. He turned and saw me and laughed. He said, catching his breath while I caught mine, "Grandfather? . . . why do you . . . chase me in a baseball game?"

"Grandson . . . I need . . . for you . . . to ride . . . my pony . . . in a race."

313

"The roan mare?"

"Yes."

"*Enjuh.* We will win. Show me the way."

"Come."

The cowboy was waiting with his pony at the flagpole, and he had his own little man to ride for him. He said, "I's beginnin' to think I was gonna git your money without havin' to race. Ya'll ready?"

I showed Eugene the tree and explained the race was to the tree and back. I tightened the cinch on the saddle and said, "This pony likes to finish fast. Stay just behind the cowboy pony until you're around the tree. After that, let her run when she wants. Race starts when Burbank throws his hat down."

Eugene smiled and nodded. He vaulted into the saddle, took the reins, and rode up next to the little man, an old cowboy with a great bush of white hair under his nose, his face, like mine, shadowed with the many creeks and valleys of old men. He was even shorter than Eugene, but I could tell from his big chest and thick legs he was still heavier than Eugene. He nodded and grinned at Eugene, who smiled back, and gave him a military salute. White Eyes and Indians had come to watch, and money started changing hands in the crowd betting.

I said to the cowboy, "Race start when Burbank throw hat down?"

He nodded and said, "That'll work." He turned to the old man on his horse. "You hear that, Jonas?"

The old man said, "I heerd it. Let's git to ridin'."

I said to Burbank. "You start race? Throw hat down."

Burbank grinned and stepped out where Eugene and the old cowboy could see him. The crowd got quiet. He put his hand on his hat and yelled, "Ready?"

Eugene and the old man nodded and leaned forward in their saddles.

Burbank's hat swooped down, and they were off in a cloud of dust and flying clods and gravel. I felt excitement flow through me like water off a cliff, and I had to yell and wave my arms in the pleasure of the moment. Ten dollars was much money, but even if we lost, the excitement was worth it.

Eugene rode the roan as I said he should and kept its nose just behind the saddle of the old man. I could tell my pony wasn't straining to keep up, and the old man was letting his pony run as it wanted.

They rounded the tree and headed back.

Eugene still had the roan where I said to keep her. They ran on, coming closer fast, then in the blink of an eye, the old man had a quirt out and urged his pony forward. It looked for a moment that the cow pony would run off and leave my roan. For an instant, my heart seemed to stop, but Eugene had been ready and leaned further forward in the stirrups, his head halfway to her ears. He gave a low war whoop, and my roan shot forward through the cow pony dust, an arrow leaving a bow, and was suddenly half a length ahead. The quirt raised dust from the cow pony, and it slowly pulled even, maybe even a nose ahead of the roan.

I was shaking my fists and whooping as the ponies thundered toward us. A hundred yards away, the cow pony still had a nose lead. I thought it would probably win. Then I saw Eugene loosen the reins and whoop again, and the roan came up and moved into a head's lead with less than twenty yards to the flagpole. The cowboy, Burbank, and I stood side-by-side and watched the horses pound past the flagpole. It was close, but we all agreed the roan had won. I felt drunk, as if I'd just had a good swallow of whiskey. The cowboy turned and stuck out his hand. I took it and we pumped twice.

He said, "Well, Chief, you got a damn

good pony. But if ol' Jonas had weighed ten pound less, you'd a lost."

"*Hi yeh.* You come next harvest. Maybe we race again."

"Yes, sir. 'Spect I'll try ya again. *Adios.*"

"*Adios.*"

A few suns after the Fourth of July feast, I worked in my melons in the cool of the morning before the sun in the soft, blue sky turned to a hot, blinding fire. A rider rode up and dismounted at my house. He waved at me, and I waved back. He sat at the edge of the breezeway to wait for me. Zi-yeh brought him a cup of coffee, and Eva sat and talked with him like she was a grown woman. Eva always made me proud of her. As I crossed Cache Creek, I decided the rider was George Wratten. *He must have news.* I stepped lively.

Teniente Beach had told Wratten to come tell me that in two moons, there would be a big feast called an exposition at a big White Eye village to the north called Omaha. Wratten said the feast celebrated the White Eyes taking land west of the great river. The feast would last two moons. Many White Eyes would come from far away to see things that are symbols of people and places that were once on the land. Those in charge of the feast wanted the Blue Coats to send Apaches with other Indians to show how they lived in the long-ago days before the reservations. *Teniente* Beach planned to send about twelve Chiricahuas, the last fighting warriors, from Fort Sill, and he wanted to send Naiche and me, if we would go. Thirty Apaches from San Carlos also planned to come.

I said, "Many White Eyes come? We sell what we do? Keep money?"

Wratten laughed. "Many White Eyes come. Sell what you want. Keep money."

"*Enjuh.* I go. You say five suns before we go. I ready."

"I'll tell you five suns before you leave. We go in about two moons. I'll tell *Teniente* Beach you'll go."

"*Enjuh.*"

Already I was thinking about what I should make to sell before we left.

Teniente Beach allowed *di-yens* for the White Eye God to come tell the Chiricahua leaders their story about the Jesus road. They told how they wanted to build a house they called a mission at Fort Sill for their people to come and help us. We asked, "How would they help us?" They said they wanted to teach us the Jesus road, and if we

318

agreed, to help our children with a mission school.

We talked among ourselves and decided to ask the Jesus road *di-yens* to give us a school for our children so they did not have to go far away to Anadarko or Chilocco to learn White Eye secrets. Since I was a *di-yen,* the others asked that I speak our desire to the White Eye *di-yens.*

After the council began again, the White Eye God *di-yens* agreed to build a school as part of the mission. I stood and spoke for the leaders. "I, Geronimo, and these others are now too old to travel your Jesus road. Our children are young. I and my brothers will be glad to have the children taught about the White Eye God."

The White Eye *di-yens,* who were named Wright and Roe, said they understood. As soon as the Blue Coats approved, they would build a mission school and work to have it ready to teach our children by next harvest. Then they made a talk to their God. We hoped their work would get done. Their work would keep our children from going away to school. I thought it would be a fine thing for Eva to stay home while she learned the White Eye magic.

Chapter 29
The Jimmie Stevens Offer

Teniente Beach had put us on wagons and sent us to Rush Springs to mount iron wagons headed for the great feast called the Omaha Exposition. Riding in the wagons reminded me of the day General Miles sent us to Bowie Station for our long, stinking ride in the iron wagons to Fort Pickens on the white sand in the big water. I remembered that we had been in captivity twelve harvests. Miles had told Naiche and me it would be no more than two harvests. Miles had lied about that and many other things. I was feeling my years. I thought we should be allowed to return to our own country.

I expected there would be many opportunities to sell my things — my hat (I had brought many), autographed pictures and postcards, bows and arrows, even buttons off my shirt (on which I sewed new ones between stops) — on the way to the exposition, and I was right. The story of the

White Eyes' fear of the Apaches at Fort Sill, when the Blue Coats left to fight the Spanish in Cuba, had spread far, and crowds came to the places where the iron wagon stopped for wood and water. They all wanted to see the fierce Apaches and especially, they said, "Wily old Geronimo." I frowned at them and made money. I thought it was sad the iron wagon ride didn't last longer than it did so we could make more money, but I made much more money over many suns at the exposition.

The Blue Coats who came with us guided us to the Apache section of the Indian village at the exposition. We were to live in tipis and eat in a common place. We had spaces where we could speak to the White Eyes and sell what we had carried with us. I brought a full trunk; others brought less and didn't sell as much as I did.

The Apaches from San Carlos arrived after us. Naiche recognized a distant relative, and as we spoke with our brothers, we learned not much had changed at San Carlos. A young man, Jimmie Stevens, led them because he spoke good Apache. His father, George Stevens, was a White Eye, and his mother was a White Mountain Apache.

I didn't recognize Jimmie Stevens when Naiche asked me if I knew him. Naiche told me Jimmie Stevens was the son of George Stevens. When I looked puzzled, he reminded me of the Mexican sheepherders we'd killed at Ash Flats when we were riding to free Loco and his people at San Carlos sixteen harvests ago. We had stopped and asked for food and were offered a few sheep from the flock. I didn't like sheep meat. I liked horsemeat better and had a nice pony in their corral slaughtered to eat instead.

Naiche, with a crooked grin, told me the sheep belonged to George Stevens, and the sheepherders we'd killed worked for him. He said the pony I'd killed had belonged to Jimmie. I thought, *Would a White Eye be my enemy because I ate his pony, especially if he had many others he could ride? Better I face this now than wait for an ambush later.*

I decided to wait until we had our first meal together and then try to get this Jimmie Stevens on my side and make him forget I had taken his pony and killed his father's Mexicans. White Eyes often forget many things if they think there is much money to be made. I remembered a raid from the long-ago times where many silver and gold bars were taken. We had no use for the silver and gold and hid it in a cave with other things we didn't need. It was much more money than any pony was worth. *Maybe,* I thought, *I can get my freedom with this gold and silver and make Jimmie Stevens my friend.*

Our first meal with the San Carlos Apaches was in the evening, and the White Eyes holding the exposition sent cooks, who gave us steak and potatoes and squash and melons. The food was good. I liked it and watched for a time when I might speak with Jimmie Stevens alone. After a while, the San Carlos Apache who sat and ate next to him stood and wandered away after finishing his pan of food. I walked over and squatted by him.

"Ho, Jimmie Stevens. You know me?"

"I know you, you old devil. You're the great Geronimo. You raided my father's sheep camp sixteen years ago. Killed some herders and ate my prize pony on the way to San Carlos to break Loco an' his people out. Some say you kidnapped 'em, forced 'em to go. I ain't never forgot it — or that pony, either."

"Hmmph. You remember good, Jimmie Stevens. It was time of war. I wanted to kill all in camp except Apache herders, but

Naiche and Chatto say no. Bad time. I make war no more. Live in peace. Live in a house with daughter and one wife at Fort Sill in the middle of Comanche and Kiowa land they give us."

"You sound downright peaceful now, Geronimo. What do you want from me?"

"You speak straight, Jimmie Stevens. *Enjuh.* I tell you straight. In the long-ago time, my warriors and I, we attacked a Mexican packtrain for rifles and bullets. Kill all. Find few rifles, but many bullets. Also find many gold and silver bars. Hide what we no use in a cave. Cover what we leave with rawhide and then rocks. We no need gold and silver bars. Hide all in cave. Never return. Gold and silver bars are still there. No one claims.

"I am prisoner far from my own country. I want to return to my homeland. Live and die at Fort Apache. You leader there now. Maybe you get me back home from Fort Sill. You do this? I show you cave where those long-ago times gold and silver bars lie. All yours, you do this. I no want. Want only to live in my own country. What you think?"

Jimmie Stevens frowned in disbelief, but his smile was filled with White Eye greed.

"You ain't forgot where that there cave is?"

"Cave in Blue Mountains. I know place. Always remember."

Jimmie Stevens scratched his chin in thought while I watched him. The expression on his face made me think of a hungry man smelling cooking meat. *Maybe,* I thought, *I see my own country again.*

"Let me think on it, Geronimo. Maybe we'n work us something out."

"*Enjuh.* I see you again, Jimmie Stevens."

Soon, Naiche told me Jimmie Stevens came and told him about my offer, seeking his advice on whether to trust me. Naiche said he looked at Jimmie Stevens, smiled, and slowly shook his head. Naiche said, "I tell Jimmie Stevens, maybe this raid happened. Maybe it didn't. I don't know about it. But on this I bet money. You go to Blue Mountain cave with Geronimo, you no come back. You die with a sharp knife between your ribs or your throat sliced from ear to ear. You disappear like gold and silver he promise. Geronimo no come back, either. He lives rest of life in Blue Mountains. Geronimo powerful *di-yen,* great warrior, but sometimes he lies."

At first, I tried to be mad at Naiche for saying this, but after a moment, we both sat and laughed together. Naiche knew me very well.

CHAPTER 30
FACE TO FACE WITH MILES

The White Eyes gave the Apaches a place with canvas-covered wickiups where we lived and could sit and be seen in the shade of army tents with the sides rolled up, make our things the white men and their women and children wanted to buy, and sell what we had. I worked on my bow and arrows and sold them with my name tracks painted on them for ten dollars, but mostly I sold my picture where I wrote my name in White Eye tracks on stiff paper the White Eyes called postcards.

The things I brought with me from Fort Sill or made at the exposition, the White Eyes wanted to buy every day, and I thought, *White Eyes are fools to buy these things, but I'll take their money.* The women and children who came with us dressed as they did in the long-ago days, but most of the men had been in the army and wore their uniforms.

I dressed as a White Eye businessman might and refused to wear what I had worn on the warpath. Still many White Eyes wanted to see me, and they came to the Apache tents in the place called "Indian Congress." So many wanted to ask me questions about how I was captured and what I thought about it that I asked Frank Mangas to be my interpreter. He had been to the Carlisle school to learn the source of White Eye power. I thought he did good giving my answers to the White Eyes' foolish questions, better even than the official interpreter, Jimmie Stevens, who couldn't or wouldn't devote any of his time to interpreting for me.

About a moon after we settled in our place, Jimmie Stevens came to me. He tilted back his flat-brim hat and, grinning, said, "Geronimo, I got some interestin' news for you."

"What news?"

"Tomorrow's a special day, kind of like a big Apache feast day. Tomorrow is *Army-Navy Day.* Big chiefs for the army and navy are coming to look at the exhibits. Bet you can't guess the name of the big chief who's comin' to represent the army."

I shrugged and made a face. "Who comes for the army? I don't know."

Jimmie Stevens laughed and, with a sneer, said, "Why it's the man who captured you, General Nelson A. Miles. You wanna take the day off, so he don't see ya when he comes around?"

I stared at Stevens and thought, *Ussen is good.*

"Ho! General Miles?" I thought, *He never takes us. We surrender because he promises things he never does. He speaks big lies. I wait many harvests to look him in the face and say he is liar.* "The sun Miles comes is big medicine. I welcome him. You bring Miles here, Jimmie Stevens?"

Stevens slowly nodded and kept his attention on my face. "Yes, sir. He's supposed to sit in the stands and watch all them play battles your boys do for Captain Mercer out on the Sham Battlefield. When he's done watchin' the battles and lookin' at all the Indians, I'll see if he'll come by to see the Apaches. I reckon he'll want to since you were enemies and he won. He'll want to see you up close and personal, 'specially with you selling all the stuff you do. How much money did you make today anyway?"

"Hmmph. *Enjuh.* You bring Miles. Maybe we talk. Sixty-four dollars I take from White Eyes today."

Steven's jaw dropped. "Damn! That's

good money. More'n I ever seen for a day's work."

"White Eyes buy plenty pictures. I make my name in White Eye tracks on them. They pay more. Even sell bow and arrow with my name. White Eyes not smart. Give money away. Yes. Good money."

White Eyes watching the Indian-Blue Coat play battles sat on long rows of planks. The plank rows went up like stairs so each one on a row saw over the heads of the ones in rows below. The seats for the big chiefs gave them the best views of the battles. They all had a good time watching the play battles in which the Indians, of course, always lost. I watched the play battles and laughed. If this is the way our grandfathers fought the White Eyes, then they deserved to be slaves. They didn't fight to be free as much as proving their bravery by counting coup or taking scalps. I thought, *What good is bravery while you watch the White Eyes take your land, and you do nothing? It's better to die than do nothing to save your freedom.*

The sun bright and the sky a deep, cloudless blue, the plank rows filled with thousands of White Eyes. I watched them come. I would not play in these battles for them. The big chiefs and their men filled their places, but I was too far away to recognize Miles.

The play battle that sun finished with much smoke and dust and many "dead" Indians. The White Eyes showed their appreciation in the strange way they do by slapping their hands together. Then the Indians in each group were marched up to the reserve seats. There, the big chiefs looked them over and saluted.

When the Apaches went to the review seats, I walked with the Chiricahuas. When they stopped in front of the big chief seats, I ran to stand in front of them and looked where the big chiefs sat. I wanted to find Miles. Instead of calling him the liar he was, I wanted to make him my friend. I thought he might be talked into sending us back to our own country. Standing in the front, I soon saw Miles and was surprised. He had many decorations on his coat, and the hair on his head and face was white. I ran up the steps covered with white canvas to the row where he sat. Soldiers were starting to stand around him and reach for their pistols, but Miles held up his hand and said it was all right.

I stuck out my hand and I said, "Now, General, I'm glad to see you."

Miles grinned and half stood as he reached

331

for my hand, but then I grabbed him around the shoulders to give him a hug like men do who have not seen each other for a long time. He waved a soldier out of his seat beside him and said, "Sit here with me, Geronimo, and watch the rest of the Indians come by. Then we'll talk."

I sat down and said, "General Miles is a great chief." There were many men around us making tracks on paper and talking about how Miles and I had smoothed over our differences. I still thought Miles was a liar, but I hoped, if I acted good, the Chiricahuas might get to go back to their own country.

It was obvious I was being set up to play the fool as the last Indians appeared before General Miles and Jimmie Stevens approached and spoke.

"Ho! Geronimo. You see General Miles and sit beside him today to see all the other Indians."

"Ho! Jimmie Stevens. Glad to see my old friend General Miles. It's a good thing to see many famous warriors and their people."

"That's a good thing ain't it? The chiefs holdin' this here Omaha Exposition and the reporters here think this special day would be a good time for us all see you face General Miles, tell him he didn't capture you, that you surrendered. Then we'll all have a chance to hear what he thinks. The White Eyes call this kind of talk between two people a debate. Would you face General Miles in a debate over whether you was captured or surrendered?"

I stared at Stevens as if he had lost his mind. "I face my friend General Miles anytime, anyplace. I say to his face, we surrendered. He never captures us. He makes promises if we surrender, promises he never keeps."

Jimmie Stevens glanced at General Miles, who grinned and nodded.

I said, "Where we talk? Frank Mangas, who interprets for me every day and went to Carlisle school and was in the army, will be my interpreter."

Miles shook his head. "I won't use an unapproved interpreter. Stevens, you be the interpreter."

Stevens made a face. "All right, General, I'll be happy to be the interpreter, but Geronimo has to pay me a debt before I'll do it."

Miles frowned. "Why does Geronimo owe you anything?"

Stevens looked at me and frowned but spoke to Miles as everyone close enough to understand what was being said leaned in to hear every word. "Sixteen years ago Geronimo, leading over seventy warriors, came riding to free Loco and his people at San Carlos. They stopped at my father's big sheep camp at Ash Flat and took many sheep to eat, but Geronimo liked horsemeat over mutton, and he killed my fine sorrel pony I had in a nearby corral for his supper. Then they got the drop on the herders and killed nearly all of them. Naiche wouldn't let him kill some of the children and their mothers, but he wanted to kill them, too."

Miles crossed his arms and shook his head as he stared at me. "Geronimo, I think you ought to pay Jimmie Stevens for his prize pony you took many years ago."

"Hmmph. How much you want for your pony, Jimmie Stevens?"

Stevens scratched his chin, looking at the toes of his boots. "Well, it was a long time ago. I reckon fifty dollars would do it."

I shook my head. This fool's game he played reminded me of horse trading. "Too much. I don't have that much money."

Stevens stared at me and said under his breath, "Yes, you do. I know you're lying." He looked at Miles and then around at the big crowd gathered in close taking in every word. "General, looks like I ain't gettin' any money for my pony outta Geronimo today, but as a favor to you and the rest of these folks, I'll go on and interpret for you. Geronimo, you go first. Stand and deliver in your best Apache."

I walked to the stairs covered in white canvas and looked over the big crowd of people and then General Miles sitting on the first row and smiling with his arms crossed. I had never stood before so many White Eyes and White Eye chiefs before. It made me nervous. I noticed my hands trembling. Since our surrender and Miles's broken promises, I had longed for this time. I hoped Ussen would tell me what to say. I tried to speak. "For . . . for . . . uh, for ma . . . ma . . . many har . . . harvests, uh, uh." Something had locked my tongue; I could only stutter.

Then from the ground level where the Apaches in their soldier uniforms knelt, I heard Naiche among them, calm and quiet, speak in Apache. "Stand strong, Geronimo. At last, you face the Promise Breaker. I know you're not afraid to speak. Speak up, old man, before they make you sit down, and you disgrace us all."

Naiche's words gave power to my need. I felt my Power from deep within me rise to my tongue. I stopped sweating and shaking and said with my voice filled with my Power, "Twelve harvests ago, General Miles's soldiers chased me and seventeen warriors all over Mexico, New Mexico, and Arizona. They were many. We were few. He never captured or killed one of us."

I saw many men the White Eyes call reporters use their marking sticks to make fast tracks on paper as Jimmie Stevens turned my Apache words into those of the White Eye tongue. I knew his words did not match mine well, but they told the story I wanted to tell.

"One sun we rest on a flat-top mountain in Mexico where the river you call Bavispe turns from flowing north to flowing south. A young warrior saw scouts for *Teniente* Gatewood come to speak with us. I wanted to kill them, but Yahnozha and Fun would not let us. They admired the scouts' courage. Hearing the scouts, we agreed to talk with *Teniente* Gatewood, who brings words from General Miles. We hear the words and agree to meet with General Miles to talk surrender so we get our families back again.

"General Miles said we'd be reunited with our families in five suns. But they'd already gone to Florida. We were separated from our families for more than eight moons.

"General Miles said we'd be two harvests

in exile in the East. Many of us died in the places called Florida and Alabama and at the school that is called Carlisle. My own wives and children left me there for the Happy Place. I am a *di-yen* of Power. But I can't stop the White Eye worms that kill our people, and neither can the White Eye *di-yens*.

"Now we live at Fort Sill. We live better than we did in the swamp country. We have cattle, and we grow crops. We live in houses. Our Blue Coat keepers pay us for our labor. Still, we've been prisoners far from our own country for twelve harvests. Still, too many of us die."

General Miles still stood smiling and nodding at my words, but the reporters stood quiet and listened, and I felt like I was in a deep, quiet place facing the darkness.

"General Miles says we have our own reservation with much grass and good water, and the White Eyes stay away. This place, Fort Sill, the White Eyes say they'll give us pretty soon now, but we see more and more White Eye settlers come. Maybe this is no more land for Chiricahuas. Still, we're prisoners, not on our own land. Give us this land now, General Miles. We want to work our land. No more will we make war on the White Eyes.

337

"All this General Miles promised us if we surrendered. We surrendered for these words. He has not kept a single promise. General Miles didn't capture us. We surrendered to his lies. This we told General Stanley in San Antonio, who made tracks of what Naiche and I said and sent them to the Great Father in Washington, who learned General Miles had lied to us and to him."

General Miles stopped smiling and, looking at Jimmie Stevens, shook his head a little. Then I knew my words he interpreted didn't match what I had said in Apache, and General Miles smiled again, nodding.

I said, "I'm a prisoner far from my own country. The acorns and piñon nuts, the quail and wild turkey, the giant cactus, and the palo verdes all miss me. I miss them, too. I want to go back to them. This is all I have to say."

General Miles turned and looked at me after he saw the faces of the quiet White Eyes and Blue Coats in the rows above us. He grabbed hold of his coat collar, leaned back a little, and began bragging in the White Eye tongue.

"Yes, Geronimo, I lied to you to get you to surrender. I lied to make you stop spreading death and destruction all over Arizona and New Mexico in the United States and northern Sonora and Chihuahua in Mexico. I lied to stop you from killing every white man and Mexican you met. I learned to lie from the great *nantan* of all liars — from you, Geronimo. You lied to Mexicans, Americans, and to your own Apaches for thirty years."

General Miles laughed. "White men lied to you only once, and I did it. It's a beautiful thought you have to return to Arizona. You speak like a true poet, but the men and women who live in Arizona don't miss you. They don't miss the murders and fear. Folks in Arizona now sleep at night. They have no fear Geronimo will come and kill them. I saved your life, Geronimo. If you had returned to Arizona a prisoner, they would have hung you and all your warriors to the nearest tree. The acorns and piñon nuts, the deer, quail, and wild turkey, the giant cactus, the palo verdes — they'll have to get along as best they can without you."

General Miles, smiling, looked around at the crowd and saw smiles and nods from the Blue Coats sitting there with him, but the people with the sticks making fast tracks stared at him and slowly shook their heads. Jimmie Stevens had a half a smile and a one-eyed squint. He said, "Thank you,

General Miles and Geronimo, for your versions of what happened. We leave it to the court of public opinion to decide which of you speaks the truth, but Geronimo, no one believes General Miles lies to us."

From the Apache soldiers kneeling below where I stood, I heard Naiche speak in Apache in a low voice, "You speak well, Geronimo. You shame the Blue Coat *nantan. Enjuh!*"

The Chiricahuas and I left when the Omaha Exposition closed in the Season of Earth Is Reddish Brown. We were glad to leave. Cold winds off the *llano* blew on our canvas-covered tipis and made us glad we had warm houses waiting for our return. Besides, fewer and fewer White Eyes came to visit us than in the warm seasons. I had made more bows and arrows than I could sell, and I had sold all the pictures I had with my name tracks on them and all the hats in my trunk. No more money was to be made. It was time to pack up and go back to Fort Sill with the soldiers *Teniente* Beach sent to escort us back. There were wagons waiting for us at Rush Springs when the iron wagon left us there, and after a long, cold ride back to Fort Sill, it was good to see my woman Zi-yeh and daughter Eva standing in the door with a bright, yellow lantern held high to welcome me back.

CHAPTER 31
MY POWER FADES

Suns through the seasons passed quiet and sure. I tended my garden in the warm seasons, led my village, trained my daughter and grandson, and helped Zi-yeh, who grew weaker. I spoke often with my nephew Dak-lugie about his work with our cattle and putting up fences to keep our cattle from wandering into Comanche or Kiowa cookpots.

In the Season of Many Leaves after the Omaha Exposition, Mike Dahkeya, the husband of my daughter Dohn-say, who had gone to the Happy Place, and father of my fine young grandson, Thomas, also rode the ghost pony to the Happy Place. I took Thomas into my house. He was a little younger than my daughter Eva, but they were good together as brother and sister. Mike Dahkeya had been a good husband for Dohn-say, a strong warrior for me and Chihuahua, and a proud father of Thomas and his other two children, who also had gone to the Happy Place. Our family would miss him. I sang many songs to Ussen for Mike Dahkeya that he might soon reach the Happy Place.

At that time, the Jesus followers were building their mission and a school for our children in a place the Blue Coats called the Punch Bowl. A harvest after the Omaha Exposition, they finished the schoolhouse. Then many of our children no longer had to leave their families to attend school at Anadarko. Between them, the teachers taught nearly sixty children. Now the young ones could stay with their families and still learn the magic of the White Eyes.

The three lady teachers the Jesus followers sent were good women who respected us, but they also wanted to show the children the Jesus road. I thought, *Let the children learn about the White Eye God.* I didn't care.

A harvest after the school in the Punch Bowl started, at the beginning of the Season of the Earth Is Reddish Brown, the Jesus follower teachers and their *di-yens,* who first had made council with us, started meeting every seventh day to talk to the White Eye God and the one they called Jesus. Chiricahuas who wanted to learn how to follow the Jesus road were invited. Many of the People went to these meetings.

Noche, who had told General Miles to send Kayihtah and Martine with *Teniente* Gatewood when he came to talk with us, became a Jesus follower and told me he was now a member of the Dutch Reformed Church. Noche was an army scout, and I thought of him as a traitor to his People, and we all knew what he was. When I heard that Noche was becoming a Jesus follower, I shrugged and thought his walking the Jesus road was not a loss. I was wrong.

Noche drew Power through this church and spoke to other leaders and encouraged them to come into the church, too, and grow in Power as he had. I didn't think anything much would change. I was the *di-yen* with Power. I counseled Chief Naiche. The People always came to me when they wanted to see Ussen's Power, not the Jesus follower *di-yens*. I was wrong.

Noche spoke a long time one day to Chihuahua about becoming a Jesus follower. Ramona, Chihuahua's daughter, who had married my nephew Daklugie, had become a Jesus follower when she was at the Carlisle school, and she, too, made strong persuasive words to Chihuahua about being a Jesus follower.

Chihuahua asked me what I thought about being a Jesus follower. I told him the god of the Apaches was Ussen. Maybe the White Eye God and Ussen were the same with different names. I didn't know. I told him my Power came from Ussen, not Jesus. Chihuahua said he would think on my words. Four days later, when the Jesus followers met, Chihuahua and his family became Jesus followers, and I felt my Power among the People grow weaker as more leaders chose the Jesus road and went to the Dutch Reformed Church.

Naiche, from the age of twenty-three harvests, had always considered me his *di-yen* and counselor, even if we sometimes did not agree. Anytime anyone in his family needed help, he always asked me to come with my medicine. Soon after Chihuahua chose the Jesus road, Naiche came to my house one evening after our meal. He said we needed to talk. We walked down to Cache Creek and, in the music of the water flowing over the rocks and the singing of frogs and tree peepers, we smoked a cigarette to the four directions.

The light from the falling sun was nearly gone, and we made a small fire for warmth and light. After I tossed the finished cigarette into the fire, I said, "Speak. I will listen."

Naiche nodded his head and said, "I've heard the Jesus followers, Noche, and Chihuahua. They say Jesus won't hold the evil things that we've done in our lives against us if we ask him and if we're truly sorry for doing them and live our lives for the good of others. Do you believe this?"

I shrugged. "I'm not on the Jesus road and don't plan to be. I think you'll find the way we believed long ago about Ussen is not much different from that of the Jesus followers. We both believe in a Happy Place, but in our beliefs, you live there for all harvests in the way you left here, and Ussen gives us special Powers to help the People."

Naiche nodded. "I've killed many men. Some tried to kill me. Others I killed because I couldn't let them tell the army about us. Others, because I was drunk. I've killed Mexicans, men, women, and children, and White Eyes — shot them, cut their throats, hit them in the head with rocks, put arrows in them, and made them scream for Ussen and quick death when I tortured them and let the sun burn out their eyes. If I saw something I wanted, I took it, and I killed them if they said I couldn't have it or tried to stop me from taking it. I've had women, not my wives, but I never forced them. I've drunk much whiskey and danced all night. I've told lies. I beat my wives and children when they displeased me. I even shot one of my wives. Remember that time when she ran to the White Eyes to get away from us the last time we surrendered to Crook?"

I nodded and said, "I remember. Are you sorry about these things? It's what warriors do. It happens in war. Ussen is not displeased with us when we act this way in war."

Naiche smiled, shook his head slowly, and looked at his hands. "Ussen may not be displeased, but I am. I have bad dreams, Geronimo. I hear the screams of those I tortured and smell their flesh burning. I see the blood on my hands and arms of all those I killed or told my warriors to kill. Sometimes the dreams of the killings are so powerful, I wake up covered in sweat, thinking it's blood. I remember the looks on the faces of my wives when I beat them. I haven't done these things for a long time. None of us have done them, not since we surrendered. Still, I drink whiskey when I can get it, and I know you do, too. But the next morning I wish I hadn't drunk it because my head throbs in pain. Do you dream these things, Geronimo?"

I shook my head. "Not yet. Not those kinds of dreams. I dream often of going back to the land of my father. I dream of killing myself, like Victorio did, when I'm out of bullets and enemies come. But the dreams of regret for what happened in the old wars, they leave me alone. Maybe they stay away because I am a *di-yen* and use my Power for the People. You never found your Power. Maybe you need a vision quest to find it, so Ussen can give you Power for the People and take the dreams away."

Naiche stared at me. "Noche and the Jesus followers say Jesus does this if I'm sorry for what I've done, say I believe he is the son of the White Eye's God, and walk the Jesus road. Chihuahua says now that he is a Jesus follower, he sleeps good all through the night, every night. Noche, the scout, the traitor, he says Jesus helps him do the right thing. In my dreams, I swim in a river of blood from all those I've killed. Soon, I dream, it will drown me. Will Ussen stop these dreams? The Jesus followers say Jesus will make my life smooth again, and the dreams will come no more."

I knew then I could say nothing that would stop Naiche from becoming a Jesus follower. I could only speak the truth, as I knew it, about Ussen. I rubbed my hands in the little fire's smoke and warmth and then rubbed my face. "Ussen might stop the dreams if you seek their end in a vision quest. He will do what is best for the People."

"The Jesus followers say Jesus always does what is best for each one of us if we say we're sorry for our wrongs and walk his road."

I shook my head. "I don't know. I haven't been on the Jesus road. I don't know if Ussen wants me to walk that road or not. I will stay with Ussen. You must decide what is best for you."

Naiche nodded and stared awhile at the disappearing fire in the now black night that had no moon. Naiche looked at me, his face etched by the orange light from the coals of the dying fire, and said, "I will walk the Jesus road."

Naiche soon made his vow to walk the Jesus road and was welcomed into the Dutch Reformed Church. Naturally, his family went with him. He told me later that the black, haunting dreams went away and returned no more. His family got along better, and his wives were happier. He was so pleased with his life on the Jesus road that he changed his name to Christian Naiche and later named a son the same thing in honor of Jesus.

The traitor, Chatto, decided after Naiche started walking the Jesus road that he would follow it, too. Carlisle students who had returned to their families as Jesus road followers also became members of the church. Among them were my cousin Jason Betzinez, the Benedict Jozhe family, James Kaywaykla and his wife, Naiche's daughter Dorothy, and, of course, Ramona Chihuahua, who had married my nephew Daklugie. However, Daklugie kept his beliefs in Ussen and did not walk the Jesus road, but he always went to meetings at the church with Ramona. As the number of church members increased, the People seemed to care less that I was a powerful *di-yen* who could do big medicine for them.

I felt my power with them growing weaker and slipping away. *Perhaps,* I thought, *this has nothing to do with Ussen. It's the road all old men walk.*

The next harvest after Naiche decided to walk the Jesus road was a bad time for us all. In the Season of Many Leaves, Mangas, a fine warrior and leader for his People, breathed his last and rode the ghost pony to the Happy Place. As a village headman, he was in the Blue Coat army as a scout. He was buried in the Blue Coat place for the dead with a big ceremony. In the Season of Large Leaves, Chihuahua went to the Happy Place. Chihuahua, still walking the Jesus road when he left riding the ghost pony, had a big Jesus ceremony where they buried him, and Naiche spoke to the people for him.

Within half a moon after Chihuahua went to the Happy Place, the Blue Coats let White Eye settlers take much of the Comanche-Kiowa lands for their farms and ranches. I wondered what would happen to all the Indians on our part of the *llano* when the Blue Coats left Fort Sill. I thought the Blue Coats would let the settlers drive us away too. Maybe then they would shoot us all rather than give us the land we had been promised for many harvests.

That harvest, I was taken to the exposition in Buffalo, New York. They paid me forty-five dollars for every moon I was there to ride my pony three or four times a day in the "Arena of Geronimo" as a representative of the Chiricahua Apaches. I counted forty-two tribes there, but few seemed warlike, and we Chiricahuas were called "the

351

scourge of the plains." The chiefs of the exposition said I was the Indian the White Eyes wanted to see. Who told the Whites Eyes we were from the plains, I don't know, but we didn't go to the plains often. My own country was on the headwaters of the Gila River in the eastern Arizona and western New Mexico mountains.

The Blue Coat chief over us at Fort Sill sent soldiers with us to be sure the White Eyes didn't panic like they did at the Omaha Exposition when Jimmie Stevens took us for a ride in a wagon in the corn country and we lost our way. The cornfields all looked the same, and we stayed lost on those roads through the cornfields until someone came and showed us the road back to Omaha. The sun had fallen when we returned, and already those who make tracks in the newspapers were certain we had escaped and were again killing many people as we rode for Arizona. *Ha, most White Eyes are fools.*

I took Thomas Dahkeya with me to the Buffalo Exposition. The old warriors the White Eyes wanted to see along with me were getting weak, and few could go. The young ones had work to do and could not or would not go. Those who did go were not famous in the newspapers. Many White

Eyes visited us in Buffalo, but they sat on benches to watch me ride.

We had been there about two moons when the Great Father McKinley, who saw us in the Omaha Exposition, came to the new exposition and was shot by a fool. All the White Eyes wanted to see where the Great Father was shot. They forgot the Apaches were there. Even so, I was able to sell a few of my photographs with my name tracks on them, and my grandson's eyes stayed big, seeing all the new things and the great crowds of White Eyes.

One day at the exposition, a White Eye with a big bush of hair under his nose and wearing a great, fringed buckskin coat, leather pants, big brimmed hat, and big boots came to where I sold my pictures. He bought a picture with my name tracks. Then he asked if he could sit and talk with me. He looked harmless, and I nodded yes. I motioned for Frank Mangas, who was a good interpreter, to come help us talk to each other.

The White Eye stuck out his hand, and I gave it three good pumps. He said, "Howdy, Mr. Geronimo. My name is Pawnee Bill. I travel with Pawnee Bill's Wild West Show. We show the people what the West was like with cowboys and Indians twenty or thirty years ago by actin' out the way things was. I watched you ride and like what you do with your pony. Ever'body knows who you are and wants to see the baddest Indian in the country. Ain't no doubt it's you. I think you could make a lot of money in my show. How 'bout workin' with us?"

"You pay money when I ride in your show?"

"Yes, sir, we pay money."

"How much you pay?"

Pawnee Bill made a face, scratched his chin, and then smoothed and twisted the long hair under his nose.

"Well, sir, I reckon we could start at one hundred dollars a month, and, if you was as popular as I 'spect you'll be, we could increase that some. How's that sound?"

"Hmmph. You pay for pony, my food, and place to sleep?"

"Why shore. That'd be part of the deal."

"I sell my picture. Keep money I make there?"

Pawnee Bill stared at the floor. Then he nodded. "Long as you do your part of the show, you'n sell as many pictures as you like and keep the money."

"How long show last? This exposition five moons. Show last that long?"

"We go from place to place to put on the

show and generally travel six or seven moons."

"Hmmph. You talk to army. They say I can go, I go."

A big smile filled Pawnee Bill's face. He stuck out his hand, and we pumped three times again. "That there's the best news I heard all day. I'll get the army fellers to let you go, and I'll send word to you in four or five moons about what we gonna do."

I nodded. *"Enjuh."*

He tipped his big brimmed hat as he stood up. "Be seein' you, Geronimo."

CHAPTER 32
CAMP MEETING

With each passing season, my Power as a *di-yen* among the people became less. Many of the people had become Jesus followers. When they became sick, they prayed to Jesus, not Ussen, and they asked the White Eye *di-yens* to heal them. They didn't need me anymore. Even those who were not Jesus followers went to White Eye *di-yens* because they believed White Eye medicine was stronger than mine, unless a witch was attacking them. I knew White Eye *di-yen* medicine was sometimes strong, other times my medicine was stronger, and the People knew it. Still, they wouldn't ask me to be their *di-yen.*

One day as the sun was falling into the *llano,* painting for Ussen great colors of reds and oranges and purples on high thin clouds, and the frogs, tree peepers, and insects on Cache Creek had begun their night songs, I sat in the breezeway of my house enjoying the coming of the night and smelling the meat and other good things Zi-yeh was teaching Eva to cook for me.

I heard splashing in the creek, and in the low golden light, I saw the dark outline of a rider approaching my house. I could tell from the way he rode, it was Naiche.

He rode up to the breezeway and swung his arm parallel to the ground in greeting as he said, "Ho, Geronimo. I see you."

I waved back. "Ho, Naiche. Come and smoke with me. Soon Zi-yeh and Eva have food for the evening meal. Join us."

With a little grunt, he swung out of his saddle, one with no silver on it, a nice one for herding cattle like the White Eye cowboys used, and sat down beside me as I began to make a cigarette.

"The smell of fine cooking fills your breezeway, Geronimo. I'm glad you asked me to join you at your meal. Yes, let's smoke and talk while your women cook."

I lighted the cigarette, smoked to the four directions, and passed it to Naiche, who smoked and passed it back to me. The way of the People said that we first speak of other things besides his business. We spoke of how the cattle herd grew, how well my nephew Daklugie made improvements and managed the herd, and how much hay had been cut.

At last, Naiche said, "You know, Geronimo, we don't see you much. You go to parades and fairs all over Oklahoma. Sometimes you even go to much greater things that last more than a moon, like the exposition in Buffalo. Many White Eye reporters come to speak with you. The artist Burbank who painted us and helped me learn to paint comes first to see Geronimo. But many of our people don't see you."

"Hmmph. Why should they? Many have become Jesus followers. They have no need of my Power or me. Why, even you, Naiche, who gave me some of your chief's rights, have no need of my Power anymore. We're no longer at war, and you are first among the Jesus followers. If People come to me, I'll help them with Power Ussen gave me in the long-ago days. But they don't come. They're Jesus followers. They no longer know Ussen or receive his gifts."

Naiche rested his elbows on his knees and, bowing his head, stared at the ground. I could see the side of his face, and it appeared that his lips moved, but I heard no sound. Maybe he prayed to this Jesus. I didn't know. Then he said, "Your people, even the Jesus followers, need you. God needs you to help them. Soon we put up the big tent and have our camp meeting in the Punch Bowl. We camp there by the big tent and go under it every night, mornings, and some days after the time of no shadows to hear the words of Jesus from the *di-yens* who have his Power. They can read us his words from the long-ago times written in the big black book of little tracks and tell us what they mean. They are good words, Geronimo. They tell us how to live in a good way so we are happy and can hear God speak to our spirits. Why don't you let Zi-yeh put up a little tipi for you and your family when the big tent rises? Come listen to what the *di-yens* with Jesus' Power have to say. The one they call Wright is Choctaw, and the one who speaks most often is called Bergen. They know the Jesus road. My life is better since I am Christian Naiche. I know you'll learn from them. I have. Come and see."

I stared up at the stars now faintly appearing in the black sky, and thoughts about this God Naiche said made his life better filled my mind. Before I said anything, the screen door to Zi-yeh's kitchen creaked, and Eva called to us in the soft darkness, "Father, Mother says the meal is ready. Come and eat with us. We welcome our chief, Naiche."

I said to Naiche, "Come, let's eat. I'll

think on these things you tell me. Maybe I'll listen to the *di-yens* in the big tent."

Naiche nodded, *"Enjuh."*

We went to Zi-yeh's meal, and, like White Eyes, sat in chairs around a table to eat what she and Eva served. Zi-yeh and Eva modestly welcomed Naiche. It had been a long time since he was in our house. The room was filled with good smells of fried beefsteak, onions, green beans, potatoes, squash, and baked bread. Since Eva had gone to the mission schools and Naiche had been a soldier in the White Eye army, they had learned to use knives and forks when they ate. Zi-yeh and I still used our knives and fingers, but we all drank our coffee from metal cups.

Before we ate, Naiche bowed his head over his pan of food and closed his eyes. I thought he was enjoying the good smells at first, but then I saw his lips moving and started to say something, but Zi-yeh shook her head for me to be quiet, as though she knew what he was doing and would tell me later, so I stayed quiet.

Zi-yeh had become a Jesus follower after Eva was born, but she was in a different tribe than Naiche. Her tribe was Catholic, the tribe of the Mexican brown robes. It was different from the tribe of Naiche's

Jesus followers, the Dutch Reformed Church, who didn't wear robes.

After Naiche left, Zi-yeh explained to me that when he bowed his head over the food, he was thanking God that he had something to eat and for all God had given him. It was a prayer he said every time he ate. I understood why he thanked his God for food, but not why he waited until he ate it. When Ussen gives you food, then you should thank him and prepare it after it is given is up to you. There was much to this Jesus I didn't understand. Maybe Naiche was right. I should come to the tent meeting and listen to what the Jesus road *di-yens* had to say.

I thought for several days about what Naiche had said about the Jesus followers and how he had become happy following the Jesus road. Before Naiche visited, I told those who came to me for help that only Ussen could give them Power, make them happy. Some believed me; others did not. They had also heard the Jesus followers. Now I had heard a powerful Jesus follower and thought maybe I should find out if what Naiche had said about Jesus was true. Maybe if I heard the Jesus follower *di-yens,* then my Power among the people might get stronger. I didn't see much difference between what we said about Ussen and what the Jesus followers said about the White Eye God. Whatever I learned about Jesus, it might help me increase my Power among the people.

One day, as I worked with my squashes and pumpkins in the early morning before the sunlight came warm and bright and the morning water on the plant leaves and fruit still glittered, I argued with myself over whether I should go and hear the Jesus road *di-yens* under their big tent. One side of me argued that if I went, I gave them more power. The other side said I needed to learn about this Power that had turned Naiche, Chihuahua, Noche, and even Chatto into Jesus followers. Unless I knew about this Power, Ussen could not tell me how to become strong again.

Finally, I decided I would go and listen on the last night of the camp meeting. I rode my pony to the tent Zi-yeh and Eva had set up there. I came to the tent when the sun was at the time of no shadows. I saw Zi-yeh and Eva sitting with a group of women who were sewing and chattering like a flock of birds in the brush. After feeding my pony his grain and brushing him down for the day, I put him in the rope corral with the other ponies.

I saw some people sitting at their tents point at me and say something to others close by. I didn't care. I wanted to learn what these *di-yens* were telling them. I was resting in the shade in front of Zi-yeh's tent in the early midafternoon when a shadow blocked the sun near me, and I raised to an elbow to see the Jesus *di-yens*.

They stuck out their hands for a shake, and one said, "Ho, Geronimo. I'm Frank Wright, and this is Doctor Bergen. You and I spoke about four years ago when you told us your People wanted a mission school for the children and it was good for them to learn the Jesus road. Welcome to our camp meeting. Is it all right if we sit here and talk with you awhile about Jesus? Are you coming inside the tent tonight?"

I stood up and took their hands, pumped them twice, and motioned for them to sit down with me on my blanket. "Ho, Frank Wright and Doctor Bergen. Maybe I hear you tonight. Naiche says it would be a good thing for me and the People to hear what you have to say about Jesus."

Wright, who sat down easily on the blanket, ran his fingers through his flint-black, shining hair to push it out of his eyes, and faced me. His eyes were quick and bright, and in his smile, I saw no deception. "Geronimo, I have prayed and have much hope that you would come tonight and hear the words of our master, Jesus the Christ, that you'll come to understand how his spirit can help you live a better life through love and help for others. Jesus wants what is best for each of us. He wants us to know God and what the Happy Land is like. He wants us to know God as he knew him and to give us a good life while we live here, not just in the Happy Place. He is the beginning and the end of all we are and all we can be. He has taught us how to be free of sin. Do you want to be free of sin, Geronimo?"

"What is this you call sin?"

"Sin is whatever you do that separates you from God. It takes away your freedom to be close to God and what will make you happy."

I thought, *Of course I want freedom, but what I want is to be in my own country.* I said, "I want freedom. I want to be free again."

Wright nodded. "Yes, I know you do. To be truly free, you have to give your life to Jesus."

"I want my life. Why would I give it to Jesus?"

"Because when you give your life away, you get it back again in full measure, like a cup of meal packed down and running over. You give it away, and it comes back to you better."

"Hmmph. This I don't understand. I give life away to get it back. Maybe you tell me and the others this when you talk tonight?"

Wright smiled. "Yes, we'll tell everyone about giving their lives to Jesus, and how they will get them back again clean and better than before. Our friend Bergen talks tonight and will tell you how Jesus will make you happy in your life. Look at the lives of your friends who have come to Jesus, taken his road, and walked his path. You see how much better their lives are now. Your chief, Naiche, is so happy with his life that he has taken the name Christian. He says his life, even as a prisoner of the White Eyes, is much better now than when he roamed free."

"Then I want to learn about this freedom. Tonight I hear you."

Wright smiled and nodded. "Good. We'll be looking for you."

CHAPTER 33
LOOKING FOR THE JESUS ROAD

When the sun began falling into the edge of the earth, the people camping around the big tent, and those who visited that night from far away, started inside the tent. There they took seats in the rows of many chairs, all facing toward a raised place for the speakers to stand and be seen. I went inside the big tent with Zi-yeh. The people all dressed pretty, men in their White Eye vests and coats with ties, and the women with their shawls and nice, long dresses like the one Zi-yeh wore.

I guessed only half the people were Apaches. The other half dressed like Comanches and Kiowa, who still wore their best clothes, some dressing like their grandfathers and mothers. Unlike my People, who were still prisoners, the Comanche and Kiowa women wore bright shawls, and their good jewelry was in silver and blue stones. I saw some wearing fine, beaded moccasins, the blue beads standing out in the pools of yellow light made by lanterns hung on the big tent poles. Some women carried their babies in their arms, the edges of the babies' blankets pulled over their faces so they slept easily. Others brought on cradleboards their babies, black eyes shining and seeing all that happened. There was a gentle murmur of talk and laughter between friends and neighbors as the rows of chairs filled.

I sat on a chair in a row near the front. Many of the Jesus followers with big smiles on their faces stopped at my seat and told me how glad they were Zi-yeh and I had come, and they all said this without deceit in their eyes. I was glad to see them, and they made me glad I had come.

Before Bergen spoke, Wright offered prayers to the White Eye God and Jesus, asking that our ears and hearts be open to what was said and that we be given understanding of what they were telling us. He said these things through the interpreter Wratten, who could speak in our language almost at the same time the White Eyes were speaking in their tongue. Others interpreted in Comanche and Kiowa. They spoke at the same time, but their voices did not interfere with what Wratten said for those speaking to us in the White Eye tongue.

A song leader stood in front of us all and led us singing songs about blood, Jesus, love, and the cross. The titles of some of these songs were a mystery to me. When they sang "When the Roll Is Called Up Yonder," those around me sang from memory and in their own tongue, but they carried the same rhythm, and I could feel the singing making me glad in my heart. Then they sang a song about the torture of Jesus, "Beneath the Cross of Jesus," and I wondered what some of the words meant, but I sang along anyway. I liked hearing the singing. It had Power. I thought, *Maybe when my strength among the People returns, I should have groups sing when I make medicine in order to increase my Power.*

When they had prayed and sung enough, the *di-yen* Bergen stood up to speak. First, he prayed that he might say the words God gave him in the spirit for which they were given. He opened the thick, black Bible the Jesus followers often carried.

Bergen said, "This reading is from the Gospel of John, Chapter fifteen, verses nine through fourteen. Jesus is speaking to his disciples. He said to them:

9. As the Father hath loved me, so have I loved you: continue ye in my love.

10. If ye keep my commandments, ye shall abide in my love; even as I have kept my Father's commandments, and abide in his love.
11. These things have I spoken unto you, that my joy might remain in you, and that your joy might be full.
12. This is my commandment, that ye love one another, as I have loved you.
13. Greater love hath no man than this, that a man lay down his life for his friends.
14. Ye are my friends, if ye do whatsoever I command you.

I thought, *I know what it means to die fighting with a friend against an enemy. All Apaches know what this means. Is what the black book says any different?*

Bergen finished reading and then said, "I pray God will open our ears for the reading of his word. Warriors all know what it means to die fighting a common enemy with a friend. Some of you elders sitting here have lost friends while you were fighting a common enemy. In the days when warriors went off to raid or war, women guarded the camp, and sometimes some of the women, too, lost friends fighting a common enemy. But this kind of death, fighting an enemy with a friend, is not what Jesus is talking about.

"What is Jesus talking about when He says in this scripture that no man has greater love than to lay down his life for his friends? Who were Jesus' friends? Were they those who called him teacher? Were they the rich and powerful? Were they ones he knew and had lived with since he was a child? Were they the soldiers who kept their boots on the necks of his people?

"Have you ever tried to do business with someone who says, 'Friend, let me give you a good price for that,' and you know that's the last thing he'll do? Is that the kind of friend Jesus is talking about? Has anyone ever called you friend, only for you to discover harvests later that they told you lies about something between you? Can these people be your friends? Who are the ones Jesus calls friends?"

Hmmph, I thought, *these are honest questions. But his followers tell me Jesus lived in the very long-ago days. How would we know who his friends were?*

"Jesus says in the Gospel of John that we are his friends if we do what he commands us."

Is Jesus speaking from the Happy Place?

Do all the Jesus followers have ghost sickness?

"What is it Jesus commands us to do? Does he tell us to pray twice a day? No! Does he tell us to cheat our neighbor? No! Does he tell us we must go to war for God? No! Jesus said in the Gospel of John, Chapter fifteen, verse twelve, 'This is my commandment, that ye love one another, as I have loved you.' It doesn't matter what race or color you are, whether you're a prisoner or a keeper of prisoners. It doesn't matter whether you're a man or a woman; it doesn't matter if you're a warrior or a *diyen;* it doesn't matter if you're a chief or the least of warriors. Jesus' commandment is to love each other as he has loved us."

I have never heard a ghost speak like this. This is good to know.

"How do we love each other as Jesus loved us? Jesus said for us to do for others as we would want them to do for us. Jesus said to love God before all others. Jesus said the greatest love one could show was to give up their life for their friend. Giving up your life for a friend can mean many things. It can mean using your whole life for a God-given purpose, such as teaching people or caring for someone who is very sick for a long time. It can mean staying straight and true to God and what we hear him telling us. And it can mean actually dying for your friend.

"Before Jesus, the world of men was wrapped in darkness. Men's eyes were closed to the evil and crooked way they lived, and the darkness was killing their spirits, killing their very souls. Jesus came to bring us light and to take away the darkness. Before Jesus, most men never knew or saw God in their lives. But Jesus let the evil of men try to kill him. He suffered, and he died for his friends that they might see the light that shows the goodness of God, but after three days in a grave, he came back. Evil couldn't kill him."

I've never heard of anyone in a grave for three days and coming back. This Jesus had very powerful medicine. Maybe I can learn it.

"Jesus said he came from God and that God was his father."

No wonder Jesus had so much Power. The White God made Jesus' mother pregnant. This is very strong medicine.

"Fathers love their children. What father would not destroy someone who made his child suffer and then killed him? God, the Father of Jesus, let this happen that men might know the evil in which they live, that they might be sorry when they saw what that evil did to God's son, and that they might come to see Jesus through their love for him and for each other. It was a terrible price to pay through the suffering and death of Jesus. It was a horrific test of Jesus' faith in God for him to bring us to the light of God in order for us to become sons, like Jesus, of the living God. Jesus died for us. He was our friend who showed us his greatest love. He asks only that we love each other as he has loved us. Jesus died on the cross that we might know the way, the truth, and the life."

If I am to be a great medicine man, then I need to know this way, truth, and life.

"Now I tell you, my friends, that this is the road Jesus walked. He gave us the best way to live in harmony by helping and loving those around us. He taught us to love each other as he loved us. That is his road. He took our places and suffered for us on the cross so we would not have to. Your white brothers have built you a mission here near your villages at Fort Sill so you might know this. They've worked hard that you might walk Jesus' road and know the love of God. You have only to serve Jesus, and in serving Jesus, walk his road. As the scripture says here in the Gospel of John, Chapter fifteen, verse ten, 'If ye keep my commandments, ye shall abide in my love; even as I have kept my Father's commandments, and abide in his love.' We have to only believe this and do as Jesus taught us. We will have satisfied our debt to him, and God won't leave us in darkness if we do this.

"Brothers! If you're broken in your life, come and walk the Jesus road, and he will heal you, for he has already taken your punishment. Love your brothers and be made whole. There's no other way. Come to the front here with me, and we'll pray together, and your life will be new again. Come to the front to pray with me while your brothers sing for Jesus in your life."

I sat and listened to every word Bergen spoke. I listened without moving, had many thoughts, and knew what he said was true. It was like Ussen, the one who Bergen called God, had shot one of his arrows into my heart, and I knew the truth. That night, there were many people God shot with his arrows and convinced them to walk the Jesus road. They came to the front to pray with Wright. I knew this power would make me a better *di-yen* and help me lead the people.

After Wright prayed, I stood with my arms raised and turned to the People. I said, "Hear me! When the missionaries came to

374

us the first time and wanted to build a mission and school, I said to them, 'I, Geronimo, and these others are now too old to travel your Jesus road. But our children are young, and I and my brothers will be glad to have the children taught about the white man's God.' Tonight I'm still glad our children are taught about the white man's God. But I was wrong. I'm not too old to travel the Jesus road.

"In the long-ago times, I made war and killed many white men, women, and children, and I killed every Mexican I could. I took everything I could from them. I am sorry now for those days. They should not have happened. They wouldn't have happened if I had known Jesus then and had walked his road. Those days are gone now. They will never return. The God of the whites has great Power. He's our Great Father. He gave the dead Jesus back to us. He's our friend. I see this tonight. The only way to Power is to walk the Jesus road. The Jesus road is best for us. Now we begin to think that the Christian white people love us. This is all I have to say."

Wright and Bergen prayed and sang with the People and agreed with some of them that they should have the baptizing ceremony to walk the Jesus road. After the meeting was finished, many came to me and said how glad they were to hear what I had to say and thanked me for it. Even Naiche, Noche, and Chatto were all smiles as they took hold of me and squeezed my shoulders. I began to think that now maybe my Power with the People would return.

When the tent emptied, Wright and Bergen sat with me, and we talked. I told them I thought the Jesus road would lead me back to Power and how the singing had made me ready to hear. I saw Wright and Bergen look at each other as I spoke, and I wondered what they were thinking as Wratten interpreted my words in English. I told Bergen I thought his talk was very good and helped me understand how Jesus could help me. Again, Bergen glanced at Wright and nodded as I spoke.

Wright said, "My brother, you have come far this night. Doctor Bergen and I believe you need to learn more about Jesus before we ask you to accept baptism. Waiting will make it more meaningful for you. We ask that you and Zi-yeh come to the church on Sundays and listen to what is said. Will you come?"

Since there were many things about what they were teaching about Jesus I didn't know, I nodded and said, "Yes, I know there's much to learn about this Jesus road. We'll come when Zi-yeh is able, but the worms the white di-yens call TB, are taking her. She must rest often in her bed."

Wright hugged me and said, "We will pray every day for God and Jesus to help her. You aren't far from the Jesus road."

As we left the tent, we heard a group sitting on the mission school porch singing a song I was told was called "Nearer My God to Thee." I thought, *Maybe I will yet get Power from the White Eye God.*

Less than a moon passed after I learned about the Jesus road at the tent meeting. I had not started to walk the Jesus road, but I went to hear the talks from the White Eye *di-yens* who spoke at the mission every seven days. I wasn't ready to leave my contact with Ussen and the Power it gave me. The White Eye *di-yens* had much to say about how to live the life they believed their God wanted for us. I still thought maybe Ussen and the white man's God were the same, but if that was true, then why didn't Ussen ever speak about Jesus?

CHAPTER 34
OLD FOOL

After the White Eye chiefs saw me at the Buffalo Exposition riding my pony, they often asked if I would ride in their feasts, where all who came stood at the side of the road and watched us ride by them. The White Eyes called this a parade. I liked riding in parades where, sitting on my pony, I could see much that went on that I would miss if I stood on the ground. We Chiricahuas had ridden in parades such as those for the Omaha and Buffalo Expositions.

The new Chiricahua commander, Captain Sayre, asked if I wanted to ride in the parades where afterwards I could sell my photographs with my name tracks or anything else I had. I agreed to do this, and soon I rode in a parade in the little town, Lawton, a short ride from the Fort Sill gates, on the day the White Eyes called Fourth of July.

A couple of moons later, the White Eye

chiefs at Oklahoma City wanted me to ride in their parade, and Captain Sayre said he would let me go any place in Oklahoma I wanted, but, for me to leave Oklahoma, his chiefs in Washington first had to decide if they would allow it. The parade in Oklahoma City was a big one, and I made good money. Eva stayed home to help look after Zi-yeh, who grew weaker with each new sun. I took my grandson, Thomas Dahkeya, to watch the parade and to help me with my pony. I was getting old and slow, and the pony was young and frisky. I hadn't worked with it as much as I would have liked. It helped to have Thomas hold him while I mounted. I could control him after that.

A harvest passed. The new harvest was the time the White Eyes named 1903. Zi-yeh was even more fragile. The chiefs at Anadarko, where Eva went to the school before attending the mission school, asked that I ride in their Fourth of July parade. In a harvest or two, Eva would go to school at Chilocco. Zi-yeh needed Eva again to stay with her, so Thomas and I were given passes to ride our ponies over to Anadarko and come back. It was a good parade. I sold enough photographs with my name tracks to make the trip worthwhile.

We returned to Fort Sill the next day, an easy ride that we finished before dark. Zi-yeh and Eva, standing in the breezeway, were happy to see us return. Zi-yeh's pony had escaped from the fenced pasture and wouldn't come when they called it. I knew where it liked to hide in the trees along Cache Creek, and since there was still plenty of light, I went to get it while they cooked the evening meal.

I found the pony where I expected, put a rope around its neck, and led it back to the corral until I could find and fix where it had got out. It felt good to be out walking with a good pony. As we approached the house, I saw the women and Thomas watching for us. I decided to show them how well I could still ride. Without warning, I vaulted onto the pony with a war whoop.

The frightened pony started bucking the moment I landed on his back. In one good crowhop, he flipped me backwards high into the air. A horse had not thrown me since I was a novitiate. I was lucky I didn't have the rope wrapped around my hand or arm, because the pony might have dragged me to my death as it ran for the corral. I landed hard in thick grass on my lower back. I think Ussen used the grass to keep me from breaking my back. I was stunned, knocked out of breath, and seeing points of lights. I felt prickles go down my legs to my feet. I wasn't sure where I was or if I could move at all.

In the falling light, even the frogs and insects were quiet. They seemed to be listening as Thomas and Eva raced to help me. I lay where I landed, trying to get my breath back. I thought I might have a broken back, but the numbness began leaving my legs as Eva and Thomas lifted me up. There was much pain in my back as they helped pull me to my feet.

I refused to show them how much I hurt. Even for an old man, it was not the Apache way. But I couldn't stand up straight. I kept my arms over their shoulders as they helped me walk to our house. All the while, I was thinking, *Old fool, old fool.* I went to bed without eating but assured the children and Zi-yeh that I would be back on my feet soon. Zi-yeh had been a good medicine woman when she ran with me off the reservation and had taken care of my war wounds for many harvests. She gave me a tea she made with willow bark, and the pain went away.

In the moon the White Eyes call July, I lay

unmoving on my bed twelve days and nights. My children and wife kept me company, but no one else came to visit me. The air was hot, and my body leaked water like it was covered with many little springs. Black dreams, old memories of loss and war, came often and made me wonder why Ussen had spared me to continue this suffering all the rest of my harvest times. My dreams of our far land and dying like Victorio sometimes came, but not often.

I had been a powerful warrior and a *diyen* with great power even in my young days when I rode with Mangas Coloradas. Mangas taught me much about war and dealing with the White Eyes and Mexicans. My body bathed in water from the heat, I smiled when in my fevered mind I remembered how I had taken my first wife, Alope. Her father asked many horses as a bride gift, expecting that I would never gather that many before someone else, more powerful and experienced, offered even more for her. But I knew where a great *hacienda* kept their horses, and I had only to kill three *vaqueros* to get all the horses I wanted. Alope's father stared at my bride gift, the seven ponies he said he wanted, with his jaw hung down in disbelief while Alope came and mounted behind me before I rode off with her to go to the place where we spent our first times together before moving near my mother's tipi.

I remembered finding my mother, sweet Alope, and our three children, all younger than ten harvests, dead by the hand of the Mexican army and how grief tore at my heart until Ussen told me I would not die by bullets and gave me even more Power. I remembered the blood of my family, and I crushed Mexican heads with rocks, shot them from ambush, and slit throats as I took my vengeance. But it was never enough to satisfy my feeling of loss.

I thought of my wives taken in slavery. I remembered other wives who died in the fighting, and others killed by White Eye diseases, and how bad I felt that I couldn't bargain them back into the land of the living. I thought of children I had lost. There were many. I groaned in torment, asking Ussen why my family had suffered so much, yet I still lived. I asked Ussen why I had been thrown into darkness, alone and abandoned by my people. But nothing filled my ears, nor did my Power speak to me. All I heard was silence.

I thought of all I had learned listening to the church *di-yens*. They said I lived in sin. I knew this. I broke their rules, drank, and got drunk when it pleased me. I didn't remember to please God with a life unfettered with rage and uncontrolled desires. I wasn't always awake to hear God's voice. I still hated Mexicans, and I had little use for the White Eyes. But the Jesus road said all men were brothers joined together loving God and doing what he wanted. Even so, I thought how happy the Mexicans would be if they could see me now paying for my foolish mistake. I wanted the White Eye God to help me, but I didn't know how to ask Him for this help. I was alone in the darkness, trying to find the Jesus road like a blind man tapping in the prairie grass with a stick.

Suns passed. I gained enough strength that I could shuffle slowly and balance against the walls to get to one of Zi-yeh's kitchen chairs to eat at the table. Frail Zi-yeh looked after me with the strength of a much younger woman, but she coughed often with a deep growl in her chest, and many times I saw blood on the cloth she used to cover her mouth. I knew it was not long before she would ride the ghost pony to Ussen's Happy Place. The thought of her leaving us hurt more than the pain in my back and legs. Eva and Thomas, good children, part of the generation of hope for the Chiricahuas, looked after my horses and field of pumpkins, melons, yellow corn, and kafir corn.

One night as we ate our evening meal, Thomas said, "Grandfather, in two suns the camp meeting begins in the oak grove on Medicine Bluff Creek. Tomorrow I want to play baseball with my friends who have come with their parents, if you'll let me go. I have all my work done in the stable and field. We have a good time playing baseball. Will you allow me this time to play with my friends?"

I nodded. Baseball was a weak White Eye game that was good for teaching how to judge flying balls for catching and hitting, but nothing better at all. I thought a good rock fight or using slings was better. "You've helped me much, Thomas. Go and have a fine time with your friends."

I glanced at Eva, but she slowly shook her head. There were things for young women to do together, but she would stay and help Zi-yeh. She hadn't yet had her womanhood ceremony, but I vowed that after she did, I would give a big dance and feast for her and invite everyone: Apaches, Comanches, Kiowa, even our White Eye friends to come and know what a fine young woman she was and how much I valued this daughter.

■ ■ ■ ■

After I returned to my bed, I lay down and didn't move. Black dreams of families killed, battles lost, and the blood of babies came again, and I awoke deep in the night with the moon bright and shining through my window and my lower back in great pain. I remembered Thomas telling me at our evening meal that tomorrow the camp meeting began. I wondered if it was time for me to leave the darkness, do what the missionary *di-yens* required of me, and start down the Jesus road.

CHAPTER 35
A NEW HEART

I lay in my bed smelling the coffee and good food Eva and Zi-yeh made and listening to the meadowlarks calling as they searched for insects in the prairie grass. I struggled, trying to decide whether or not I should go to the camp meeting and commit to the Jesus road. There was not much difference between Ussen and the White Eye God. Maybe the way the White Eyes thought of God was a clearer picture of Ussen. I didn't know if this was true, but I knew I had to leave the dark place where I was living.

As we sat drinking the last of the coffee after the morning meal, I said, "I'll go to the camp meeting after the time of shortest shadows. Thomas, I need you to saddle my pony. Then bring him to the breezeway, and you and Eva help me mount."

Zi-yeh bowed her head and rubbed her forehead like it ached, and the eyes of Eva and Thomas grew wide.

Thomas shook his head and said, "I'll obey you, Grandfather, but with your back, can you even mount a pony, much less ride one for the time it takes to get to the camp meeting?"

I stared at Thomas and felt very old. "Yes, I can ride and stay on the pony. I've ridden great distances with bullet wounds, torn muscles, and broken bones that hurt as bad or worse than my back and groin do now. If old Nana, with his arthritic legs, could stay on a pony during his Victorio revenge raid, then I, too, can ride a pony, even with my back and leg pains. Bring me the pony at the time of shortest shadows."

He nodded he understood, and Eva said, "Father, you must be very careful. You might hurt yourself and never get better."

Zi-yeh raised her head and said, "Husband, if God wants you at the camp meeting, he'll get you there. I pray you don't suffer much on the way."

I took her hand and said, "Zi-yeh, you're a good woman. Pray for me as you please. The suffering I can stand, and if I find what I seek, it will be worth it."

She whispered, *"Enjuh."*

Thomas brought the pony to the house breezeway. I tried not to groan, but I did, as

I shakily stood on a box with Eva holding me so I didn't lose my balance, and she helped me get my right leg high enough to slide into the saddle. I couldn't sit up straight in the saddle, but by supporting my weight on the saddle horn, I got my toes in the stirrups and kept my weight forward so my back pain was not as bad as when I leaned back. Even in this bent-forward way, I could manage the pony with the reins. Before I rode off toward Medicine Bluff Creek, I told my family I would be back that night and might need help getting in the house.

The ride seemed to take a long time. Streaks of pain sometimes flew up my back, and the sun, bright and shining, added its heat to my misery. The thirst filling my throat grew. I wished I had a canteen or a smooth creek pebble to keep in my mouth. I said to myself many times on that ride, *This Jesus road is a hard one.* But I had to get to the missionary *di-yens* and leave the darkness that had filled my life.

I learned later that Thomas followed behind me in case I fell off the pony and needed help. I went slow, just guiding the pony but letting him walk as he chose. I didn't have enough strength in my legs to even slap its sides and make him move along. We came to the camp meeting after two circles of the long White Eye clock hand from the time of no shadows. It had taken me much longer than I had planned to get there, and I was barely able to stay on my pony. Some of the People watched me ride up to the big tent, but they didn't know I was about to fall off my pony. The water coming off my forehead was so heavy, it nearly blinded me as I slid off the pony and held on to the saddle horn until enough strength came for me to stagger into the tent and find a chair.

Naiche was speaking to three or four of the men near the speaker's stage when he saw me come in the tent. He came, sat down beside me, and said, "Geronimo, I'm glad you're here, but your face shows much pain. You should be resting in your house."

I sat with a bowed head, waiting for the pain in my back and legs to hide. The White Eye *di-yens* who were holding the meeting and a few others gathered around us. They squeezed and patted my shoulders, acknowledging they were glad I was there. I began to speak in the tongue of my father, and Benedict Jozhe interpreted for the White Eye *di-yens*.

I looked up at the faces around me and croaked, "I'm in a dark place. Enemies killed some in my family or took them into slavery. Memories of blood and killing in revenge fill my dreams. A need for revenge fills my heart. My heart has never been satisfied. Many suffered because of me. Sins fill me. I'm separated from God. I want to find Jesus, walk his road, and have the past rubbed out."

I had never before seen such a look on Naiche's face. He seemed on fire with happiness and goodwill. He put his arm across my shoulders and gave them a squeeze. The White Eye *di-yens,* and others gathered around us, were all smiling, lifting their hands, and saying, "Thank you, Lord," and "Amen and amen." It was the first time I had felt the darkness lift and felt at peace with myself in a long time.

Naiche sent a boy driving his wagon to tell Zi-yeh and my children that I would stay at the big tent and not to worry. I had a place to sleep and eat with his family. But Zi-yeh and the children returned in the wagon before dark, put up our family tent near the big tent, and made us a meal before the evening service.

I attended every service, learning about Jesus and his road. Between services, the White Eye *di-yens* and my brothers in the church came to sit at my tent. They told me what it meant to them to live a life where God could speak to them and they could hear him, how helping others without expecting payback was what God wanted, how without the shedding of blood there is no forgiveness, and that is why Jesus died for us, and how forgiving those who wronged you was much better for your spirit than revenge.

These were new, hard ideas for me, but I thought on them much and came to understand their wisdom. They spoke of what life after death, as a spirit, was like, as their Bible described it. I had killed many people and seen many dead, but I had never seen this thing they called spirit. I knew now I would have to look harder to see this spirit. I didn't know how I had missed it before. They spoke of the power of praying and how God blesses us when we do. I have always prayed to Ussen and believed he protected me. They also prayed that the pain in my back would be eased, and it felt to me that it had.

On the night of the last service, I shuffled to the front, a bent-over old man supported by his stick, where the speakers stood, saying all who wanted the Jesus road should come forward and ask for it.

I said, "I'm old and broken by this fall

I've had. I have no friends, and my people have turned from me. I'm full of sins, and I walk alone in the dark. I see that you White Eye *di-yens* have a way to get sin out of the heart so we can hear God, and I want to take that better road and hold it till I die."

The *di-yen,* the Choctaw Walter Roe, sat and talked with me about what I believed about God and why I believed it. I had listened to the *di-yens* speak about Jesus and God many times since last harvest, and my eyes were clear in how I understood Jesus and God. Walter Roe nodded and smiled approvingly at my answers and said I was ready for their ceremony of baptism, and that it would take place in seven suns at the baptizing pool in Medicine Bluff Creek. After this ceremony, I would become a Christian like Naiche and the others, and I knew the light on the Jesus road would drive away my darkness.

Rather than go back home, Zi-yeh and Eva kept our little tent in place, and we waited seven days there where the big tent had been for the baptizing ceremony. Friends who walked the Jesus road came, and we talked all that time about what it meant. I asked them what they believed about the Christian idea of heaven and life after death, and how these beliefs were different from what the Apaches thought about Ussen and living in the Happy Place. I believed what I had learned, but I didn't understand how heaven was different from the Happy Place, and they all had a little different understanding of heaven and how it was different from the Happy Place. I knew I had much to think over and learn.

Near the mission school and building in the Punch Bowl, Medicine Bluff Creek made a turn and formed a shaded pool about waist deep, which the Christian *di-yens* used for the baptizing ceremony. The day before my ceremony, which took place after their services, the *di-yens* came and told me what to expect, how to dress — they wanted me to wear a shirt and pants, no breechcloth as I would normally wear for swimming. They didn't think it appropriate for men to be seen in just their breechcloths. I didn't think that should have been a problem since God must have known us before we were born, but it was their ceremony, and I didn't question it.

For the ceremony, a big crowd of the People who walked the Jesus road, and some who didn't, gathered on the creek bank next to the baptizing pool and sang Jesus songs. I thought the singing was powerful and encouraging. They sang "Blessed Assurance" and "Lord, I Want to Be a Christian" before the *di-yen* waded into the baptizing pool and raised his hands to pray. He said many words to God and gave thanks that I was ready to follow Jesus. Then he motioned for me to come to him in the pool, his helpers holding me until my feet were steady on the rocky bottom, and I could move to him.

When I reached the *di-yen,* he steadied me with his arm around my shoulders, raised his right hand, and asked if I believed Jesus was the risen Son of God. After I said I did, he lowered me under the water, which was supposed to symbolize my burial, and raised me up to symbolize Jesus raising me from the dead. The crowd on the bank began singing "Guide Me, O Thou Great Jehovah" and "Come Thou Fount of Every Blessing."

As I came out of the water, they were still singing and Naiche, with a great smile, embraced me, and the women and children held on to my hands. I had not been this happy in a long time. I thought, *This Jesus road is good to walk.*

CHAPTER 36
ZI-YEH RIDES
THE GHOST PONY

Zi-yeh was so weak that, while we waited at the mission for my baptism ceremony, Eva and Thomas did most of the work around the tent while she rested. After my baptism ceremony, they took down our tent, and Na-iche sent a boy to drive a wagon and take us back home. On the way home, Zi-yeh rested on the folded tent while the rest of us sat where we could see her and watch the way home. The disease attacking her was growing stronger and now lay on her face in the shape of a great red butterfly, its body aligned with her nose, its wings on either side of her face. She wanted to hide it by covering her face with a thin cloth she could see through. I told her to use it if she must, but no one of any worth would say or think anything about the redness whether she covered it or not. She finally decided not to hide her face, and I told her she was wise.

Two moons passed. I prayed for a long time every day that Ussen or the White Eye God would heal Zi-yeh while she rested, but the red butterfly on her face wouldn't go away, and every sun she grew weaker. Thomas planned to leave for school at Chilocco, and Eva would spend her days at the mission school, so they wouldn't be at the house to help us. I asked Eva to teach me what to do as part of the woman's work to keep up the house. Every day, like a good woman, I swept out the house, washed the dishes and pots with which I cooked, prayed for Zi-yeh, and then took care of our ponies and other livestock and worked in the pumpkin patch.

In those days, I knew the prayers by our Christian brothers for us reached God. My pain was disappearing, and as I worked in the house, I grew stronger. But I saw Zi-yeh growing weaker, growing closer to riding the ghost pony. God wanted her.

In the moon the White Eyes call September, I drove our wagon carrying Thomas and his trunk of supplies and clothes to Lawton, where he mounted the iron wagon to the Chilocco Indian School. Zi-yeh, Eva, and I would miss him, but it was best he learned White Eye secrets. What he knew might save us all one day. Eva had decided she would continue at the mission school near our village so she would be near her mother when Zi-yeh needed her.

Women came and stayed with Zi-yeh when I worked gathering crops or performed my duties as head of the village. Men from the church came and helped me with the harvest, and we gathered all we had in the Season of Earth Is Reddish Brown before cold ruined it, and the Ghost Face with its dark, cloudy days, wind, snow, and ice came to lie heavy on us.

I paid a woman, a widow, to come and stay with us and help Zi-yeh when Eva was at the mission school. Zi-yeh had become so weak, she could not get out of her bed. It was hard to watch her wasting away, harder even than when I had to watch Chappo die at Mount Vernon. I prayed often for her, but my Power had grown weak, and I could do nothing for her even by asking God.

I wanted God to hear me, and I wanted to hear him. I followed the rules the church said we should follow so we could hear God and Jesus when they spoke to us, and they would hear us when we prayed. I didn't drink whiskey anymore. As the soldiers said, I was sober as a judge, which I was for my village. I didn't play Monte or poker card games anymore because the church *di-yens* said it was not what God wanted and that it made our hearts so greedy for money, we couldn't hear God speaking to us. I didn't race horses, either. Watching my horse in a race made me become someone who was ready to fight, as though I was ready for war. Then after the heat of the race, I really didn't want to fight anyone. I needed to listen and hear God and Jesus speaking to me, and I wanted them to hear me when I prayed, especially for the sake of Zi-yeh. I followed all the rules the mission *di-yens* gave me.

During the Ghost Face of the harvest time the White Eyes called 1904, the White Eye *di-yens* with strong medicine came often from Fort Sill to see Zi-yeh. They gave her medicine they called laudanum and other things, and I sat beside our bed watching her with the woman I paid to help me look after her. The White Eye medicine let her sleep, but as the rain came to make the grass green and the wind grew warm, I knew soon she would ride the ghost pony. Our friends came often to see us, mostly to visit her, and the widow kept food on the stove and the coffee pot full to serve them if they were hungry.

One day the sun was bright and warm, there was a light scent of wildflowers in the air, and birds were beginning to make their nests in the prairie grass. I sat with a blanket over my shoulders at the edge of my breeze-way between the two rooms of my house. The widow was helping Zi-yeh wash, and I stayed away from the sleeping place to give them privacy. I saw a man on a horse, a soldier, his hat pulled low over his eyes, jogging across the fields toward my village. By the time he crossed Cache Creek and headed for my house, I could tell it was Captain Sayre, commander of the Chiricahuas at Fort Sill.

Sayre rode up to me and made a sign of greeting by waving his forearm and hand parallel to the ground. "Ho, Geronimo. It's a good day to feel the sun warming us. Is Zi-yeh any better?"

"Ho, Captain Sayre. The sun feels good after a cold winter. Zi-yeh is still weak. I have a good place to sit, see the light on new grass, and hear birds sing. Join me."

Sayre nodded and swung down from his horse, a big black one I would have stolen when I was free. With a grunt and blow from puffed cheeks, the captain sat down beside me. I said, "There's coffee on the stove. A widow I hire looks after Zi-yeh. I'll get it myself if you want some."

He shook his head. "No, I had several cups at my office this morning."

We listened to meadowlarks whistling and talked about the Ghost Face Season, how mild it had been, and what a good job Daklugie was doing as manager of the Chiricahua herd. Then he said, "I've received notice from the War Department that there's to be a world's fair in Saint Louis called the Louisiana Purchase Exposition this summer and fall. They plan to have a big exhibit of Indians from all over the country in addition to wild people from all over the world. Naturally, they've asked that you come as part of the Chiricahuas representing Fort Sill. Mr. McCowan, chief at the Chilocco Indian School, where your grandson studies, will be in charge of the exhibit. I've agreed you can go as long as you're under his supervision. I think they'll pay you about a dollar a day and let you sell your pictures and tracks on paper and all the other things you make. McCowan says you can keep the money you make. What do you say? Are you interested in going?"

I stared out over the prairie and thought about how I had enjoyed the things I had learned at the fairs at Omaha and Buffalo, and taking White Eye money for things I would have thrown away. I said, "Yes, I'll go, but I can't go to the fair as long as Zi-yeh lives, even if Eva is with her. If I do go, perhaps this man McCowan will let my grandson, Thomas Dahkeya, now at Chilocco, come with me to help with what I sell."

Captain Sayre smiled. "Mr. McCowan has already said he planned to have the students from Chilocco there. I'm sure he'll be happy for Thomas to help you. We're talking about the group from Fort Sill leaving in about two moons. If Zi-yeh . . . no longer needs you, then we'll all leave together. If you need to stay, then come when you can."

"Hmmph. Captain Sayre is a fair man. I come when I can."

He nodded. "*Enjuh.* I'll tell Mr. McCowan you'll come. He'll be sure there are places for you to live and from which to sell your things. I have to get on back to the command post. Much business to take care of there."

We stood up together. He held out his hand, and I gave it two solid pumps. He said, "We'll talk again when I know more. I hope Zi-yeh feels better soon."

I nodded, but I knew Zi-yeh would be lucky to last another moon.

I borrowed the mule the Chiricahuas shared to plow my land for my next melon and pumpkin crop. The soil, a reddish brown, had always produced good crops for my family. I was halfway through with my plowing on a day when Eva didn't have to go to the mission school, when I saw Eva appear in the breezeway and motion for me to come to her. I unhitched the plow and came running and leading the mule.

Her face filled with sadness, she called out to me, "Hurry, Father! My mother mounts the ghost pony."

I tied the mule to the house and went to kneel beside Zi-yeh's bed. Her breathing was labored, and her eyes, closed. I took her hand. Her eyes fluttered open, and she looked at me. "Husband, I go to the Happy Place. I trouble you no more." I was shaking my head when she closed her eyes and breathed her last.

Eva, standing behind me, whispered through her tears, "Goodbye, Mother. Safe journey. Your suffering, it is finished."

Zi-yeh had become a Christian at Mount Vernon Barracks and was a member of the

Catholic tribe. Captain Sayre sent a talking wire message to a Catholic *di-yen,* who came the next day. He made a ceremony for Zi-yeh at her grave in the Apache Cemetery near where many of the other Chiricahuas from the long-ago days were buried.

I looked around as he spoke. The place was a garden, growing wooden army grave-markers all around us, each the same size and shape. The markers had name tracks carved in them, so those who could read the tracks knew whose bones rested in that place for the times to come and for the memory of the ones left behind. After the *di-yen* spoke for Zi-yeh, they lowered her box into the ground.

I watched Zi-yeh's box disappear into the dark hole and wondered how long it would be before they lowered mine.

CHAPTER 37
THE SAINT LOUIS LOUISIANA PURCHASE EXPOSITION

About a moon before the Fort Sill Chiricahuas were supposed to go to the Saint Louis Fair, I was enjoying the sun and listening to the wind rustle through the bosque trees along Cache Creek and hearing the birds call in the prairie grass as I sat on the edge of my breezeway. A man in fine White Eye clothes came riding down the road to my village, crossed the creek, and, after looking at each house, headed for mine. He rode up to where I sat and said, "Howdy, I'm lookin' for Mister Geronimo."

"Why?"

The man grinned and said, " 'Cause I have business with him."

I studied the man for a short time. He looked harmless as most White Eyes do. "I Geronimo. Speak."

The man, who made no move to dismount, only nodded and said, "I thought I recognized you. I saw you in Buffalo at the world's fair and have seen your photographs a number of times. You planning to go to the world's fair in Saint Louis in about a month?"

"Hmmph. I go."

"Good. Good. I think you talked to Pawnee Bill about being in his Wild West Show after you were at the Buffalo Fair, and you said you'd do shows with him if the money was right and the army approved?"

I nodded. "Army say no to Pawnee Bill. I no go in his Wild West Show. He say he pay good money, say I can sell my pictures and other things to make more money. Army say no."

The man nodded as I spoke. He said, "Yes, sir, the army turned down his proposal. Now, with this fair in Saint Louis, the army probably won't say no. It's been proposed that all the Wild West shows do reenactments of the old days for the crowds, using the same Indians who were in the actual engagements. I'n tell ya, the army ain't said no yet. Naturally, Pawnee Bill would want Geronimo in his show. You still interested in doing it?"

"Maybe so. I be in McCowan show. He pay same to me he pay Quanah Parker — dollar a day — and I sell my pictures and other things. How much Pawnee Bill pay?"

The man grinned and reached inside his coat pocket to pull out two long *cigarros*. He reached down from his horse and gave me one. We lighted them and blew smoke to the four directions. Then we talked business.

He said, "Well, if Mr. McCowan is payin' you a dollar a day, that's about thirty dollars in a moon. Just like he told you in Buffalo, Pawnee Bill will pay you a hundred dollars a moon, plus money for your food and stabling your pony, 'cause he'll want you to ride for sure. He'll also let you sell and keep all the money you make for your pictures and things. What do you say?"

As a breeze rippled through the grass a few houses up the creek, small children laughed and played at hide and seek. I heard a horse nicker out in a nearby pasture and thought, *This is a good day. Soon I make much money.*

"For this money, I ride for Pawnee Bill when army say so."

The *cigarro* clamped in his teeth, the man said, "Pawnee Bill is looking forward to making some money with you, Geronimo. He'll let you know what we're gonna do as soon as the army says you can come."

I took a puff from the cigarro and nodded. *"Enjuh."*

He grinned and gave me a little two-finger White Eye salute off his white hat with a wide brim.

"*Adios,* Geronimo. I'll be talking to you again here pretty soon."

I nodded, and he rode off back down the road to Fort Sill.

Captain Sayre and McCowan made plans and met with the ones going to Saint Louis. They wanted to discuss how we would travel and what we would do at the fair in Saint Louis. Captain Sayre planned to send George Wratten with us to get us settled in, get us started in what we did, and show us how to get what we needed when we needed it before he returned to Fort Sill.

I said nothing about my talk with the man from Pawnee Bill, but I asked McCowan again how much we would be paid in a moon. When he said about thirty dollars, I said it ought to be one hundred dollars a moon. He just smiled and shook his head.

The day before the Fort Sill Chiricahuas were to leave for Saint Louis, the man from Pawnee Bill still had not told me their plans to use me in their Wild West Show. I knew if I went with the others, it was certain I couldn't make money with Pawnee Bill. Thus, at the last meeting that day with

Captain Sayre, I said, "Thirty dollars a month is not enough money. I want a hundred dollars a month, or I won't go to Saint Louis."

Sayre crossed his arms, stared at me, and shook his head. "Then, Geronimo, you're not going to Saint Louis. You agreed to thirty dollars a month like everyone else. If you go, that's what you'll be paid. There's no bargaining about the money you'll be paid."

The Chiricahuas going to Saint Louis left the next day to ride the iron wagon. I stayed at my house at Fort Sill. I worked in my squash, melon, and pumpkin patch and with my pony, because I knew he had to be in good shape and smart to be in Pawnee Bill's Wild West Show. I stayed close to my house, expecting the Pawnee Bill man to come soon, but I never saw him again.

A moon passed and Captain Sayre came riding to my breezeway again. He said, "Geronimo, we should talk."

"Come sit breezeway, Captain Sayre, it cool. Speak. I listen."

Sayre dismounted and tied his horse to the hitching rail by the house. Without a word, he sat next to me, pulled paper, made a cigarette, and we smoked to the four directions. He said, "I'm curious, and others are angry. Why did you suddenly demand more money before the rest went to Saint Louis?"

"Pawnee Bill man say he pay hundred dollars a moon for me in his Wild West Show at Saint Louis. Why not make more than McCowan offers? I go as soon as Pawnee Bill man says the army lets me go."

Sayre pushed back his hat and squinted in the bright sunlight as he scratched his beard. He slowly shook his head. "It's like I told you before. The army isn't going to let you earn money from any commercial business like Pawnee Bill's Wild West Show. If you don't go to McCowan's exhibition, you're not going to Saint Louis, and any money you might have made with the pay and your other things will be gone."

I knew Captain Sayre spoke true. I had decided the same a week earlier after the Pawnee Bill man still had not come to speak to me. Sayre would know about army approval when the Pawnee Bill man would not. I was an old fool in more ways than one. I wanted to get on Sayre's good side before it cost me more.

I said, "Then I have made a bad mistake, Captain Sayre. If you let me go now, I'll do it without pay if I can sell my photos and my grandson can help me."

He crossed his arms and looked at me as he grinned. "You can go, Geronimo. I'll take you myself tomorrow. McCowan will pay you, too. We'll protect you from people like Pawnee Bill trying to make money off your name. People at the fair will be glad to see you. Be ready at dawn, and I'll come with a wagon for you and your trunk. I know it'll take you a while to get all your stuff together, so I'll head on back to my office. Glad we had this little talk."

"Hmmph. Glad, too, Captain Sayre. Ready at dawn."

The World's Fair Indian Exhibit in Saint Louis had a big building with a wide walkway down the middle. On one side were booths for Indians to do their work, and on the other side was a set of rooms for Indian children of different ages to show how they were taught in the schools. McCowan put me in a booth by myself between a booth of Pueblo women grinding corn and making bread and a booth of Pueblo pottery makers. In my booth, I had a table from which I could sell photographs with or without my name tracks, and I made bows and arrows on which, for extra money, I also made name tracks.

Indians who appeared in the exhibit lived in little villages of lodges like their native tribes once used. The Apaches used tipis, and McCowan had a nice one for Thomas and me. It was a big, white tipi, bigger than any I had owned when our people roamed free. Thomas lived in the tipi before I came. He was surprised when I ducked through the tipi door the first time, and a big smile spread across his face. We sat and talked for a time. He was anxious to help me in the booth and looked forward to getting out of the classroom where he had to sit until I came.

After I began working in my booth, more people began coming to the Indian Exhibit, and McCowan, who was angry when I wouldn't come without more money, now helped me make more money by sending my pictures and other things by messenger to people who couldn't come to the fair but wanted them anyway. Sometimes he took me or had someone else take me to see shows by tribes I had never heard of.

There were strange men with red caps and great curved knives in a made-up fight, who my escort called "Turks," and he called their knives "scimitars." I could see that, even though they were just playing at fighting, they would be hard to kill in a hand-to-hand fight.

One time the people with me took me into a little house that had four windows, and we all sat down. We waited, and soon our little house went high in the air, and the people down on the fairgrounds looked no bigger than ants. One of the officers with me gave me his glasses (I often had such things I took from dead officers in Mexico and other places), and I could see the big river, brown and covered with boats, and even lakes and mountains far away. I looked in the sky but saw no stars. I finally put the glasses down, and as they were all laughing at me, I began to laugh, too. Back on the ground, we watched many of these little houses going up and coming down, but I didn't understand how they traveled.

Thomas and I lived this way for a moon. One morning, I began my work in the booth early. There were arrows I needed to finish to go with a bow McCowan was sending by the messenger named Mail, who would leave soon. I was looking down the shaft to judge its straightness when a shadow grew on the wall. Someone stood at the entrance to my booth. I turned to tell them to go away for a while, that I was busy, but what filled my eyes was not a fair visitor but a beautiful, slender Apache girl in a fine, fringed buckskin gown.

I smiled and nodded at her. I said, "I see you. Now I work. Soon we talk?"

She was about Eva's age, maybe two or three harvests older, and she looked familiar, like someone I had known in the long-ago times. I hated growing old and losing my memory. I should have died fighting a long time ago.

The young woman smiled, squared her shoulders, stood straight, and said, "Good. I can wait. I want to watch you work."

CHAPTER 38
LENNA

I finished my arrows, humming my riding tune, while the young woman, smiling and waiting patiently, watched me trim the fletching and put a final smoothing on the shafts near where the head should be if I had put one there. As I worked, I tried to remember where I might have seen her before, but my mind was a dry well.

Thomas hurried into the booth, smiled at the young woman, and then said, "Are you ready for the messenger? Mr. McCowan says the one who ordered the bow is anxious to have it."

I gave the bow and arrows a final look and nodded. "Ready. Take them."

"I'm on the way. Be back soon. Can I bring you coffee?"

I nodded. "Coffee is good. Maybe the young woman here would like some?"

She smiled and said, "Yes, thank you for bringing it."

415

A pretty girl being pleasant and gracious with him made Thomas stick out his chin and nod in pride as he went out the booth gate.

As Thomas disappeared in the shadows down the walkway, I said, "I am Geronimo, and here is where I make my bows and arrows for the White Eyes and sell my pictures and signed name. You look familiar, but my memory is bad now. Where have I seen you before?"

She sighed, looked at the floor, folded her hands together like the Christians do when they pray, and held them in front of her chest, upon which the strings of little blue stone beads hanging from her neck lay. I could see the smile playing at the edge of her lips as she said, "I didn't look like this fifteen harvests ago, Father. Perhaps I remind you of my mother."

I stared at the past, now come to take me, and heard the wind fly from my lungs as memories of a young Mescalero woman I had taken and later divorced to save her and our child from White Eye disease and Blue Coat treachery flew about in my mind.

"Lenna! Can it be you? Grown to womanhood already? You make an old man very happy to see you."

"Yes, Father, Lenna. I've longed to see

416

you since I was a young girl and my mother told us of your many battles with the Mexicans and White Eyes. Now the White Eyes want you at all their fairs and parades. Everywhere White Eyes and Indians know and respect you. I've always been proud to be your daughter."

I hugged her. She smelled of desert flowers, good and clean, and her buckskin was as soft as cloth. I sat down on a box holding some of my supplies and motioned for her to sit on another near me. "You've grown to be a beautiful young woman. I'm very proud of you. Have you been to White Eye school? Can you read their tracks and make them on paper? Have you taken a man?"

She shook her head. "I haven't taken a man, but there's one I want. He's a good man. I still go to the White Eye school in Mescalero. Maybe I go one more year before I marry. Yes, I can read and make White Eye tracks on paper. I know some of their secrets, but there is much to learn."

I could hear the distant echoes of the Indian hall beginning to fill with visitors in its cool air and shadows, and saw sparrows leaving their nests high in the rafters to get out the great doors to the hall. The day looked and sounded like all the others at the fair, but to me it was an especially good one.

"Tell me of your mother. I never saw or heard from Ih-tedda after she left Mount Vernon with you. I've often wished to see her again. It was hard to send you back to Mescalero, but I knew if I didn't, you would die from some White Eye disease, or the army might decide to execute us all."

"Mother is well, but she's no longer known as Ih-tedda. A few days after she came back, grandfather married her off to a retired scout, Old Cross Eyes. He named her Katie Cross Eyes, and he took the name Old Boy."

I knew Ih-tedda's father was right to marry her off quick and save her reputation, and it was hard to find a husband for a divorced woman. Still, I hated to think another man had Ih-tedda and this beautiful young woman to look after his house. I sighed and shook my head a little. Lenna must have seen me and shrugged her shoulders.

"Wait, Father, there's more. Ih-tedda had a baby, a little boy, seven months after Old Boy took her. She registered him with the Mescalero agent as Robert Cross Eyes. Old Boy walked around with his chest out for months, telling the young men they'd better hope they were as strong and productive as he was when they were his age."

I didn't know what to think. All these years, and I had never heard of Robert. "Are you sure Robert was born seven months after she was given to Old Boy?"

Lenna nodded and leaned into me. "Yes, Father, I'm sure. Robert wants the famous Geronimo to be his father and begs Mother to tell him the truth, but she insists that he is Old Boy's son."

"Well, he might be my son. Was he a big baby when he was born?"

"Yes. Grandmother told me he was a big baby, but Katie just looks away and says nothing."

"Hmmph. Maybe someday I meet your brother. Then I know if he is my son."

Thomas, smiling and nodding to people walking down the middle of the exhibit hall to see the now open booths, came carrying a jug of coffee like we usually had, and he had an extra cup for Lenna. He pulled our cups out of a box where we kept them and poured us all a cup before pulling up a box and sitting down with us. The number of White Eyes on the walkway increased, and a few paused at my booth's gate, saw we were talking, and moved on to visit the Pueblo booths on either side of mine.

I nodded at Thomas and said to Lenna, "Thomas is my grandson. He lives with me at Fort Sill when he isn't at McCowan's school at Chilocco. His mother was my daughter Dohn-say, whose mother was Chee-hash-kish, stolen by the Mexicans many harvests ago. Dohn-say was at Fort Marion in Florida when you were a baby there with your mother, but I know you're far too young to remember her."

I lifted my hand toward Lenna and said to Thomas, "Lenna is the daughter of Ih-tedda, my Mescalero wife. I sent her back to her father in New Mexico to escape Blue Coat captivity. Lenna is your aunt."

Thomas's mouth dropped, and his brows rose. He said, "I've heard of her mother and her little girl. It makes my heart glad to see you."

Lenna nodded and smiled. "Ho, Nephew! At last, we meet. I'm proud to see a grandson of my father."

A small crowd started to gather around my booth gate, and there were White Eyes pointing at pictures and bows around my table. Time to make money.

I said, "Lenna, why don't you stay with Thomas and me in the tipi we have? It's the big one with the red blanket door among the Fort Sill tipis. There's plenty of room. I

420

don't think McCowan will care. The White Eyes are anxious to give me their money. Now we must entertain them."

Lenna shrugged. "I much want to speak with you and Thomas some more. If my sponsors and the Mescaleros agree, I will come. Now I get out of the way. My heart is full from seeing you again, Father, and meeting Thomas." She, with poise and grace, arose from her seat, and the crowd parted for her as she left the booth. My heart was happy to know I had such a daughter.

McCowan told us to sort out where Lenna would stay with the Mescaleros. The Mescaleros were glad to say they had one of their own, a daughter of Geronimo, staying in his tipi. Part of her time, Lenna passed out pictures in the New Mexico building, showing the White Eyes the land was a good place to visit. I noticed when I first saw her that her eyes looked a little red and swollen, and in a few days they were worse, so bad she had to spend most of the time resting in the tipi and applying medicine to them a White Eye *di-yen* gave her.

Still, even with her sore eyes, we spent many good evenings together learning about our lives since she and Ih-tedda had returned to Mescalero. She told me of her young man, a Lipan named Juan Via, who was quietly courting her and that she expected to marry him as soon as she completed her last months in the school at Mescalero.

She bowed her head, as though embarrassed, and told me she had joined the Catholic tribe of Christians at Mescalero. I laughed and told her that I was a Christian now in the same church with Naiche and others at Fort Sill, and that I thought my life was better because of it, but following the church's rules was hard, and I had much to learn. She said she was glad I followed the Jesus road and wished I could meet her *di-yen.* She called him Father Migeon.

I told Lenna about her sister Eva, who was also in the Catholic tribe, and was at Fort Sill staying with Daklugie and his wife, Ramona, while I was at the fair. Eva had worked hard to look after her mother, Zi-yeh, before Zi-yeh rode the ghost pony to the place the White Eyes called heaven. Lenna said she had dim memories of Zi-yeh and how she had been kind to her.

Lenna asked if Eva had her eye on a young man yet. I laughed and said many young men often rode slowly by my house. Some even offered to help me in my squash and pumpkin patch. But Eva had not yet had her womanhood ceremony, so young men courting her was not now serious. I planned to give Eva a great feast and celebration and invite all the Indians in and around Fort Sill after her womanhood ceremony. I was sure there would be many more who would want her. I didn't tell Lenna that I didn't want Eva to marry and that she wouldn't, either. I had trained her to obey. Women in my family had a hard time at childbirth, and marriage was dangerous for them. I had divorced Lenna's mother to save them from the Blue Coats and disease. Now I had no say in what Lenna should do, but with Eva I did.

After two moons, Lenna and Thomas left the fair to return to their schools. I was lonely without them and wanted to see Eva. I asked McCowan to return to Fort Sill for a moon, but he said for me to work at the exhibit for a moon, and then I could return to Fort Sill. He promised to send me back by way of Chilocco, so I could visit with Thomas and stay there as long as I liked before going on to Fort Sill. McCowan and I had become friends. Lenna promised to keep me informed about her life, that of Ih-tedda, and especially Robert, who I wanted to meet.

I told Daklugie what Lenna had said about Robert. Since he knew how to ask about checking on birth records at Mescalero, he wrote to ask the agent. The messenger tracks he received made certain everything Lenna had told me. Robert Cross Eyes had been born in August 1889. Ih-tedda and Lenna had left Mount Vernon Barracks in the Season of Ghost Face. The White Eyes said that was early in the month of February in 1889. Ih-tedda and I had been together many times before she left. I knew Robert could be my son.

Chapter 39
Lieutenant Purington

I stopped at the Chilocco Indian Boarding School to visit with Thomas on my way back to Fort Sill. The land was flat and near a brown river, and the wind blew all the time. The buildings were big, made of gray stones stacked high. As at the other White Eye schools for Indians, the children had to wear clothes so they looked the same, and the boys had to have White Eye haircuts. Thomas told me he was learning much and thought he would be satisfied staying there.

We walked together to see the school buildings and how the White Eyes taught the children there. I had learned much watching the classes in the Indian Exhibit during the trip to the Saint Louis fair. Now Chilocco School promised to show us more secrets of the White Eyes. I told Thomas to learn as many White Eye secrets as he could, and perhaps Ussen or the White Eye God would give him Power to become a strong leader for his people. I had much hope that Thomas would be my legacy to the Chiricahuas. After a few suns, I left Chilocco and went on to Fort Sill.

It was good to see my daughter Eva, who came home from school every day to help me. She was growing into a fine young woman, and I knew that soon I must have a big feast and dance to celebrate her womanhood ceremony. I wished Zi-yeh were still with us and strong. She would have been very proud, as I was, of our fine daughter.

I had missed helping with much of the harvest, but I had made much money selling my photographs with my name tracks on them and on my bows and arrows. Eva and I would have enough to eat in the coming Ghost Face and Season of Little Eagles.

The sky was gray and overcast, and there was a feel of snow coming in the winds rolling across the plains into our village. I rode my pony to George Wratten's store to buy a few things Eva and I needed and to catch up on new stories told about the people. When I walked through the door, the warm air from the stove in the middle of the room and the smell of good things on the shelves and in barrels greeted me. Wratten saw me come in and waved me over to speak with him.

Wratten said, "Ho, Geronimo! It's good I see you. Lieutenant Purington wants to see you."

"I do nothing. Why does he want to see me?" I had not yet met *Teniente* Purington since he had replaced Captain Sayre while I was at the Saint Louis fair. I didn't think this was a good sign. Maybe the army chiefs had decided to shoot me. I thought about leaving.

Wratten shrugged his shoulders and said, "Not sure, but I think it may be about riding in some big parade in the Season of Many Leaves. Go see him. I'll go with you, if you like."

Wratten and I had our differences, but he was always willing to help the People. "Hmmph. *Enjuh.* When we go?"

"I think he's in his office now. Let me get Eugene Chihuahua to look after the counters and customers up front, and we'll head out."

Teniente Purington waved Wratten and me through the open door of his workplace in the big Fort Sill building where the Blue Coat chiefs like to stay. We pumped hands as White Eyes do when they meet, and then he motioned to chairs in front of his desk as he sank into a big one he used for working and sitting at the desk. He put his feet up, made a tent with his fingers, and grinned like a coyote waiting at a rabbit hole.

We all sat and stared at each other for a couple of breaths before Purington said, "George, I appreciate you coming over with Geronimo. I have an important invitation for him, and I want to be sure he understands its importance."

I understood most of what Purington said, and Wratten knew that, but he nodded and played the game. "Yes, sir, I understand. I'm happy to interpret for you. What do you need to tell Geronimo?"

Teniente Purington's lips curled in an arrogant smile to show his teeth under the big bush of hair under his nose. I already didn't like Purington, and I could tell he didn't like me. *Enjuh.* We would start in the same place. Purington wouldn't even look at me, but looked up at the ceiling.

"Tell Geronimo that the new President, I believe the Chiricahuas call him the 'Great Father,' is Mr. Theodore Roosevelt. Mr. Woodworth Clum is helping to organize the big inaugural parade in Washington, D.C., on March fourth of next year. Mr. Clum has informed me the president wants to show how the Indians are acquiring civilization with the government's help. The plan is to have six wild Indians of the old order riding their horses come first, followed by students from Carlisle Indian School. Among the old order Indians, the president wants, among others, Quanah Parker from the Comanches, American Horse from the Oglala Sioux, and of course," he said, raising his hands up prayerfully toward the ceiling and laughing, "the great warrior Geronimo from the Chiricahua Apaches, if he will go."

Wratten understood our tongue better than any White Eye I had ever known, and he could interpret almost as fast as he heard the speaker. I often thought his ability to interpret was a gift from Ussen to our people. As soon as I understood what *Teniente* Purington was asking, I wanted to smile, but I kept my face straight. I thought, *So I ride in a parade for the Great Father. Perhaps I can speak to him, convince him to let me and my people go back to the land of our fathers. We've learned to make war no more. We cause the Great Father no trouble.*

It was like awakening from a dream as I heard Wratten say to me, "What the *teniente* offers is a great honor, Geronimo. You'll ride with five other famous chiefs, including your friend Quanah Parker. What do you say?"

I stared at them with my arms crossed and my face straight. "How much does the Great Father pay for my ride in parade? I want my nephew Daklugie to go as my *segundo,* my number two, and you, Wratten. I want you to go also so I can speak my best to the Great Father, if he will hear me."

Teniente Purington frowned when Wratten told him what I said. He said under his breath, "Damned impudent Apache. Beaten into the dust and still he speaks like he owns the world." Purington stared at me as he learned back in his chair and ran the fingers of his left hand over the sides of his face. I stared back and didn't blink.

Teniente Purington leaned forward, resting his elbows on his desk. "All right. I was going to ask you to go with him, Mr. Wratten, and if you will, I would be most appreciative. I'll send Daklugie also. He's a leader, manages the cattle herd well, and he needs to see this parade. The government will pay all your transportation costs, including those for the horses to be ridden in the parade, meals, a place to sleep, and pay, as he was at other major events, one dollar a day. What does Mr. Geronimo say to that?"

When Wratten finished interpreting, I nodded and said only, *"Enjuh."*

Purington said to Wratten, "Of course, the army will pay your travel expenses, too, plus a little extra for you to coordinate shipping and for looking after Geronimo and Daklugie. Is this acceptable to you, Mr. Wratten?"

Wratten glanced at me, nodded, and said, "Yes, sir. I'm glad to help in any way I can. It'll be a pleasure to watch Mr. Roosevelt's parade. I think he's been a good president so far."

Purington stood up from his desk and stuck out his hand as he said, "The army appreciates your service. I'll let you know as I learn more about arrangements and schedules." He gave Wratten's hand a good pump, and when it was my turn, I again pumped Purington's hand twice.

Wratten and I talked about the trip on the way back to the store and what had to be done to get ready. He thought the trip would take fourteen or fifteen suns, and we would need to be ready with our ponies five or six suns before we left. I tried to remember what I had at home in my box of things to make war caps and medicine hats.

For the Great Father, I would make a fine bonnet to wear with many eagle feathers. There was much to be done to get ready for the big parade and many plans to be made, but even as I thought of these, my mind made the words I would give to the Great Father asking him to send us back to the land of our fathers.

Chapter 40
Great Father Roosevelt

The medicine hat I made for the Great Father's parade was a fine one. It was made of goatskin that fit tight on my head. It had the white breast feathers of the eagle so that they stood up on the ridge of the crown, and there were symbols I fixed or painted on it, and no one but I knew what they meant. Two long pieces of buckskin attached to the crown reached below my knees (when I was mounted, they reached below the stirrups of my pony). On these strips, I placed many eagle plumes and fine colored cloth. We also mounted silver and beads on the horse's bridle and leather.

Eva stayed with Daklugie's wife while Daklugie, Wratten, and I went to see the Great Father. Ramona and Eva made sure our best buckskin suits and moccasins had perfect beadwork, and we packed them with our medicine hats. The day before we left,

Wratten went with me to see *Teniente* Purington.

Teniente Purington looked like Coyote, grinning at us with clenched teeth. He said to Wratten, "Well, boys, you leave in the morning. I assume you're already to go with your horses and packed trunks."

Wratten and I both nodded. Wratten said, "Yes, sir. Plans and schedules are made, trunks are packed, and horses and their gear are ready to go."

Purington picked up a small piece of paper. He handed the paper to me and said to Wratten, "This is a check made out to you, Geronimo. You can get cash for it at the bank in Lawton. It's for all of your travel expenses, including the shipping of your horse to Washington." Speaking straight to Wratten, *Teniente* Purington said as he shrugged his shoulders and his Coyote grin got bigger, "This is all the money he gets. If he runs short of money, then he'll just have to walk or starve. Does he understand this?"

Wratten looked at me, spoke as an interpreter, but winked with the eye Purington couldn't see, and I nodded. "Yes sir, he understands. That's all the money he will get."

Purington grinned again. "Good, good, good. I hope he spends it wisely and doesn't run short. Gentlemen, I hope you have a fine trip." Then he laughed aloud and said, "Please give my congratulations to the president." I saw nothing at which to laugh at in what Purington said, but Wratten made a big smile and saluted, and we left for the bank in Lawton.

Wratten had taught me that the best place to save money was in a bank. With money I had collected by going to the world fairs and selling my pictures and name tracks, I had more money than I had ever had before.

At the bank, Wratten started to take all the money the check said to give, but I said, "No, save most. I make more on train and at parade."

He smiled and nodded. "Okay, how much do you want to take with you?"

I held up a finger. "One dollar."

Wratten laughed and nodded. He put all the money from the check in the bank, except for one dollar that he folded and slid into my shirt pocket.

The next morning, Wratten, Daklugie, and I boarded the iron wagons at Lawton and rode north. After a while, the iron wagon turned toward the rising sun. The White Eyes seemed anxious to see me and pay for my name tracks. Strange people, the White

Eyes are.

I made much money selling my tracks and my pictures to White Eyes when the train stopped at stations, and they crowded up to my window to stare at me like I was some animal they had never seen before. I didn't care. I took their money and laughed at them to myself.

At one station, we had to go to a different line of iron wagons than the one on which we rode. Wratten had a hard time getting me though the crowd, and the iron wagon we were supposed to be on nearly left without us, but I sold many pictures with my name tracks, and even buttons off my shirt. I sewed new ones back on between stops.

The iron wagon first took us to meet the other chiefs who had gathered at the school Daklugie had attended. There we practiced riding in front of other Indians and the Indian students, who marched like Blue Coats, playing drums, flutes, and other instruments. We took a day or two to learn how fast to ride our ponies. Later, Daklugie showed us around the school and a farm where he had worked and learned much about cattle. Then they loaded us all on an iron wagon that carried us to Washington, the place of the Great Father's parade.

On the morning of the parade, it rained, but then it stopped, leaving fine, thin water smoke hiding the streets and buildings. I had planned to ride as I had when I made war, wearing a breechcloth and showing respect to the Great Father by wearing my best belt, medicine hat, and moccasins. However, an old man can suffer much in the cold air and wind. I decided it would be better to wear a shirt, vest, and jacket, and even then keep a blanket over my clothes.

Daklugie brought our horses around, and we mounted and rode with the other chiefs to our place in the parade line. After a while, as the water smoke slowly vanished in the sunlight, there was a big ceremony for the Great Father in front of the great house where the subchiefs held council.

The Great Father ended the ceremony with a talk of many words, and when he was finished, there was much music played and many drums beaten. Then the Great Father mounted in a big, black, iron wagon that didn't need an iron road, and he rode forward to lead us past the unending numbers of White Eyes, who waved their hats, threw them up in the air, and made yells of joy for him saying, "Hooray for Teddy Roosevelt," and "Public hero number one."

They grew quiet as the army band and their instruments went past.

Behind the band, the five chiefs and I passed. Again, the White Eyes made whistles, waved their hats, and yelled, "Hooray for Geronimo!" Some yelled "Public hero number two!" Some even left their seats to watch the parade and ran along the side of the road yelling, "Hooray for Geronimo," holding their arms high and shaking their fists.

I thought they might be trying to take me, and I saw no soldiers to protect us. I was ready to ride off if they did, but none came into the street where we were, so I kept riding. Wratten told me after the parade that the White Eyes left their seats, for which they had paid much money, to run alongside us because they wanted to see me, and that next to the Great Father, I was the most popular man in the parade.

The White Eyes are strange people. A few harvests earlier, they would have been happy to see me dragged through the streets. I wished I could have brought more of my pictures to sell. I could have made much more money. I bought a trunk to bring back new clothes and gifts for Eva, paid all the costs that were demanded of me, and still had much money to put with the hundred and seventy dollars Purington gave me.

In the three days after the parade, the White Eye chiefs showed us the great stone buildings for their councils. We saw monuments to their great men, including the great stone spike pointing high into the sky and named for the first Great Father, and *casas* holding their treasures from their long-ago times.

On the fourth day, we saw the Great Father and spoke to him in private council. It was a time for which I had waited for many harvests, and I had thought often and long about what I might say to convince the Great Father to let me and my people return to the place of my birth, the great canyon from which came the waters of the Gila River, there to live in peace undisturbed by the White Eyes. The other chiefs, too, had requests of the Great Father. My friend Quanah Parker wanted to ask for pardons so some of his friends could work in the councils. We all were ready when he sat down with us to listen to what we had to say. Wratten was with me. I knew he would say what I wanted in the best way to the Great Father.

My hopes were high when I pumped his offered hand, and he said, "Delighted! Tell me what I can do for you and your people."

439

I didn't hesitate to answer him.

"Great Father, I look to you as I look to God. When I see your face, I think I see the face of the Great Spirit. I come here to pray you to be good to my people and me. I fought for many harvests to protect my homeland. Did I fear the Great White Chief? No. He was my enemy and the enemy of my people. His people desired the country of my people. I wouldn't let them have it without shedding much blood and giving many lives.

"My heart was strong against the Great White Chief. I said that he should never have my country. I defied the Great White Chief, for in those days, I was a fool. I had a bad heart and was ready to kill all who came close to my land or crossed my trail. I ask you to think of me as I was then. I lived in the home of my people. They trusted me. It was right that I should give them my strength and wisdom.

"When the soldiers of the Great White Chief drove me and my people from our home, we went to the mountains. When they followed us, we slew all we could. We said we wouldn't be captured. No. We starved, but we killed. I said we would never yield, for I was a fool.

"So I was punished, and all my people

were punished with me. The white soldiers took me and made me a prisoner far from my own country. My people have died from many diseases in this far country. They were kept in places where they couldn't see the mountains and under big, tall trees where they couldn't see the sun. Many die even now that we live in the land of the Comanche, Kiowa, and Kiowa–Apaches. Fort Sill is a much better place than the first three places, but still we die.

"Great Father, other Indians have homes where they can live and be happy. My people and I have no homes. The land where we are kept is bad for us. We grow sick there and die. White men are in the country that was my home. I pray you to tell them to go away and let my people go there and be happy.

"Great Father, my hands are tied as with a rope. My heart is no longer bad. I'll tell my people to obey no chief but the Great White Chief. I pray you to cut the ropes and make me free. Let me die in my own country, an old man who has been punished enough and is free."

I had said all I knew to say to the Great Father. He studied my face for a few breaths. His eyes were kind and easy to see through the spectacles hanging on the bridge of his nose. He said, "Geronimo, I have no anger in my heart against you. I even wish it were only a question of letting you return to your country as a free man. But there is much hatred against you from the white people who live there now. If you went back to your country, they would want to kill you for your past crimes against them. You would have to fight them to save your lives. I would have to interfere between you. There would be more war and bloodshed. This hasn't happened for many years. Your people are few, and many of them would die unjustly if this happened. It's best for you to stay where you are. I'm sad to say this. I understand why you want to go to your homeland. I'll confer with the commissioner of Indian affairs and the secretary of war about your case, but I don't think I can hold out any hope for you. That is all I can say, Geronimo, except that I'm sorry and have no feeling against you."

As I stared at him while Wratten spoke his words to me, my heart fell as a flat stone slowly turning, falling, falling in a deep pool of black water. I thought, *Someday, someday, Great Father, you'll let my people go.*

CHAPTER 41
EVA'S WOMANHOOD CEREMONY

After I spoke to the Great Father about the freedom of the People, I knew I would die a prisoner. I decided to keep asking to return to my own land until I could ask no more. I didn't sleep good for a long time after we returned from the Great Father's parade, and I sometimes gambled and drank when I thought no one, especially from the church, watched.

Three moons after we returned, Purington sent me to a show for a special day at the 101 Ranch for men who worked for newspapers. There were many there, some said sixty-five thousand. Whatever the number was, it was not as many as watched the Great Father's parade, and they all sat in one place.

There were iron wagons at the 101 Ranch like I had seen at the Great Father's parade. These wagons didn't run on an iron road, and they had demons growling in metal boxes that somehow made them go. We had been taught about hell in church, and I thought, *The White Eyes must go to hell often to take prisoner the demons they use to make the iron wagons move.*

I had my picture taken in one of those iron wagons. I wore a top hat like Chihuahua had at Mount Vernon, and I sat like I was driving the other war chiefs sitting in seats around me. The White Eyes thought it was funny for Geronimo to be wearing a top hat and driving what the cowboys called the Locomobile. Many pictures were taken of us in the Locomobile. My friend Edward Le Clair, a Ponca Indian, sat next to me in the Locomobile and wore an exquisite beaded vest and headdress. The vest used fine buckskin for its base, and it had many clever patterns of colored beads against white ones sewed on it. I told him how magnificent I thought his vest looked, and before the end of the day, he gave it to me. It became one of my favorite things to wear on special occasions. I was glad I went to the 101 Ranch.

In the last harvest, before I had gone to the Saint Louis Exposition, I had become friends with Stephen Barrett, chief of the schools where the White Eyes living near Lawton and Fort Sill sent their children.

One day, he helped me interpret my Spanish into an understandable White Eye tongue when I was trying to sell one of my war bonnets to an Anglo visitor. We became passing friends, but later I learned Barrett had been wounded by a Mexican and realized we had much in common, for my body carried many scars from Mexican bullets.

After that, I went to his house one day, and we spent a long time in the shade drinking cold, sweet and sour juice he called lemonade. I liked the lemonade, but it was not as good as whiskey. I told him some of my stories about fighting and killing Mexicans. Then we visited several times, he to my house, and I to his, telling many stories.

After I returned from the 101 Ranch, Barrett brought a friend of his to visit at my house. His friend, an old, white-haired, Anglo man named Greenwood, was a chief of schools in Kansas City, a place where many iron wagons stopped. Out of respect, I treated Greenwood as formally as I would any chief I didn't know. He told me he and General Howard were friends and that Howard had spoken of me to him.

It was good to know someone who knew General Howard. Howard was a good man. He gave Cochise the reservation and agent he wanted, until the chiefs in Washington decided the people of Cochise couldn't have their mountains and land anymore and gave them to the White Eye settlers, after making the Cochise People move to San Carlos, but Juh and I got away and left for Mexico. *Greenwood, I thought, must be my friend and not just a chief if he knows General Howard.*

I invited Barrett and Greenwood to sit in the shade while I cut a watermelon I had cooled in a nearby spring. We ate big chunks of melon and had a good visit, with Greenwood telling me about his friend General Howard. When we finished, I told Barrett and Greenwood to come anytime they could. I would be glad to see them.

Soon after Greenwood left, Barrett came to visit. I liked Barrett. He spoke straight, and he was a good marksman. He could hit targets about as well as I could. Again, we ate cool watermelon, and he asked if he could write and publish some of the stories I had told him since we had started visiting. I knew I had to be careful with these stories. The stories I had told him might give other White Eyes an excuse for punishing the Chiricahuas further. After I thought about it, I said to Barrett, "No, you must not use the stories I've told you. There are Mexicans and White Eyes who would use them to further punish us. I have to be careful. But I like you. I have a better way. You write what I tell you, and I'll tell you the story of my life, if you pay me and if the army officers in charge of us don't object. You get their permission and an interpreter, and I'll tell you the entire story of my life. Yes, we can make much money."

Barrett thought this was a fine idea and went to Purington to ask permission to write my life story as I told it to him. He told me later that Purington made a frown that looked like a black thundercloud and said, "No! You can't do that. Geronimo has killed many people and destroyed much property, and the army has spent much time and money taking him prisoner. He ought to be hung rather than making money off the story of his murders. Go away and forget about writing Geronimo's stories."

However, I had told Barrett about talking to the Great Father after riding in his parade. He knew the Great Father could tell the army what to do and that he would remember me. Barrett sent the Great Father tracks on paper asking to let me tell him my story and sell the tracks on paper. The Great Father sent tracks on a paper that agreed I could tell my story to Barrett. In a few days,

Purington told Barrett the Great Father had granted permission for me to tell my story and for him to come to Fort Sill for instructions on how the army would approve what Barrett wrote.

I spent much time deciding what to tell and how to tell it. I knew there were many lives at stake. My words had to be written exactly as I told them to a trusted interpreter, or the law might come after my brothers and me, or some brother might kill Barrett, thinking Barrett was trying to get him in trouble. As long as it was clear the words were mine, there would be no danger to Barrett or me. I told Barrett he could take notes, but that he must write what I spoke. If he had questions, then I would answer them later with the questions and answers in the Apache tongue, and he must use an interpreter I trusted. I suggested Daklugie, and Barrett was happy to use him when he agreed to help us.

Late one sun in the Season of Large Leaves, I sat in my breezeway with Eva as we watched the sun disappear and listened to the calls of the *googés* (whip-poor-wills) in the brush by Cache Creek. I was thinking about what I would tell Barrett.

Eva was working on a piece of beadwork.

448

Soon she would have to get a lantern to do more work as the smooth night settled in on us. I heard boards creak in the breezeway behind us. I was getting too old to live. In earlier days, I would have known someone was there before I heard the creaks. I looked over my shoulder and saw the dark outline of a woman in a long dress. As she came out of the dark shadows, I recognized Ramona, wife of my nephew Daklugie.

"Ho, Ramona. I see you. Come sit with us and enjoy the night."

"Ho, Grandfather. I can't stay long. My husband wants to sleep, and the children play around the house. I have good news for you."

"Hi yi! I always like good news. Tell me!"

"During your last trip, Eva's womanhood came. Now we must do her ceremony, and I've heard you say you planned to have a big feast with singing and dancing to celebrate it. Have my ears heard these stories correctly?"

I turned and looked at Eva, who sat shyly looking into the dark with a hint of a smile at the corners of her mouth. I laughed in my pleasure. At last my little daughter had become a woman, ready to take a man and give us children and grandchildren, but like shadows from dark clouds drifting across the desert, the memories of the hard times the women in my family had when having babies passed through my mind. I wouldn't let them shadow this happy time and put them aside.

"Yes, Ramona, you have good ears, and Daughter, I'm very glad for you. At long last, you're a woman. We'll have a great feast with all our friends to dance and sing with us to celebrate this best of times. Ramona, since her mother has left us, will you serve as her attendant? How long before we should plan to hold the womanhood ceremony? What do you need me to do? Where —"

Ramona laughed. She held up her hands to stop me. "Yes, Grandfather, my sister Emily and I will be her attendants and guides. We've already talked about when we should hold the ceremony. Eva's mother had already begun helping her with her gown, and we worked more on it while you were at the Great Father's parade and at the 101 Ranch. There's much to prepare, but I think the ceremony and festivities could begin on the second full moon from now if you approve."

I looked at my young daughter, now a woman, smiling in joy at me. I remembered our days at Mount Vernon and how I used to pull her around the camp in a little red wagon and let her buy anything she wanted in the trader's store. I thought about all the hard work she had done, helping her mother before Zi-yeh had ridden the ghost pony, and what a help she had been to me since Zi-yeh had left us. I thought, *Maybe after this ceremony, I ought to get another woman.*

I said to Ramona, "We'll have the best of socials and dances to celebrate this great time. Invite all the Apaches to the festivities. My friend Quanah Parker and many Comanches and Kiowa will come. We have much work to do. Buy what you need, and I will pay."

Eva murmured, "Thank you, Father. You make me happy that I'm your daughter."

Ramona said, "*Enjuh!* This ceremony, feast, and social dancing will be a good time, Grandfather."

The next day I spoke with Naiche about the festivities and where to hold them. He was happy Eva had come to womanhood and offered to help in any way he could. Near Naiche's village, we picked out a level place on the south side of Medicine Bluff Creek, where we could cut the grass close in a big circle.

For Eva's ceremony, Naiche agreed to

lead the singing, and I would lead the dancing with the *di-yens* conducting the ceremony. Women from every Apache village helped with the cooking. I told all the village chiefs to tell their people they were invited. The ceremony would begin the night of the first full moon in the time the White Eyes called September 13, 1905. I visited my friend Quanah Parker and invited him and our Comanche and Kiowa friends, and I even asked my friend Barrett to come. I planned to start the story of my life I promised to give Barrett in the next moon after Eva's ceremony.

Ramona and her sister Emily would help and guide Eva through the ceremony. Emily, a few months older than Eva, had married a few moons before we began planning the great social, and I learned later that she already carried a child in her belly. I decided to have photographs made before the ceremony so we could all remember the girl who became a woman. George Wratten knew a good photographer in Oklahoma City who agreed to come to Fort Sill and make the photographs. The one I wanted with Eva, Ramona, and me was not made. Ramona had a sick child then and could not leave her, so she asked Emily to stand in her place for the photographer, and so I had the picture done of Eva and Emily, a niece like Ramona, with me to remember the good time we would have.

Eva had a fine womanhood ceremony. Naiche knew just the best songs to lead in the singing, the *di-yens* with me leading the dancing, and Ramona and Emily guiding Eva in what she should do and how she should act were all signs of great Power present at the ceremony. The ceremony lasted four nights. Each night, the masked dancers came, and each night the people danced and had a fine feast. I was glad.

On the fourth night, when the ceremony finished and Eva was considered a marriageable woman, we danced all night. A big fire was built in center of the close-cut circle in the field, and as the moon rose, we all joined hands around the fire and danced in a circle with the masked dancers. Then there were dances of a circle within a circle, and as the fire died down, the men made their circle into wheel spokes that ran from the fire to the outer circle of women. Sometimes the spokes moved with the circle, sometimes against it, sometimes at the same speed, sometimes slower, depending on the songs that were sung.

As the moon reached the top of its arc

and began falling in the southwest, baskets of food were laid in a line out from the ceremonial place, and we all ate while the masked dancers completed their dances.

When the dance began again, the old ones left the dance to the young people to begin the lovers' dance. The drums stopped, and what the White Eyes called the flageolet music started. I have no such word as flageolet. It is just a flute the young men learn to play to sometimes court their women. It has many voices and can be made to sound soft or played very fast.

This night several were played together in good harmony and there were also one or two Apache fiddles to add their voices. The fiddle is made from a piece of dry yucca stalk. A string of horsetail hair was stretched over it and passed across a specially shaped sound hole. The instrument was played with a horsetail hair bow. As the fiddles and flutes played, they made a dreamy sound that seemed to touch the young people as the young men made a circle around the fire and the girls made an outer circle.

One after another, the girls would dance to the inner circle and pick a young man to dance with as they formed the spokes of a wheel, doing two steps forward and one back while the couples held hands and looked at each other. I saw Eva dancing with a young man with whom she looked pleased. He was taller than most boys his age, but he had big hands and a strong face. I didn't remember him ever riding past our house. She must have met him in mission school. I grew sad and realized that soon I must have a talk with her about marrying and how dangerous it would be for her. Eva had been taught to obey. I knew she would do what I told her.

As the sun began rising, the dancing stopped, and there was a final meal as the young men who had been picked by the girls to dance with them gave them presents, and a few announced they were ready to marry. Eva stood with her young man, her head bowed, but I saw her smiling and knew soon he would ask to speak with me.

The women began gathering what was left and making the ceremonial site clean again. Barrett mounted his pony, telling me how impressed he was with our ceremony and generosity. He thanked me for inviting him as I swung up on my pony, something I'd thought I might never be able to do again two harvests earlier.

As we rode toward the sun, Barrett said, "Geronimo, I think Eva is a beautiful young woman. There'll be many young men asking you for her."

I said, "Watching tonight, I think Eva may already have chosen her husband."

"Well, she's a little young to marry yet, I think. But good for her."

"Hmmph. Soon we know. Soon I have to decide."

As our ponies broke into a jog, I began singing my favorite riding song.

O, ha le
O, ha le
Through the air
I fly upon a cloud
Toward the sky, far, far, far,
O, ha le
O, ha le
There to find the holy place
Ah, now the change comes o'er me
O, ha le
O, ha le

CHAPTER 42
SUNS OF CHANGE

Less than a moon after Eva's womanhood ceremony, Barrett hired Daklugie to interpret my life story from Apache into the White Eye tongue. I wanted Barrett to use Daklugie as his interpreter, because Daklugie would know things I didn't know that the White Eyes would find unacceptable.

Our first meeting was one morning at my house in the Season of Earth Is Reddish Brown. Eva had already left early for the mission school. I expected we would sit around the table Eva and I used for eating while I talked and Barrett listened and wrote what Daklugie told him, but Barrett brought another man with him that day.

I said, "Who he? Why here?"

"Geronimo, this is Mr. James. He's a court stenographer and can make tracks on paper much faster than I can with my notes. I know you said to use no one else to write or hear your words, but I'm just too slow and will have to remember most of what you say. I might not get it right. Won't you reconsider and let me use Mr. James?"

I shook my head. "No speak. He go, or I go."

Barrett took James over in a corner, and they spoke in low voices until James nodded and left. Barrett turned to Daklugie and me. "Mr. James is gone. No others with us."

"*Enjuh.* Write what I have spoken, and do this without questions. Write only what you remember and without any other help. After I have spoken and you have made your tracks on paper, I'll come to any place you say, and listen in Apache to what you've written. Then I answer questions and maybe add any more to what I remember telling you.

"Each day I speak, I have in mind what I want to tell, and I tell it straight. I speak at any place I say — here, Daklugie's place, over yonder, out in the woods, or even riding horses across the plains. Understand?"

Barrett puckered his lips as if he wanted to whistle and nodded. "This I understand."

Daklugie couldn't understand why I wanted to tell my stories to a White Eye, rather than the way we had always done before — tell them over and over around the fire until the children could repeat them word for word. What Daklugie didn't understand was that I wanted our people, other Indians, and even White Eyes to understand our struggle for survival.

There were many things Daklugie and I had to consider when I told my story to Barrett or anyone else. First, we were prisoners of war, and we believed that a change in the army commander in charge of us might mean execution for everyone. None of us had a sense of security, so nothing could be said that might be incriminating and used against anyone. Second, we thought Barrett might be a spy trying to get information that couldn't be found by any other means. Third, we knew Barrett had problems getting government consent for the project and had to get approval from the Great Father, President Roosevelt. This might mean the government wanted me to admit something. This I would never do. I believed my Power would let me see what would happen in the future if I spoke in a certain way.

I motioned Barrett and Daklugie to sit at the table where I poured cups of coffee that I made from what Wratten sold at the agency store and then mixed with ground piñons. Then I sat down with them. "Now we start."

■ ■ ■ ■

Daklugie interpreted my stories as I told them to Barrett during the Seasons of Earth Is Reddish Brown and Ghost Face and into the Season of Little Eagles. Barrett often read back to me what he had written from our last meeting. Sometimes he forgot much, other times very little, but as long as he told the stories without making up lies to fill in what he forgot, I didn't object and neither did Daklugie. We discussed our comments in front of Barrett, since we were able to speak our minds in the Apache tongue without him knowing our thoughts.

I soon tired of these talking sessions and would have stopped, but I had given my word to Barrett to give him my life story, and so I did. After I finished in the Season of Little Eagles, Barrett spent much time organizing what I had spoken and rewriting his original words for the book he would give to the army to approve. Daklugie read what the army approved and told me there were many errors in this book, like Barrett saying I was a chief, when I was never a chief. These kinds of errors didn't hurt the People. I didn't care.

Even though Daklugie and I were very

careful not to endanger any of the People with my stories, there were some warriors, warriors who had fought by my side like Lot Eyelash, who believed I had betrayed them and started believing the lies Chatto and others told about me.

Early in the first suns of the Ghost Face during the time I told Barrett my story, I rode to George Wratten's trading post to buy *tobaho* and supplies for Eva to do her housework and cook. George was working behind his counter when I came in, but there were no other customers, not even one or two standing around his stove to get warm. He stopped to talk with me awhile, and we had a smoke and spoke openly as friends.

The door opened, and a rush of cold air blew past us. George nodded welcome to the three people who had come in and walked to the warm stove. They smiled and nodded back, a young man and woman and a woman old enough to be their mother. I especially liked the older woman, who looked very young in my old eyes. The older woman's eyes studied me, almost to the point of being rude and too forward for a woman, and a faint smile pulled at the corners of her mouth, but I didn't care. I hadn't had a woman in a long time, not since moons before Zi-yeh had ridden the ghost pony, and the staring woman stirred me. *Ha,* I thought, *maybe I haven't lost all my Power.*

The young man spoke to Wratten, motioned toward the women, and pointed at the one I liked. They spoke in the White Eye tongue too fast for me to follow, but I heard words like Mescalero Reservation, mother's uncle, and a moon's visit, while I continued to study the woman out of the corner of my eye, and she watched me with arms crossed. The young man thanked him and turned to leave.

Wratten, who had been watching the woman and me looking each other over, came around the corner of his counter and said to them, "Why don't you stand by the stove and let me introduce you to the famous Geronimo, who a harvest ago rode in the Great Father's parade and went to the Saint Louis World's Fair."

I stepped up to them and nodded. The older woman with the sparkling eyes was smiling big and nodding. She made a little bow to me, "I've seen Geronimo's photograph in the agent's office at Mescalero. I'm honored to meet such a great warrior."

I nodded, "And who is this fine woman?"

Her light skin turned a little red. "I've forgotten my upbringing. My name is Sousche. I'm a widow. We came from the Mescalero reservation in New Mexico to visit my old uncle, Yo'íí (He Sees It), who married a Chiricahua woman and lives in Chatto's village." She introduced the other woman as her son's wife, and the young man as her son, Nawode Nádilgheed (He Runs Fast).

I was looking at Sousche when I said to Nawode Nádilgheed, "Maybe you will approve my visiting your mother at your uncle's house."

He smiled and lifted his hands in a shrug. "Of course. We're always honored with a visit by the great Geronimo."

Sousche, smiling and looking very pleased, said, *"Enjuh!"*

That night I visited with Daklugie and asked if Eva could stay with him and his family for a moon. He frowned and asked why, and I told him I planned to have important business at my house for a while. He laughed and looked pleased when I told him what that business was.

Later that night, I told Eva I had business at the house and would need for her to stay with Daklugie and Ramona and their children for a moon.

She nodded. "I hear and obey, Father." She said nothing more.

I knew she must be curious why I wanted to be by myself for a moon. "I met the niece of old Yo'íí at Wratten's store today. She is a widow and attracts me. I visit her tomorrow. Perhaps soon she comes back here with me to stay, and you'll have help to cook and make straight the house."

Eva smiled, even laughed aloud. "Father, you take a bride when you're your age? You put the stallions in the corrals to shame. Your woman and I will work together for you well if you take her. This I promise."

Sousche returned to my house with me after I visited her four times at her uncle's house. I spoke with her son and offered him a pony for her. They spoke together by themselves for a while, and he agreed she would be my woman. We crossed Cache Creek and rode up to my house before the sun had fallen on the fourth day I visited her.

She made our supper while I cared for the horses. It was a good meal of steak, gravy, potatoes, acorn bread, and coffee. In our bed, she pleased me, and I think I pleased her — at least she didn't complain. We slept close together and shared our warmth. I was glad to find a new woman who cooked good and made me feel like a young man again.

When Eva returned to my house, she and Sousche were friendly, and I saw no bad blood between them for a moon, but then I saw Sousche begin treating Eva as if she were a slave, and I didn't like it. Eva didn't complain, but as I watched them together, I saw my new wife being more and more lazy. When I told her I didn't like what I saw, she shrugged her shoulders and said older women needed to train younger ones to be good wives and didn't have to work as hard. I'd had many wives in the times before I surrendered to the Blue Coats. I was not a fool.

Another moon passed, the Season of Little Eagles was beginning to show green grass on the prairie, and meadowlarks called from the wet spots where rainwater collected in the old buffalo wallows. Sousche's interest in me in our bed went away, too.

One day after Eva had gone to school, I said to Sousche, "Your desire for me and my household is gone. You do little or nothing all day. I won't beat you as I would have in the old days to make you serve me in a good way. It's time for you to go. Go."

She raised an eyebrow, looked at me, then

465

around the room, and back to me with a smile. She said, "Old man, you're an old, broken-down pony. Ha! I ride you no more. Saddle my horse. I put my things in a sack and go to my uncle Yo'íí. If you want to reconcile, I'll be there for a moon before I return to Mescalero."

I fingered my walking stick for a few moments, thinking I would beat her, but I remembered from walking the Jesus road that it was better not to strike those who did evil to you. I said nothing, shook my head, and walked out and saddled her pony. *At least,* I thought, *I'll be rid of her.*

The sun was pouring its last light through the cold air in my breezeway as I sat wrapped in my blanket and stared toward the land of my birth, wishing I had kept fighting the White Eyes, wishing I had some good White Eye whiskey, and watching Eva walk up the path to my house.

Eva came to the breezeway and looked around. She said, "Father, where is Sousche?"

"Gone. I sent her home. She has no place here with us anymore."

Eva's face was part frown, part smile. She sat down beside me to watch orange and purple color the clouds on the far horizon.

"Why did you send her away?"

"She was lazy. You did all the work. She didn't keep me warm when the nights were cold."

Eva nodded. "I didn't mind doing all the work if Sousche satisfied you. She seemed to, but I'm glad you sent her away. I'll still do all the work, and I'm happy to look after you. I'm still learning how to be a good woman with a man in the house, but my mother taught me much, and I learn good things at the mission school."

The light grew dimmer, and the sky was turning dark orange and red. I made a cigarette, smoked to the four directions, and then handed it to my daughter, only three seasons past her womanhood ceremony. Her eyes widened as she took it and smoked. I had never done this with her before, but I wanted her to know I wanted to speak of serious things.

She smoked and handed the cigarette back to me. I said, "I think you chose your man at your womanhood dance. Most women do. We should have talked before then, but I've had many distractions."

She nodded. "I know, Father. Yes, I know who I want, and he wants me. He's a very good man. I've watched him since we were children. We'll be happy together. I see him every day on the way to school. Soon he comes to you with a bride gift. I want you to accept it."

Stars came to the soft blackness above us, and in the low glow on the horizon, we could see steam come from our mouths as we talked. I said nothing for a while as we listened to the night birds and rustle of mice in the grass.

"Father?"

I said, "Your young man must not offer a bride gift. I won't accept it. You can't marry."

I heard her breathe hard, trying to pull air into a body that had lost for a moment its life rhythms. I knew her eyes were filling with tears. When she finally spoke, she had regained her balance. "But why, Father? I don't deserve to be treated like this. Why are you doing this?"

"I know you aren't happy with this, but it is for your life that I speak. Listen, and I will tell you a story. My sister Ishton married the great warrior Juh. When Daklugie was born, she strained with him four days and nearly died. I went up on the mountain and prayed for her. Ussen heard me and said she and the baby would live and that I would die a natural death."

We heard dogs barking and the clink of

harness chains as men brought their teams to the barn.

"Other women in our family have died or nearly died having children. My Power says if you try to have a child, both you and the child will die. You must not take a husband. Hear me and obey me. Do you understand?"

She sat there a long time in the darkness, saying nothing. I waited. Out of the darkness she said, "I hear you. I'll make us something to eat." She pushed herself up and went in the house. Soon I heard the clank and rattle of the iron doors on the cookstove. The sun had been long. Much had changed.

CHAPTER 43
RETURN TO SUNS PAST

I tried to follow the church *di-yen's* medicine to stay on the Jesus road. It was hard, and sometimes I wandered off the path to the White Eye God. As Zi-yeh lay dying, I'd found some White Eye whiskey and drank it when I hadn't had any in many moons. The whiskey felt better in my belly than in a bottle.

Of course, I wasn't alone sneaking a drink. I saw even the good Christians like Naiche and Chatto take a swallow or two when they thought no one looked. They were only fooling themselves. Many knew they drank what was forbidden by church *di-yens* but said nothing. I started to drink the whiskey again when I could get it, which was not often. Twice the Blue Coat police put me in the guardhouse for being drunk. Once they found me passed out at a horse race with an empty bottle in my hand. And I admit, I had enjoyed a few games of Monte — and won — while I was there, too. It shamed me when they let me out three days later and some friends from the church watched me leave the guardhouse.

That harvest in the Season of Large Leaves, a new Christian *di-yen*, Leonard Legters, came every seventh sun to the mission and spoke words about the Jesus road. I saw that he soon wanted to take for his woman one of the teachers, Maud Adkisson, who had been at the mission school five or six harvests. The White Eyes have strange customs for men taking women for wives, and they make it much harder than it needs to be, but that is their choice.

One sun, Legters spoke to me at church and asked if he might visit at my house where we could talk by ourselves. I told him to come any morning after school started, and we could sit and talk alone at my table while drinking coffee.

Three days later, we were sitting at my table, drinking from speckled blue coffee cups Zi-yeh had found many harvests ago at Mount Vernon. We spoke of those in the church and life as we lived it. The Chiricahuas were still prisoners of war wanting to go home. Legters's Apache was much better than my White Eye tongue, and he understood our custom for making talk about little things until we finally reached the point of his coming to speak with me.

He said, "Geronimo, I've heard stories of you being so drunk the soldiers put you in the guardhouse for three days. Is this true?"

I nodded. "I had gone to sleep with a whiskey bottle in my hand. It was all gone, but I drank it."

He said with wrinkles forming on his brow and his eyes narrowing, "There are other stories of you playing Monte and winning much money and betting on horse races. Are these stories true?"

"Hmmph, they're true."

"I also understand you still do the work of a *di-yen* in trying to cure some sicknesses and even had a big dance for your daughter's womanhood ceremony."

"I use my Power as Ussen grants it to me to help my People."

He slowly shook his head. "There's also a story of you living with a woman for three moons without marrying her in the church, and she left you."

"Hmmph. We were married in the Apache way. We divorced in the Apache way. It's none of a church *di-yen's* business how a man handles his women. You won't tell me this. I had wives before you were born, and

472

they were all good women who gave me children."

Legters raised his brows and started to speak, but I said, "I haven't done well following the *di-yen's* medicine for staying on the Jesus road. This I know."

Legters shook his head, looked at the roof, and sighed. "My friend, you've wandered far off the Jesus road. We all make mistakes. That's why we can ask God for forgiveness. If we're truly sorry we made those mistakes, then he'll wipe our record clean and help us find the Jesus road again. I'll pray with you now if you're sorry for your mistakes and won't do them again. Will you pray now? Waiting to ask forgiveness is not a good thing. You might die in the next hour and be lost eternally in the fires of hell because you didn't pray and ask God for forgiveness for leaving the Jesus road."

I realized then that the way I thought about God and used prayer were different from what Legters wanted me to believe.

I said, "You need to understand the way I think, and probably the way many Apaches think, of your White Eye God and our Ussen. Before the missionaries came, our contacts with Ussen and to those of our tribe were all each one needed to know about Power. But the God of the Jesus road

473

says we must honor all men, except maybe Mexicans, and our prayers go to Him through the ghost of his son Jesus.

"Apaches believe there is a life after this one, but I've never known what part of us lived after we died. I've seen many men die and many decayed human bodies, but I've never seen the part called spirit, and I still don't understand where the spirit is on the Jesus road. We Apaches believed that doing our duty to our tribe made the next life more pleasant, and we hoped, in the next life, the way our families and tribes lived would begin again.

"Since I've been a prisoner of the White Eyes, I've heard the Jesus road beliefs and in many ways believe they are better than what my fathers believed. But you must understand I've always prayed, and I know the great god Ussen has always protected me.

"I believe going to church and having Christian friends is a wise way to live and makes me do right things. I believe the church has helped me much during the short time I've been a member, and I advise all my people who aren't Christians to study its beliefs because I think it's the best way to learn to live right."

Legters smiled and showed many white

teeth as he reached over to affectionately squeeze my shoulder. "You aren't far from the Kingdom of God, Geronimo. You and your people just need to give up your pagan ceremonies and superstitious beliefs and walk the straight way every day, and you'll be on the Jesus road again. Won't you pray with me now that you'll do right?"

I thought about what Legters said as I stared at his kind eyes. Then my Power from Ussen gave me words. I slowly shook my head and said, "No, I won't pray to the White Eye God. I've always prayed to Ussen. The rules for the Jesus road are too strict. We can't enjoy our lives as we did when we were wild and free. I want freedom again. I'll return to the beliefs of my fathers. This is all I have to say."

Legters puffed his cheeks and blew. "Then I and all your friends will pray for you. We'll pray that your eyes will be opened and you'll see the light from the one true God and come back to us to stay on the Jesus road. Call me whenever you have need. Good day, sir."

I was surprised to see Legters leave so quick, but I said, "I see you again, Legters."

The crops had been gathered, and Eva and I led a peaceful life after my talk with

Legters. I even continued to attend church, and he said nothing. Perhaps he hoped I had prayed to the White Eye God and changed, but I had not. I was invited again to the 101 Ranch late in the Season of Large Fruit, and *Teniente* Purington agreed to let me go.

Before I left, Lenna sent me tracks on paper that Eva read to me. Lenna said Ihtedda had gone to the Mescalero Agency and declared that Robert Cross Eyes was not registered right, that his name should be Robert Geronimo. She said Robert was then in school at Chilocco. Daklugie had told me of hearing stories from children he knew in Chilocco, who said a new student was telling others he was a son of Geronimo.

I was determined to see this son I'd never known I had until Lenna had told me about him. Daklugie agreed with me that this Robert might be my son. I asked Purington if I could go to Chilocco, which was about thirty miles northeast from the 101 Ranch. I could go on my way back to Fort Sill. I told him I wanted to visit my grandchildren, and he agreed.

I didn't like the visit to the 101 Ranch my second time. I thought it was supposed to be another Oklahoma celebration like they

476

had done for reporters my first trip, when I got to ride in a Locomobile and shoot a buffalo. On this second trip, the celebration was more like a Wild West show. They paid me money to sit at table with a heavy ball chained to my leg and an armed guard on either side of me. People paid money to walk by and look at me. I looked back at most and wished I had a rifle, but I said nothing. At least I could sell my photographs, for which I made good money.

My friend McCowan, who was in charge of the Saint Louis Indian Exhibit where I had met and spoken with Lenna, was chief at Chilocco. He had agreed with Purington to be in charge of me during my visit. It was good to see him again. We drank coffee from a pot on a hot stove in his big workroom on the second floor of one of the stone buildings I had seen before when I had come to visit my grandson Tom Dahkeya at Chilocco.

After we laughed and talked for a while about our days together in Saint Louis, he said, "I suppose you've come to visit with your grandson Tom Dahkeya. He's very smart. Let's see . . . oh yes, I think his group is learning carpentry today. I'll send one of my assistants to find him for you."

I held up my hand before he could rise from his chair. "Wait, friend. There is another boy I want to see first. Robert Cross Eyes."

McCowan leaned back in his chair and frowned. "Why do you want to see Robert Cross Eyes?"

"Robert Cross Eyes is the son of a woman I divorced and sent back to Mescalero in order to get her and our daughter Lenna out of that Mount Vernon death camp many harvests ago. You remember Lenna. She came to Saint Louis for the Mescaleros and lived with me and Thomas."

McCowan was nodding and rubbing the jawline of his smooth boyish face with his thumb and forefinger.

"This boy Robert is her brother. He was born seven months after my woman left Mount Vernon. Her father married her off to an old man named Old Scout Cross Eyes a few suns after she returned to Mescalero. When the boy was born, she registered him with the agency as Robert Cross Eyes, but he could be my son. I want to see him. When I see him, I'll know if he's my son or not."

McCowan, with the smallest of smiles, nodded and stood up, straightening his coat. "I understand. Let me get an assistant to find Robert Cross Eyes for you. You may use my office to talk with him if you like."

I nodded. "McCowan is a friend."

I sat waiting with my back to the door. I could see who came through the door from reflections in the window glass. I waited quiet and ready, like a hunter watching for a deer. I didn't wait long before the door creaked, and I glanced up to see the figure of a boy about the age of a warrior novitiate. As soon as I saw the figure in the glass, I had no doubt Robert was my son. Ussen had blessed me. All my other sons had died. Now one I'd never known I had, had just walked through the door.

I turned and said, "I see you, Robert."

For a moment, his mouth dropped open, and I heard him jerk in a swallow of air. He said, "I know you. You're Geronimo. Your picture is everywhere. How . . . why — ?

"I heard stories you were here and that you say you're the son of Geronimo. Is this true?"

He frowned. I could tell he was deciding whether to lie or not. "Yes, I claim your name and believe you're my father. I look like my sister you spoke to in Saint Louis. I don't look like Old Boy, who my mother insists is my father. I feel the pull of your life. Whether you claim me or not, I know your blood is in me. I am your son."

I pushed up out of the chair and turned to face him. He stuck out his jaw in defiance and tilted his head back. He didn't move as his eyes followed my approach. I stopped an arm's length from him and studied his face, his bright eyes, his big, strong wrists, and his small but powerful hands, as I thought, *Truly Ussen has blessed me.*

"Yes, Robert, I see much of your mother's face in yours. I also think I'm looking at a reflection in still water when I look at you. My Power thanks Ussen. I don't doubt you're my son." He grabbed my shoulders and hugged me, holding on as if he were a tree leaf clinging to its tree in a storm.

CHAPTER 44
AZUL

I returned to my village soon after meeting my grown son Robert for the first time and introducing him to my grandson Thomas Dahkeya. I didn't feel close to Robert, but I was sure he was my son. I said he should come stay the summers at Fort Sill, so we could get to know each other. He was quick to say he'd come to Fort Sill.

I had much to think about through the seasons of Earth Is Reddish Brown and Ghost Face. I was happy I'd met Robert and now had a son who, along with Thomas, could carry on the family. Eva's children could carry on the name, too, but I couldn't risk it. I would not let her die trying to have a child. Better to be a tree with no fruit, than a dead one with no leaves. I had trained her well to obey, but I knew she was angry about my decision to forbid her marriage. She used any excuse to stay away from my house. I missed her, but I knew that one day she would understand why I did this hard thing. I wanted her to understand this sooner rather than later, but how to help her, my Power wouldn't tell me.

The talk I had with Legters haunted me. I expected the church doors would be closed to me every time I went. I didn't want to leave the Jesus road, but I didn't want their *di-yens'* medicine to stay on it either.

I thought often and dreamed of how much I wanted to return to the land of my fathers in the mountains at the headwaters of the Gila River. If the Great Father wouldn't let my People go, then who would?

I thought of all the great things the White Eyes had built and that I had seen at the expositions and how my People had to learn White Eye secrets or be wiped out, never to be seen again in the great white flood swirling around us. How best for all of us to learn these things?

As the seasons turned through Ghost Face, I thought on these things until my head hurt, and the voices in my mind spoke loud with many arguments.

In the Season of Little Eagles, a warm, dry sun came that spoke to the coming of new life. The birds on the prairie called and whistled as they made their nests and mated, and there was a scent in the air of flowers beginning to bloom. I decided I would go that night and build a little fire among the trees on Cache Creek, about halfway between my village and that of my brother Perico, his village a little south of mine. There I would pray to Ussen for guidance on all the things that filled my head with so many questions and worries.

The night was cool, and I sat next to the fire wrapped in my blanket as I bathed in sage smoke, sprinkled sacred pollen, and prayed that Ussen would speak to me or give me a sign for those things about which I worried and prayed. The fire began to burn low and still Ussen had not spoken.

I sat praying with my eyes closed, letting my mind float free as it called to Ussen. The heat from the fire still warmed my face when I heard feet moving toward me in the darkness, feet softly crunching the dried, brown prairie grass left by Ghost Face under the shoots of new green grass. I opened my eyes and stared toward the sound floating through the darkness toward me.

At the edge of the fire's circle of light, a figure painted by shadows appeared, a woman. In the orange glow of the fire I saw she wore a black skirt and blouse and had a dark blanket over her head and shoulders. I nodded slowly in recognition. Out of the shadows stepped Sunsetso (Old Lady Yellow), a widow who lived in Perico's village. I didn't understand why everyone called her Azul, which is Spanish for blue. I knew who she was, but I had never known her husband, who had died some seasons ago. I knew her well enough to speak or nod as we passed on trails or met in Wratten's store.

She said, "Ho, Geronimo. I knew it must be you. Only you would now sit outside in the dark, bathe in sacred smoke, scatter yellow pollen, and seek Ussen with his Power. Shall I wait while you continue to seek Ussen? I would ask your guidance."

"Come, Azul. Sit by my fire. I will hear you. My prayers to Ussen still float in the air. He hasn't yet spoken to me." I patted a place beside me, so I didn't have trouble hearing her and threw a little more wood on the fire, making bright orange sparks rise high in the darkness toward the milk river of stars above us.

She came and slowly squatted over the place I had patted, and, fixing her blanket under her, she sat down with a grunt. Her face was solemn, filled with experience and wisdom. She smelled good, of soap and crushed flowers, and her hair was long and still black, gray not yet taking it, even though she was past the age many women still keep the black in their hair. She made me feel as a young man again around young women. I liked her.

"Speak, Azul. I will listen."

"Hear me, Geronimo. My heart needs your wisdom. I have no man. This you know. I serve my niece's husband Guydelkon and his two sons, Arthur and Paul, Jr., in the village of Perico. Guydelkon's wife has gone to the Happy Place, and Guydelkon has no other woman to help him. Our neighbors are on the Jesus road. They ask me often to join them. I don't know yet whether to join them or not. I've always followed the religion of the People with my man. Now I'm alone. I don't know what to do. I feel no pull toward the Jesus road. I know you go to the mission church, but I also know you don't always follow the White Eye *di-yen* medicine to stay on the Jesus road. You enjoy yourself. I think that's a good thing. What do you think that, I, an old woman, should do?"

I don't know where what I said next came from unless it was my Power speaking. "I think you should take an old man, like me, and live so life gives you some pleasure." When she heard this, she frowned, then covered her mouth with her fingers to hide a laugh. I said, "In some ways, the Jesus road is better than the religion of our fathers. It reaches beyond our tribe to all people, except maybe the Mexicans, who I think can't be reached, to say the White Eye God is for everybody. Join the church. They look after their widows until they die, and they look after orphaned children until someone else takes them for their own children. But the medicine their *di-yen* says is required to stay in the Jesus road is too much for me. The rules are too strict. I want to enjoy my life now while I have it, not wait until I wander as a ghost in the Happy Place. I want to drink a little whiskey. I want to race my horses. I want to play cards. I want to be free, but this I'll never be as long as the White Eyes have me. Maybe I run away so they send me to the Happy Place when they find me. I'll be free then."

I realized I was speaking the truth, truth I prayed for but didn't want to hear. So Ussen had sent me a sign after all. He sent Azul to hear me, to goad me into speaking and hearing the truth. Maybe Ussen was the reason my Power told me to say she should take me.

Azul was a wise woman. She sat for a while, wrapped in her blanket, saying nothing and staring at the low yellow and blue flames as the new wood burned down. Then she said, "Where would I find an old man like you? Do you think he could give my life pleasure?"

I said, "The old man you seek sits beside you. I've had many wives and children over many harvests. I know good women when I see them. They stir me, and I admire them. I have heard nothing about your past, but my Power says you're a powerful woman. I would speak to you and hear you. Tell me of your life."

Her eyes, black and shiny as the finest flint, stared at mine and seemed to look into my spirit. She said, "My earliest memory is of a Mexican army raid on the camp where my mother and father lived while we gathered and cooked mescal for food. All the People who didn't run away were killed, and the children who survived were sold as slaves to great *haciendas* in Chihuahua. I was old enough to have been taught how to use a knife, and one day, I found one, a good one, and hid it away to take with me when I left. I learned Spanish, and listened to the family and travelers who stopped there until I knew enough about the land to get back to the People. One night, I took my knife, a blanket, and some corn I had hidden away and left that *hacienda.* I ran all night and then slept all day hidden in a mesquite thicket. After that day, I stayed out of sight by moving at night.

"It was two moons before I found our People. An old couple, their children gone, adopted me. Within a harvest of my return, I had my womanhood ceremony. I knew the young warrior I wanted for a husband. He had yet to take a wife, and he knew I would accept him. He brought my father a fine bride gift of four ponies, and we stayed together until Mexicans killed him during the fighting at Aliso Creek when Loco's People were headed for your camps in the Sierra Madre. I hid in one of the holes we dug in the creek bank to protect the children. When I learned my husband had been killed in the fighting, I didn't wail for him. He had gone to the Happy Place as he wanted, fighting as a true warrior. I have great respect for warriors. They have much courage and skill. You're a great warrior, Geronimo."

Off in the distance, we heard coyotes yipping and night birds calling. Peace began settling on me as I listened to Azul tell me of her life.

"I lived alone until four harvests ago."

"Why was that? Didn't you want anyone?

Didn't anyone want you?"

Azul smiled and shook her head. "No. There were no old men, at least none I was willing to nurse until they finally died. What old man wants an old woman, unless it's for that or to enjoy what's left of her body? No man had authority to make me marry, so I've waited until I found someone I want. No old men have I yet wanted. A young man might want to learn how to mount a young woman well, using an old woman, and stay with her for a while, but the *diyens* say old women are bad for young men. So I lived alone."

"What happened four harvests ago so that you stopped living by yourself?

"My grandniece, daughter of Guydelkon, had been looking after her father and two young brothers since her mother went to the Happy Place six harvests earlier. Four harvests ago, my grandniece went to the Happy Place and left Guydelkon and his two boys without a woman to help them. Guydelkon could find no one he liked. He asked me to come look after them, since we were both alone, and I went. Now I live with Guydelkon and his two sons over there in Perico's village. Guydelkon and sons are good men and hard workers, but I have become lonely without a man of my own.

So you see my interest in the old man who might be interested in me. Do not test me, Geronimo. Do you speak of yourself in this way?"

I looked in those black flint eyes and nodded. "Yes, Azul. I'm interested in you. I would talk with you more, that we might decide to marry."

Her smile was wide, and she said, "*Enjuh.* Come to Guydelkon's house for our evening meal when the next sun leaves. You can see how well I cook, and I can see how well you eat. Perhaps in a few nights we'll come back here with only our blankets, make no fire, and use only our bodies to keep each other warm. Perhaps then you'll decide to take me for your woman."

Azul's roasted beef, potatoes, beans, and mesquite bread were very good, and Guydelkon and his sons were happy to have me visit. Azul and I spent a few more days sharing our thoughts, and then one night, we went to the trees around Cache Creek and, under leaf buds beginning to open, shared our blankets.

To prove I still had my vigor, I took off everything I wore and crawled in the blanket in the cold night air. She, too, removed her clothes. It was hard to see the many wrinkles and ridges in our bodies, but we both knew they were there. Despite our wrinkles, I enjoyed her, and she said she enjoyed me. Life stirred in us once more.

The next sun, I stayed with her in the house of Guydelkon and his sons. We were married in the Apache way.

CHAPTER 45
THE FREEDOM ROAD

As with all good times, the suns passed too swiftly, galloping ponies escaping across the prairie. Azul and I lived on one side of Guydelkon's house, the kitchen side, of course, and he and his sons lived on the other. We were content. Azul and I went to church together. The church *di-yen* welcomed Azul, but after I told him we were married in the Apache way, he said we should ask forgiveness from the White Eye God and marry in the Christian way. I told him I would think about his words, and Azul and I would talk, but I knew we wouldn't do this.

Teniente Purington sent for me early in the Season of Many Leaves. He said he had a message McCowan had sent him from Chilocco on the talking wire. Robert had told McCowan I had invited him to spend the summer with me at Fort Sill. McCowan wanted to know if I still wanted the boy to come.

My mind was on other things when I took Azul to wife, and I hadn't remembered my invitation when I began living with her. Azul and I wanted to be alone when we went to our blankets. I told *Teniente* Purington to tell McCowan to let the boy to come. I would find a place for him. I asked Daklugie if Robert could stay with him and Ramona and their children. Daklugie said, "Any son of my uncle will be welcome to stay with me, but I must ask Ramona first to agree." He did and Ramona said she, too, welcomed a son of Geronimo.

In the warm evenings, before Robert came, Azul and I went for walks along Cache Creek after the evening meal was finished. Sometimes we carried a blanket for things better than walking. We often spoke of what we most wanted for the rest of our lives.

One evening as we lay in the dark listening to the insects and water animals, Azul said, "I enjoy the peace and good husband I have. I'm content here."

"Hmmph. I enjoy and want you for my wife, but if I speak with a straight tongue, I want my freedom. I want to live in the land of my fathers when I die. I've asked the

Great Father to free us, but he will not. He says the White Eyes who now live in our country want to take revenge against us for fighting for our land in the first place. He can't let us go. It would mean more blood would flow if he did. I wish I'd died fighting, shooting my last bullet at enemies and putting my own knife in my heart."

In the night's moonlight and deep tree shadows along the creek, I saw Azul shake her head. "I'm glad you live, Geronimo. You make me feel like a young woman again. There's more to life than a good death, but I understand the flame that burns in you. If you ever find a chance for your freedom, you take it. I want it for you. Don't worry about me. I'll be satisfied knowing you've found what you want."

"Azul is a fine woman. I'm glad I have her."

My friend Quanah Parker sent word that I should come visit him in his big Star House and ride with him in the town of Cache Fourth of July parade. We had ridden together in the Great Father's big parade two harvests earlier in Washington. It was good to ride with Quanah Parker. He knew how to ride better than me and do tricks with his horse. He had been a great warrior before he surrendered to the White Eyes. *Teniente* Purington agreed I could go, and since Cache was so close to Fort Sill land, he said he would let me go unescorted if I returned to Fort Sill by dark on the day of the feast and told Wratten I was back. This I said I would do. I answered Quanah Parker and said I would come and ride with him for the great White Eye feast they called Fourth of July.

It was an easy ride, ten or eleven miles as the White Eyes count distance, to Quanah Parker's Star House. I rode along across the prairie singing my favorite riding song, feeling the hot, good sun on me, and thinking about the long-ago times and how our lives had changed since the White Eyes had swarmed like locusts across the land. I thought of Azul and how Ussen had used her to bless me and speak to me even though I went to the White Eye church. I knew Ussen had not forgotten me.

I came to Star House, a big *casa* with many rooms and big, white, pointed symbols for stars on its red roof. A boy came from the barn to take my pony, and Quanah Parker pushed open a screen door, a clever thing that let cool air in the house but kept insects out, to come out to meet me. With stiff joints, I swung off my pony and laughed as he came up, and we clasped shoulders as brothers.

Quanah Parker and I talked long into the night sitting on his porch, smoking, and taking little tastes of whiskey from a bottle he kept hidden there. I wanted to drink it all, but Quanah wouldn't let me, saying there would be more tomorrow after we sat straight on our horses in the little parade for the White Eyes.

We spoke of rumors washing over Fort Sill that the army had decided to keep the land, and the Chiricahua would have to leave all the hard work we had done building houses, developing fields of corn, pumpkins, and beans, cutting timber, stretching fence, and increasing our cattle herd. Quanah Parker had already agreed to give the Chiricahuas the land when the army left, if the army extended Fort Sill lands east and west by the same amount he gave us, so the Comanche and Kiowa would have the grazing land they needed for their herds. But now the White Eyes were taking much of the Comanche-Kiowa reservations and turning the land over to the White Eyes. There was little or nothing the Comanches under Quanah Parker could do for the Chiricahuas anymore.

Daklugie had long said that if the Chiricahua had to leave Fort Sill and could not return to our homeland, then we ought to go to Mescalero in New Mexico. He wanted to visit the Mescalero Reservation to learn if the Mescalero land could support a big cattle herd. Daklugie was certain he would like what he saw, and that the Mescaleros would want us to come live with them because they needed more people on their reservation to keep the White Eyes from taking it away.

Maybe so, but I knew the White Eyes would never let my people go to New Mexico as long as I lived. Their fear of me was as strong as the stink of death after a close battle. I thought, *If I disappeared, then the White Eyes would let my people go. Maybe I could go back home on my own, and all would think I was dead. My disappearing sounds like it has a reward for getting me back to the Gila and for moving the Chiricahuas west to Mescalero. I must think on this.*

The next day, Quanah Parker and some chiefs from other tribes and I rode into Cache in our best outfits and on our best ponies for a little parade for the White Eye feast of Fourth of July. The White Eyes along our path stared at us. I knew they must have been wondering where to hide if we broke loose and went after them. It made me feel good to know we still had this power over them. The White Eyes whooped and hollered as we rode by. There were even some pistols fired to make noise. I was glad I had trained my pony not to rear or buck at unexpected sounds.

We left the White Eye festival when the sun was at the time of no shadows and returned to Star House. Quanah Parker found a new bottle of whiskey, and he and I sat together in the shade of big trees and had a few swallows. The White Eyes did many things wrong, but they made very good whiskey. His wives and servants had made a big feast for many visitors to Star House.

Some of his White Eye friends who rented pastureland from him had been invited. When they stopped to speak with him, we hid our bottle, but they offered us drinks from their little bottles. Quanah Parker introduced me to all of them, and I gave each a strong hand pump. Most said they had seen me before and knew who I was from earlier feasts and horse races at Fort Sill, but as they spoke to Quanah Parker, they kept their eyes on me, studying me like they might a rattlesnake.

I thought, *It's good you White Eyes watch*

me as an old man. When I was younger, I might have killed you, but now I only think about it, unless you get close enough for my knife.

Quanah Parker and I nipped at his whiskey bottle. I drank more than he did, until I saw the sun was down halfway from the time of no shadows and the far edge of the earth. I said, "My friend, I have to return to Fort Sill before dark. The sun says I must go. I've enjoyed the whiskey and talks with you. This visit is good for me."

Quanah Parker said, "It's good to see you, my friend. We've spoken of many things. Let us hope they happen well." He called for a boy to bring my pony and waved after I mounted and headed east.

I headed back to Fort Sill thinking over and over, *Disappear and return to the land of your fathers.* I rode well out of sight of Star House following the iron wagon tracks until I stopped at the second stream the trail crossed. I smoked to the four directions while I sat on my fine sorrel-pony racer, thought about what to do, and looked in both directions up and down the trail back to Fort Sill. I saw no one and turned south, riding in the near dry stream. My pony made clear tracks in the muddy stream, but the whiskey made me feel good and made me forget how to be sly and cautious with my trail. I thought, *I'll never get my freedom if I don't try.* I planned following the stream south until I reached the Red River. Then I would follow the Red River west until I could ride for New Mexico.

I turned to look at my back trail and wondered if I saw a ghost. The old man with the long, gray beard with a scar running through it, wearing his long, black coat covering a pistol in a shoulder holster, who I had first seen at the town where I sold my first button, sat on a big black horse, not fifty yards away, smiling at me. The only thing I had to defend myself with was my little butcher knife sheathed inside my vest, its butt end just outside the button seam. I asked Ussen to let me die a brave man.

I called to Gray Beard as I reached to rub my belly as though scratching. "I see you many times before. What you want? Who you?"

Keeping his hand on his coat near his pistol, he nudged his horse to walk toward me and stopped when we were about ten yards apart. He stared at me for a few breaths and then croaked in a deadly, whispery voice, "My name is Grayson. General Miles hired me to keep an eye on you and to be sure you never escape, even if I have to kill you. He'll never accept the idea that he caught you and then you got away from him like you did from Crook in eighty-six." He grinned like Coyote, showing his big, white teeth surrounded by the gray beard. "What's it gonna be, old man? You turning east back to Fort Sill, or am I the man who killed Geronimo?"

I could only think, *Thank you, Ussen*. I might have been old, but my knife-throwing arm was still quicker than a striking rattlesnake. My fingers closed on the end of the butcher knife handle, and it flew for his heart as he put his hand on his pistol. My throw was good, straight, and hard. The knife buried in his chest all the way to the handle. His hand froze on the pistol, and it cleared its holster, but he never raised or fired it. His eyes big with surprise, he slumped forward, a little patch of blood around the knife buried in his heart, and breathed his last.

Holding on to Grayson so he wouldn't fall off, I led his horse over four rolling rises on the prairie before I pulled him off in brush at the bottom of the rise and left him lying there. I pulled my knife from his heart and wiped it on his shirt. I wanted to take his pistol and holster, but I knew better. I didn't even take his money. I unsaddled his horse, leading it down the bottom of the crease between the hills to a little pond of water that must have been an old buffalo wallow. I killed it there and left it for the wolves and coyotes. A loose horse always goes back to where it came from. I wanted to be far away when Grayson and his horse were found. The smell of blood and death were strong there. It stirred my memory of the old days and made me wish again I had never surrendered. At least Grayson would never again fill my eyes.

That night I hobbled my pony to graze along the stream, but I dared not make a fire, even a little one. I had put some of Quanah Parker's wives' good meat and bread in my coat pockets before I left, and I ate that while the darkness came and the sound of things that lived along the creek began to sing. I found a place to sleep for a while in the roots of a big tree and took my rest.

The moon was near setting, but the sky was not yet turning gray. I washed in a still pool beside the stream, caught and watered my pony, and then saddled him with a loose cinch while I waited for the dawn and finished the food I had taken from Quanah

Parker's feast.

With the whiskey no longer affecting my thinking, I wondered how far I'd get. After all, I'd left a trail even a White Eye could follow. Soon the sky turned gray, and there was a dim crack of light in the darkness. I prayed to Ussen, tightened my pony's cinch, and followed the creek south.

I stayed near the stream. As the sun rose higher, the heat was like that in a sweat lodge. I took off my coat and shirt and tied them behind my saddle. I stayed in the shadows to keep hidden as much as to keep cool. By the time of no shadows, I stopped beside a nice pool in the creek, let my pony drink, and kneeling on one knee, I looked up and down the stream, before I, too, took water.

I was ready to remount when a voice came out of the brush downstream. "Ho! Geronimo, are you lost? We look for you." My spirit fell. The scouts had easily found me.

"I'm not lost. I return to the land of my fathers. Come with me."

"Do you have a gun?"

"No! I have no gun. I go back to the land of my fathers and won't harm or bother anyone on the way."

An army officer and three scouts came out of the brush. I knew my eyes were becoming very bad. I had not seen any of them until they moved. The Blue Coat officer rode up to me and said, "Geronimo, you've violated your parole to visit Quanah Parker. I have orders to find and return you to Fort Sill. If you give me your word to come peaceably, I won't put you in chains."

I nodded. "I come. No chains."

Teniente Purington was angry that I had gone south, but he couldn't decide if I was trying to escape or, being an old man, had become confused about the way home. Finally, he sent me home rather than to the calaboose and told me if I violated a parole again, I'd be caged up for a long time.

I shook my head and said, "No more."

Azul was very happy to see me back as she fluttered around her kitchen. She said she had been worried about me, but she guessed my being missing was the result of what we had talked about in our night walks. She was sorry to see me come up the village trail and realize I still wasn't free. That night it was especially good to be back together.

Azul and I spoke of freedom and a return to the land of my fathers many times. I knew the only way I could go was if the Great Father let me. I had asked him to let us go home after his big parade two harvests earlier, but then he had said no. Two harvests had passed since then. Maybe he had thought about it and changed his mind.

I wore my best suit and went with my son, Robert, acting as my interpreter, to my White Eye friend in Lawton, the *di-yen* who knew how to put my pictures on glass or paper. I asked him to make me a photograph to send to the Great Father. While we waited for the images on paper to dry, I sent Robert to bring a reporter to write what I wanted said to the Great Father.

The reporter came to learn what I wanted. Robert told him I wanted to send my new picture to the president with a note, if the reporter would write as I said. When he smiled and said he would do this for me, I reached in my pocket and held up gold money for him to take, but he said he didn't want money to do this for me.

Enjuh. A good White Eye to write to the Great Father for me will write what I said.

I said, with Robert giving him the White Eye tongue, "I want a good picture to send my good friend, President Roosevelt. I know you remember me. I rode in your big Washington parade two harvests ago. You said then that I could not return to the home of my father, that too much blood would be spilled between the settlers and Apaches. Maybe so, sometime the president will say, 'Go home, old Geronimo. You killed many white folks, but now Jesus has made you good. You're a good man all the time, and the army will hold you no more.' I listen for you like I do the voice of God."

I wrote my name on the picture and the White Eye reporter said he would send it to the president if I would give him a picture, too, and I did.

CHAPTER 46
END OF MANY ROADS

I had much regret I didn't escape to the land of my fathers and had returned to Fort Sill in shame with a soldier escort after a two days hiding in the *bosque* along the creeks. But I was happy I had put blood on my knife from this man Grayson, who General Miles had stalking and watching me all these years.

A few suns after I returned, I played cards with old friends. Someone, I don't remember who, gave me some whiskey. I drank nearly the whole bottle before I passed out. The Blue Coats found me asleep, smelling of whiskey, by the side of the road on the way to Guydelkon's house and put me in the calaboose for three days.

It was not a good time for the church *diyen* to learn I had been drinking. He said Azul and I had not yet done a marriage ceremony as the White Eye God said we must. Now he knew I still played cards and drank whiskey, and that I didn't pray for the White Eye God to help me. These things said to him that I was no longer near the Jesus road and should no longer be a member of the church.

He discussed this with the Chiricahua church leaders, and on the last day of the camp meeting that season, it was announced that, while Azul and I were always welcome at church, I had been suspended from church membership until I repented of my ways and got back on the Jesus road. Azul and I left the church and did not return until the next camp meeting a harvest later.

That harvest Robert stayed at Fort Sill most of the time in the Seasons of Large Leaves and Large Fruit. We visited often, and although we still weren't close, like my grandson Thomas Dahkeya and I were, I came to like the boy more every sun he was with us. He was well-behaved in Ramona's house, and because Eva stayed there, they came to be good friends.

Eva planned to go to school in Chilocco late in that Season of Large Fruit, and Robert said he would return to school with her and help her learn school customs so she would do well quickly, and for this she was grateful.

One day about a moon before Robert and Eva left for Chilocco, for reasons I never knew or understood, Robert, without asking, took Daklugie's best pony. He rode it to death in a race over the prairie. Daklugie, his face red with anger, told me Robert must live somewhere else. He said, if Robert didn't get out of his sight for a time, he might kill him.

I sent for my nephew, Eugene Chihuahua, who had become chief of his father's village, joined the Seventh Cavalry as a scout, and married Massai's daughter, Viola. They had buried four children, if my memory was correct. At the time I sent for him, I think they had only one child then, about a year old.

Eugene came the same day I asked to see him. The sun was nearly gone, spreading its light in oranges and purples across the western sky when we heard his cavalry boots thudding in the breezeway of Guydelkon's house. He stood at our door, cleared his throat, and waited for me to come greet him.

Azul made us a good evening meal, and we all had a good visit discussing Fort Sill gossip while we ate. What I had to discuss with Eugene needed to be done in private, so we sat drinking our coffee on the end of the breezeway, listening to the peepers and frogs and insects in the brush and trees along Cache Creek, while Azul made her cooking place clean and Guydelkon and his boys visited neighbors.

Eugene finished his coffee, sat the cup beside him, placed his elbows on his knees, and, staring out into the velvet night, asked, "How can I help you, Grandfather?"

"What do you think of my son, Robert?"

Eugene rolled a cigarette, lighted it, and we smoked to the four directions. Since his father, Chihuahua, had gone to the Happy Place, Eugene, now the headman in his father's village, acted like a chief should and was deliberate in all he said and did.

After we smoked, he crushed the remains of the cigarette with his bootheel and said, "Robert is a good boy but not yet a man. I've seen him let his feelings carry him beyond where his head says he should go. He took Daklugie's best pony without permission and literally rode him into the ground. Daklugie is so angry, he wants to whack the boy every time he sees him, and it has caused a bad spirit in his house. Daklugie asked if I would let Robert live in my house. I've spoken with Viola about it, and she's willing to have him come if he acts right. He tells me he's very sorry and that it will never happen again. I have no reason to doubt him. So he now lives with us. He causes Viola and me no concern so far. Why do you ask, Grandfather?"

"Daklugie told me he was very angry about what Robert did, and that Robert must live somewhere else. I thought he wanted me to find Robert another place. Now I see we both had the same thoughts, and he has already spoken with you. *Enjuh.* I'm glad the son of the great warrior Chihuahua gives my son a place to sleep in his lodge. I'm grateful you and Viola help him."

"We're glad to do this, Grandfather. I think one day he'll make a fine man."

We sat together in the darkness, listening to the night animals, saying nothing as the moonlight began to fill the tall grass.

Eugene sighed and stood up. "It's time for me to return to my family. You're a lucky man to find a woman like Azul. Her food is good. Don't worry about Robert. He'll be a good man. Soon I see you again, Grandfather."

I nodded. *"Enjuh."* And Eugene disappeared into the night shadows.

One morning early in the Season of Large Fruit, Kaytennae came to see me before

Azul was ready with our morning meal. Kaytennae was the headman in the village where my blood sister Nah-dos-te, had lived with the great Chihenne chief, Nana, who had been Victorio's number two. Nana had gone to the Happy Place within two harvests after we left the swamps and great trees of Mount Vernon, and Nah-dos-te had continued to live there in another house after the house of her and her husband had "accidentally" burned soon after he rode the ghost pony.

No one wanted the ghost of Nana to come back. Even Captain Scott said nothing about the fire. Nah-dos-te was a loved and respected widow in the village of Kaytennae, who had been Nana's number two. Azul and I visited with her often, but I could tell she was growing weak and slept more than she should.

I was sitting in the breezeway enjoying the golden light from the sun sweeping over the prairie, listening to the ducks singing their songs down on Cache Creek, and smelling the good smells of Azul's cooking meat, when I saw Kaytennae cross the creek and ride for my house. Even in the early morning light, I saw his face filled with sad news. He rode up to the breezeway but did not dismount or sign all is good.

He said, "Geronimo, I come in sadness. Just before the moon fell in the prairie horizon, I heard old women wail. Your sister now rides the ghost pony. You are a *di-yen* for Ussen. Do you want to do the ceremony for her fast travel to the Happy Place?"

I groaned deep in my heart and stared at the yellow grass beginning to shine in the sunlight. I loved my sister, a fine woman, fit for any chief, any warrior. I said, "Kaytennae, I thank you for bringing me the news of my sister leaving us. Yes, I'll do the ceremony. It's what she wanted."

"*Enjuh.* We hold the ceremony tomorrow at the place where all Fort Sill Apaches rest in the bosom of the earth. I'll make the arrangements and send word to you for when you must be there."

"Kaytennae leads his People well. I come when you say."

Kaytennae nodded and turned his pony toward his village. I puffed my cheeks and blew as I went inside to tell Azul that Nahdos-te had left us on the ghost pony, and that I would make the ceremony for her at the place the Apaches were given for placing their dead under wooden army markers.

Late in the Season of Large Fruit, my friend, Spybuck, a Shawnee leader, invited me to a big Indian gathering on the land of their ceremonies near the new railroad town of Collinsville northeast of Lawton. It was about the same distance to Collinsville as to Chilocco. To get to Collinsville, we had to pass through first Oklahoma City and then Tulsa. George Wratten told me about the new machine the *Oklahoman* newspaper had just put in place to support many newspapers at one time.

The same Lawton reporter who sent my note to the Great Father Roosevelt asking for my freedom was with the others and me, including Wratten, who were going to Spybuck's great ceremony.

We took the train first to Oklahoma City. The reporter and Wratten spoke to each other of the new great machine that could print so many newspapers so fast.

Maybe, I thought, *this machine can carry my words to Great Father Roosevelt.* I said to Wratten, "I want to see this great machine that is so fast in putting word tracks on paper. We'll be in Oklahoma City for two circles around my watch before the train takes us to Tulsa and Collingwood. Can we go?"

Wratten looked at the reporter and repeated what I had said. The reporter smiled, shrugged, and said, "I'll call the *Oklahoman* when we get to the station in Oklahoma City and learn if we can visit."

The reporter used the talking wire when we arrived at the train station, and the voice on the other end of the line said, "Bring him and his party on. We'll be starting the evening edition pretty soon." The reporter hired a velocipede to carry us to the building where the machine was.

Outside the building, I saw long black ropes attached to the building that came off the limbs of great brown poles marching toward it. They were ugly. When we went inside the building, the floor seemed to hum, and we could hear something like the clank and slam of iron pieces and the low rumble of a long collection of iron wagons. There were smells I didn't recognize and some like those in the air after the lightning arrows fly from the Thunder and Wind gods. I thought maybe I had made bad mistake coming to see this great machine the White Eyes had created.

The chief who was in charge of the machine explained to me through Wratten that after adjustment, the machine would take paper off great rolls hanging beside it at one end, print the words for the day, and, when finished printing, fold the paper and run the ready-to-sell newspaper out the other end. This sounded impossible to me, but I had learned the White Eyes could do many things that sounded impossible.

After the chief finished explaining what the machine did, he led us to the great room where the machine worked. It was loud, and its noise hurt my ears. The smell of oil and the tart smell of paper and ink were strong. The machine had many wheels of different sizes with teeth around the edges. I saw the paper pulled off a great roll and into the machine on one end, and the printed paper holding many tracks came out folded on the other end where we stood. The chief pulled a paper out of the stack and gave it to me. It was still warm, but I liked the smell of the paper and ink. I was amazed and impressed that the White Eyes could make such a machine.

We went to another room where quiet seemed to hover in the air. I said, speaking in their tongue to the reporters there, "In paper, write letter to Great Father in Washington. Say, 'Geronimo got religion now. Geronimo fights no more. The old times he forgets. Geronimo wants to be prisoner of war no more. He wants to be free.' Tell the Great White Father that. Tell him in the paper."

Soon after we left seeing the printing press, the train to Tulsa came. From there we went on to Collinsville. A man Spybuck sent picked us up at the train station to carry us to the ceremonial grounds in a big, red velocipede that reminded me of the Loco-mobile at the 101 Ranch. It, too, smelled of oil and blew smoke out its back, and the howling spirits that made much noise moved it along a dusty trail of small stones lined with Indians from many tribes in paint and feathers and their best dress leathers. The many Indians and whites who came to watch reminded me of the great Saint Louis Exposition three harvests earlier.

The sun was about a hand width off the horizon when the Indians sat in front of a wooden platform for those who would speak to them. Chief Spybuck stood and spoke. He said this dance and gathering would the last kind of ceremonial he would lead. Then he asked me to come and speak to the crowd and give them my advice for the future. The crowd grew very quiet, and I spoke from my heart.

"Brothers! I'm glad to see so many of you and see you playing the old games. I shall not keep you long, but you've asked for my advice. I say our way of life is gone. Your children must travel the white man's road. Schools and churches will help you and them. That is all I have to say."

There were many campfires scattered across the darkness, and we danced and sang all night. I thought, *These dances have been a large part of our enjoyment in the past. They won't soon be ended.* It was the same thing I had thought at Eva's womanhood ceremony. I was glad I had been at both of them.

Back home, a few suns later, Wratten waved me over to him at his store and held up a newspaper like we had seen in Oklahoma City. He said, "Well, Geronimo, the paper we saw being printed in Oklahoma City printed what you told them to, and they say they sent a letter along with a copy of the paper to President Roosevelt. What do you say to that?"

"I say, *Enjuh.* Maybe the Great Father in Washington will change his mind."

CHAPTER 47
WITCH!

Early in the Season of Little Eagles in the harvest time the White Eyes call 1908, my grandson Thomas Dahkeya, the last living child of my daughter Dohn-say's family, went to the Happy Place. He had lived longer than his brother Joe and sister Nina and his mother and father, but the sickness that took his family finally took him too. He helped me much with my work at the expositions, and we had continued to grow close, even after he had begun school at Chilocco four harvests earlier. He was at Chilocco when my daughter Eva and son Robert began school there two or three harvests after he had started.

Although I had seen it happen many times, including with my own children, Dohn-say and Fenton; and two wives, She-gha and Zi-yeh, while we were captives, I couldn't understand why members of my family kept leaving for the Happy Place

519

when they had lived so few harvests. In my life, I had thought I was headed to the Happy Place many times, and I still wished I had died fighting.

I was in a dark place for two or three moons after Thomas went to the Happy Place. I thought often of Thomas riding the ghost pony. My mind couldn't focus on work for the day. I looked for my knife when I was working on bows and arrows, forgetting I had it in my hand, or, forgetting I was wearing my hat, I looked for it, blaming Azul for hiding my knife and hat. She was patient with me while young friends watching me work laughed at me. I felt a fool, an old fool. It was like I was in a dark cave surrounded by smoke. I could smell the smoke, but could not see the cave walls that held me.

One day I realized how weak Eva looked in her mourning and sadness at the funeral for Thomas. I had thought then that she just grieved for Thomas, but as I thought more about it, I realized her looks were from more than grief. She, too, was getting sick. How could this be?

Then it came to me that maybe my children and grandchildren might have been witched and made sick by an enemy, and I had many enemies. The more I thought about this, the more I believed it was true. I had to stop the witch before it sent Eva to her death and then started on Robert and Lenna.

I needed the kind of Power, which I didn't have, to find and identify the witch before it could do more harm. I needed someone who had the Power to identify witches. I remembered Lot Eyelash, who as a novitiate had ridden with me and held horses during raids and fights when the People had left San Carlos to live in the Blue Mountains. General Crook and the scouts went to the mountains to take us back to San Carlos. The White Eyes called that harvest time 1883. Crook sent Lot Eyelash to the Carlisle school with about fifty other children.

Lot Eyelash stayed at the Carlisle school until he visited family at Mount Vernon during Ghost Face six harvests later. After another harvest had passed, he returned to live with his family. He joined the army and was in Company I with the rest of the Chiricahuas. He married Edith Jones and had a child, but both Edith and the child died in a short time. Then he married Gotsi, his mother in-law. They had a daughter, but she died early, too, along with Gotsi, in a bad fire. Lot Eyelash knew the same sorrow

I knew in losing family so young and so quick.

Two or three harvests ago, Ussen had given him Power and ceremonies to identify witches. Lot Eyelash would be a good *di-yen* to help me learn who had been witching my children and wives and making them die before their time.

I told Daklugie what I thought about a witch attacking my children and using Lot Eyelash as a *di-yen* to identify who was doing this bad thing.

Daklugie frowned and slowly shook his head. He said, "Geronimo, you may be right about your children dying from being witched, but it is dangerous to use Lot Eyelash."

I frowned in confusion. "Why not use Lot Eyelash? He has Power. He knows what it is for children in his family to go to the Happy Place too young. He has ceremonies to identify witches."

Daklugie nodded. "Yes, all you say is true. But remember how angry some people got when you told Barrett your stories? They were afraid you might tell something from the old days that would get them in trouble. You remember how careful we had to be when you told those stories?"

"I remember what you say about others

being angry, but we never got anyone in any trouble."

"You speak the truth, Uncle. However, our friend, Chatto, who thinks of you as an enemy, kept the others stirred up, especially men like Lot Eyelash, who rode with you. They're afraid of what the White Eyes might do to them after they read your book. He should know that nothing would happen to him now if it hasn't already. All the Blue Coat chiefs have read the book. They know what you said. I don't think Lot Eyelash understands this. He's not your friend."

"Hmmph. My nephew speaks words to think on. I'll consider them."

I spent restless nights and days thinking about what Daklugie had told me. It made sense to stay away from Lot Eyelash if he was angry with me about the book. I was ready to forget using him when a friend with two grandchildren at Chilocco visited them and reported back to me that when he had been there, Eva had been sick in bed, but Robert seemed strong. I knew then I had to do something quick. I went one evening to see Lot Eyelash, who lived in Chatto's village.

We sat in his breezeway, watched the moon spread its white light on the little mountains behind the village, and talked for a while of the old days in the Blue Mountains and of rumors that the army would soon take back Fort Sill land, leaving us with nothing after all the years we had worked to build our houses, farms, and cattle herd. At last, Lot Eyelash said, "How can I help you, Grandfather?"

After I rolled a cigarette and we smoked to the four directions, I said, "I have much sorrow. My grandson Thomas Dahkeya and my wives and children here have all gone to the Happy Place. They were too young. I shouldn't have lived longer than my wives and children. I think a witch must be making them sick so they die. I need to know who this witch is and end its curse before my other children, Eva, Robert, and Lenna, are taken. I know you have Power and you have ceremonies to find witches. I offer you two ponies, a fine blanket, and whatever you need for your witch-finding ceremonies to sing at a big dance I'll give at the first full moon in the Season of Large Leaves, if you agree."

Lot Eyelash crossed his arms, his face blank, and stared out into the white light in the darkness. He nodded. "Grandfather is very generous. I thank him, but I would do this Sing to help him for no gifts. I'll need a big fire and drummers, who I will instruct before your dance, and golden pollen to do my ceremonies."

"Hmmph. I understand. The dance will be held on the first day of the first full moon in the Season of Large Leaves where I had Eva's womanhood ceremony near Naiche's village. I'm glad you'll help me find this witch with your ceremonies. I'll send Robert with the golden pollen and ponies next sun."

"*Enjuh.* I sing to find the witch for you."

The fire was a big one, bright yellow and orange, and the moon had risen out of the star-filled, cloudless sky, sending bright, soft light across the prairie, our fields, and the place of the dance. I had invited all the villages to come for the ceremony to identify the witch who was after my family. Most old Apaches came, but not the Christians, who didn't believe in witches and thought I should just pray to the White Eye God to save my children.

Lot Eyelash led the People dancing around the fire, feasting and singing until the moon reached the top of its arc, and then Lot Eyelash disappeared for a time. They all sat down and quietly waited for Lot Eyelash to reappear and continue the witch-finding ceremony that might last until sunrise if his Power did not direct him to the witch's identity.

Lot Eyelash suddenly appeared out of the shadows as if he were smoke off a bubbling pot. He led the People in a dancing movement two steps forward and one back around the fire from east to south four times. Each time, he stopped them when he reached a new cardinal direction, where the drummers played a different rhythm as he sang the same song and sprinkled sacred pollen. When he finished leading the dancing around the circle for all directions, he prayed to Ussen for Power to see the witch who was attacking my family. He sang a long song, asking for guidance and that his eyes might be clear.

After he finished his first song, Lot Eyelash led the dancers and moved from east to north in a movement around the fire again four times, each time stopping at a new direction and sprinkling the golden pollen, and again singing the same song he had when they danced in the other direction. The fire began to burn low, but he didn't summon more wood. In the slowly closing ring of orange light, he began his third song, the drummers using a different rhythm than they used for the first two songs.

I grew curious. In all my years as a *di-yen,* I'd never seen such a ceremony. Lot Eyelash must have had a great revelation when Ussen showed it to him. Those who had danced before Lot Eyelash began singing were now watching and listening to Lot Eyelash more out of curiosity rather than reverence for his singing. Something didn't seem right.

Lot Eyelash suddenly raised his hands to the sky and cried, "Ho!" The dancers stopped and stared at him, their eyes wide with expectation. The drummers stopped. There was no noise except for the low crackling of the wood on the fire. Slowly, Lot Eyelash's hand made a fist with his forefinger pointing out. His hand came down and stopped. His quivering finger pointed directly at me.

He yelled, "You did it! So you could live on!"

Everyone stared at me, scarcely breathing. In my long life, I had suffered many wounds from bullets, arrows, and stones, but none hurt like the shaft of Lot Eyelash's accusation that I was the witch killing off my children so I could live longer. I remembered Daklugie's warning about Lot Eyelash and felt like a fool. My fingers curled around the handle of the long knife hanging in a sheath under my vest, but then I relaxed.

I stood and walked into the circle of firelight toward Lot Eyelash. His eyes grew wide, and he took a step back as I approached. But I stopped within four paces of him and turned slowly to look at the dancers and, to make sure they could see me, I pulled off my hat.

I said, "Lot Eyelash! I don't know where you got your witch-finding ceremony, but it wasn't from the same Ussen who has given me Power. This Power I have used for the People all my years. I would never take the lives of my children to extend mine, which I risked many more times than you ever have when you made war as my novitiate. I know, after all these years, neither would any of the Powers Ussen sent me demand their lives to lengthen mine."

Lot Eyelash haughtily raised his chin to look down his nose at me and said through clenched teeth, "I have said all I am going to say."

"Good. Then the dance and ceremony are done. Go and say no more."

I thought many times of Lot Eyelash and his ceremony. If it *were* a true ceremony, how could it be so wrong? In the Season of

Large Leaves, when the nights were warm and filled with the sounds of insects, peepers, and frogs, Azul and I took a blanket and lay together in our favorite spot by Cache Creek and comforted each other.

As we rested, we spoke often of the Lot Eyelash ceremony and if he had done it right when he identified me as the witch. I knew what he found was a lie, but I couldn't decide if he had played me for a fool or if Ussen was playing me for a fool.

When I voiced this thought, Azul laughed her deep, throaty laugh and said, "Regardless of Ussen or Lot Eyelash, Coyote waits." The Trickster was always waiting to play a trick on the unsuspecting.

One night I said to Azul, "A few harvests ago, I joined the Christians and told those who asked that the Christian religion was better than that of my father's. Then I decided the missionary rules for staying on the Jesus road were too strict and I would return to Ussen. Perhaps this is the way Ussen tells me not to return to Him. Perhaps I should talk to the missionaries about coming back to the Jesus road."

Azul was quiet for a long time. I thought maybe she had gone to sleep, but she finally said, "Yes, perhaps you should talk to the missionaries about returning to the Jesus road, if that is what you truly want."

I thought, *Wise woman. Is the Jesus road what I truly want? This I needed to think on. What do I really want?*

After all my years, I still stuttered when I tried to answer that question. I decided I wanted to protect my children and wife above all things. Perhaps the White Eye God was more powerful than Ussen. The White Eyes had grown very strong and prospered under their God. Maybe I should go back to the Jesus road but never forget Ussen.

When the time of the camp meeting came, I rode my pony there to speak with the missionaries. I met in the shade of big oak trees by Medicine Bluff Creek with Legters and the big chief missionary who spoke at every camp meeting. Naiche and other Chiricahua church leaders were there, too.

Legters prayed to the White Eye God to guide us all in this meeting that the lost soul, Geronimo, might find his way back to the Jesus road. After he prayed, the missionary and Chiricahua leaders sat quietly with their eyes closed and their lips moving with prayers. I had seen this ceremony often. Even the children did it, but I still didn't understand its purpose. When all eyes opened, Legters looked at everyone and then at me.

He said, "Brothers, Geronimo has come to me and said he wants to return to the Jesus road. We're here to talk with Geronimo and understand his mind and ask the Father for guidance." Then he turned to me and said, "Speak to us, brother. Tell us why you seek the Jesus road again."

I looked over the solemn faces, saw Naiche, and spoke to him as if we were alone. "In the Season of Little Eagles, the grandson I had come to love as if he was my own son went to the Happy Place. My heart was heavy with sorrow. An old man should not outlive his children, but I have. I came to believe a witch must be cursing and taking them. I had a big dance, and a *di-yen* with the Power to identify witches sang and led the dancing. He led three songs and then pointed to me and said I did it. His medicine is bad. It speaks lies. I have thought much about this. Now I know I must follow the god with the most Power."

Heads slowly nodded in the group around me. Legters started to speak, but Naiche raised his chin and said in a low, rasping voice, "Tell us, Geronimo, do you still drink whiskey?"

"Yes, I still drink whiskey. An old man sometimes needs his medicine."

531

"Do you still believe in Ussen, or have you returned to Jesus?"

"Both I believe. If the White Eye God is in three parts, then I do not understand why Ussen couldn't be a fourth part."

"Do you still play card games like Monte, games of chance?"

"All of life depends on chance. Why not understand chance with games?"

"Will you marry Azul as the White God directs?"

"Azul and I are happily married in the Apache way. There's no need to do the White God marriage ceremony. He knows our hearts are good for each other."

"Do you still wish to die fighting?"

"Yes. That is how I want to die. I want to die fighting like a warrior, but Ussen has told me that won't happen."

Naiche stared at me and slowly shook his head. "Return to Ussen, Geronimo. You're not ready for the Jesus road."

I looked at each in the group, and they all slowly nodded in agreement. I stood and looked at each one again and then walked toward the corral where I had left my pony.

I heard Legters call after me, "Geronimo, wait! Stay with us! Jesus will save you."

I kept walking.

CHAPTER 48
NEVER SURRENDER

A break in winter weather brought the People and White Eyes out of their houses to Lawton for supplies. It was a warm day for the Ghost Face Season, too cold for an old man to sit outside all day, but I was too full of pride to sit beside the stove in the store where I sold my things.

I had come to Lawton to sell my photographs and bows and arrows my friends and I had made, and I sat outside on the boardwalk with a blanket around my shoulders, enduring the cold, waiting for a foolish White Eye to give me money for my toy weapons. Apache children would have thrown the arrows away as too weak or too crooked for hunting or shooting contests, but I made good money selling them to curious White Eyes who wanted to remember me as, they said, "the most feared Indian in captivity."

I sat outside most of the day in the cold

533

air and felt a chill in my center, and my joints were getting stiff. I was moving slow. In the middle of the afternoon, I saw Eugene Chihuahua coming down the street. I immediately knew who he was, even in a Blue Coat uniform. With a puffing grunt, I pulled myself up to speak to him when he came near.

I pulled a five-dollar gold piece out of my pocket and gave it to him. "Grandson, I need some whiskey. Take this money and get some for me."

Eugene smiled. I hadn't seen Eugene or his wife, Viola, since midsummer when they had agreed to take in my son Robert until he went back to school in Chilocco.

"I want the whiskey to warm my insides and to reward myself for a good day of taking White Eye money for meaningless toy weapons and my signed photographs."

"This gold piece could get us both in a lot of trouble," Eugene replied, "but I'll see what I can do, Grandfather. I'll be back in a little while."

Nodding, I smiled and murmured, *"Enjuh."*

In those days, selling whiskey to an Indian was punishable by hard labor in the penitentiary. I knew Eugene had friends in the Seventh who would buy the whiskey for

534

him, but his uniform fit so well and tight, he couldn't hide anything under his coat without it being noticed. I wondered how he would get it back to me.

A few minutes later, Eugene returned and said, "Grandfather, I need to swap horses with you for a little while. You're still riding that fast sorrel I rode for you in that race a while back, ain't you?"

I smiled. "I still have him. He's tied 'round back of the store here. He's a good pony. I could have killed a lot of White Eyes and gotten away riding that pony in the old days."

"I'll tie my pony in his place. You use mine while I'm using yours. Meet me on the road out of town at the bridge across the creek when the sun is a hand width off the horizon."

"*Enjuh.* Don't forget the whiskey."

Eugene grinned, and went to swap ponies.

Riding Eugene's pony, I saw him coming in a hurry and, like an old fire horse, I took off down the road to Cache Creek as fast as I could make his army mount run, which wasn't nearly fast enough to stay in front of my fine pony. Eugene caught up with the slow, army pony in the long evening shadows. He held up a bottle of rye as I grinned, swung my arm forward, and somehow coaxed the army mount to run a little faster.

The wind had died to nothing in the low light as we entered the timber and brush along Cache Creek. We found a place under the bare limbs of a big oak where we could make a little fire and drink the rye without being seen by people in the village houses. After we watered and rubbed down the horses and hobbled them in the brown winter grass, I sat down between the roots thrust out from the bottom of the tree and leaned back against its trunk. I cradled the whiskey in the crook of my arm, waiting for Eugene to dig a pit, gather some wood and twigs, and start a little fire.

In a while, he rubbed his hands in the warmth of the flames dancing over the little pile of wood. I smiled, handed him the bottle, and said, "Here, Grandson, you open it. My fingers are too cold and stiff to get that cork to move."

The cork was tight, and it took him a few hard twists to pull it out. He handed the opened bottle back to me. I held it up, looked at the tawny, amber liquid in the firelight, smacked my lips, and took a couple of long of swallows before handing it back to Eugene. I licked the last precious drops off my lips, saying, "Hmmph. That's good. I've needed some all day. The White Eyes know how to make good whiskey."

Eugene took a small sip and handed it back to me. He had to be careful, because the Blue Coats would never tolerate a drunken Indian in a Seventh Cavalry uniform. I took another big swallow and held the bottle as I looked at him. "Grandson, you're big and tall. I don't remember you being that big when you came to Guydelkon's house to talk about keeping Robert. You're your father's son. Your sister Ramona took my nephew Daklugie for a husband, and your father found you Viola Massai. Massai was a great warrior, the only one to escape the Blue Coats on the train to Florida, but he's long gone now. Is Viola Massai a good woman for you?"

Eugene nodded. Off in the distance, through the grove of trees standing like sentinels around us and the murmuring creek below us, we heard cows bawling and a couple of dogs barking in a village over the hill. I took another swallow and pulled my coat closer.

The whiskey loosened my tongue, and I started to ramble through my years of memories. "I've had many wives, maybe ten or twelve, but your grandmother Francesca, she was the bravest. She killed a mountain lion with her knife even after it chewed her up pretty good and tore off part of her scalp. She looked so bad after that, she wore a big bandana around her face to hide her scars. No man wanted her, but I did. I took her for a wife. I loved her bravery. She was a strong woman. I wish she were still with us.

"I had to divorce Ih-tedda and send her back to Mescalero. She was young, and sending her back to the reservation got her out of the Blue Coat prison. I wanted her, and she wanted to stay, but I told her to go. I kept Zi-yeh instead. She went to the Happy Land soon enough. Now I only have Azul, my last wife, living with me.

"Eva, my daughter with Zi-yeh, still lives. She goes to the Indian school in Chilocco, but she looks like she's getting sick. She has signs of the worms the White Eye *di-yen* calls tuberculosis. She wants to marry some young man there, but I won't approve. She'll die in childbirth if she marries. Women in our family always have a hard time bearing children. I can't let her die for no baby. It would die, too, if she did."

Eugene slumped back next to me and puffed his cheeks. He said, "Life is hard for all of us under the White Eyes, but it is hardest for the old ones."

Far away, the yips of coyotes made a night song, and the wind rattling the branches above us, making them click together like bones in a sack, paused. I looked up through the bare limbs and saw patches of stars changing shape as clouds gathered over us.

Eugene reached for the bottle and took a long swallow before handing it back to me. He said, "Viola is a good wife. My father picked her. He made me marry her, because he decided I would be chief and had to live with our People here. First, I wanted to marry Belle. She was a friend of Ramona at the Carlisle school, but he said no. He said I couldn't marry some woman and move off to live with her family, wherever they are, and still be a chief here. Then I wanted a beautiful Shoshone woman who already had a child, but he said no. I have to stay here. It's a hard thing to be a future chief and a chief's son. Your life is not yours. It belongs to the People."

I took another long pull on the bottle and slumped down further between the big oak roots, trying to get comfortable. "Grandson, we have to do what Ussen gives us to do. It's always for the People that He gives us gifts of Power, and we do what we do. All our lives belong to the People. It's the only way we can survive. We have to put each other first."

We swapped the bottle back and forth, taking smaller sips to make the whiskey last longer. We talked about the old wild and free days and the fights we had with the Mexicans and White Eyes, and the warriors we had known. Despite the whiskey warming our bellies, the wind had a sharp chill and made my head hurt a little. I looked up through the branches again and could no longer see any stars. The sky had filled with clouds. Eugene staggered up and got a little more wood for the fire, made water, and got our horse blankets to keep the cold away.

When he returned to the fire, the bottle lay empty between my boots, and I was coughing with a deep, barking growl from my chest. He laid my blanket over me. I nodded thanks and, staring out into the darkness, said, "Grandson, I made a big mistake many harvests ago."

"What was the mistake, Grandfather?"

"I surrendered." I coughed up phlegm and spat it into the fire. "I should never have surrendered, especially to that lying Blue Coat, Miles. I should have killed as many White Eyes and Mexicans as I could before they took me. I should have fought to the last warrior. I should have died like Victorio, sticking a knife in my own heart, not like some kicked-around dog on a chain. But long ago in my Power vision, Ussen told me I would die a natural death, and so it will be."

I wheezed and coughed some more and murmured more to myself than to him, "Never surrender . . . never surrender . . . kill more White Eyes, kill many Mexicans. Alope, my mother, and children will be avenged."

Eugene stuffed the blanket around me before lying down in his. It had been a long day. Gradually, the whiskey made me sleep.

CHAPTER 49
THE LAST DREAM

A cold, drizzling rain awoke me. I could barely see the black, staggering outlines of the surrounding trees in the dim, gray light. Dawn was coming fast. I began coughing hard, and I had a wheezing gurgle deep in my chest. My face was hot.

Eugene awoke and looked up at me, and I said, "Grandson, I've been sick all night."

"Why didn't you get me up, Grandfather?"

"I thought the whiskey would soon make me better. No need to wake you if it did, but it didn't."

He shook his head. "I'll saddle the horses, and then I'm taking you over to the Apache hospital where a Blue Coat *di-yen* can give you some medicine."

I sucked in a gurgling breath, stood up, and put my wet hat on. "All right. The Blue Coat *di-yens* know how to make good medicine, but if you go in that Apache hospital, you don't come out alive. The

People are afraid to go in there, but I'm not afraid."

The soldier in charge of the hospital desk led us to a room with a bed and said he would go find a doctor. Eugene helped me take off my hat, coat, and boots and had me lie down on the bed until the doctor came.

The doctor was an old military surgeon. Most of his hair gone, he wore silver frame glasses across his long, hooked nose. He knew Eugene from when he played baseball on a soldier team. He didn't even have to use his listening ropes after feeling my hot face and hearing my breaking wheeze. He said, "Mr. Geronimo, you have pneumonia. Stay in that bed, and we'll do all we can for you."

"Hmmph. I stay. Sometimes Blue Coat medicine is strong. Will I leave this bed alive?"

The doctor slowly shook his head. "I don't know. We'll do all we can. I'll be back this afternoon, and I'm sending you some medicine now to make you feel better."

I coughed hard and spat in a pan next to the bed. *"Enjuh."*

Eugene stepped out into the hall with the doctor and closed the door, but I could hear them talking. Eugene asked, "Sir, how much time do you think he has?"

"It's bad. I've seen it this way in other Apaches. They don't last more than three or four days when they're like him. I'll send a nurse with some laudanum. Give him a spoonful in a glass of water. It'll make him sleep."

"Yes, sir, I will."

I heard the doctor walk off down the hall. Then I heard Eugene say to someone, "Ho, brother! I need a favor. Can you help me?"

"Hey, Eugene. I not see you in a long time. What you need?"

"You know where Geronimo lives?"

"Sure. Everybody knows Geronimo lives with his wife Azul in Guydelkon's house."

"I need for you to ride over there right now and tell Azul Geronimo's here in the hospital, sick with pneumonia. She needs to come quick. Can you go tell her that?"

"Sure. I'm leaving right now."

Daklugie and Azul came quick. They stayed with me all that day, and Daklugie stayed all that night. I heard that many Apaches came to the hospital to see me, but the nurses and orderlies wouldn't let them in. My family never left me alone and rotated in shifts of one turn of the shortest pointer around the clock face.

Eugene asked Daklugie to make Apache medicine for me, and he did. Eugene made medicine, too, but he prayed as a Christian, and his medicine wasn't as strong as Daklugie's. The doctor and nurses did all they could, but it wasn't enough. Pneumonia lingered on me like a curse. I knew it was my time as I drifted in and out of sleep, growing steadily worse.

The dream came like a fog lifting out of my mind. I knew this place. I'd rolled in the sand here often when I was a child. It was the place of my birth. I had to tilt my head far back to see the tops of the ridge cliffs forming the canyon where my People lived. On the canyon floor, the blue water ran fast, and the pines and junipers reached high to gather the sun falling on their branches.

Here my people had brought their tipis, fine buffalo skin ones traded from the Jicarilla, Lipan, and Mescalero, who often had to fight the Comanches for them. For this, we'd paid a high price. The women and children were happy. They laughed and joked much as the women prepared food for the Ghost Face and the children played the games boys play to be warriors, and girls play to be women wanted by a husband. The warriors sat and smoked, planned raids, and gambled, playing hoops out on a flat bench by the water, or card games like Monte in the shade of tall trees. The Great Father had given us our freedom, and we had returned to the land of our fathers. It was the best of times.

I heard the sound of many horses coming up the canyon and felt the earth tremble from their pounding hooves. A warrior on his pony charged into the camp. He screamed the Blue Coats had come to take us back to our prison camp. The Great Father no longer wanted us here. We had left the White Eyes alone. We'd done nothing wrong.

I decided, *I won't go. I'll fight this. Where is my rifle? Where are my warriors? Where are my People? We'll fight until we are no more.*

I called my People to follow me and headed for the high ground. The tremble of the earth grew stronger, and the sound of many horses running hard came down the canyon toward us. The warriors stayed with me up high behind rocks from where we could shoot and kill many. The women and children ran on, climbing higher and higher, up out of the way of bullets. They climbed to the top of the canyon and sat to watch what would happen.

The Blue Coat captain leading the unending columns held up an arm and stopped the charge. He rose in his stirrups and looked around the deserted camp until he saw me watching high in the rocks. "Geronimo!" he yelled. "The Great Father says you and your people are no longer welcome here. You must return to Fort Sill!"

"No! He gave us this land. We won't leave. You go."

"Come peacefully, or many will die."

"Then many will die, but you will die first."

Faster than an arrow to a bow, my rifle came to my shoulder and struck down the Blue Coat captain, hitting him square in the chest, yanking him back to fall slowly off his horse. It was a good day to die.

The Blue Coats were off their horses and behind the rocks along the river, sending a rain of bullets that cracked and whined in the rocks around us but wounded no one. Many Blue Coats we hit, and others came forward to take their place or to carry the bodies away. There were unending columns of them. The smoke from many rifles filled the canyon, making it hard to see.

A ricochet hit a warrior in the head and killed him, and a hard rain of lead from the Blue Coats fell on us. Others were hit and soon died, covered in blood. Some women high up on the ridge who saw their men fall wailed in sorrow, but others climbed down into the rocks amid the whine and splatter of bullets against the stones, found their husbands' rifles, and took up the fight, before they, too, went to the Happy Place.

We killed, and killed, and killed some more. Heads exploded, and chests burst in fountains of blood, but there was no end to the Blue Coats or their bullets. Our rifles were hot, their loading gates almost too hot to push bullets in, but still we shot them. I refused to surrender.

I heard fewer shots from those around me, heard the clatter of rifles falling to the ground, and even the clicks of empty rifles. The smoke from many shots filled the canyon and rose up to us, making it hard to breathe. My dry throat begged for water.

"Water!" I cried.

"Here, Grandfather. Let me raise you up a little so it goes down your throat." Daklugie slid his hand under my back and raised me to the cup he held to my lips.

I drank a couple of swallows, coughed, and lay back. My eyes opened, and I frowned as I studied Daklugie's face, as though trying to see him through a fog. "Is that you, Nephew?"

"Yes, I'm Daklugie, Uncle."

"Where are Eva and Robert? I wait for them before I fight my last fight. I should never have surrendered."

"They're coming as fast they can from their school, Uncle. I think soon they come."

"*Enjuh.* If only Ussen would let me die fighting like Victorio."

I drifted off for a while and then opened my eyes, gripped Daklugie's hand, and said, "My nephew, promise me that you and Ramona will take my daughter Eva into your home and care for her as you do your own children. Promise me you'll never let her marry. If you do, she'll die. The women in our family have great difficulty giving birth, as your mother had. Don't let this happen to Eva."

Again, I drifted for a little while, still holding Daklugie's hand. Daklugie was patient and waited for me to come back, and soon I did. I coughed and growled deep in my chest. I looked at Daklugie. "I want your promise."

Daklugie said, "Ramona and I will take your daughter and love her as our own. But how can I prevent her from marrying?"

"She'll obey you. She has been taught to obey. See that she does."

During the night, I drifted in and out of

consciousness, but when I was lucid, I said several times how sorry I was I had surrendered. I spoke of warriors who had always been loyal and of some whose loyalty failed.

The Blue Coat chiefs realized no more bullets came from us on the cliffs. They began ordering their men to stop firing and waited for the cloud of gun smoke to leave the canyon.

I looked around the rocks. Only two or three others still lived. Their guns were empty. They had no more cartridges. They had pulled their long, sharp knives and stood looking at me. They were ready to die. They would not be captured or surrender. Good men. Great warriors. I pulled my knife and waited while the smoke cloud vanished. Soon sun filled the canyon, casting light on many dead Blue Coats, but many more, as far as I could see, were ready down in the canyon to come for us.

I laid my empty rifle down and gripped the bone handle of my long knife. I put the point between my ribs for an easy thrust straight into my heart and fell forward against the rock covered with strikes from the many Blue Coat bullets that Ussen would not let kill me.

A brilliant flash of light came like the sun exploding, but in the blink of an eye, it collapsed to bright point of light, growing dim and settling into perfect blackness. Somewhere in the darkness a voice sang.

O, ha le
O, ha le
Through the air
I fly upon a cloud
Toward the sky, far, far, far
O, ha le
O, ha le
There to find the holy place
Ah, now the change comes o'er me!
O, ha le,
O, ha le

EPILOGUE

Geronimo rode the ghost pony at 6:15 a.m., February 17, 1909. His funeral at the Indian Cemetery at Fort Sill, scheduled for 3 p.m. on February 18 had to be delayed for half an hour while the procession, over a mile long, waited for his grief-stricken children, Robert and Eva, to arrive by train from the Chilocco Indian Boarding School. Geronimo had wanted to see them one last time, but Lieutenant Purington, the army commander for the Chiricahuas at Fort Sill, had sent a letter rather than a telegram to tell Robert and Eva their father was near death and they needed to come. The ghost pony that carried Geronimo raced past the slow letter to his bedside.

Virtually all the Apaches attended Geronimo's funeral. Fort Sill gave its soldiers half a day off to attend the funeral, and nearly the entire village of Lawton attended.

Naiche stood at the graveside and gave

Geronimo's eulogy in Apache. Naiche recalled incidents on the warpath and praised Geronimo's bravery and skill as a war leader and spoke of how he had been loyal to the peace once he surrendered. He said Geronimo had refused to accept Christianity, thus being an utter failure in the chief thing in life. Naiche ended by urging the assembly to profit from Geronimo's mistake. Eugene Chihuahua served as interpreter for the formal service conducted by Reverend Leonard Legters of the Dutch Reformed Church, where Geronimo had once been a member.

Geronimo's unquenchable desire for freedom and the preservation of Apache lifeways, while learning new knowledge, lives on in his people. It is their best and greatest tribute to their most well-known and popular leader.

ADDITIONAL READING

Adams, David Wallace. *Education for Extinction,* University Press of Kansas, Lawrence, KS, 1995.

Ball, Eve. *In the Days of Victorio: Recollections of a Warm Springs Apache,* University of Arizona Press, Tucson, AZ, 1970.

Ball, Eve, Nora Henn, and Lynda A. Sánchez. *Indeh: An Apache Odyssey,* University of Oklahoma Press, Norman, OK, 1988.

Barrett, S. M. *Geronimo, His Own Story: The Autobiography of a Great Patriot Warrior,* Meridian, Penguin Books USA, New York, NY, 1996.

Debo, Angie. *Geronimo: The Man, His Time, His Place,* University of Oklahoma Press, Norman, OK, 1976.

Delgadillo, Alicia, with Miriam A. Perrett, *Fort Marion to Fort Sill: A Documentary History of the Chiricahua Prisoner of War,*

555

1886–1913, University of Nebraska Press, Lincoln, NE, 2013.

Gatewood, Charles B., edited and additional text by Louis Kraft. *Lt. Charles Gatewood & His Apache Wars Memoir,* University of Nebraska Press, Lincoln, NE, 2005.

Haley, James L. *Apaches: A History and Culture Portrait,* University of Oklahoma Press, Norman, OK, 1981.

Hutton, Paul Andrew. *The Apache Wars,* Crown Publishing Group, New York, NY, 2016.

Opler, Morris Edward. *An Apache Life-Way: The Economic, Social, and Religious Institutions of the Chiricahua Indians,* University of Nebraska Press, Lincoln, NE, 1996.

Opler, Morris, Edward. *Apache Odyssey: A Journey Between Two Worlds,* University of Nebraska Press, Lincoln, NE, 2002.

Opler, Morris, Edward. "A Chiricahua Apache's Account of the Geronimo Campaign of 1886," *New Mexico Historical Review,* Vol XIII, No. 4 (October 1938).

Robinson, Sherry. *Apache Voices: Their Stories of Survival as Told to Eve Ball,* University of New Mexico Press, Albuquerque, NM, 2003.

Sánchez, Lynda A. *Apache Legends and*

Lore of Southern New Mexico, History Press, Charleston, SC, 2014.

Scott, Hugh Lenox, edited by R. Eli Paul. *Sign Talker: Hugh Lenox Scott Remembers Indian Country,* University of Oklahoma Press, Norman OK, 2016.

Skinner, Woodward B. *The Apache Rock Crumbles,* Skinner Publications, Pensacola, FL, 1987.

Sonnichsen, C. L. *The Mescalero Apaches,* University of Oklahoma Press, Norman, OK, 1973.

Stockel, H. Henrietta. *Survival of the Spirit, Chiricahua Apaches in Captivity,* University of Nevada Press, Reno, NV, 1993.

Stockel, H. Henrietta. *Shame and Endurance: The Untold Story of the Chiricahua Apache Prisoners of War,* University of Arizona Press, Tucson, AZ, 2004.

Sweeny, Edwin. *From Cochise to Geronimo: The Chiricahua Apaches, 1874–1886,* University of Oklahoma Press, Norman, OK, 2010.

Thrapp, Dan L. *The Conquest of Apacheria,* University of Oklahoma Press, Norman, OK, 1967.

Turcheneske, John Anthony, Jr. *The Chiricahua Apache Prisoners of War: Fort Sill 1894–1914,* University Press of Colorado,

Niwot, CO, 1997.

Utley, Robert M. *Geronimo,* Yale University Press, New Haven, CT, 2012.

Worchester, Donald E. *The Apaches: Eagles of the Southwest,* University of Oklahoma Press, Norman, OK, 1992.

ABOUT THE AUTHOR

W. Michael Farmer's in-depth historical research and southwest experience fill his stories with a genuine sense of time and place. His first novel, *Hombrecito's War,* won a Western Writers of America Spur Finalist Award for Best First Novel in 2006 and was a New Mexico Book Award finalist for Historical Fiction in 2007. He has published short stories in anthologies, and award-winning essays. His novels include: *Killer of Witches,* a 2016 Will Rogers Medallion Award winner, *Mariana's Knight,* 2017 New Mexico–Arizona Book Award winner for Historical Fiction, and *Blood of the Devil,* 2017 New Mexico–Arizona Book Award finalist for Adventure-Drama and Historical Fiction. In 2018 *Mariana's Knight* and *Blood of the Devil* were awarded 2018 Will Rogers Silver Medallion Awards for Western Fiction, and his book of historical essays, *Apacheria: True Stories of Apache Culture,*

1860–1920, won the 2018 New Mexico-Arizona Book Awards for Best New Mexico Book and Best History–Other.